I Give *it a* Year

Also by Helen Whitaker

The School Run

I Give *it a* Year

HELEN WHITAKER

First published in Great Britain in 2021 by Orion Books,
an imprint of The Orion Publishing Group Ltd,
Carmelite House, 50 Victoria Embankment
London EC4Y ODZ

An Hachette UK company

1 3 5 7 9 10 8 6 4 2

A CIP catalogue record for this book
is available from the British Library.

ISBN (Mass Market Paperback) 978 1 4091 9547 4
ISBN (Ebook) 978 1 4091 9548 1

Printed and bound in Great Britain by Clays Ltd, Elcograf S.p.A.

www.orionbooks.co.uk

To Ian

Chapter One

31 December, 11.59 p.m.

Ten . . .

The telly blares with the sound of pissed-up revellers as the camera pans down the Thames. Fifteen years ago, I would have been there with them, having spent all evening jostling for a spot and dying for a wee so I was in a good position for the countdown.

Nine . . .

I'm so glad I'm not on a packed riverbank, drinking Prosecco that's only cold because the temperature is Baltic and pretending to have a good time while worrying about how busy the tube station will be post-midnight.

Eight . . .

At least Jack and Sav are asleep. Finally. The best thing about having young kids is that you can use them as a convenient excuse to get out of things you don't want to do. 'Sorry, no babysitter!' is the best get out of jail card of all time.

Seven . . .

Even if most of the time it's a total ball-ache having no babysitter, because it means you can't do things you genuinely want to do either.

Six . . .

But New Year's Eve definitely doesn't fall into that category. I'm not even bothered about sitting here alone, watching the countdown on TV, while Adam is up in Sheffield.

Five . . .

It's not as though he's up there having a good time. Having to get on a rammed train from London on New Year's Eve to give your thirty-seven-year-old brother a talking to because he's possibly-maybe-almost-certainly been barred from another pub in the city centre, and they want some money for damages otherwise they're pressing charges. Cheers, Gabe. Happy sodding New Year.

Four . . .

That's a point. I bet Adam had to pay the landlord. Not that he'd have mentioned it to me. He always gets funny with me if I bring up lending Gabe money.

Three . . .

'Lending.'

Two . . .

The last time he did it he didn't even tell me, and I went overdrawn on the joint account paying the deposit for Center Parcs.

One . . .

Thousands of people scream 'HAPPY NEW YEAR' and hug each other as Big Ben bongs in the background. Fireworks erupt, filling the screen with colour and smoke, and the BBC presenter out on location tries to finish her link above the din.

'The British public was assured that the great clock's bongs would be temporarily restored during important national events, such as New Year and Remembrance Sunday, until restoration work is completed.'

I drain the dregs of my white wine. The rest of the bottle is in the fridge and for a second I contemplate getting a refill, before yawning and remembering that, despite it taking until 10 p.m. to wrestle the kids into bed, they will almost certainly be up pre-6 a.m., as is the unwritten law when you've been left to parent solo and have imbibed more than two units of alcohol.

Instead, I flick off the telly and fire a message to Adam.

Hope it's not a nightmare up there. Happy New Year. X

He's probably already asleep at his mum's house, back in the single bed in the room he used to share with Gabe.

The patch of floor in front of me simultaneously lights up and chirrups. Bloody kids! Adam's iPad lies abandoned, screen up, on the carpet, half concealed by Christmas toys that they've already got bored of. My text appears in the corner, obscuring part of the photo on his home screen, a selfie where we're all smushed together in front of the London Eye. You can barely see the wheel because it's all grinning faces, or in Jack's case, him anarchically shouting 'poo' when Adam said, 'Everyone say cheese.' I pick up the tablet and put it on the table while I look for its case, clearing a few other stray toys from the area. The house looks like a bomb-site, with discarded superheroes, cardboard boxes and foot-shattering bits of Lego all over the carpet. The kids have insisted on keeping every single bit of tat from every Christmas cracker, so there's endless plastic crap spilling out from the toy drawers we're now resigned to having in our once relatively stylish living room.

I pick up the debris – Sylvanian, Sylvanian, Spider-Man wearing a Sylvanian's outfit (Jack will be livid) – and find the case underneath the Millennium Falcon. It's plastered with fairy stickers, which makes me grin. Sav's handiwork. Adam will look very cool reading the *Guardian* on his iPad on the tube when he goes back to work on Thursday. The screen lights up again as I pick it up. Another message. That it's simply from 'J' makes me look more closely. I can only see the preview.

Thanks for partying with me like it's 1995 again . . .

Who's J? And what party? He's with his brother, sorting out yet another catastrophe of Gabe's own creation. That's what he said anyway. Maybe he went out for a drink after clearing up Gabe's mess and bumped into someone he knew. I can't begrudge him that. What's a night off from the kids if you can't have a spontaneous night out at the pub?

But that doesn't tell me who J is.

Heart fluttering, there's a second when I don't want to know, but my suspicions quickly take over and I swipe the screen open, tapping the passcode – Jack and Sav's birthdays – onto the landing page. My stomach plunges as the full message appears, along with the rest of a thread that goes back way further than tonight.

Thanks for partying with me like it's 1995 again. Shame I have a flight or we could have got drunk and seen in the New Year together properly – although sparkling water and a king-size at the Hotel du Vin is a bit more glam than cider and sneaking into my old bedroom back at my parents'. x

1995. A flight. An old bedroom.

In 1995, Adam was a sixth-former in Sheffield. And he was going out with a girl called Jules. Amazing Jules, who broke his heart when she went off to a different uni, and whose brilliant career as a pilot was mentioned on one of our early dates and has provided fodder for my lower self-esteem moments ever since.

Adam's reply is almost instant.

Safe trip. Text me when you get back x

He hasn't replied to my message.

The tablet trembles in my hand so I grip it a bit tighter. I can hear whooping and music outside, through the walls of our North London terraced house and drifting along the street, but even through the bangs and whistles the sound of my own breath catching is louder. It feels like my body is pulsating but my mind is clear, focused. Because I instantly know it's not going to turn out to be a misunderstanding. He's never even mentioned seeing Jules, so how can it be? I swipe my shaky finger down the page to reach the start of their conversation. It scrolls and scrolls and scrolls, new messages loading up every time I think I've got to the top, my eyes blurring with tears as they settle on the odd word or phrase as messages whizz past.

In me
Beautiful
Fucking sexy
Can't wait

It looks like sometimes they've exchanged several messages a day, and sometimes days have gone by with no contact. Eventually, the window bounces, going back no further. Five months ago: 5 August, 11.07 a.m. A blue bubble showing that Adam sent the first message.

Hi, this is my number these days.

Seven words that blow apart my night. My year. My life.

Chapter Two

1 January, 4 p.m.

I've been sitting in silence for hours when I hear his key turn in the lock. When the kids are running riot I usually yearn for quiet, an hour to myself, but today – when I've packed them off so I could wait alone for Adam to come home – the silence makes me feel as though I can't breathe. The door slams and I jump, as if I haven't been poised for his entrance all afternoon. What I mean to do is thrust the tablet into his hands the second he walks through the door, while saying something damning that an imagined crowd of similarly wronged women (on *Oprah*? OK, more like *Loose Women*) would greet with thunderous applause.

Instead I rush into the hallway and stop dead at the sight of him. He looks normal. Like, completely normal. His dark hair is streaked with the same few strands of grey; his chin is dotted with the same patchy stubble I used to tease him about. He doesn't look like a man who's been shagging a hot pilot.

'You wouldn't believe the state of the train back,' he's moaning, as if I could give two shits. 'A signal delay on top of the typical New Year's Day chaos meant we were diverted to Doncaster and all the ticket reservations were cancelled. There were people crammed in every spare centimetre of aisle.'

He leans in to give me a perfunctory kiss, not noticing – or at least not mentioning – that my face looks like a crumpled-up paper bag from the combination of crying and swigging the vodka I found at the back of the freezer. As he does, I flinch, and my voice cracks as I choke out, 'I found your texts. Are we over then?'

In a split second his whole face changes. He looks exactly like Jack when he's been caught doing something he shouldn't, knows there's no denying it, but is going to lie anyway. I'd laugh, except I spent until 7 a.m. sobbing and reading his sexy back-and-forth with Jules, before trying to hold it together in front of the kids this morning on no sleep and no answers.

'What texts?' he says, his hand frozen where he's only half unzipped his coat. 'What are you talking about, Iris?'

The fright on his face ignites a deep guttural anger that sonic booms around my body from somewhere inside my chest.

The *fucking* coward.

'You're lying,' I say. 'Don't you dare lie to me on top of what you've done.'

I wish his train had crashed on the way back from Sheffield and he'd died. Actually, I don't. But only because then I'd have to listen to people telling me what a great husband and father he was, and what I want *everyone* right now to know is what a burning trash-fire scumbag he really is.

He's still staring at me, saying nothing, just looking scared. Big grey eyes questioning what I'll do next. 'Are you going to say anything?' I ask, in a way that leaves no room for ambiguity. He needs to speak. *Yes? No? I've made a terrible mistake, Iris, I lost my phone weeks ago and it's someone else sending sub-Tinder-level sexts to my high-school girlfriend.*

He's not looking at me; he's still fumbling with the zip of his coat. He opens his mouth to speak but all he says is: 'Where are the kids?'

'Fran's,' I spit back. Somewhere beneath the pulsating rage and the full-body fear, there's a pang of guilt – for the kids and for poor Fran, who texted me at 5.30 a.m. when she was woken up for the day by her twins with the sort of mum-moan about having a shit night's sleep that deserves a reply full of solidarity for her suffering. Instead she got a hysterical phone call from her best friend that resulted in having two more children dumped on top of her own three on New Year's Day.

The blood is pumping around my body, crashing through my temples. Self-loathing is churning in my stomach, a hangover-esque paranoia pressing at the back of my eyes. But it's not paranoia because it happened. My anger shrivels back into hurt as quickly as it appeared. Darts of dread fire through my brain. *Is he leaving us? Is that why he isn't saying anything?*

Adam looks around the hallway like a spooked animal looking for an escape route. We painted it four years ago, in a knock-off shade of the mousy Farrow & Ball one that David Cameron painted that stupid writing shed. It's all shabby now, having been scraped by the kids' scooters and grocery bags every time we've carried anything through it to the kitchen, all the mundane stuff you do when you've been married forever and haven't got enough time to be careful. The grubbiness of normal life, not sex-in-a-fancy-hotel life.

'Why did you do it?' My voice is so wobbly the whole sentence vibrates.

He finally turns to face me.

I can't tell if he's crying or I'm seeing him through my own tears, but his face is crumpled, blurred. 'I'm sorry,' he says after what feels like a thousand years, his voice shaking. I leave the pause to stretch out while I wait for the rest. Either a barrage of apologies and excuses, or the alternative. Him saying he's sorry because it's over. It doesn't come quick enough and in the end, I can't help but fill the gap.

'Sorry about what? Which bit? Shagging someone behind my back, or getting caught? Destroying our marriage or the fact that you're only now telling me it's over?' My voice is anguished. 'Say something, Adam. *Tell me.* Isn't it enough to do this to me without leaving some sort of *X Factor*-style pause to build up the suspense?'

'Can we go into the lounge?' His rucksack is still on his shoulder. I don't want it in the house. A bag of laundry from his sordid affair. That he'll drop into the basket along with all the other clothes, expecting someone – me – to wash it.

'If you're going to leave me, I don't want it to be in the living room.' This suddenly feels very important and I don't know why. Maybe because last June after Mum told me about her cancer, Adam held me there while I cried. In my head it still seems like a place of sanctuary.

'I'm not going to leave you,' he says quietly. He finally drops his bag and rubs his left shoulder. It's been giving him gyp for weeks. The aches and pains of being over forty, I joked with him the other day. I offered to make him an appointment at the osteopath. *For his sex injuries*, I think now. He rubs his hand over his stubble. Takes a big breath. He's stalling. 'I don't know what this . . . thing is. Was.'

'Was?' I spit it out. 'As of midnight, it looked pretty ongoing to me. Did you dump her while you were on a stationary train in Doncaster?'

'No.' His eyes drop and he fiddles with his coat zip again before giving up on it. I can see his hands shaking. Good. 'But I will end it. It's not what you think.'

'Do tell me what I think, Adam. No, *do*.'

'It's been a difficult few months,' he says, stepping closer towards me. I instinctively step back. 'Don't you feel that?'

It has. Mum's illness came without warning, the full horror coinciding with Sav starting school in September, which she's decided she hates. Earlier in the summer, Adam's work decided to make them all reapply for their jobs – without necessarily being guaranteed one at the end of the process. 'Difficult' is an understatement; I'd say it's been hideous. But I didn't start fucking someone else as an escape. I started running.

'Are you telling me you had an affair because you've been stressed? With that logic I should have been shagging both the Hemsworth brothers by now.'

'Who are the Hemsworth brothers?'

I forgot that Adam's too worthy to know anything about pop culture. He didn't have a TV when we first met. I should have dumped him then. 'It's irrelevant,' I snap. 'Don't change the subject.'

His eyes flare with a spark of annoyance. 'Well, what do you want me to say? Nothing I say now will be right.' He sighs. Rubs his chin again, as though the whole conversation is making him weary. 'I didn't mean for it to happen—'

'Which time?' I interrupt. I'm not having him getting defensive, not when he's the one in the wrong. 'Or at all?' I can't get my words out fast enough. It's as though I'm trying to speak while running; I'm not taking in enough breath between words.

He at least has the respect to look ashamed. 'No. Yes. Neither. We ran into each other. A while back. And we stayed in touch. It wasn't . . .' His eyes flick over me, and I want to cry at the casual judgement. All I can think about are the pictures I saw of Jules last night while deep-diving into her Instagram feed and how I nowhere near measure up, particularly not right now. She's all jet-setting around the world for beach sunset set-ups and cocktails in Miami. Shiny, almost black hair, with tanned skin and liquid brown eyes. She's a cross between the actress who plays Wonder Woman and a Kardashian sister, except without the identikit pillow face. Photo after photo of her looking curvy and strong while sipping green juices, hiking up Runyon Canyon in LA or wearing her hair braided in front of waterfalls. It's like she has one of those Insta-husbands following her around to take eight thousand versions of the same almost perfect shot until they get the right one, except if she had a husband, she wouldn't be shagging mine, would she? Maybe she would. After all, she's sodding Wonder Woman.

'It wasn't a thing,' he finishes. 'Not to start off with.'

'No, not until the twenty-sixth of August, to be exact.' Adam looks at me as though I'm being facetious, but I'm not. The date is seared into my brain, along with the text.

Wow. I wasn't expecting that. We should talk. I feel like I'm 17 again.

And her reply:

Go back to your wife. We'll speak soon. X

He did. Go back to his wife, that is. But he went back to her too. Again and again.

'Iris.' He reaches a hand towards me.

'Don't.' I flinch and angle myself away. 'I've read the messages. I know what you said to each other.' I also know the one thing neither of them has ever said. It's my only port in this storm of emotion. They have never said they love each other. Not over iMessage anyway.

I don't want to know the answer but I ask him anyway. 'Do you love her?'

Adam's eyes fly open in shock. 'What?'

'Please don't make me say it again.' Tears are falling down my face and I swipe at them with the raggedy cardigan-shawl thing I only ever wear around the house. 'Is she The One? The one that got away and you never got over? I knew she broke your heart but that was . . .' I work out the years in my head; Adam's forty-three in June. 'Twenty-five years ago. If you've been waiting for your moment to win her back, like some sort of pathetic Friends Reunited story, then now's the time to say.'

'No, she's not . . . The One or whatever,' he mumbles, reaching out for me again. This time I slap his hand away.

'Get. Off. Me.'

He cradles his hand in the other, a wounded look on his face as though it genuinely hurt him.

'She was someone, you know she was, I told you about her. I don't think I would have ever left Sheffield if it wasn't for her.' If Adam's trying to get sympathy for his hard-luck-northerner-done-good story, he's picked the wrong time. Raised by a single parent, absent father, blah blah blah.

'Yet you're willing to throw away our family for her. And what, let your kids be raised by a single mother, while you fuck off to travel the world with her.'

My missile wounds him just as it was supposed to and colour rises to his cheeks. I can see by the way his face hardens that he's angry. 'I would never abandon the kids and you know it.'

'Do I?' My voice is icy. I'm finally getting a foothold in this conversation and talking like someone in a TV show who knows exactly the right thing to say and how to hit his weak spots. Good. Yet each bit of malice I throw at him makes me feel worse. I don't want to be a character in a script with the person I love. Loved. Whatever. 'I'm not sure I know you at all. I certainly don't know what you want. So what is it? Do you want to stay married or have I done you a favour by finding out?'

His voice stumbles. 'Iris, please. I'm sorry, my head's been all over the place. You and I—'

'YOU'RE STILL NOT ANSWERING THE QUESTION,' I scream at him, and he recoils as though I'm about to hit him. As though *I'm* the one who's problematic. Something snaps inside me; my patience, my heart, who can tell. 'I want you to get out,' I decide. I hate this conversation. I hate how powerless I am to influence its outcome. I hate that he's not begging me for forgiveness.

'What?'

Now I've said it out loud I don't know how I could stand to have him here to start off with. 'You need to leave. I'll tell the kids you had to stay at your mum's a bit longer.' My mind starts whirring with the logistics. 'They don't need to know you've come back yet.'

'Where am I supposed to go?'

'I hear there's another lovely Hotel du Vin in Wimbledon,' I snarl, picking his bag up off the floor and throwing it at him. It's not heavy but he reacts by dramatically stepping back. Two days ago, I would have taken the piss out of him for that, and we'd have laughed about it. Now I think he's pathetic. 'It's not my problem where you go. I just know that I can't stand to have you here right now.'

'But we haven't sorted out . . .' He stops. 'This,' he finishes lamely.

'No, *we* haven't,' I say. 'Because I've been waiting for you to decide if you love me, if you love us, if you want to stay. And I'm no nearer to an answer. But I've realised that it's not just up to you, it's up to me too, and all I know is that I can't think with you here.'

I squeeze past him, adding another scrape to the hallway wall with my belt as I keep as far from physical contact with him as possible. Another marker of family life. Perhaps the final one. But I can't think about that right now so I open the front door instead, a blast of freezing January wind rushing in from a day that has got dark having barely got light to start with. And then I fix my expression into one more solid than I feel. 'Go, Adam. Get out.'

He takes a tentative step towards where I'm standing on the threshold. 'But what about Jack and Sav? They're back to school tomorrow and I'm supposed to be dropping them off. I want to see them.'

He's right. During the week, I have to leave for work a full hour before him. Our entire family routine relies on Adam doing the school run in the mornings.

'I'll come by and get them in the morning,' he adds. 'They'll worry if I'm not here and you won't make it to work on time otherwise.'

'They won't worry, because they're going to think you're still at your mum's. It'll be weirder if you turn up for the school run. And I don't need you to. We'll manage.' I have no idea how we'll manage. My heart twists again. 'I'll ring you in a few days and we can talk. In the meantime, you can think about what you want.' I start to usher him towards the door, but he holds his hand up, desperate.

'I don't want to leave. I want our family. I want us. We need to talk about it.'

The right words, but at the wrong time. Why didn't he say any of this earlier, when he could see I wanted it all to be a big mistake?

'I can't talk to you now. I can barely stand to look at you.'

'Please, Iris.' His eyes are frantic, searching my face for a different response.

Am I really about to chuck him out? What if he goes straight back to Jules?

Then you've answered your own question.

I look out into the street. The lamp-posts have all come on and it's deserted. Everyone keeping out of the cold and nursing their hangovers with a takeaway and a film. How I wish that was us. 'You need to go,' I say flatly. 'You don't get to say when the time is to talk about it.'

He closes the rest of the gap between us, passing me and going through the door, but then he stands in front of me on the doorstep, his tall body tensed and still.

'You can't make me leave.'

I shiver and summon up all my strength. 'No, I can't. But hardly anything you've said since you got home makes me think you care about saving us, so if you won't do the one thing I'm asking for then I know it's over. Give me some time to think and to keep things normal for the kids.'

He pauses, stares at me for a second longer, before nodding solemnly in assent. 'I'll phone them later and pretend I'm at Mum's.'

It's this small act of complicity that threatens to overwhelm me. To protect them, I have to protect him.

I shut the door before I can see which direction he goes in and then sit down on the stairs, looking at the door, half expecting him to come back. I pull my phone out of my pocket. My husband is gone. Who can I say that to? I'm ashamed and embarrassed. Fran already knows the bare bones, but I can't ring her when she's with the children. I'll fill her in when she drops them off in a couple of hours. Until then I need to sort out the practicalities, like how they're getting to school tomorrow. More than anything, I wish Mum was here. For many, many reasons. Am I going to have to pull a sickie on the first day back of the year, when I'm going to be expected to be refreshed and on it? I swipe my phone open, and sniff as hard as I can while wiping my face on my cardie. I think of Jules in her body-con sportswear, hiking. Under my baggy cardie, I'm wearing a slogan T-shirt that says 'Give Peas a Chance' that Jack (Adam) bought for my birthday two years ago, and boyfriend jeans that look cool when people like Rosie Huntington-Whiteley wear them with heels and slouchy tops, but on my pear shape make me look like a middle-aged refugee from an Avril Lavigne gig.

Don't think about Jules.

Another sniff and I think about the one person I can depend on, stabbing at the contact. The phone quickly connects.

'Happy New Year, Iris.'

'Happy New Year,' I reply, my voice thick from suppressed tears. I force myself to sound perky. 'Adam's been called up to a family crisis in Sheffield, but the kids go back to school tomorrow. Dad, I don't suppose you'd be able to help me out for a couple of days, would you?'

Chapter Three

2 January, 7 a.m.

'I want a Curly Wurly!'

'No, Jack. I said NO,' I snap as I slam closed the kitchen cupboard, narrowly avoiding his fingers and wincing at my own carelessness. 'Toast or cereal.'

'I hate toast with seeds in it,' he mutters, just as I remember we don't have any bread anyway.

'Fine. Cereal it is.' I shove a box of Cheerios in his direction. He deliberately doesn't catch it and the box tips, Cheerios skittering all over the counter. He starts laughing.

'JACK!'

'You're the one who pushed it over.'

It could be a typical weekday morning, with me endlessly losing it, when Sav comes into the room, climbs onto a seat at the kitchen table and says, 'Where's Daddy?'

My heart squeezes. She's sitting there all sleepy in her favourite unicorn pyjamas, completely unaware of the way our lives have collapsed.

'I told you, sweets, he's at a work thingy. He's got to meet some important people about raising some money for his charity.'

The doorbell goes, saving me from any further explanation, and I run into the hallway to answer it.

Even though he was here on Christmas Day – eight days that now feel like eight years ago – Dad's slightly wrinkled shirt and could-do-with-a-wash chinos (Dad is of the generation that thinks you should look smart even when at home) seem bigger, baggier. Registering this spears guilt through my anguish. I haven't seen him enough. Does he even know how to work the washing machine? The iron? Mum didn't like him meddling with 'her' appliances, which took care of both the laundry *and* any responsibility he might have felt about being a 'new man', as he occasionally called it.

He waits on the doorstep for me to let him in, clutching the little wheelie suitcase (cabin baggage-approved size) Mum got in the sale at Debenhams a few years ago. Mum would have used her key, then started tidying up as she made her way from the hall to the kitchen.

'Come in,' I say, swallowing him in a massive hug as he steps into the hall. He looks inordinately pleased to be here. The hug takes me as much by surprise as him. He's never been a big man, but now my 5'6 seems to completely dwarf him. He hugs me back, almost sagging against my weight, and we stand there for a minute holding on to each other. Did I even hug him on Christmas Day? The last time I can remember doing it is at Mum's funeral, a fact that makes me want to burst into tears.

'I'm glad you're here,' I say. Which is true. I want my mum, but I miss my dad too. Steady, constant Dad, looking perplexed whenever I talked through a drama with Mum but not saying anything, just helping out with practicalities like offering lifts or discreetly taking the kids to the park so I could vent. I want him to lead me to the sofa, sit me down and tell me what to do. Whether to leave Adam or to fight for my marriage. Or to simply agree that there's nothing worse than the hurt and humiliation I feel right now. But I also don't want Dad to know what Adam has done or to ponder why he might have done it. Mum and Dad always had a running joke that I was a bit of a drama queen, but during a row once, Dad told me that I was 'hard work'. I've never forgotten it. He might have felt guiltier about the time he smacked my bum for deliberately smashing a plate when I was four – and of course that's the memory I'd wheel out whenever I was pissed off and threatened to call Childline – but it's that off-the-cuff remark when I was fifteen that has burned the longest. Maybe I am hard work. Maybe I'm too much. Maybe Adam craved someone more self-sufficient, less needy. Or better looking, more successful, sexier.

Dad pulls away from the hug with an awkward clearance of his throat. 'Sorry I couldn't come any sooner. There were no trains running from Weybridge yesterday, New Year and all that. I didn't want to bring the car, wasn't sure about parking permits.'

'God, don't worry, it's fine.' This morning would have been way easier if he'd been here last night, but I might also have had to talk to him properly. It's probably better all round if I only have twenty-five minutes before I have to leave the house. 'Cuppa?' I say, just to be saying something, and to get us out of the hall and into a situation where I can feasibly leave for work.

'Lovely,' he replies, parking his suitcase and following me to the kitchen.

'Gan-Gan's here!' Sav shouts, jumping up from her chair and hurling herself at Dad's legs.

'Steady, Sav,' I say, holding out an arm to stop Dad from falling over. A trip to A&E is probably the only thing that could make life worse right now.

'Hello, Iris darling,' Dad says, leaning down to hug her.

'I'm not Iris, I'm Savannah,' Sav says, bursting out laughing. 'Silly Gan-Gan.'

Dad laughs too but I see a flicker of insecurity in his eyes. He's always done that, got everyone's names mixed up, but lately he has been doing it more. Sign of getting old. I usually ignore it; he won't like Sav drawing attention to it.

'Thanks again for coming, Dad, it's a big help. Adam . . .' I'm not sure I'm ever going to be able to say his name again without my stomach lurching. 'His boss sprang this stupid trip on him. Who does that on the first day back of the New Year? A training course in bloody' – where did I say? – 'Portsmouth.'

Dad's face crinkles in confusion. 'I thought you said it was a family crisis up north. I hope everything's all right.'

That's right. How did Adam manage to have an entire affair when I can't even get this one story straight? And why am I the one having to cover for him? I choke out a small laugh.

'Yeah, I assumed it was something to do with Gabe – you know what he's like – when he told me about it at the last minute, but no, just his boss assuming he could drop everything and rush off. He's got to give some training to a sister charity down there, so they can learn how to deliver the events in schools. He might have to go to Sheffield at the weekend though.' Too late I realise that this isn't what I told the kids. I'm babbling and can't stop.

Dad chuckles, not noticing the prickling sheen of sweat that has formed over my cheeks and forehead. 'Or Adam forgot to tell you,' he says. 'You know what us blokes are like, pretty rubbish at organisation.' Dad sits himself down at the kitchen table and Jack instantly starts chatting to him, while I turn away and flick on the kettle, discreetly wiping my tearful face with a damp tea towel. 'Your mother had that big calendar with everything marked in – birthdays with ages, holidays, appointments, the days all the bills were due. God forbid I sprang something on her. Except I always did, of course. Those conferences I had to go to, I always completely forgot about them until the day before. She was at home anyway though, so it never threw her too much, apart from the annoyance. But it's not the modern way, is it? Not the done thing to stay at home any more.'

The subtle dig registers, even on top of the warm memory of Mum always being at home.

I let it go, not trusting myself to answer, and discover Jack has topped his bowl of Cheerios with chocolate raisins.

'What? It's only like having a bowl of cereal with chocolate bits in it,' he says, his cheekiest, most insolent look on his face.

'We don't buy cereal with chocolate bits in it,' I reply tightly. 'Because it's bad for your teeth.'

'Oh, let him just this once, Iris,' Dad interrupts, and the only reason I don't kick him out there and then is because I need him so much right now.

The triumphant look Jack shoots me reminds me so much of Adam I almost gasp. I force my mind to run over all the small tasks I need to do before school. Mornings are Adam's domain. Were. What do I need to remember so they stand a chance of leaving on time?

'Grandad's going to take you to school because Daddy's away,' I explain.

'I DON'T WANT TO GO TO SCHOOL,' Sav instantly shouts. She's hated it ever since she moved up from pre-school to big school and we – Adam – has this routine every morning. I don't have time for it now.

'Dad, I have to go in twenty minutes,' I say, looking down at my crumpled pyjamas. I haven't showered since New Year's Eve and I can practically feel the grease working its way along my hair. It's blonde and bobbed and looks all right when I have time to style it, but it also needs washing every day if it's not going to resemble a flat, oily helmet.

'So let me run you through everything. Sav likes a bagel for breakfast.' From the side of the microwave I pull out a Dulux paint chart that I swiped last time we were in B&Q. I point to two starred shades, Trench Coat and Caramel Latte. 'These are the parameters of how toasted it should be. Any darker or lighter and she won't eat it.' I clock the incredulous look my dad is giving me and hold his gaze. 'I know. But believe me, I am saving both your time and your sanity. The butter must be spread right to the edge. Jack has his Cheerios. He's not supposed to have chocolate on them, so he definitely can't have anything else after that, regardless of what he tells you.'

'Noted,' Dad replies, winking conspiratorially at Jack. Jack blinks back because he hasn't mastered winking yet.

'Dad, seriously, the dentist said we had to be strict with his sugar intake.' Whatever. Not today.

'Their uniforms are . . .' Festering at the bottom of the washing machine. I walk over and open the door before fishing them out and throwing them in the tumble dryer, ignoring the waft of damp coming off them. 'Drop-off is at eight fifty; no earlier, but before nine. Then they're both in tea-time club so you can get them any time before six; *no* later or they will fine me and/or ring social services. I'll ring them and tell them to expect you, as you'll need a password to pick them up. Can you give them their tea? I'm usually back to do the pick-ups but I have, er, a meeting.' I don't but I know if I text Fran – and maybe Nat – she'll meet me for a drink. We couldn't talk last night when she dropped the kids back, and it took every last bit of my strength to get through the bedtime routine without breaking down. I couldn't risk Jack or Sav overhearing me sobbing on the phone.

'Tea, right-o,' Dad says. 'Sausage rolls, I think.'

I start to tell him no way and that they need vegetables but instead grit my teeth. This is not a normal day. These are not normal circumstances. The rules do not apply. Adam broke them all.

'When's Daddy back?' Sav asks, throwing me. It's Wednesday and I've only thought as far as tomorrow, maybe the weekend. My stomach drops.

'I'm not sure,' I say noncommittally. If I'm not worried, they're not worried. That's the idea anyway. 'I'll ask him.' I pull out my phone, trying to look casual even though my heart is thumping.

FaceTime the kids when you get this. FYI you're going to a course in Portsmouth, then potentially back to your mum's at the weekend.

Blue ticks. He must have his phone in his hand. Why?

Portsmouth? Why Portsmouth?

Fury pulses through me.

I don't know, Adam. It was the first place that came to mind. I'm not as good a liar as you.

My phone vibrates.

Adam would like to FaceTime.

'Oh look, it's Daddy!' I call, my voice dripping with insincere cheer. 'I have to go and get ready for work.' I hand the phone wordlessly to Jack and leave the room before anyone can see yet more tears dripping down my face.

Chapter Four

2 January, 6 p.m.

'Have you heard from *him*?' Fran is holding two empty wine glasses upside down between her fingers. She flips them over and pours out two large white wines in one fluid movement. We're at our usual All Bar One in King's Cross, which is on the way home from my office in Paddington, Fran's in Clerkenwell and Nat's in Canary Wharf, but also far enough away from all of our houses that we're unlikely to see anyone we know. The Christmas decorations are still up, despite party season being a distant memory and the piety of Dry January being in full swing. The barman looked positively thrilled to uncork the bottle, probably because it was a change from squeezing fresh lime into soda.

I blow out a big breath, one I feel like I've been holding in all day, and make a grab for my drink before she's finished pouring, so it ends up all over the table. 'He messaged me this morning to ask if he'd be taking the kids to school tomorrow.' One message. Business-like. That's all I got. It was like a punch to the gut.

'And?' Fran starts fiddling with her hair, swirling it first into a ponytail and then a messy bun before feeling along her wrist for a hairband to secure it. Fran is all hair. Big, glossy, dark brown hair that I think is to die for but she swears is the bane of her life because she has to plan around having enough time to wash and blow-dry it. Left to its own devices, it takes two days to dry.

'I said no. I don't want him anywhere near me or the house at the moment. I feel sick every time I think about him.'

'Fucking prick,' says Fran, swigging her own drink. The phrase has become a reflex. 'I still can't believe he wasn't grovelling to you yesterday.'

'Maybe he doesn't want to,' I say. 'His only communication has been about the kids; he didn't ask me to forgive him. I've spent all day trying not to cry at my desk.' I take another massive gulp of my wine. Earlier, at work, as I kept my head down and tried to avoid the 'How was your Christmas?' chat, I swore I wasn't going to drink. My head was foggy enough after another night of next to no sleep, but now I can't stop myself.

'Did you tell anyone at work?'

'You're joking, aren't you? Happy New Year, everyone! My husband's been shagging his childhood sweetheart and now I don't even know where he's staying. Imagine if annoying Sophie' – my work nemesis – 'got hold of it. She would love nothing more than to play the role of chief comforter, while slowly extracting all the details to parse out as gossip dressed up as concern.'

My job – which I usually love – is for the National Trust. I'm a Philanthropy Manager, which involves looking after our high-rolling donors, nurturing the relationships between the Trust and its wealthiest benefactors, and organising special events and tours. It's busy and intense, with *a lot* of one-to-one meetings and phone calls – pretty unusual in a world that now runs on texts and emails, but many of our benefactors are older, and they want the personal touch when they're dropping tens of thousands of pounds on a cause. I like meeting people and loathe being trapped behind a desk, so that's one of the reasons I enjoy it. Usually. Fran – a freelance financial writer who rents a desk in a co-working space – sometimes willingly goes days without speaking to another person in a professional context and thinks I'm mental.

'Thankfully a lot of people aren't back in until next week. I had two meetings where I was expected to listen rather than contribute, and then I went to the Pret furthest away from the office to cry in the toilets for half an hour. I dodged most of the Christmas chat, and told the people who did corner me that it was hard because it was the first one without Mum.' Which is true. Christmas was already wrong before all this kicked off. 'I'm not going to be able to avoid telling people forever, though, am I?'

Fear and humiliation, fear and humiliation – my mind is pinballing between the two. My marriage is failing for the most cliched of reasons and I don't know what to do.

'I don't want anyone to know what he's done. Even you knowing makes me feel like a failure.'

Fran slams her glass back onto the table. 'You're not a failure, Iris. He's a fucking prick.'

'Is he, though? I want answers, but what if the answer is that I'm a shit wife?'

'You're not a shit wife,' she replies instantly, leaning back into her chair. 'And you don't need to tell anyone – definitely not some nosy cows at work – if you don't want to. It's none of their business—'

'But it doesn't stop people talking about it, does it?' I interrupt. I've done it myself; everyone has. I'm painfully aware that this is hot gossip. It will have every coupled-up person I know examining their own relationship and talking about my marriage as if it's a cautionary tale. There have never been any secrets about the reality of marriage, and marriage after children, between me and Fran, but that doesn't mean what she says to me is the same as what she says about me when she's alone with Liam. The idea of her – of anyone – talking to her husband about me and Adam is revolting. I imagine them saying things like, 'Well, she did work very hard,' or 'He did spend a lot of time in the north,' dissecting our lives for the pitfalls to avoid if they want their own marriage to work out.

At that moment, Nat walks in. 'Sorry, sorry,' she's saying as she approaches the table. 'I had to pick up Georgia and get her tea before I could leave the house again. Mark had to work late.' Mark always has to work late, but as usual we both ignore the implication that under normal circumstances, he would be more involved in his child's daily care.

'I'll get another glass and Iris can fill you in,' Fran says, standing up.

'No, no, I'm fine for now,' Nat replies, pulling up a chair. 'Dry January, you know how it is.'

'Good for you,' Fran says, picking up her glass and shooting Nat a look that makes it clear she's disappointed with her lack of camaraderie. Nat opens her mouth to say something else but clocks Fran's expression and shuts it again.

'It's OK, I can't stay that long either,' I say gloomily. 'Dad's there and I haven't told him what's going on. He thinks I'm at a meeting.' I take another slug. It's nice wine.

Too nice for me to be throwing down the back of my throat as quickly as possible during the forty-five minutes I have before I need to head home. 'I can't face it.' Dad will be so disappointed, maybe even disapproving. He and Mum met at nineteen, were married for fifty years, and were still sickeningly in love when she died. The fact that I didn't even meet Adam until I was thirty-one means I can never measure up to that level of first love or lifelong commitment. And now, Adam has decided I'm not what he wants after all. He changed the rules while I wasn't paying attention.

'Have you thought about what you're going to do?'

Bless Fran. The assumption that Adam has fucked up and it's entirely my decision what happens next is true friendship. But maybe Adam doesn't care if he's forgiven. Nat's eyes flit towards me but she doesn't say anything. She looks nauseated though, which is about five per cent how sick I am about it all.

I gesture at my phone, which is still resolutely silent. 'It's not like he's on his knees, begging to come back, is it? For all I know, he's with *her*.' As I say it, a spear of pain and self-pity slices through me and Nat grabs my hand to squeeze it.

'He's hiding,' says Fran, with a confidence I don't share. 'You caught him and now he's terrified of what you're going to do. You have all the power.'

'Do I?' Of all the things I feel – small, sad, inadequate, pathetic – powerful isn't one of them.

'Yes.' Fran looks annoyed with me. 'You have the kids, you're in the house, you're getting on with things without needing him to be involved.' I'm not sure shipping my dad in as a temporary nanny counts as getting on with things in a strong, independent woman sort of way, but I keep quiet because Fran's in full flow. 'Meanwhile, he's sitting there realising exactly what he's lost and how much work he needs to do if you're going to consider continuing in your marriage. Listen, I wanted to show you this.' She pulls her phone out of her bag and swipes the screen. 'Read that,' she instructs, thrusting a news article into my face as Nat leans in to look.

Women happier after divorce, new survey claims
By Hanna Williams

***Metro*, 25 September 2016**

The key to finding happiness as a woman? Getting divorced. Contrary to the lonely divorcee cliché, a new UK survey has revealed that 53% of women reported feeling 'much happier' following divorce compared to only a third of divorced men.

The survey of 1,060 divorced men and women, commissioned by The Times, asked thirty personal questions about respondents' lives and reasons for divorce to ascertain their feelings following marital separation.

Women were more likely to use celebratory language, such as 'glad' and 'fulfilled', and talked about being 'free to be myself'. Men were more likely to speak of 'failure' and 'disappointment'.

Women were also more likely to say they were happy single and weren't looking for another relationship (61%) compared to 47% of men, although both men and women spoke of 'freedom' and 'new beginnings'.

The top reason for splitting up was the respondent or their spouse 'changing as a person', but most of those surveyed gave multiple reasons. The second most common reason was 'mutual unhappiness'. A partner meeting someone else was cited by 34%, but wronged spouses take heart: of those extra-marital relationships, only half survived.

The biggest piece of advice all those surveyed gave was 'don't get married', and if you do tie the knot and it isn't working out, don't feel as though you're stuck. 'Get a divorce sooner rather than later,' said one respondent. Maybe singledom is the real happy ever after?

'The end? Turns out divorce was the first chapter.' Writer Poppy Quayle on how life began when her twenty-year marriage imploded.

'This article is nearly three years old,' I say, handing Fran's phone to Nat so she can read it properly.

'That doesn't mean it's not still true; if anything it's probably *more* true.'

I see Nat's eyes skimming over it. 'Fran, this is a bit premature, isn't it? Who's talking about divorce?'

Fran shoots her another look. 'Well, we're not *not* talking about divorce, are we?'

'He's ended the affair though, hasn't he?' Nat asks. 'Like, she's gone, done, dumped. He's promised you that, right?'

'He hasn't promised me anything,' I say dully. I've been obsessively checking Jules's Instagram today for any evidence of either heartbreak or triumph, and there's been nothing. Not even one of her 'sunrise as seen from the cockpit of a plane – oh, by the way, have I mentioned I'm a pilot' specials. 'I haven't spoken to him.'

'He will, though. I'm sure he knows what a massive mistake it's all been. Of course it is. You're such a good couple,' she carries on. 'And you have to think about the kids too. It's so much better for them if their parents are together.' And just like that my hackles are on high alert.

How would she know what's better for my kids? How dare she?

'I'm not going to do anything on a whim, Nat,' I say, spitting the words out like tiny pebbles. 'I can barely think at all right now.'

'You're in shock,' Fran cuts in. 'Of course you are. All I'm saying is *you* should be using this time to decide what *you* want.'

'I want to not feel like this.' The wine has hit my bloodstream. I'm getting maudlin. I was aiming for numb but it's making me muddled, as though I'm on the cusp of what a trashy women's weekly magazine would describe as a 'boozy breakdown'.

'No. Remember you don't *need* him.' Fran slaps the self-loathing down. 'Separate yourself from the hurt, the humiliation and the shock.'

I choke out a bitter laugh. 'That's basically who I am right now. Without that triumvirate, there *is* no me.'

'Iris.' Fran fixes me with a look. An 'I don't have time for this' look. Which she doesn't. She has an eight-year-old and three-year-old twins. The childcare jiggery pokery she's had to enact to meet me here at short notice proves it. Nat too. Her job as an HR manager for a bank is full on and Mark never does his share. The flexible working she negotiated after having Georgia is constantly stretched to its limit. Fran, Nat and I have a standing monthly wine date, which we Doodle into our diaries two months in advance to make sure it happens, but that meet-up isn't scheduled for another two weeks.

'Think about this: if he hadn't cheated, how would you feel about your marriage?' She holds up a hand as I start to speak about my life falling apart, quelling my rising panic about how and where I could afford to live if I was a single parent. 'Not as a reaction to what he's done or what will change in terms of the house and kids if you split – what would *you* want to do? Where do you want your life to be in, say, a year's time?'

She takes a sip of wine and gives me a small, tight, supportive smile, one that's weighted with the knowledge of every conversation about our marriages we've had in this exact bar over the years. 'You get a say in it too, and you don't have to make a decision right now, but think about it. Would you want to stay together?' The smile gives way to an enquiring look. 'Or would you want to go?'

Chapter Five

7 January, 10 a.m.

'You've been quiet. Did you have a good Christmas?'

Sophie is standing over my desk, one eyebrow raised expectantly, wearing an 'ironic' jumper that says 'January Blues' on it. I quickly pull the headphone out of my left ear and minimise my browser window, where I'm watching a TED Talk that Fran sent me titled 'How Not to Let a Break-Up Break You'.

'Happy New Year, Sophie,' I reply wearily. 'And yes, fine, thanks.'

'You look . . .' She lets that hang in the air for a moment. 'Have you had that cold that's been going around?'

I consider my outfit. Grey trousers and a black woollen sweater, about as far from the bright tailored dresses I like to wear for work as possible. And my face is probably as grey as my jumper. Any make-up I applied this morning will have seeped into my deepening worry lines, and I'm so tearful I couldn't risk any eyeshadow. She might as well say I look like shit.

'No.' I hope that shuts her down, but she nods and waits for me to ask about hers. I can't bring myself to. Every office has a martyr and ours is my fellow Philanthropy Manager, Sophie. She's always lamenting things that nobody else cares about, like running out of the speciality teabags that only she drinks and acting as though it's incredibly unfair that she has to pay for them out of her own pocket, even though we all chip in for the PG Tips. I have analysed my feelings towards her many times and there's nothing in particular I can pinpoint about her that is 'bad', which in turn makes me feel antifeminist, but I've come to the conclusion that it's not unsisterly for someone to piss you off. She just *is* annoying.

'I know you've only just sat down' – her eyes flick to the clock on the office wall above my desk, a pass-agg acknowledgement that I am late, as I have been every day since I came back to work after Christmas – 'but there are some urgent donor emails that Vanessa says need actioning within the hour and they need your input.'

There are always some urgent donor emails to deal with, particularly in January when we run through our donor activity for the year, and book in events to try and retain our big spenders after their charitable donations at Christmas. Meetings upon meetings upon meetings to ensure everyone feels appreciated – and we hit our targets. Usually I thrive on it, the good sort of stress, but the problem with being a team player and a mucker-inner is that everyone notices immediately when you stop mucking in.

I pull up my inbox and try not to wince at the two hundred unread messages that glare out at me. Anything I can't get to during the day I usually clear in stages in the evening or over the weekend, so that I stay as close to inbox zero as possible. I'm forever missing vital plot points in Netflix dramas because I've got one eye on my phone while watching something with Adam. It's the only way of keeping on top of the queries and requests that come from donors who are spending a lot of money and aren't used to having to wait for a response. It also means that my colleagues now expect me to reply swiftly, even out of office hours. I know – rod, own back and all that – but it's part of the reason I have been promoted twice since starting here, and our director Vanessa refers to me as her rock (usually when she wants to palm off a job, but even so).

However, this weekend all I could think about – between the activities with the kids I jam-packed into it to avoid thinking about why Adam hadn't been in touch with me, other than that one attempt to take them to school – was Fran's question. I drove myself mad wondering where he was, who he was with, while refusing to break and message him first. It wasn't him who had to deal with Jack's questions, Sav's questions, *Dad's* questions, about where he was and when he'd be back. It wasn't until yesterday morning, Sunday, when the sun crept out for a couple of hours, Dad offered to walk the kids down to the park, and I had some headspace to think, that he finally kicked into gear.

Can I speak to the kids?

They're out.

I didn't say where and I didn't say who with. Why should I?

We should talk too.

Anger thudding through my chest, I started to type 'oh should we', but instead I ignored him, not knowing if it was a half-hearted attempt at reconciliation, or if he was trying to pin me down so he could end our marriage.

I wasn't ready to find out. I don't know how you ever prepare for something like that.

My phone buzzes and I jump, but it's Dad with one of his sporadic misspelled texts. I can never work out if he doesn't know the grammar or just can't find it on his phone.

SAV was supposed.to.HaVe a costume today? Got upset at school when. Wasn't.One.X

Shit. It was 'wear green to go green' day today. Total contradiction seeing as it meant buying a cheap new outfit most likely made in a sweatshop and destined for landfill, but still.

Sorry Dad. My fault. Completely forgot. Tell her we'll sponsor a bear or something instead.

. . .

TEDDY BEAR?

No, it was a dress-up day to raise money for the environment. We can do something for an environmental charity instead. I'll explain later.

'So . . .'

I jump, realising Sophie is still looming over me, her right hand hooked through 'her' work mug. ('For everything else, there's Prosecco,' it says. I want to smash it on the floor.)

'What?' I snap.

'The emails,' she says.

'Are you going to stand over me while I write them?' I don't bother grinding the edge off my voice. My phone lights up again on my desk and both our sets of eyes flit to it. My heart stops. Adam.

Iris, please. Talk to me.

I flip the phone over so hard that two people turn around to see what the banging is. The 'please' is the first bit of wheedling he's done. Fran warned me this would happen. That bit by bit my sadness would give way to anger. Well, forget bit by bit, it's more like a deluge. Total silence and a simpering text asking to talk, no apology, no evidence that he's ended the affair or has any intention of doing so, and he expects me to drop everything when he knows I'm at work. He knows the beginning of the year is manic here. All I can think is, *how dare you*. How dare he decide this is all on his schedule? Why does he get to call the shots? WHY?

'Right,' I bark at Sophie, channelling the pulsing anger into a voice that hopefully makes me sound efficient and on it, rather than batshit crazy and borderline hysterical. 'I'll get to those emails now, Soph, then finalise the guest list for February's donor brunch for Vanessa to approve before I proofread the invitation and send it off to the printers.' I force myself to smile at her. 'I'll schedule a team catch-up for this afternoon so we can all get an update, much more efficient than loads of side-chats.' I angle my swivel chair away from her so she's in no doubt that our conversation is over, and look at my screen until my breath evens out and the blood stops pulsing through my temples.

I'm not a passive player in this. I refuse to let this situation just happen to me.

You're right, we do need to talk. Once I've finished my appointment with the solicitor tonight, I'll let you know a time.

Pressing send evaporates any sense of victory, replacing it with the now familiar fear. I put my phone on silent and shove it in my bag, scanning my inbox again. One from Vanessa re: Lucas Caulfield. Usually seeing that name would be our office cue to start gossiping about him – well, what little we know. He's a legendary figure because he gives so much money to the Trust, but is insistent on remaining anonymous. He never attends any of our donor drinks receptions, and has so far politely declined our invitations to visit the Trust's properties. However, we have his name, so as soon as he came onto our books – along with the exact six-figure number that he donates per year – we immediately Googled him. Vanessa made a big show of saying we shouldn't, before joining the others around my desk where it took about three clicks to discover that, not only is he a filthy rich partner in a venture capitalist firm, who made his fortune investing in a meat-free burger bio-engineering start-up that's being lauded to help solve climate change, he's also gorgeous. Vanessa will want a quick response to this one, so I quickly skim the email to see what action we need to take.

From: Vanessa Meldrum
Date: 7 January
To: Iris Young; Sophie Carmichael; Taylor Lowry; Lynette Simpson
Subject: Fw: Site visit
Dear Vanessa
Happy New Year to you too. And thank you so much for your kind offer of guided site visits during 2021. I have a window in my schedule on 25 Jan – early afternoon – and would love to visit Chatterstone House. Anon of course, no embarrassing donor

introductions to the staff. Assume this works?
Best
LC

Vanessa has been schmoozing him for months so will be livid about the date he's picked; her daughter is getting married in Mauritius that week which means she won't be able to lead the visit. The question is who will? I feel a reassuring flare of ambition and write down 'Chatterstone visit?' at the top of my to-do list. Sophie – tediously – is right though. I need to see what urgent responses are needed for the two hundred other unread emails I should have already caught up on, before I brainstorm how to impress 'LC'. If I'm about to become a single parent I have to be good at my job, and I'm already starting the year on the back foot. I hover the cursor over the first one.

But before that.

I turn around to make sure Sophie isn't hovering around my desk again and type 'divorce + lawyers + London' into my search bar.

Chapter Six

7 January, 6.15 p.m.

'How can I help you today?' asks Tabitha Douglas of Douglas, Douglas and Reid. She's about fifty years old with a sleek black bob and wearing a grey skirt suit with a purple shirt, the very image of what would come up if you were to Google 'capable professional woman'. She has been talking weeping women (I'm speculating) through the divorce process from her chic office in a Regency terrace in Holborn since nine this morning; many of them, like me (again I'm speculating), having booked free consultations as part of the firm's New Year's special offer. Divorce lawyers do January sales – who knew? It turns out everyone does, because for the first time in my forty-one years, I'm completely on trend. The *Metro* article I read during the tube ride here told me that so many people consult a divorce lawyer on the first working Monday of the New Year that it's been dubbed 'D-Day'. My marital anguish isn't even unique. I should have known when the first two solicitors I called were fully booked. It took me three attempts to find a female one with an after-work appointment.

'I wanted to get some advice on how to file for a . . .' My voice disappears as I try to get out the word 'divorce'.

Tabitha doesn't bat an eye as I visibly tense under her gaze, and that calms me down.

'I'm exploring my options,' I say carefully, trying hard not to blurt out the whole mess. I remind myself she's a solicitor, not a therapist. 'I found out my husband has been having an affair and I want to know where I and the children stand, should I decide to leave.'

'I see.' No judgement, just a brisk nod and a soft but penetrating stare. 'I'm so sorry, it must have been a terrible shock.' There's a certain warmth beneath her words but not enough to set me off. Which I like. She's no-nonsense, exactly what you want in a divorce lawyer. I've got Fran for the other stuff.

Besides, my sob-story probably barely even registers. Imagine the stories of abuse she's listened to. Only in this situation could my lowest moment seem comparatively positive. Husband cheats; wife leaves; assets and custody split; the end.

As Tabitha explains that the divorce process begins when one party sends their petition to court, I glance around her neat office. Law books line one wall with filing cabinets – custom-made, not the battered and squeaky grey metal type we've got at work – running along the opposite one. All I can think about are the lives contained within them. Hundreds of families, many that were once happy, distilled into an inventory of each horrible moment you experienced and every crappy piece of furniture you bought together. Dissolved.

Do I want to be here?

'Should you decide to go ahead, I will talk you through each step of the process,' Tabitha is saying. 'There will be several financial factors to take into consideration, the priority being, of course, any children, and your custody arrangements. If you can agree on these areas, then the process should be relatively quick and trouble-free' – she catches my grimace – 'which I appreciate isn't the same as being painless. Do you work, Mrs Young? And does your husband?'

'Yes,' I croak. All this information has made it seem very real very quickly. 'I'm a Philanthropy Manager for the National Trust, and he's a Project Manager for a charity that goes into schools to teach teenagers about gender equality.' The irony of my cheating husband having a job that people always coo about for its 'goodness' is not lost on me here. 'We earn roughly the same amount of money—' I stop. 'Roughly' is no longer going to cut it, not when – if – our finances are going to be subject to scrutiny. What would my life be like financially if we broke up? How would I manage? 'I earn three thousand pounds a year more than he does.'

Tabitha nods again.

'We share the childcare, we always have. I wouldn't be looking to take them away from him.' Or would I? Shared custody would mean not seeing Jack and Sav for half the week. How would I even make their school week and my working life function without Adam around to do his share? But not having them with me is unthinkable. Of all the mini tragedies of the past few days, the prospect of this one is most painful. Spending half the week alone, and then half the week with them but without a partner to share the minutiae of everyday family life. So many memories unshared and lost, because they only exist with the person who knows the rest of the story. To think about what I might forget without Adam reminding me overwhelms me with sadness.

A small voice pipes up inside my head.

You don't have to leave.

But who stays?

Beyoncé. Beyoncé stayed. And then she wrote an award-winning album about it. I hold in an urge to laugh. Something tells me I'm not going to mine my best creative material out of this whole shitty mess. Or look better in a sequinned leotard than ever.

'Have you discussed separation with your husband yet?' Tabitha asks, interrupting my stock-take of all the reasons I'm inferior to Beyoncé.

'No. We're not, er, in touch at the moment.' I omit that I don't know his forwarding address.

'I know it's a lot to take in.' Tabitha looks briskly at her watch and then stands up. It's a discreet move but my free consultation is clearly over, and she needs me to either hire her or bugger off.

'Do give me a call if you have any further questions, or if and when you decide to proceed. Our office shan't follow up for discretionary reasons.' She chances a small smile of solidarity.

I automatically smile back, though it's the sort of smile you do with your mouth but doesn't reach your eyes.

I shake her hand – I don't know if mine will ever stop trembling – and then find myself on the step outside the heavy black door. It's freezing and raining. The kind of hideous January evening that makes you want to get home and cosy with your family, your people, your husband. But instead, here I am in the pouring rain, running through my options outside a solicitor's.

I'm in my forties, I remind myself; this is when people start getting divorced. It's so normal it's almost expected to happen.

Not to me.

Another wave of sadness crashes over me. I want Mum. At least there's Dad, waiting at home with Jack and Sav. I try to hold on to the thought of them while I rummage for my umbrella. From the kamikaze childcare regime Dad's been practising over the last few days, there's a good chance the kids will both be up when I get back. For once I don't care that it'll send their routines all out of whack. Umbrella up, I fumble one-handed for my phone to tell him I'm coming back, and to not put them to bed until I get there, finally landing on it as I dismount the steps.

There are sixteen missed calls from Adam.

Chapter Seven

7 January, 7.30 p.m.

'Can you forgive me?'

I can see the strain around Adam's eyes, and the crease in his brow that seems deeper than the last time I saw him. He looks desperate, devastated, shattered. He looks how I wanted him to look a few days ago. Anxiety thrums around my body as I take in the sight of him after five long days, and I wonder how I look to him. Broken? Bitter? Or does he barely think anything of me at this point? I didn't know he was shagging someone else, so how would I know anything any more?

We're in the pub around the corner from our house. The hipster one we never come to because we're always with the kids and they don't allow them, but that we sometimes look into yearningly on a rainy Saturday when we'd love nothing more than to be able to nip in for a quiet drink and a read of the papers. We're at a corner table, him on the seat that runs along the wall and me perched on a stool, further away. I couldn't bring myself to sit next to him; it seemed too intimate.

'I don't know.' It's true, I don't. I want all of the detail about Jules and I want none of it at the same time. I don't know if I'll ever be able to look at him and not think of her. 'Do you even want me to forgive you?' More than anything, I want *answers*. 'I love our family, Adam. Loved how it was. It kills me that you didn't.'

'I did! I do.' He leans forward hard onto the table to emphasise his point, causing the table and both our drinks to tip up. His beer and my lime and soda slosh over the table towards him and he jerks back to avoid the spill. I don't do anything to help clear it up.

'Then why?' I say.

He looks twisted, broken. 'I don't know,' he says finally.

I start to cry. It's all I seem to do these days. 'That's not good enough. It makes it worse that you would ruin everything for no reason. You were supposed to be one of the good ones.'

He *was* one of the good ones. I thought he was anyway. We didn't meet until we were in our thirties, when we were supposed to have got all the crappy relationships and bad behaviour out of the way, and an internet algorithm had filtered out the worst of the mediocre and/or unsuitable men. Adam transitioned into being my boyfriend only a few weeks after our first date. He was kind. He was respectful. He was a grown-up. None of those qualities sound very sexy, but when you also fancy the pants off the person in possession of them, they really are. I didn't just fall hard in love with him, I felt like I'd hit the jackpot.

'I wish I had something more I could tell you,' he says in a quiet voice. 'Something better that explains why I've been so fucking stupid. I could lie to you, petal – keep lying – but I don't want to.'

'How do I know you're not?' I interrupt, and his eyes widen in fear. 'I have no idea when you're telling the truth these days, so how do I know this isn't another spiel?' I shift my stool a few inches further away from the table. The liquid on the surface is edging in my direction now. 'And don't call me petal.'

No one else calls me that. It's the nickname he gave to me because, Iris. He always says it in a Geordie accent because it's not a Sheffield thing, even though I used to joke that to someone born in Surrey like me, all northern is the same.

He looks as though he's going to lean towards me again then seems to reconsider, folding his hands into his lap instead. 'All I know is that I've never been more scared than when you sent that message saying you were seeing a solicitor.'

'Why? You've barely been in touch. Complete silence. You were gone. Consulting a solicitor is the logical next step when your husband has an affair and you don't hear from him.'

'I thought if I hassled you it would make you angry. I wanted to give you space.'

'All that lovely luxurious space,' I say scornfully. 'Also known as trying to keep everything normal for Jack and Sav, lying to Dad, trudging to work. Where were you?'

'What?' He looks taken aback. It's obviously not the question he was expecting.

'Where were you? When I sent that message.'

'At work.'

Is he being defensive? 'You know what I mean. Where have you been staying?' I'm watching him for even a flicker of shifty eyes, a fidget, a rogue twitch.

'Calum's.'

I almost snort out a laugh. 'Calum's! Where even is Calum's right now?'

Adam gives me a small, grim smile. Calum and his topsy-turvy living arrangements are a source of endless fascination to us. Were. He's one of Adam's uni friends who never quite got his act together. He moves around between guardianship properties – buildings due to be knocked down or converted which need tenants to stop squatters from taking over. It means the buildings are occupied and the tenants only have to pay minimal rent, mainly because they're still set up as, say, a care home or a school rather than a private rental property. It suits Calum because he still harbours the dream-slash-delusion that he's going to be a successful musician one day, and won't get a 'proper' bill-paying job to subsidise his rock-star dream. But unfortunately, he's not that good.

'He's in an old infant school in Kentish Town. It's pretty hard to use the loos.' Adam gestures somewhere just above his shins, demonstrating the height of a tiny child's toilet. We almost share a conspiratorial smile. Then I remember all over again.

'Not with . . . her then?'

'No!'

He looks outraged at the suggestion, but does he flinch? I can't tell. I let a long shaky breath out. Where does a successful pilot even live? Near Heathrow or Gatwick, presumably.

'Don't say it as though it's an outlandish suggestion. You've been gone six days, Adam. SIX DAYS. Where was I supposed to think you were?'

'You told me to leave.'

'I told you to leave the house. I didn't tell you to evaporate into thin air. And I definitely didn't tell you to shack up with your mistress.'

'I didn't! Iris, I promise, no. I was with Calum. You can ring him.' He holds his phone out to me and I want to snatch it, unlock it and devour everything inside it. He's changed the password or the settings, or both, because the iPad doesn't sync to it any more. I know, I've checked. Surely, he would have deleted any incriminating messages before handing it over to me like this.

'It's all right. I believe you.' I reconsider, because I don't. 'Unlock it so I can see who's in your message lists.'

Does he look taken aback? Like he wasn't sure I was going to call his bluff? Again I can't read the expression on his face. It's hard to keep one eye on him and one eye on the names as I scroll down his call log: me, his mum, work. Then a few numbers not saved as contacts all come up in a row.

'Who are these?' I ask sharply, hating myself for needing to know.

'Volunteers for a workshop we ran at a school on Friday,' he says, arms folded across his chest. 'People who work at Morgan Stanley and had signed up to be mentors. I swear. I had to go to the reception to meet them and then sign them in as they arrived.' The call times tally with his story. But.

I flip to his WhatsApp. Me, Calum, a group of his uni mates trying to sort out a weekend they're all free to meet up. Adam hasn't responded to any of the suggested dates.

His text inbox, his email, Messenger, Twitter DMs: all clear. What does it mean, other than that he cleaned house before coming to meet me?

'There's no need for you to be suspicious,' he says, taking an anxious sip of his drink.

'"Suspicious" implies something is unfounded,' I fire back, sliding his phone across the table.

'I haven't been in touch with' – he tries again – 'Jules since I told her it was over. I told her I couldn't contact her again.'

Couldn't, or wouldn't. My brain hurts from trying to interpret his choice of words. I want to know how she took it, what she said. If she slagged me off or tried to convince him to change his mind. Maybe she didn't care and walked away without looking back. Pilots are pretty renowned for their laissez-faire attitude to fidelity, aren't they? Maybe that's the only reason he's sitting here now. She didn't want him anyway. Or maybe it's not even over.

I don't say anything.

'Please, Iris, I promise.' His eyes search for mine, but I still can't look at him.

'We never come out for drinks, do we? Not on our own.'

That confused face again. As though he can't keep up with the topics my scattergun brain lands on. He should try being in it.

'Not for a while, no,' he says evenly.

'Was that why you cheated? You got bored with me because we're so domestic and dull that we barely even have time to come to the pub?' I know I sound pathetic, but I want to know, for there to be a reason.

'No. I can't explain it. It just felt like something that didn't have consequences. It was completely separate from us, from what we had. I didn't expect—'

'To fall in love?' My voice is a scratch, dreading the answer.

'NO! For it to impact our life together,' he says miserably. 'I know it sounds inadequate. I didn't think of it as something with a future. I wasn't thinking at all.' We sit in silence for a minute. The pub is quiet. The only other punters are a couple eating some small plates and a group of four women who keep ordering drinks and squealing. From the looks of the endless selfies with her ring finger held aloft, one of them has got engaged. I try not to hate her.

'Are you going to leave me?' Adam asks. His voice wobbles, which makes my insides crumble before solidifying into something sharp.

'You already left me. Left us,' I snap back. 'And after your dad did it to you, too. How could you? You were always so adamant that he was a scumbag, so how are you any different?'

Adam goes pale, as though he's been winded. It's a low blow, but I want to hurt him the way he has me. Adam's dad boomeranged in and out of his life for years and did it all – drinking, gambling, cheating. His mum kept kicking him out and taking him back, before he buggered off for good when Gabe was nine and Adam fifteen. He still lives in Sheffield and makes zero effort with either of his children. Hasn't for years. Running into his dad unexpectedly is often the start of Gabe getting up to some nonsense.

Adam looks down at the table and when he looks up again, he's crying. 'Fuck. I'm like him, aren't I? What have you told Jack and Sav?' He's properly weeping now, pulling his hands through his hair and worrying the skin around his hairline. Panicked. 'Do they hate me? Shit. Iris, I thought I was doing the right thing by giving you time to think, but do they think I've abandoned them? If they thought about me the way I think about Patrick' – Adam never calls him Dad – 'I'd never forgive myself.'

'They don't. They wouldn't.' I toss him the packet of tissues from my bag. One of them. I'm currently keeping Boots in business. I want to pull him in close to me and then bang his head against the table while shouting, *SO WHY DID YOU DO IT THEN?* 'You're a good dad.' He is. He's a great dad. I sigh. 'You're just a shitty husband.'

'Can I come back home?' he says quietly. 'I need to see them.'

I pull another pack of tissues from my bag and start mopping up the spillage, concentrating on getting it all so I don't have to focus on his face. He dries his eyes, squeezes a tissue around his nose, but he's still all blotchy. I can see his chin wobbling as he presses his lips together to contain his emotion.

'I would never stop you from seeing them, Adam, whatever happened between us. We'd work out an arrangement. They need their dad.'

'I didn't mean that. But I do appreciate you saying it,' he adds hurriedly. 'I meant can I come home, now, with you, and we try to work this out.'

'Oh.'

My brain is liquid. An hour ago, I was seeing a divorce lawyer. A week ago, I thought I was happily – or not unhappily – married. Who knows what I'll think later today, never mind next week?

'I don't know,' I admit. 'What would that even look like? Even if you came back, it wouldn't be the same. Might not ever be the same. Fran thinks I should kick you out for good.'

'And what do you think?' he asks, eyes red-rimmed and making no attempt to stop his lip trembling now. He gets on with Fran, but we're not one of those couples that only socialises with other couples. There are 'our' friends – ones we've made as parents since Jack and Sav came along – but we also have our own. Fran is my friend, my ally.

I shrug. 'I wish I could be as sure as her about what the right answer is.'

We're in marriage purgatory. I think of all the books stacked next to my bed. Self-help guides on work-life balance, on asking for your worth at work, on parenting, on self-love. Where's the one that will solve this for me? Then I think of the children and telling them that Adam isn't coming back, seeing the fear and insecurity on their faces. Of them asking why Daddy left them.

Stick/twist, stay/go: the two thoughts are speeding around my brain from the second I gasp awake to the minute I finally get my twitchy mind to stop at night.

Fran's words come back to me again. What do I want my life to look like in a year's time?

'*If* you came back – and I mean *if* – it would be a trial.'

Adam looks so elated that I start to thaw. A tiny bit. Trying can't make me any sadder than I am now, can it? I'm not ready to let my marriage go.

'Yes, of course. Whatever I need to do. Tell me.' He leans forward again, an eager look on his face.

'You'll have to sleep in the spare room. I can't have you back in our bed. Not yet. Maybe not ever. I can't make any promises.'

'Sure, sure.'

'No contact with *her*.' I gulp away the nausea. 'Ever. Blocked on all channels—'

'Of course, I told you—'

I hold up a hand. 'I haven't finished. That's the basic housekeeping.'

He stops, chastened. Nods.

'You leave your phone unlocked at all times. If I want to look at it, I can. And we go to couples counselling. If we have any chance of getting past this, we need to work out why it happened to start with.'

His brow furrows. I've said for years that Adam should see someone about all his dad stuff – when Jack was born, his anxiety was through the roof over whether or not he had it in him to be a good dad – but he's always refused. Doubly ridiculous considering his work, a charity that challenges toxic male stereotypes to help teenagers break free of dangerous patterns.

'And it can't just be going through the motions to "keep me happy",' I continue. 'You commit to it. Committing to therapy is committing to us. I need to see some sign that you're committed to us.'

'How long do we need to do it for?'

I shoot him a look. 'How should I know? How long does it take to cure a marriage?' Or end one. 'All I know is that this time next year I want to be a lot happier than I am right now.'

'OK,' he says eventually, before swallowing a mouthful of his beer. 'A year then. We sort this out – give it a proper go – over the course of one year.'

A year? That seems like nothing, not in the grand scheme of things, but twelve months is also too long if it's twelve unhappy months. That means it's probably about right in terms of coming to any big decisions. 'A year,' I agree. Then one final thing comes to me. 'And Dad stays a bit longer.'

His eyes widen. I don't know why I want Dad there, but I do. I'm frightened of going home to just me and Adam, or of how hollow the promise of commitment will seem when we get back to our house, which is full of responsibilities and no time to deal with the mess our marriage has become.

'OK,' he says again, looking anything but in agreement. But what else can he say? Our relationship is no longer a democracy. I'm in charge and I have the nuclear codes, so I'm making my demands, regardless of what he might think is right or best. I'm the Donald Trump of our marriage.

Something that feels exactly as much like winning as the accolade sounds.

'Then you can come back, for now.'

A smile spreads across Adam's face, as though that's it, we've cleared the slate. 'We can spend this year working on our marriage, so next year you're happy again,' he says enthusiastically.

'Uh. Well, yes, one way or another.' *One year to become happily married or ready to get divorced*, I think. He clinks my glass and I go along with it.

'I'm coming home,' he says. 'It is what you want, right?'

'Yes,' I say, giving him a weak approximation of a smile in return. Because I do, but it's not that simple. I want my husband to come home, but I also want it to feel like home again. Can we make that happen? Can one year save us?

Chapter Eight

7 January, 8.30 p.m.

'Olives, is it?' Dad says as I plonk some bowls down on the kitchen table, and I resist the urge to tut. I'm preparing what Adam and I refer to as 'a picnic tea', AKA a ploy to make the random selection of leftovers in our fridge into an appealing meal, which is our only option given how late home we are. The kids love having Grandad here because he never tells them off. I, however, bear the full brunt of his opinions and judgements, usually centred around things he deems 'unnecessarily middle class', and apparently olives represent me becoming a bit hoity-toity. See also: fizzy water, pesto and hummus. For some reason he's decided to be offended on Mum's behalf about me serving things to the children that I never had when I was growing up.

'Yes, Dad,' I reply in a tight voice. 'Olives. But there are plenty of other things.' I fan an arm out over the table, a gesture that *might* be perceived as sarcastic if you were looking to construe it that way. 'Bread rolls, cheese, crisps, salad. Many different choices.'

He peers at the salad. 'What's that?'

'Rocket.'

He makes a shape with his mouth that I interpret as disapproval.

'Shall we eat?' I don't wait for a reply. 'JACK! SAV!'

'Grandad had his slippers on today when he picked us up from school,' Sav shrieks, as she runs in and starts piling food onto her plate.

'I was in a rush, that's all,' Dad says, smiling indulgently.

'I want to sit between Daddy and Grandad,' she says, gesturing for me to move away from my usual seat. Charming. 'Daddy!' she shouts, as Jack and Adam trail in from the living room. Jack is studiously ignoring him to convey his annoyance that he's been gone so long. He throws himself into the other 'spare' seat at our six-person dining table, the one I think of as Mum's, leaving a gap between him and the seat I have been relegated to. We're all lopsided, but I'm the only one who notices. Maybe it's because it's me who's the outsider. It feels that way, with Sav looking from Dad to Adam like there's nowhere she'd rather be. After all, I'm the one who's lost her seat.

'Not just crisps, Jack. Have some cucumber too.'

He rolls his eyes at me and picks up the thinnest sliver of cucumber he can find. He jostles another plate while reaching for some pigs in blankets I found at the back of the freezer, and the bread rolls go flying. He doesn't even attempt to pick them up. I do it instead, to give me something to do because I know I won't be able to eat anything. But I don't want anyone to notice me not eating, because I also don't want my children to think I have food issues that they might internalise.

'JACK! Pack that in!' Adam's voice roars out. Jack is gnawing at his crisps like a hamster, crumbs spilling across the table onto Dad. Jack freezes. His dad has only been back twenty minutes and he's getting bollocked. A part of me is glad they won't see him as the returning good guy of the household.

On the way to the fridge to forage for some vegetables, I pick up my phone to surreptitiously start Googling marriage counsellors. There are a couple of messages – one from Fran, telling me to let her know how the meeting with the solicitor went, but I swipe it from the screen. I'm not ready to talk about my decision to put divorce on the back burner with her yet. I have a feeling that she'll disapprove. Another emotion layered on top of all the others. There's a calendar invitation from Sophie too.

From: Sophie Carmichael
Date: 7 January
Attendance required: Iris Young, Vanessa Meldrum, Lynette Simpson, Taylor Lowry
Subject: Lucas Caulfield donor visit meeting, 16 January 10.30
To talk through the logistics for Lucas Caulfield's visit to Chatterstone House on 25th.
Iris, we put this in the diary today, but you'd already gone. I can catch you up tomorrow in advance of this meeting, if you can make sure you're in on time.

Cheeky cow. It's a time blocked out to talk about the visit, the details of which are all in Lucas's own email. Why do we need a pre-meeting meeting? Sophie's obviously flexing to show how on it she is and make me look bad by implying I skipped out on the working day. I left *ten minutes* early to get to my appointment with Tabitha, and made a big song and dance about having toothache so that everyone would believe it was an emergency dentist appointment. I stab my finger on the 'accept without comments' response.

I flip back to Google, and the list of marriage counsellors in our area. I don't even know what I'm looking for. All the websites seem to use stock photos of middle-aged people looking pensive. I mean, I guess that's us, but how do we know who's a good fit? I click on one and grimace. In what universe would someone think Comic Sans is an appropriate font for people seeking life-changing therapy? No.

One is called 'Transformations', which sounds like a plastic surgery clinic. Also no.

I click on another, which has an office near us in Finsbury Park. It has soothing pastel shades across the banner and a shot of two people laughing. I scan their list of offerings: psychosexual therapy, pre-marital counselling, couples counselling. There are ratings and reviews. Apparently, they are award-winning. How do you win a therapy award? Most cured patients? Everyone a solid one hundred per cent on the Happiness Index?

'Dr Croft gave me the tools to change my life, I'm so grateful,' says one happy customer. If we go here will I be so content that I'll be moved to write a TripAdvisor-esque review of my therapist?

They have twenty-five therapists on their books but no explanation of how it works. Do you pick or get allocated one? I scan their names and decide it definitely needs to be a woman. I don't know why, it just does. Adam will have to go along with it—

'Something more interesting on Instapics, Iris? I thought you said you wanted dinner.' The tone of Dad's voice reminds me of when I was a teenager and he was trying to 'encourage' me to do my homework. Fine, I'm lurking by the open fridge while they're all eating their dinner, but I'm instantly irritated. 'You can't expect the children to get off their screens if you're addicted to yours.' He looks for back-up to Adam, who gets halfway through an agreeable nod before my glare hits his eyeline and he goes back to his breadsticks.

'A message from work that I had to reply to,' I lie. It comes out without any effort. Is this how Adam did it?

'They shouldn't be bothering you now,' Dad mutters. 'It's bad enough that you have to leave at the crack of dawn and keep missing the kids' bedtime, without them encroaching on what time you do have with your family.'

'There's stuff I need to catch up on that I haven't managed to get done, Dad. It's hard when Adam's away.' It's hard when Adam's here too. Constant juggling and my attention being pulled all over the place, but I don't say that. I'm too annoyed that Dad doesn't mention that Adam being away for work encroaches on *his* family time. I know he doesn't approve of me working full-time. He's never said it outright but comments like this are semi-regular. Mum stayed at home, ergo I should too. Never mind that we couldn't afford it if I wanted to. Or that it would drive me utterly bonkers with boredom.

I stuff a slab of Brie into my mouth to avoid answering and slide back onto my chair. I look over at Sav. She's practically falling asleep on her plate, unsurprising considering it's almost nine o'clock and we're only just having dinner. Poor kid. Usually our household runs like a military operation. Back from after-school club by 6.30 p.m., tea, then a bath, then books, then in bed by seven thirty. Jack gets to stay up while Sav has her bath and then has his books afterwards. But the past few days have been chaos, and every time I've been back late, she's been in a sort of post-fatigue delirium. She slumps her little head onto Dad's shoulder, fluffy blonde hair all stuck up with static and breadcrumbs dotted around her mouth.

'Shall I take you up?' I ask, gesturing for Dad to pass her over to me. She fastens her arms around me like a chimp and nods into my armpit.

Adam starts to stand up. 'I'll do it,' he says.

'No,' I snap back, and Dad glances sharply at me.

'He's only just got back, Iris,' he says, with the kind of chuckle that sounds light-hearted but is in fact a judgement. 'No need to start giving him a hard time already.'

I can't help myself. 'Yes, what a royal bitch I am to my kind husband who does fifty per cent of the childcare like some sort of actual hero.'

Adam's eyes meet mine, willing me to be quiet and not grass him up in front of Dad and the children.

'You said bitch,' Jack cackles. 'How come you can say it and I can't?'

'Because Mummy understands irony,' Adam says quickly, 'and she's being silly.' He forces out a laugh and Dad joins in. If he thinks I'm going to thank him for defusing the situation, he's wrong. I blank him, but Dad is oblivious anyway, too busy analysing the plate Adam's now holding out in front of him.

'It's quiche, Dad. Even you can't have a problem with sodding mushroom quiche.' I don't wait for anyone to reply, instead sweeping out with Sav in my arms, talking softly to her while carrying her up the stairs to the sanctuary of her tiny bedroom, where there's just enough room for a child-sized bed, a chest of drawers, and a patch of floor big enough to sleep on restlessly if you need to keep an all-night vomit vigil. I click on her night light and pull the curtains shut before depositing her on the bed, and wrestling her little limbs out of her clothes and into some fleecy unicorn pyjamas. Then I pull the duvet over her and sit next to her bed on the floor, watching as she snuffles about to find a comfortable position.

She hasn't brushed her teeth, I remember, and I think, not for the first time this week: fuck it. Then I remember that I told Adam I wanted him in the spare room, but that's where Dad is. The only place left is the sofa bed in the living room, and that raises too many questions. So, he'll have to stay in our bedroom. My first request already denied.

I pull the vomit-vigil sleeping bag out from under Sav's bed and locate a flat soft toy dog that doubles as a sort of cushion when you need it to. Her breathing slows down, so I know she's on her way to sleep. When we first moved her into this room after being in with us for seven months, I'd come in two or three times a night to check she was still here and still alive, even though we had a baby monitor with a screen. I'd wake up abruptly in between her feeds and couldn't go back to sleep if I didn't reassure myself that she was OK. Sometimes I'd sit where I am now, watching her and listening to her dream and snore.

I quietly roll out the sleeping bag and climb into it, exhaustion bearing down on me. It's as though the constant adrenaline of the past few days has finally seeped out of my system, and I'm left drained and unable to get up. I don't want to go out there and apologise to Dad for being an arsehole. I don't want to go to our bedroom and face whatever awkward bed-sharing set-up we'll have to work out. And I don't want to think about what giving my marriage a 365-day deadline means. If I worked consistently hard at my job for a year, I'd expect a promotion. In this situation, is staying or leaving the promotion?

I'll stay here for a bit, I decide.

Sav murmurs, 'Night night, Mummy,' as she finally drifts off and I close my eyes, enjoying being in a place where everything is fine as long as I can hear the regular in and out breath of my sleeping child.

Chapter Nine

Transcript of initial assessment with Adam and Iris Young by Esther Moran, 15 January

Iris: Hi, hello, we're, er, here for our session. Our first session. I'm Iris.

Esther: Hello, Iris, have a seat. I'm Esther.

Adam: Adam. Hi.

Esther: Do sit down.

Iris: So how does it work? Do you take notes? Who talks first?

Esther: I'm sure you'll have a lot of questions—

Iris: Sorry, I'm a bit nervous. I'm not sure about this, telling a total stranger everything about us.

Esther: Of course, that's perfectly natural. To start off with, I'd like to ask you both why you think you're here.

[silence]

Adam: Well. This is awkward.

[silence]

Iris: [nervous laugh]

Esther: OK, to put it another way. If your partner was here alone, what do you think they would say? Iris, why don't you start.

Iris: Adam's been having an affair.

Adam: Wow, straight in like that.

Iris: What? It's true, isn't it? There's no point in being coy. We wouldn't be here if you hadn't had an affair. I wouldn't have to come to a therapist if it wasn't for that. I found out about the affair two weeks ago, and I wasn't sure if I wanted to separate or stay together – I'm still not if I'm honest – but I want to try and see if we can move past it. I'm hoping you can help with that.

Esther: And how do you feel, Adam?

Adam: The same. A hundred per cent the same. I want to move past it. It was a massive mistake and I don't want to break up with my wife or break up my family.

Esther: Have you had any sort of relationship therapy before?

Adam: No, no, nothing like that.

Iris: We've never needed it. We've always been happy. Before, anyway.

Esther: OK. I'll tell you a little bit about the sessions here. I'm a relationship therapist and I specialise in what's referred to as Emotionally Focused Therapy or EFT. It specifically works on talking about and empathising with each other, so that's something to keep in mind as we talk. The emphasis is on listening to each other and letting the other person speak so that you can find out what they're thinking about something, rather than making assumptions about what that is. An affair is obviously a seismic event in your marriage so we'll be talking about that, and as we work through it, it will likely stir up even more emotions about other things.

Iris: [low laugh] I'm not sure I've got any more emotions to stir up.

Esther: After a betrayal that's bound to be the case. One question to ask yourselves now is, 'What do I want to get out of the sessions?'

Adam: I want my marriage back on track. I don't expect Iris to forgive me straight away, but I'm hoping over time we can get there. And, well, we've set ourselves a deadline.

Esther: What sort of deadline?

Iris: A year. I – we've – decided to give it a go until the end of the year. To work on our relationship and see where we are then.

Adam: Which has got to be a good thing, right? Because we need to give it some time.

Esther: [pause] It's important to bear in mind that time isn't necessarily a healer when it comes to betrayal. You can't assume you will feel better as weeks or months pass, as though it's the flu.

[silence]

Esther: I can see you both looking worried, so I'll explain. The only way to move past a betrayal is through what we call the 'three Rs': responsibility, remorse and reconciliation. Iris, I can see you looking over at Adam as I'm talking. This is natural as you feel like the injured party. He needs to accept responsibility for the betrayal and show remorse for doing it. However, this won't be a space in which there are goodies and baddies. The aim is for you to feel as though you're on the same team. And that's what I'll work through with you here.

Adam: [pause] OK.

Esther: Without dealing with the problems in your relationship, old betrayals can be triggered at any time. These sessions will give you a place to discuss how you feel about past and present issues.

Iris: The issue is that Adam cheated, and I don't know if I can ever trust him again. That's the problem we're here about. [pause] What do you mean about past issues? We're here to talk about Adam's infidelity.

Esther: Trust is a large part of a healthy relationship. Adam, is that true? Is that what you would say is the issue?

Adam: I take responsibility for it, and I'm sorry. We need to know how to fix it. How to go back to the way it was before.

Esther: Let me unpick that for a moment. Fixing, or rather healing, is something we will definitely work on. But back to the way it was before isn't necessarily something to strive for. For you to get to this point, something wasn't working. Moving forward, your relationship will need to evolve. The process means a willingness to change and each looking at your part in past problems.

Iris: What do you mean 'my part'? What is this? Are you saying it was my fault Adam cheated? [starts to cry]

Adam: It's not you. I was an idiot.

Esther: That's not what I'm saying, Iris. Of course Adam needs to accept responsibility for his being unfaithful—

Adam: I do! I have. I am. I'm so sorry.

Esther: But for you to reconcile, you both need to be open to the process, and to empathise with the other. I must also tell you that I can't guarantee you will stay together, but through these sessions, you will be able to work out if staying together is what you both want, and if you do, how to deal with any issues that come up in the future – because they will – with empathy and love for your partner. It's about listening to each other, attending to each other's feelings, and accepting what they are telling you. So, what do you think?

Chapter Ten

15 January

I want to simultaneously punch a wall, push Adam into the road, and scream at every stranger dawdling in my path as we leave the suburban house in Finsbury Park that Esther practises her wishy-washy therapy from.

Both look at our part in past problems?

How dare she imply it was my fault? I speed up to get to the bus stop, passing cars whose windscreens are crusty with ice, and Adam has to rush to keep up with me, but I'd happily leave him here. I can't believe he can't feel the seething anger radiating out of my body in his direction. So, this is what therapy is going to be. Some woman telling me that it was something in our marriage – something *I* did – that led to the 'seismic event' of Adam shagging his high-school girlfriend behind my back. And not 'assigning blame', but somehow making me feel as though *I'm* to blame using that same philosophical framework.

I stop abruptly outside the mini Sainsbury's and then stride in. 'We need to get something for dinner,' I blurt out, and leave him standing there while I head to the ready-meal section.

I'm pretending to weigh up a lasagne versus a fish pie when he catches up with me.

'Lasagne?' he suggests quietly.

'It's not going to work,' I tell him. He glances at the two ready meals in my hands.

'I'm not talking about the food,' I add.

Adam leans against the fridge and looks pensive, as though he was expecting me to say something like this. As the session went on, I withdrew every time Esther asked me something, and by the end I was practically mute.

'I can see why you might think that,' he says, 'but that's only the first session. She must have to do that patter to make sure I don't get scared off because I think everyone's going to gang up against me.' He fixes a look on me and drops his voice. 'We can't give up before we've started. What would that even mean? For us.' He's stopped talking but he carries on looking at me, until I get the message that he's got something else to say but is holding back.

'What?' I snap.

'It's that you were the one who said I had to commit to it, so . . .' He falters as my eyes laser in on him. 'So don't you have to commit too?'

My stomach plunges. 'That's not fair.'

'Why?' he says, in a level voice that mirrors the ultra-calm tone Esther was just using on us both. 'Because you thought it would be all about me getting told off and made to pay?'

'No.' That's exactly what I thought. It's not fair that there's a whole part of his life that he kept secret for months, and yet he can see through me in seconds. 'OK, fine. I hate that you get to nit-pick our past and tell me that our marriage, which I thought was happy and functional, wasn't.'

'It was, Iris. Overall. I wouldn't be trying to save it if it wasn't.'

'How big of you. And I'm supposed to be grateful, am I? Do you know what I can't stop thinking about?'

Adam looks pained. We're *that* couple having a row in the supermarket, voices getting higher and tighter while people awkwardly step around us to get to their evening meal deals.

'Are you getting that one?' a man in a suit asks me, pointing at the lasagne and forcing Adam to move his weight from where he's still blocking the fridge. There are no more left on the shelf.

'I haven't made my mind up yet.'

He continues to wait and I face him down. 'Are you going to stand there while I decide?'

'Well, if you don't want it, I'll have it.'

'Will you?'

'For God's sake, Iris.' Adam grabs it out of my hand and gives it to the man with an apologetic smile, who raises an eyebrow at him in solidarity for having to deal with what is clearly a 'difficult' woman.

'Why the fuck did you do that?' I hiss the second he moves off.

'Why does it matter? We'll have the fish pie.'

'WHY DO YOU GET TO DECIDE?' I scream at him. I throw the fish pie back on the shelf and pick up a hotpot. I hate hotpot. I focus on breathing and browsing the rest of the rapidly depleting selection around us. We're both standing completely still while people nip past, getting on with their lives.

After a minute he says, 'What can't you stop thinking about?'

'I keep remembering moments from the summer, ones I thought were happy – not like, Instagram-hashtag happy, but normal – and I can't stop wondering if secretly you were on your phone writing messages to her, or trying to think up an excuse to leave so you could see her or call her. Or when I was with Mum and she was' – I blow out a breath – 'dying and I was sitting with her. What were *you* doing? I thought you were with the kids, keeping our life going, when you might have been, I don't know, *sexting* her or something. I keep thinking about you being with me, or with us, but not really being with us. I don't know which moments were real and which moments weren't, and so they're all spoiled.'

I look away from him, and out through the sliding doors back onto the high street. It's a leafy part of Finsbury Park, with nice terraced houses that all seem to have scaffolding up and signs flapping from them advertising whatever loft conversion company is doing the job. We'd have moved here like Fran if we could have afforded it, but we couldn't, and instead our therapist works here.

I'm so sick of talking. Me! Usually I love it. I can sit and analyse things for hours with Fran, we love breaking down how we feel and why, and what we can change to feel differently. But all this is doing is highlighting the things I had before but don't now.

'It's ruined, isn't it,' I say flatly. 'How can we come back from it? How can a year make any difference?'

Adam looks despondent, misery radiating off him. I look at him. My husband. The face I fell in love with, slightly softened after ten years, his jawline wobbling with emotion. I hate him.

'Don't say that. Not yet.'

I'm trying not to cry. Again. I wipe my eyes on my sleeve, force in a shaky breath.

'I love you,' he says, as a person's arm reaches between us to get to some triple-cooked chips. It freezes and quickly withdraws.

'Don't,' I say. 'You don't get to say that and expect it to solve anything, because I don't believe you.'

'I'm not expecting you to. But please let's keep going with the sessions,' he begs. 'You promised me a year.'

'And you promised to be faithful,' I hurl back. 'Turns out people lie.'

Adam's face twists. From apologetic to angry in a split second. 'You can't throw that at me every single time we have an argument.'

'Every time?' I almost laugh. Almost. 'It's been two weeks. I'll decide on the statute of limitations on it.'

'So, what's it going to be like? "Can you remember to empty the recycling, Iris?" "But you had an affair!"' he shouts. '"Could you stop working so hard at weekends and do some stuff with us, Iris?" "But you had an affair!" "Can you stop prioritising every single person in your life except for me, Iris?" "But you had an affair!"'

He stops, staring at me with barely concealed resentment.

'So much for it being nothing I did.' I exaggerate a shrug. 'It's great that Esther has opened up the lines of communication between us. If I'm such a terrible wife, why are we even bothering? Why don't you fuck off back to perfect Jules?'

When he talks again, his voice is level and quiet, which is worse than when he was screaming at me. 'Don't think I didn't think about it.'

Something inside me breaks. I have to go. I accelerate and storm out of the shop, veering right and vaguely in the direction of the tube station, but without any real plan.

'Iris, come back,' Adam is shouting somewhere behind me. 'I only said it because I was mad. I'm sorry.' His voice gets fainter and fainter as I start running, trying to leave him behind. I need some space and I need the punishing whip of the January wind, something to hit me and remind me that I'm still here, still breathing, still me, and not the person Adam said I was, a woman who drove her husband away because she didn't make him the centre of her universe.

Is that what happened?

Esther just told us we need to be on the same team if we have any chance of working things out, but how can we ever be after what he said? He has an affair and I'm still the bad guy?

Over the past fortnight I've had too much caffeine, and not enough food or sleep. My impromptu sprint quickly leaves me light-headed and my lungs burning. I duck into a shop doorway, some artisan knick-knack place that sells dreamcatchers and leather footstools for £100 a pop. There's a big SALE sign in the window, but it's dark now and closed up for the night. I stand there and look at grey ceramic coffee-pots, running through my options.

Stay. Go. Punish him. Ignore him.

I look down at my hand. I've just shoplifted a Taste the Difference hotpot. That's dinner then. I got to decide, but I don't want it. Why does that feel like a metaphor for our marriage right now?

Chapter Eleven

16 January

Fran: Maybe the answer is to level the playing field. You get to shag someone too. Then you're even.
Nat: Yes, because two wrongs always make a right 😒
Iris: That's an insane idea.

It is. But the idea is like an itch. Maybe I could let him *think* I've shagged someone. So he knows how it feels. I could see what – who – is out there. I look up Happn in the App Store and my hand hovers over the install button.

'Morning, Iris.' Sophie comes up behind me and I scramble to turn my phone face down on my desk. How does she keep *doing* that? 'It's the meeting now. You know, the Lucas Caulfield one.'

'I know,' I say, ignoring her tone. 'I'm going over my notes and will be there in a minute, which' – I look pointedly at my watch, which says 10.29 a.m. – 'is when the meeting begins, I believe.'

I grab my notebook and head to the conference room, trying to force my mind to switch from home mode to work mode, another thing that is becoming harder and harder at the moment. I slip into a chair at the edge of the room. Taylor, who is Vanessa's PA, Lynette the Philanthropy Officer, Sophie and Vanessa, our director, are all already there.

I look down at my notepad, where I had every intention of making some pre-meeting notes about how the visit would run, but didn't.

'As we all know, Lucas Caulfield has been somewhat elusive when it comes to us trying to schmooze him,' Vanessa starts. She's in her usual work uniform of fitted black trousers and black woollen polo neck. They're never bobbly or fluffy so I can only guess that she has about twenty-five identical ones at home, Silicon Valley chief-style. She looks over the top of her deliberately owlish glasses at us. 'So this is a major opportunity for some face time with him.'

Taylor giggles and Vanessa indulges her for a second. Face time with the hot millionaire does not seem like a chore. 'It needs to go well, and not only because he's already been very generous over the last couple of years,' she continues. A grim expression comes onto her face. 'I'm not going to sugar-coat it: overall, there's been a drop in donations over the previous financial year. As we know, donations ebb and flow, but this is more serious than a few thousand pounds. We're looking at a major shortfall.'

'Two of our most generous regular patrons passed away last year and willed us some money,' Sophie interrupts.

Vanessa frowns. 'They did. But no matter how generous their legacy donations were, it also means no more regular contributions from them. Additionally, we've had several big patrons withdrawing their financial support. Nothing to do with us, apparently, but Brexit has made people nervous about parting with their money – especially millionaires – which means we need to step up our caretaking of existing donors to stop others doing the same. We also *must* attract some new ones. I know how hard you all work, but I'm going to need one hundred and ten per cent from you for the next year while we battle this.'

At this, I'm snapped from my half-attentive state back into the room. I slap on my most focused expression, because there's no missing her point. Our entire purpose as a department is to come up with ways of getting rich people to give money to the charity, and since I've been here, year on year donations have always gone up. Then so do our targets. However, now donations have decreased. Which is very bad news. Anyone who thinks the charity world is gentle and nurturing has got it all wrong. It's about money, so of course it's cutthroat. I look at the others and they're all sitting straighter in their chairs too, meerkats on high alert for danger.

'What sort of shortfall are we looking at?' I ask.

'One point five mill,' Vanessa instantly replies, and there's a collective gasp. Our collective target usually goes up by five hundred thousand a year, but this means we'd need to bring in two million to meet that this year.

'We're a large department, so if we don't make up the shortfall – and then some – I'm not going to be able to justify having so many staff.' She lets that settle for a moment and then drives it home. 'I'm talking potential redundancies. We can only manage philanthropic relationships if those relationships exist, and I'm only going to need people who can attract and retain donors. Strategy meetings will be scheduled to work out how we do it, following which everyone will be given a revised monetary target based on seniority, donor losses and expectation.' Anxious glances flit between us over the conference room table. I even exchange a brief look of solidarity with Sophie. The two donors who died were our contacts, so we're both already down on what we can expect to earn this year.

'With that in mind, Lucas Caulfield's visit is more important than ever. As mentioned, not only is this the first time he's been interested in an in-person meeting, but it's a chance to wow him into upping his current endowment. It's not a brilliant time of year for a visit to Chatterstone as the rose gardens won't be in bloom, but he was insistent on the date,' she says, looking over her notes. 'Which is why I won't be able to accompany him myself. It's on the twenty-fifth.'

She looks as though she'd like to move her daughter's wedding in Mauritius. But it has been two years in the planning and don't we bloody know it.

'So.' Vanessa's glasses come off and she looks at us in turn around the room. 'I need a volunteer who is confident she can ace it.'

Taylor instantly sticks up her hand. She's been asking for more responsibility for six months. She only graduated two years ago, but she's keen and has been desperate to meet Lucas Caulfield since we cyber-stalked him. Vanessa smiles warmly at her. 'Taylor, once I'm back from Mauritius, there are several meetings I'd like you to come along to with me. I absolutely want you to start building up your own donor relationships, and you'll be getting your own annual target in due course, but let's start with you shadowing me so you can gain experience.' Taylor looks thrilled. 'However, Mr Caulfield is already twitchy about anonymity, so we need someone with a track record of handling potentially tricky donors.'

Vanessa looks at me and then Sophie, neutrally. We've both done our time with overbearing and arrogant donors, ones who've criticised every staff member, every painting placement and even the gift shop merchandise, while we've struggled to keep a helpful smile on our faces. It's got to be one of us. Nerves mingle with excitement, the first time my stomach has churned in a positive way for weeks. It's daunting, and it's clearly a test, but if there's the threat of cutbacks this is a chance to prove my worth. Imagine convincing Lucas Caulfield to up his already massive donation? It's the kind of challenge all of us live for.

'I can definitely deliver on this one,' I say before Sophie can, and Vanessa nods. Sophie's eyes bore into me, a martyred look on her face, but this is no time to be all 'no, after you'. Vanessa wants someone to demonstrate how hungry they are for the money, and I need her to know I am. Not least because if at the end of this year I decide to leave Adam, I'm going to need this job more than ever.

'Great, thanks,' says Vanessa, gathering up her iPad and notebook. 'We'll have a briefing session before you go, but you know how important this is for us.'

I nod in what I hope is my most capable-looking way.

'Sophie, there are a couple of my donors I'd like you to make contact with while I'm away. I think it's important we start the year by giving them all lots of love, so let's come up with some bonus experiences to offer.' She addresses us collectively again. 'Start examining your contact lists for how we can caretake our existing donors, and brainstorm where we can start rustling up some new ones. One-to-ones will start going into your calendars so we can strategise.'

Sophie starts scribbling in her notebook, turning her back a little away from me so I can't see what she's writing. I stand up to go back to my desk, and as I pass her, I hear a faint, almost imperceptible muttering.

'You'd better not fuck this up.'

*

The following Friday afternoon, the sky is flat and listless, but the wind is foul and sheeting through my unlined coat as I wait for Lucas Caulfield to make an appearance. After another week of overly polite exchanges with Adam, this morning I needed to summon up a bit of the old Iris – the woman who loves site visits and talking to donors about historical buildings – so I pulled out my favourite turquoise vintage skirt and a sixties wool coat, and added a slash of don't-mess-with-me red lipstick. There was a moment when I considered wearing my padded, utilitarian Uniqlo mum coat, but I need to make a good – no, a brilliant – impression, so here I am, bloody freezing and regretting my coat decision, but at least looking a bit more like me, and that's a start.

I hear the rush of the River Test in the distance and pull my coat a bit tighter. My scarf keeps whipping up into my face, but the weather suits my mood – grey and angry. In winter your eyes can be watery and your nose red, and no one thinks anything of it. Everyone's ill, everyone's cold, and everyone's eyes are cast down and buried in the front of their coats. Your life could be crumbling or you could have a virus – who's to know? I could wait for Lucas inside, but it's all about first impressions, and it looks better if I meet him at the door of this impressive eighteenth-century country house that looks like something from a primetime BBC drama. Also, the last thing I need is for him to have to hunt for me somewhere inside the building after the repeated direction from Vanessa to keep Lucas's identity strictly under wraps. I don't want any of the staff to overhear me greeting him like a stranger, when he's supposed to be my good friend and plus one for the Chatterstone experience. I think of my target session with Vanessa last week. She smilingly praised my track record for bringing in money before hitting me with a half-a-million-pound target for the year, and in the same breath telling me she didn't think that would be a problem. What else could I do but agree, despite it being almost double the amount I brought in last year, particularly when she told me Sophie had been given the same target?

Esther has suggested Tuesdays at 5 p.m. for our regular session time. Shall I confirm?

My heart sinks. Adam has not only committed to therapy but has taken it upon himself to be the point of contact, something I'd have been thrilled about if it had applied to any area of our lives before this point; say for the kids' school admin or the dentist's or the doctor's or the MOT garage for the car. But the one time he gets proactive it's to corral me into seeing a therapist I'm not sure I like, because I think she's on his side.

Can we make it 5.30? Hard for me to get out of work for 5.

. . .

This is the only spot she has left outside the working day.

Great. Just as I'm supposed to be throwing everything I've got at my job, I'm going to have to leave early on

Tuesdays for reasons I'm reluctant to disclose. We'll have to cancel some of the sessions as we go, depending on what's happening at work.

Fine.

A vehicle pulls up, one of those high-end Addison Lee town cars you pay extra for, and a man in his mid-to-late forties – who I immediately recognise as Lucas from my online stalking – steps out. He's *exactly* as good-looking as his photos. Whereas most people I've passed today have been bulked up in layers of jumpers and coats, Lucas's silhouette is refined, and he's wearing the sort of outfit that screams 'rich' without also screaming 'off-duty Tory MP' or seeming as though he's trying too hard to be cool: well-fitting dark jeans, a thin grey jumper and black Belstaff boots. All topped off with a dark grey coat – cashmere by the look of it – that he buttons up as he walks towards me. His dark hair is shot through with the right amount of grey to make him look distinguished and his facial hair treads the precarious line between scruffy and manicured. The kind of beard that Mark Ruffalo has mastered.

'You must be Iris,' he says in a deep posh voice, while striding over (excellent gait) and holding out a hand to shake. I'm painfully aware of how cold and chapped mine are but resist the urge to say so, which would draw attention to it even more.

'God, you're freezing,' he says. 'Am I late? You should have waited inside.'

'No, no, not late at all,' (he is, ten minutes) I reply cheerily, 'I've just arrived myself. Not much you can do about this January weather though, is there?'

He gestures for me to go ahead of him through the white front door, and this small bit of chivalry in this romantic setting pushes Adam back into my head.

Focus, Iris. Your job depends on this visit, this man, and this man's cash.

I start my patter to drown out the thoughts of Adam and therapy and crumbling marriages roaring through my brain.

'Despite the original priory building dating back to the eighteenth century, Chatterstone as it stands today very much reflects the taste and interests of its last owners, the artist Quentin Russell and his it-girl wife Evangeline, who was also his muse. They moved here in the thirties and held lots of extravagant parties with all the society names of the day, like the Mitfords.'

We walk through a hallway towards the morning room, passing dust sheet-covered antique furniture and an anachronistic bucket catching a rogue drip. Only a few lights are on and it's making the place seem haunted. The skeleton staff here has been tipped off about my presence, so the odd one we see – a maintenance man, a woman with a clipboard – give me small smiles. They've been told to let me lead a tour with my plus one as a dry run for bringing some VIPs here in the spring and summer, so they let me get on with it. All aside from the conservation manager, who I was introduced to earlier and is hovering nearby, clearly ear-wigging and no doubt wincing over the facts I'm mangling. I pray she doesn't go as far as correcting me in front of Lucas. It's not that I haven't read up; I have, or at least I tried to. But my eyes kept sliding over the web pages without taking much in, and now it's all getting muddled in my head. Something else I can blame Adam for: ruining my attention span.

'We're having a tour of the rose garden with the head gardener shortly, which as you know is the highlight of this property. It was planted pre-nineteen hundred, is in full bloom once a year, and contains thousands of flowers, including dozens' – hundreds? Shit, I don't know – 'of varieties of old-fashioned roses.'

'Shall we have a coffee first?' Lucas interrupts. 'I could do with getting warmed up.'

I look at my watch and quash my rising annoyance. The visit has been meticulously planned, not only because Lucas told Vanessa he was on a tight schedule and had a 'hard out' at 5 p.m., but because Chatterstone isn't technically open this week. Off-season, they schedule a break to carry out repairs and deep cleaning, so the customer-facing staff here today have been especially requested to come in for this visit. We were supposed to start with the art in the morning room and then meet with the head gardener, who will be waiting for us in ten minutes.

'Sure – yes, sure,' I stutter. 'I've arranged for us to have afternoon tea following the rose garden visit, but I'm sure we can rustle up a coffee now too.' The catering manager wasn't exactly good-natured about having to sort out a full-works afternoon tea for just two people, especially as she thinks I'm here on some sort of jolly, so I'm sure they will be delighted that I'm now messing with the itinerary. I steer Lucas back in the direction we came, looking for the café and trying to hide the fact that I don't know this house as intimately as I am pretending to. Not all the art is where it should be; I can see gaps where pieces are usually hanging, but I wave my hand at some paintings as we go past them.

'Another artist, Anthony Castle, who was very good friends with Evangeline, donated his personal art collection to Chatterstone, and it's permanently on display – mainly twentieth-century artworks, including pieces by Barbara Hepworth—'

'Hepworth's sculptures or drawings?'

'Er.' No idea.

'A drawing,' the conservation manager chips in as we pass her again. She's talking to the clipboard woman about a piece hanging in the hallway but can clearly stand my incompetence no longer. 'One of her hospital drawings.'

'Wonderful,' replies Lucas smoothly, before lowering his voice and saying to me, 'Can't say I know much about her. I saw some of her sculptures at the Tate in Cornwall once. One of them looked like two avocado halves to me. That's why I always like to have a professional show me around and tell me what I'm supposed to be thinking about all the art I don't understand.'

He says all this cheerfully and I have no idea what to say in reply. I obviously can't admit that I was expecting him to be, well, more of an arsehole. Let's face it, all the elements are there – a millionaire who insists on private tours of his charitable concerns during the miserable off-season, and sends emails that say things like, 'Assume this works?' Maybe he is an arsehole in his daily life – I highly doubt that you become as successful as he is by being nice – but I love that he's exposed himself as entertaining company as well as possessing gracefully ageing boy-bander looks.

I steer Lucas out of the conservation manager's earshot and into another room, which, thankfully, is the café. But no one is expecting us in the café right now, so it's all dark and most of the chairs are stacked up around the edge of the room. I fumble for a light switch as we enter, startling a very young member of staff who is sorting condiments into plastic tubs behind the counter. 'Back in a sec,' I call to Lucas, gesturing for him to go over to a table near the window – which fortunately has seats around it – before heading over.

'Hello. I work for the National Trust and I'm on a visit with a guest today. Would it be possible to get two coffees over there?'

The pimply boy, who can't be much more than sixteen, looks dubious. 'What sort of coffee? I've not been trained up on the machine yet.'

'What sort of coffee can I get you, Lucas?' I call over. He's standing in front of the sash window and looking out onto the manicured lawn. It's a shadow of how impressive I imagine the view is on a sunny spring day, but still pretty, even in the January gloom.

'Americano. Black, please.'

Relief. It's a basic enough order. Although when I turn back to the trainee barista, he looks stricken.

'Americano is regular filter coffee,' I reassure him, 'nothing that requires frothing milk.'

'OK,' he replies, looking less certain than he sounds. 'I'll try that and bring them over.'

'Shout if you need me to help you,' I say. 'I'm sure we can work it out between us.'

'What is it you do, Lucas?' I ask when I go over to the table. Obviously I already know, but he doesn't have to know that the phrase 'you have visited this page six times' appears under his company website when you type his name into Google from my work computer.

'Venture capitalism,' he says, with an artful, if not practised, shrug. The whole thing would seem less 'aw shucks' if he wasn't wearing a Rolex watch that cost more than the deposit for my house.

'Long hours,' I say, because I don't really understand venture capitalism and I can't think of anything else. Besides, it's better to let someone tell you what they think of their job before you offer an opinion on it.

'Yes,' he agrees. 'Today is my first day off in a month – and I include Christmas in that. That's why I wanted to come here. I don't know when I'll get the chance again. My car is waiting outside to take me to the airport after this. I have a meeting in Switzerland tomorrow morning and then one back in London on Sunday.' I marginally soften my stance against millionaires demanding tour days that fit around their schedule. 'I'll be in Geneva for all of about fifteen hours so will only see the inside of a hotel and a meeting room. I can't tell you how envious I am that you get to spend time in places like this day in, day out.'

'Believe me, my office in London is nowhere near as picturesque. The best view we have is of the National Trust calendar pinned to the wall.' I laugh and he joins in. 'But you're right, that's what attracted me to my job to start off with. The chance to see different parts of the UK and enjoy what's here.'

I'm *almost* relaxing into the conversation. Adam, Jules, the constant thrumming of rejection and sadness – it's all there, but maybe a little further in the background. I can do this. I can make light chat with a handsome man about stately homes. I can.

'Have you always worked in heritage and conservation?' he asks.

'Not until this position. I've always been in fundraising and charity work, though. I worked for a children's charity before, but when this job came up a few years ago it was a dream. I love old buildings, I love travelling and I love meeting people. Now I just have to work my way around the three hundred Trust buildings in the UK. It might take me a while.'

Lucas smiles. Slightly imperfect teeth, but very white. He seems like a man who takes good care of himself.

Everything looked after, but not so much as to be vain. Vain-adjacent.

'One a weekend, with a weekend off for Christmas . . . it would only take you about six years.'

'That's why you're a numbers person and I'm not,' I laugh back. 'Plus, one every weekend might be a bit of a stretch. I'm not sure my children would appreciate being dragged to manors and crumbly old castles – as Jack once called Lindisfarne Castle in Northumberland – every weekend.'

'You have children?'

'Yes, two. Jack and Savannah.'

I reflexively look down at my left hand. I'm not wearing my wedding ring. Pre-New Year that wouldn't be weird. I used to take it off all the time when I was doing housework or exercising, and then forget to put it back on. But since 1 January, almost four weeks ago now, it's been deliberate. If Adam and I were a celebrity couple, body language experts would be analysing our paparazzi shots and telling the *Mail Online* that my consistent lack of ring wearing is indicative of the state of our marriage. They wouldn't be wrong.

'Do you have any children?'

'No,' he says, and looks out of the window towards the rose garden. 'Hopefully there's still time for that one day.' He sounds a bit less posh as he says it, with a trace of an accent; somewhere near Fran's Warrington one.

'Where are you from originally, Lucas? Can I detect the north-west in there?'

He laughs and his eyes crinkle up as he does. ''Ey, love,' he says in exaggerated Scouse. 'I'm from Liverpool originally.' His voice switches back into the measured tenor he arrived with. 'I'm a state school boy who got a scholarship to Oxford. The accent was the first thing to go when I wanted to fit in.'

The nervous barista comes over with our coffees, his hands shaking slightly as he sets them down, which spills coffee into the saucers. I can see grounds in the spillage, so am pretty confident he didn't know what he was doing.

'Ah, good man,' Lucas says to him. I sip the coffee and stifle a cough as grit catches in the back of my throat. Lucas follows suit and I can see his face struggle not to grimace as he swallows. 'Lovely, thanks,' he says to the teenager, and I take his tact as another tick. Not rude to service staff. Even when the coffee is a sending back offence. He waits until the boy goes back to the counter and whispers, 'Shall we get out of here? This coffee is undrinkable.'

*

Ninety minutes later, we're back in the same spot. This time with the lights on, the table laid, and a full afternoon tea in front of us. It looks more like it would during the fabled springtime peak season – albeit without anyone else here. Tiny cakes and finger sandwiches are layered on a tiered cake stand, and there's a gigantic pot of tea, as well as a bottle of Prosecco nestled in an ice bucket.

My hair is a tangled mess and I'm even colder than I was before, having stood shivering in my coat while the head gardener gave us the sort of in-depth, information-packed tour that makes me confident I now know enough to jack in my job and raise roses for a living. Like everyone else here, he thought we were mad for visiting when there was nothing to see but hard ground and thorny sticks, and told us at least ten times that we should come back in the spring. Although that didn't stop him from lecturing us on how to treat the rose garden soil during the winter months for almost fifteen minutes.

'Do you want a cup of tea or would you prefer . . . ?' I gesture at the Prosecco. It's 4.30 p.m. Like me, Lucas looks cold and dishevelled, although more in a handsome, ruddy, pink-cheeked way than the runny-nose look I'm sporting.

'God, tea, definitely,' he says easily. 'I'm bloody freezing.'

I pour us both a cup and he swallows his down in almost one gulp. 'Should have asked for tea earlier,' he says. 'Thankfully that is about a million times better than their coffee.'

'Yes,' I agree, 'difficult to get hot water and a teabag wrong.' I reach for one of the cakes, but my hands are so cold my fingers end up clumsily fumbling at the éclair I was going for.

'Here, let me.' Lucas does the same thing and we both laugh while holding our hands out uselessly in front of us. 'Might need to thaw out a bit first.'

'You know what you need to do,' I say, putting on a broad but bad Devon accent in an attempt to mimic the gardener.

'Come back in the springtime,' Lucas finishes. His accent is worse than mine. 'Although I definitely will, if you're amenable.'

'Yes, of course. Drop us a line and we can make the arrangements.' I chance a joke. 'That'll probably be the next time you have a day off anyway, won't it?'

He smiles, looking a bit wistful. 'It's not that far from the truth.'

Vanessa's words come to the forefront of my mind. I need to start giving him the hard sell and lay the groundwork for a donation increase. I mean, ideally she wants me to impress him so much he'll increase his donation here and now, but years of experience have taught me that I can't bring up money right away, it's too crass. The next best thing is to learn about him and cultivate him as a contact, find out what he's interested in, what he doesn't like, and how I can prove what extra value the Trust can offer. *Then* I can sting him for some cash.

'As one of our valued donors, I can arrange another visit for you, anywhere you like, even at very short notice,' I tell him.

'Thank you. I'd like that.'

'I'm interested in which of our properties you've already been to and which you're keen to see,' I add.

He looks at me a fraction too long and I freeze halfway through pouring milk into my tea. Was that a touch flirtatious? Distracted, I end up spilling milk all over the tablecloth. Lucas springs into action and hands me a stack of napkins.

'We also host lots of donor dinners over the course of the year,' I say, scrambling to mop up the spill. If I can lock him into one of those, at least that's something to take back to Vanessa. I invite high rollers to our events all the time, but it never feels so weird when it's one of our elderly female donors. With Lucas it's like asking him out. 'Plenty of them are in London in the evening, so they might be easier for you to come along to if you're interested. Of course you can bring a guest too,' I add quickly.

Lucas gives a low laugh, plucks an éclair from the stand and passes it to me on a plate, then helps himself to one. 'Chance would be a fine thing,' he says, a trace of cynicism in his voice. He bites into his pastry. 'Did you say you were married?'

I choke on my mouthful of tea. *Christ, Iris, it's a perfectly innocent question.*

'Separated.' I demote Adam before I can stop myself.

Why did I say that?

Lucas frowns, a follow-up question forming on his lips. I go to correct myself with a mad urge to offload the whole sorry mess onto him, but my phone rings, stopping me. The screen says 'Home'. Dad should be back with the kids after school now.

'Sorry, I have to take this. I'll be one second,' I tell Lucas. He gestures for me to go ahead.

'Hiya, Dad, everything all right?'

'Mummy?' It's Jack. His voice sounds small and instantly makes my blood chill. He hardly ever says 'Mummy' any more. I'm always 'Mum' in front of his friends. 'Mummy' is reserved for last thing at night when I'm reading to him and he forgets to keep up his big-boy act.

'Jack, are you all right? Where's Grandad?'

'Grandad's hurt his hand. He was making us pasta and he spilled the water from the kettle on it.' His voice is all wobbly and he sounds like he's trying very hard not to cry. I can hear Sav shrieking in the background. 'I tried to help him,' says Jack, 'but he shouted at me and sent me away.'

'It's OK, darling. You did the best thing ringing me.'

I glance at Lucas, who is looking back at me with concern. I thought this would be a maintenance call – the kids are home, they want chocolate, maybe a bit of an argument with Dad about what's an appropriate dinner – but now my heart is pounding. I'm all the way in Hampshire and my children need me.

'Don't worry, Mummy's going to come back right now. Is Grandad there?' I say.

'Yes.' Still small. I need to get back to him.

'Can you put him on?' The line crackles as he takes the phone to wherever Dad is. I can hear him saying,

'That'd better not be an ambulance,' in a cross voice as Jack approaches.

'It's Mummy,' says Jack.

'I'm fine,' Dad says grumpily, the second the phone is near his mouth. 'Just a bit of hot water as I was draining that bloody pasta you told me they like.' Of course, my fault for asking him to make something as bougie as pasta. 'It made a bit of a mess because I dropped everything when I spilled it.'

'Grandad said the F-word,' chirrups Jack in the background, sounding more like his old self.

'I think we'll let him off this time. Right, Dad, I'm going to . . .' What *am* I going to do? *Think.* It's a fifteen-minute walk to the train station and then the trains only go every hour. 'I'm going to call an Uber and I'll be back as soon as I can. In the meantime, I'll call Adam. He's nearer so should be able to get away. Dad, I'm going to hang up so I can book a taxi. I'll ring you when I'm on my way.'

I end the call and open the Uber app. There's one lone vehicle roaming around, by the look of it. I confirm it and try not to register the eye-watering estimated journey price. Eleven minutes away. Shit.

There's the sound of a throat being cleared and I remember Lucas is sitting there, and that I'm supposed to be wowing him, but I have no thoughts in my head other than how to leave immediately.

'Everything OK?' he says, with a concerned look on his face.

'Bit of a family emergency.' I give a quick, tense smile, and try to keep my voice neutral. Somewhere below the waves of panic, I know it's wrong to involve him in my drama. 'I'm really sorry, I'm going to have to leave.' There's a moment when I hear Vanessa's – and Sophie's – voice in my head and know I shouldn't be ditching him. That I should get Adam to deal with it and see the visit through. I know I *could* do that, but I also *can't* do that. My kids need me. There's enough going on at the moment without them being unable to rely on their mum.

He nods. 'Listen, you don't want to be waiting for an Uber. Take my Addy Lee, it's right outside.'

'I can't do that,' I say, glancing again at my phone screen. My driver has now rejected the journey and there are no other cars on the screen at all. 'You need it,' I continue unconvincingly. 'What about your flight?'

'I don't need to leave for another thirty minutes,' he says, topping up his teacup as if he has all the time in the world, despite the exhausting-sounding schedule he told me about not two hours ago. 'My PA will call me another one.' He takes a sip of his tea.

'If you're sure . . .' I hover there for a few seconds, even though I know I'm going to take him up on the offer. I want to get back. To sort this.

'I insist.'

I smile again, gratefully this time, and quickly gather my things together while standing up.

'Thank you so much,' I tell him. 'If you need me to book you another car, please let me know. And drop me a line about future visits, I'd love to show you some more properties.' I'm babbling. Then I almost forget my phone, until Lucas picks it up and passes it to me. 'Also, I will obviously pay for the Addison Lee. Let me know where to transfer the money.'

He flaps his hand at me. 'Iris, it's fine. *Go.*'

'Right, yes, thank you.' I rush out and throw myself into the car.

'Hi, there's going to be a change of destination. Mr Caulfield has said it's OK if you take me to North London, please.' The driver looks dubious, but then a message appears on his phone that changes his mind.

'That's fine. What's the new address?' I reel it off and swipe open my phone.

'Hi, Dad, it's me. I'm leaving now and I'm going to ring Adam to tell him to leave work too.' Dad starts to protest, but half-heartedly. He mainly sounds relieved. I hang up, jabbing on Adam's name the second I do. It's only as we pull away from Chatterstone, and my heart rate slows, that I let myself dwell on the thought that far from making a flawless impression, and using today as recon on how best to schmooze our most important donor, I've made it all about me and ditched him in the middle of nowhere.

Chapter Twelve

27 January

'Let me get this straight,' Fran says, while struggling to breathe. 'A handsome, charismatic millionaire came to your rescue in a crisis and this is a problem?'

Fran and I are running. Very slowly. Which is an improvement on our previous 'fast walking', thanks to the Couch to 5K app we committed to in November last year with the vague promise of getting fit, having some me (us) time, and 'maybe' looking for a 10K race to enter, as befits the forty-something cliché we're embracing. We tried parkrun once, but Fran decided it was a cult, and given the level of competitive runners for an apparently amateur race, I couldn't entirely disagree with her. Instead, we do our own version on a Sunday morning when we're not dodging people trying to beat their PB.

I nod, neither trusting myself to answer nor able to, as I don't have the lung capacity.

'The rescuing, no,' I say a few metres later, although it comes out as more of a puff. I have committed to running more since seeing all those pictures of taut Jules on Instagram, but I can't help being aware of how unfit I am when I do it, not to mention all the bits of me that wobble every time I take a step.

'But the scenario as a whole, yes. I emailed him to say thank you the second I got home and made sure Dad was OK, but I haven't heard anything back from him. Shit, what if me taking the car made him miss his flight and he's pissed off?' I fret.

'Stop.' Fran holds up a hand. It wavers around in the air as she bobs along the path in Finsbury Park. 'Didn't you say he's had, like, one day off in the past year and that he had some insane schedule for the weekend after the meeting with you? He's busy! He probably doesn't have time to reply to you in between making all that money.'

'It's not as simple as that, Fran.' I've told her about the looming threat of redundancy, but she doesn't know that Lucas is the white whale in terms of meeting my target. 'I barely got to raise the idea of him coming to a donor dinner, and I have no information to take back to Vanessa about him because I legged it before I found out anything useful.' I take a couple of ragged breaths. 'It's one thing for him to be intensely private, it's another that I didn't even ask. I don't know what I'm going to say at work tomorrow.' Thank God Vanessa isn't back from the wedding festivities until next week, even though she WhatsApped me from Mauritius this morning to ask how it went. It will sit guiltily un-blue-ticked in my message folder until I work out what I'm going to say. But the others in the office will want a full download tomorrow morning.

'It was an emergency. Work will understand.' Fran squeezes my arm as we duck around a man walking a tiny yappy dog.

I think back to the meeting of doom and how I practically shoved Sophie out of the way to get the Lucas Caulfield gig. 'I don't think they will,' I reply. 'Work itself is an emergency right now. I'm supposed to be proving myself to Vanessa. Sophie wouldn't have ditched him.'

Fran snorts. 'No, instead she would have bored him to death.' She met Sophie once at one of our summer drinks parties. 'OK, here's what you do. You send him a gift as a token of gratitude – although God knows what you buy for a bazillionaire who has everything – and invite him to another all-singing all-dancing visit, all that sucky-up stuff you're supposed to be doing. Then tomorrow, you tell them a watered-down version of what happened, while hamming up your dad's injury. No one can argue with a trip to A&E with an OAP.'

Despite claiming she hates being around other people, Fran always navigates social situations deftly. She's the kind of person who'll be introduced to a stranger at a party and extract their life story – including their troubled upbringing and broken engagement – within fifteen minutes.

'You're right. I need to stop them finding out about how it ended and make it seem like we're on great terms, whilst also finding a way to actually be on great terms with him.' It seems so simple when I talk it through with Fran. 'I don't know why I'm being so rubbish about it all.'

'Hang on, I need to walk for a minute,' Fran says. We slow down and a thoughtful look crosses her face. 'It's because your confidence has been knocked. You're usually so decisive about work, but now you're second guessing yourself about everything. It makes total sense.'

I take a couple of breaths, think over what she's saying. 'You're right. I feel like I can't trust my instincts any more, about anything. I mean, look where that got me with Adam.'

'Adam's a prick.' She catches the expression on my face. 'I know you're doing this whole "giving him a year" thing, but sorry, I'm not going to think otherwise until he's proved himself.'

I pick up the pace so I don't have to say anything else, and Fran follows. 'Iris, you know I'm only saying it to make sure you know I'm on your side, right?'

'Yep, I know,' I reply tightly. I do. But it's hard to know if I'm doing the right thing if all I hear is that my husband is a wanker. 'I think you can hold back on telling me quite so often, though.' We approach her exit from the park, the one to her house in Crouch Hill, but my brain is still buzzing. 'Do you want to do another lap?'

Fran stops but starts bouncing from foot to foot. 'I would, but I think I'm going to have to go home before I wet myself.'

'Sure,' I say, 'I know you're a slave to your postpartum bladder.'

Fran has been with Liam for fifteen years; he's an old uni friend she couldn't see her way through the WKD fug to fancy while she was at university, but they got together when they both moved to London a few years later. She thought it was because they were drunk and homesick for the north-west; he thought it was because he'd been in love with her for years and she'd finally noticed him. Her life is basically a romcom. Except for the part where they tried for a second baby, ended up having twins, and she left her pelvic floor somewhere in Homerton hospital.

She pulls me into a quick sweaty hug before swerving down the trail. 'Same time next week, yes?'

She ambles away, running faster than she was with me. I've long suspected she's fitter than she makes out, but keeps pace with me so I don't feel so rubbish. Or maybe it's because she really is desperate for a wee. I pick up my feet and make my way back down towards Harringay. It wasn't the best area of London when we moved here eight years ago, but not the worst either. It was the area we could afford (and when I say 'we', I include my parents in that; I'm very much a benefactor of the bank of Mum and Dad) when I got pregnant with Jack and we needed more room than our one-bedroom Islington rental allowed. Adam mentioned moving up north, nearer where his mum and Gabe are in Sheffield, but I didn't want to be that far from my parents and our jobs. Besides, we were about to become parents for the first time, so the last thing we needed was to become surrogate parents to Gabe too. Which is exactly what I suspect would have happened.

I pound along, out of the park and down the hill past the pale Victorian terraces that line the street. Sweat on my face mingles with the cold air. This time of year always seems to drag. It's usually the combination of the winter bugs we take it in turns to come down with and the interminable wait for the weather to get better as we go stir-crazy cooped up in the house, but this year it's worse. Not just because my marriage is a raging bin fire, but because there's no Mum, and the loss is everywhere: in the absence of late-night phone calls after a Sunday night BBC drama has aired, or the garden-centre coffee and cakes I don't do any more because that was our thing, and until Sav is old enough to make a useful contribution to the lemon drizzle index I'm not interested in doing it with anyone else. The kids are growing out of the last lot of clothes Mum bought them ('Just a few bits,' she'd say, while hauling a binbag-sized John Lewis carrier into the house), and even though Sav's jumper sleeves are somewhere around her forearms now, I can't bring myself to pack them away or pass them on because they're the last of Mum. I realise I've sped up without noticing and find myself outside our front gate, out of breath and skin prickling with sweat. I simultaneously fumble my key and a tissue from the weird tiny back pocket of my leggings, and blow my nose noisily. The run has finally cleared my head of Adam and Lucas, but now it's full of Mum.

As I reach up to put my key in, the door opens.

'Dad!' I exclaim. He's pulling his roll-along suitcase. 'Where are you going?'

Dad looks at me impatiently, as though I should know. 'Home.'

'Now?'

'Yes, I've got to get back.'

'Have you? You never mentioned it.' It hadn't occurred to me that Dad might have plans. When I asked him if he wanted to stay for a bit, we never talked about how long that would be, and he seemed happy to be here. The guilt creeps in, before another thought, the one of an only child: what or who could be more important than me?

Dad opens his mouth to reply but stops, his face looking as though a familiar response is eluding him. His hand is worrying at the handle of the case. 'Got to get back,' he says again. 'For the . . . it's Saturday, isn't it?'

'Sunday. Are you all right, Dad?'

'Rod!' he shouts. 'Said I'd see Rod for darts.'

Rod is Dad's mate. They play darts together. They've known each other for twenty years and that's still pretty much all I know about Rod.

'OK.' I'm fighting annoyance, seeing as this is the first I've heard of it. Maybe Dad's looking for an excuse to leave and Rod is handily providing his exit strategy. Especially as to arrange it, Dad will have had to turn on his brick of a mobile phone, the one he keeps turned off to avoid 'wasting the battery'.

'Have you booked a train?' I say instead. I'm still on the doorstep and aware of the sweat drying into little salty crystals on my face, making it all tight.

Dad is looking past me, up and down the street. 'What?'

'What train are you getting?'

Now Adam comes barrelling into the hallway.

'Terry – there you are. Iris!' We're all staring at each other – me outside, those two inside – as though none of us can believe we've run into each other here.

'Dad says he's got to get back,' I say, shooting Adam a look. 'Everything OK?'

'I told him one of us could take him home once you got back from your run, but he said he had to go now.'

'Right. Because of Rod,' I say.

'Yes.'

Adam pulls a 'don't ask me' face. 'I went upstairs to get Sav dressed and the next thing I knew, his bag was packed.'

'Well, I'm back now, so I'll take you, shall I?' Dad peers down the street again. 'Unless you've called' – would my dad even know *how* to book an Uber? – 'a taxi?'

All I get in return for this comment is a suspicious look.

'I'll get the car keys then.' I push past both of them to get into the house, avoiding looking at myself in the hallway mirror as I reach beneath it into the bowl where we keep all the crap, including the car keys. A post-run stretch and a shower will have to wait. Adam quickly shuffles past me into the kitchen before re-emerging with

Jack's Batman water bottle, filled up, and presses it into my hand.

'You never remember to take a bottle of water when you go running. Have this for the journey.'

A small gesture, but the first time I have felt anything but resentment for him since New Year.

'Thank you,' I say, avoiding his gaze. A goodbye kiss was automatic in the past; now the idea of it is awkward, something to be weighed up rather than a reflex. 'I'll see you in a bit.'

Two minutes later I'm pulling out of our road and heading towards Surrey, with Dad sitting fretfully in the passenger seat next to me.

'It's all right, Dad, we'll be back before lunch. I'm guessing you're not meeting Rod until later anyway.'

He makes a sound that could be 'hmmm' but is less committed than that. He's looking out of the window, and occasionally gripping his seat in the way he always does when I drive him anywhere. I wouldn't mind (much), but he's the one who taught me to drive.

'Thanks for coming these past few weeks,' I say as we reach the A406.

'You don't have to thank me, I'm happy to come. I know it's not easy when you're both working so hard, trying to get the kids to school and back again too. I know Mum was always more help for you with the kids' – at this we both start to tear up, and I'm grateful we're sitting side by side rather than facing each other – 'and I'm not as good at making dinners and helping with homework, but you know I'll do anything I can.'

I'm still blinking away tears but not for the same reason as before. Dad thinks he's been helping with the day-to-day routine of two full-time working parents, mucking in like

Mum did and chuffed that I've included him. Instead he's been a vital component in stopping our entire household falling apart while we decide if our marriage is going to last. I don't want to turn him against Adam, but it suddenly seems unfair that he doesn't know exactly what's been going on.

More selfishly, I also want someone who is completely on my side yet invested in the hope that we'll be able to fix it. Fran's been great, but she hates him so much right now that it's making me question whether staying is the right decision. And if it has any chance of working, I need to commit to the process, and see it through.

'You're a bit close to that van there, Iris,' Dad says, flinching as if we're about to rear-end the vehicle in front, rather than being a mere whisker off the requisite five car lengths of stopping distance we should be keeping on a fifty-mile-an-hour-road.

I slow down as a courtesy, while simultaneously blurting out, 'We're having some problems. In our marriage. Me and Adam. There was another woman. He says it's over, but I don't know. I don't know what to think. Or do.'

We're merging down from three lanes to two, so I make a big show of checking my blind spot to prevent me from seeing Dad's reaction. Verbally, there's nothing, but he could just not want to distract me from the road.

'Stupid bastard!' he suddenly shouts, and there's a little part of me that ignites. He's furious! And then I realise he means the car that's just overtaken us, pulled into our lane and slowed right down. I have to brake hard, with Dad holding on to the dashboard the whole time and mumbling about bloody BMWs who think they own the road and shouldn't even be allowed a driving licence, probably not even properly insured. The car pulls off and I accelerate but stick strictly to the speed limit, so there's no more mistaking car chat for relationship chat.

'Dad?' I venture. 'Did you hear what I said? About Adam. And me.'

'Yes. I was thinking about it. And then that car came out of bloody nowhere.' Irritation pricks his voice again.

'Forget the BMW, Dad, it's gone now.'

'Well,' he huffs, 'I did sense there was something going on, you know, between you two.'

Despite what I've told him, I'm embarrassed. There we were pretending everything was normal, and even Dad could pick up on the tension.

'But I didn't think it was something like this. More that you were stressed out and didn't have enough time for each other. You know, you working all the time' – my jaw clenches – 'and you both leading such busy lives. I thought I might be able to help with Jack and Sav and free you up a bit.'

'You did, Dad. I'm so grateful to you for coming. It was a big help. Who knows, maybe we do need some more time for each other to work things out.' I'm falsely cheery; now I've said it, it doesn't seem like such a good idea. It's not as though Dad is chomping at the bit to tell me how wronged I am.

Dad falls silent again and fiddles with the radio until he settles on Radio 4. I'm guessing it's to fill the silence until he formulates a response. Mum was always the emotional one, responding to any perceived slight I'd had from someone at school with hugs and the pronouncement that I should 'stay away from them', even if we'd formerly been inseparable. Dad was more likely to say nothing, to the point where I wasn't even sure he was listening, only to bring it up a few hours later with some well-chosen words of encouragement or advice. I'd usually forgotten what I was upset about by then though or was back to being best friends with whoever it was, so Mum's approach was by far the more satisfying in the moment. But right now, I'll take whatever I can get, from anyone on my side. If he's not going to tell me Adam is as much of a bastard as the driver of that BMW, I could at least do with some guidance on what to do.

I keep shooting little glances at him, but he's still mulling as we hit the M25 and pull off again to get to Weybridge. By now my thighs are aching every time I press on the pedals because I haven't cooled my muscles down. Does Dad not want to get involved? I knew he could be a bit old-fashioned (see: my having a full-time career), but I didn't think he was in the 'stay with your husband no matter what' camp.

And then we're at their – his – road, and I pull into the drive. The front garden is looking overgrown, the hedges all fat and overhanging the pavement, and a honeysuckle is hanging half off a trellis attached to the garage.

'Has the garden man been recently?' I ask.

'Not much point in the winter, is there? Might as well wait until the spring to get it all tidied up.' Mum hated it when the bushes at the front got 'out of hand'. She would have got the gardener round to trim them regardless of the season, but I don't say anything. I can't browbeat him into doing things Mum's way when she's not here any more.

I unclick my seatbelt, but Dad says, 'Don't come in.' He pats my knee and makes for the door handle. 'You should get back.'

'Not even a cup of tea before the return journey?' I joke. Isn't he going to say anything else? Not even a mention of how hard it must be for me?

'Should think the milk will be off after such a long time away,' he says. All I can do is nod.

'We'll see you soon though, won't we?' I try again. 'Come over for Sunday lunch soon. Any time. You've got your key, haven't you?'

'Yes, yes, and I will. Good idea.' He climbs out and goes to get his case from the boot, slamming it down before coming around to the driver's window. I wind it down, letting in a blast of cold air.

'About Adam,' he says, brow furrowed. He seems preoccupied, but not upset in any way I was expecting or hoping.

'Yes.'

'The thing is, he's your husband.'

'Yes.'

'You love him.'

I'm not sure if that's a question or a statement, or if I do, but I say yes again.

'Then I think you'll work it out,' he says.

But how? is what I want to scream. Closely followed by, *Is that it?* No sympathy, no rage, not even an element of 'How could he do this to my baby?'

'Maybe this is another situation Mum would have been good at advising on,' I say quietly.

'What do you mean?' He looks surprised, maybe even a bit hurt.

'Nothing. I just meant . . . when you said before that Mum was a big help with some things . . . she was good at advice,' I say lamely. There's a fist of tension on my chest. Great, now I've managed to offend Dad, after all his help these past few weeks. 'Sorry, it was a stupid joke. Have a good time with Rod.'

He waves his hand in farewell and turns to let himself into the house. I sit in the car and watch him, seeing the lights going on as he potters from the hall into the living room, probably settling himself down into 'his' chair in front of the telly. I wonder how he feels going back there, knowing Mum won't be along later. When we all went to the house after the funeral I spent most of my time in the kitchen, boiling the kettle and doing all the hostessing I knew Mum would expect of me: counters wiped, teas made, seats found for her innumerable friends from her millions of hobbies – charity shop gang, bowling club, wine tasting 'girls' (as they always referred to themselves; no one was under sixty-five), book group. Every time someone came into the room I looked up, expecting her to follow them. If I'm honest, I've avoided coming over since then, using every excuse to get Dad to ours instead.

'You'll work it out,' is what Dad said. *You*. Meaning you, plural – me *and* Adam – or meaning me?

You.

Your fault.

I put the car in reverse, casting one last glance at the house that was the foundation of my childhood, with Mum at its core. What was it the therapist said? 'Time isn't necessarily a healer.' So far, it hasn't been when it comes to Mum being gone.

I make it as far as the next street before I have to pull over and cry.

Chapter Thirteen

28 January

From: Taylor Lowry for Vanessa Meldrum
Date: 5 February, 16.30
Attendance required: Iris Young
Subject: 1-2-1 meeting

The calendar invitation pops up as I approach my desk on Monday morning, and my chest immediately constricts. A one-to-one with Vanessa for the day she comes back from Mauritius with no other details given. It can only be about the Chatterstone visit. I still haven't heard anything from Lucas, even after I took Fran's advice and sent a gift to arrive at his desk by first thing this morning. Out of the corner of my eye I see Sophie coil herself ready to pounce, and I stuff in the last giant mouthful of my almond croissant purely to buy myself some extra thinking time.

'So,' she says, in that overly solicitous way people do when they want to extract gossip from you. 'How did it go with Lucas on Friday? Did you not get my WhatsApp about it?'

I shake my head and chew, shake my head and chew. 'I think my phone's on the blink,' I lie. 'Haven't seen any WhatsApp messages all weekend.'

'Weird,' Sophie replies, looking at me like 'yeah right'. 'I'm sure you'd have done an all-company email if it was a raging success though, no?' She's pulling a faux-sympathetic face, but I'm determined to give her nothing.

'It went exactly as hoped,' I say. 'As we already knew, he had barely any time so it was a flying visit, and it was the first in-person contact so we – I'll – have to build on it, but it was well worth meeting him. Well worth it.'

'Yeah, but was he fit?' Taylor laughs from her desk across the room outside Vanessa's office. Like all good personal assistants, she hears and sees everything in the office. She'd never dare say that if Vanessa were here, but then again, if Vanessa were here, Vanessa would be the one grilling me about Lucas's visit. Taylor's question is a welcome diversion and at least has a straightforward answer.

'He was as good-looking as we all wanted him to be,' I say with a smile, 'so yes, very.'

Taylor grins. 'I knew it. Rich *and* sexy. The. Dream.'

'Have you booked me a boardroom for my eleven o'clock yet?' Sophie calls over her shoulder, before turning back to me. Taylor pulls a face.

'Hope you didn't get all flustered because you fancied him,' Sophie says to me. She's smiling but there's no warmth. Shark smiling.

'Like you did when that Colin Firth film used Knole as a location and we were allowed to meet the cast,' I fire back, with the same supercilious smile. 'And no, I didn't.' Sophie and I have never exactly been friends, but now there's the threat of redundancy, I guess we're not even going to pretend we're not in competition for whatever jobs might be left after the bloodbath. Besides, *that's* not why I got flustered. 'And I didn't say I fancied him, just that objectively speaking he's good-looking. As is Colin Firth.'

Sophie makes a noise like 'whatever'. 'I'm sure Vanessa wouldn't mind us flirting if it made him pledge more money or got him to agree to the donor dinner in March.'

'We didn't get to that.' I give a small laugh, as though it's a ludicrous idea to bring up him donating more money. 'It was the first meeting – it was about cultivating the relationship, not tipping him upside down to empty his pockets.' I check to see if Sophie is buying it.

She sniffs. 'Well, I got the Kims to add a thousand pounds a month to their donation and we only met for coffee at Ham House.'

Shit. That was one of the meetings Vanessa had asked her to go to. 'The Kims always increase their donation at the beginning of the year, but good for you,' I choke out. They do, but if, as Vanessa said, our existing donors are generally being more conservative in their philanthropic pursuits, it's a good result, and it's twelve grand towards Sophie's target. Why did I volunteer for the high-stakes gig rather than go for coffee with the nice-but-dull Kims?

'They also brought along their friend who is looking for a new philanthropic endeavour. We're going to lunch next week.'

'Well done you. You must have made quite the impression.' As I congratulate her through gritted teeth, the thing I find most surprising is that apparently not everyone finds Sophie as annoying as I do.

'You must have made an impression on Lucas too,' Taylor hoots, while nodding at her computer. 'He's emailed Vanessa about you.'

'Fuck, what did he say?' I blurt, blowing any facade of detached, professional cool.

As her PA, Taylor has access to Vanessa's inbox, which usually works out well for us because Taylor is so indiscreet. She gives us a heads-up about 'the mood' on any given morning so we can work out how to manage our boss. Higher-ups singing her praises about something? It's a day you can get away with delivering bad news. Daughter emailing to ask for 'a bit more money' towards the wedding? Save it for another time.

My heart starts pounding and I glance at my own screen. There's still nothing in my inbox. He's bypassed me and my guilt gift and gone straight to my boss.

I rush over to Taylor's desk, with Sophie tailing me.

From: Lucas Caulfield
Date: 28 January
To: Vanessa Meldrum
Subject: Re: Chatterstone visit
Dear Vanessa
Thank you so much for the coffee delivery. It made up for the heinous—

This is all I can see in Taylor's browser window.

'Scroll, scroll!' I say, trying to keep the shrill out of my voice.

—heinous cup Iris and I endured at Chatterstone on Friday.

'What coffee?' says Sophie.

'I had some artisan beans and a grinder delivered to his office this morning,' I say faintly. 'Bit of an in-joke.' Sophie looks at me. I don't explain.

Taylor moves the cursor so I can scan the rest.

Thanks for the Trust's and Iris's time. Everyone was very knowledgeable and welcoming. LC.

Seconds later, the email is forwarded from Vanessa's account to Taylor's and mine.

Taylor – Coffee delivery? Organise one of those posh monthly coffee subscriptions for him and expense it. Sounds like it went well, Iris? Let's talk activations at the 1-2-1.

I breathe out, a breath I didn't even realise I was holding, and my shoulders drop incrementally.

It's fine. It's fine.

'If there's anything I can do to help out with this – or any – account, please let me know,' Taylor says, immediately Googling 'coffee subscriptions'. 'I'd love to get some donor experience.'

I nod, mentally adding 'talk to Taylor about her ambitions' to my to-do list, and scuttle back to my desk, two more emails catching my eye as I go to read Vanessa's message again. One from a couple of my favourite donors, Emmett and Viola Banks, asking for a property tour on the Isle of Wight, and one from Sav's teacher. She's been trying to schedule a meet-up for two weeks but hasn't been able to 'catch us'. Another thing to feel guilty about. Rushing in and out of tea-time club pick-ups, especially when Sav still hasn't settled at school.

I start to respond to Vanessa but then properly register the date and time of the one-to-one. Tuesday at 4.30. When I'm supposed to be in Finsbury Park for counselling with Esther at 5 p.m. One of them will have to move, but is it the marriage therapy I'm supposed to spend this year wholly committed to, or the catch-up with my boss about the career I'm also supposed to be spending this year wholly committed to?

Fuck. I shake my head at the screen, hovering the cursor arrow between the 'accept' and 'decline' buttons. I'll ask Taylor to bring the meeting time forward by half an hour and get her to reissue the invite. That'll work. That has to work. I give myself a second. The main takeaway from this morning is: Lucas hasn't grassed me up.

'In-joke, eh?' Sophie says, as she comes back to her desk and sits down. 'Let's hope he laughs all the way to the bank.'

Chapter Fourteen

Transcript of session with Adam and Iris Young by Esther Moran, 5 February

Iris: [door slams shut] Sorry, sorry. [breathlessly] I'm so sorry I'm a bit late.

Adam: Ten minutes. For an hour's session.

Iris: My work meeting slightly overran—

Adam: That's Iris for, 'I only left at the time I was supposed to be here.'

Iris: No, it's Iris for, 'I had a meeting I absolutely couldn't miss but I left as soon as I possibly could and I've had to run all the way from the tube station to get here so please give me a break.' I *told* you that this time was going to be difficult for me. I'm trying my best to make it work.

Esther: Are you OK?

Iris: I'm [pause] sorry, could you give me a second to decompress. Start with Adam.

Adam: We've already started.

Iris: Then, please continue.

Adam: Are you being deliberately passive-aggressive?

Iris: What? No. [pause] I'm sorry I'm late, OK.

Esther: It's fine, Iris. Take a moment. I was explaining to Adam that we were going to try an exercise today. So I'll start with him. Adam, how did you and Iris meet?

Adam: What's this got to do with anything?

Esther: I'd like to get a sense of your history. It also lets us discuss what you love about each other.

Adam: Um, sure. We met online. Guardian Soulmates. [laughs] That seems retro now, doesn't it? But it was still new then. In 2009 people were still a bit embarrassed about it. I think we initially told people that we met in the pub.

Iris: Did you? I was always honest about it. I mean, who cares? I was thirty-one and was so over dating that I didn't care how I met someone, I just wanted to.

Adam: You definitely didn't tell your workmates that we met online, but anyway. I'd been single for a long time but dating on and off, using the site for about a year.

Esther: What were you looking for when you joined, Adam?

Adam: To see who was out there. I had a few girlfriends in my twenties, but no one serious. When I turned thirty, a lot of my mates were settling down and it made me think I wanted in, so I joined a dating site to see.

Esther: To see if . . .?

Adam: If there was someone like that for me. A forever person. The One. I don't know, whatever you want to call it. Someone serious.

Iris: [snorts]

Esther: What are you thinking, Iris?

Iris: I'm thinking, how could he ever find The One when perfect Jules has always been the one that got away? It's stupid that I ever believed it could be me.

Adam: That's not fair.
Iris: Isn't it?
Adam: It was you – it *is* you.
Esther: We are going to come back to what you've said, Iris, so please don't feel like I'm shutting you down, but I'd like us to work through this thread first. Adam, what attracted you to Iris to begin with?
Adam: On her profile?
Esther: Yes, let's start there.
Adam: She was gorgeous in the photos. If I'm honest, that's what I looked at first. Blonde hair, dark eyes, curvy figure. Then when I read her profile, she was funny and smart too. We only messaged a few times before she suggested meeting up, which I liked. I'd been on the site long enough to have got fed up with all the admin involved in messaging people, as when it came down to it, I always decided pretty quickly once I met a person if I fancied them. She suggested going to a pub in Islington for a drink. [laughs] What she actually said was, 'Let's have one drink and we'll review after that if it's too much like a job interview.' I liked that too. So we had that one drink and she blew me away.
Esther: Is that how you remember it, Iris?
Iris: Sort of. Although I wasn't actively looking for anyone at that point. I'd paused all my dating site subscriptions but must have forgotten to do the *Guardian* one, so it took me by surprise when his message popped up.
Esther: And what were you looking for?
Iris: [low laugh] A grown-up.
Esther: What do you mean by that?
Iris: I'd done my time in the trenches with shit men. You know, the ones who give you nervous flutters because they're treating you badly but for some reason

you confuse it with love. I wasted my twenties on a bloke like that. Waiting for him to grow out of going out drinking four nights a week, and making me feel like a drag because I wanted to set up a direct debit for the bills. When I broke up with him it took about two years to rebuild my self-esteem, and I swore I'd hold out for someone who wanted the same things as me. In all honesty, the only reason I went on the date is because he asked if I was free on Friday night – in dating terms that's prime real estate. I liked that he didn't pretend he had anything better to do than meet up with a stranger.

Adam: I've never been much of a game-player.

Iris: [silence]

Esther: What was your first impression on the date, Adam?

Adam: She was so much herself. She's into vintage clothes and she was wearing this little sixties dress. What's it called?

Iris: A shift dress.

Adam: Yeah, a shift dress. It was bright green, and very cool. She seemed secure in who she was. So together.

Iris: [snorts] As if.

Esther: You don't agree.

Iris: Who's secure?

Adam: You definitely gave off that vibe.

Iris: I probably came across as not giving a shit, because I couldn't be bothered to traipse to a bar and drink an overpriced cocktail with a bloke I probably wouldn't fancy.

Adam: That's what I liked! You were wary, but hopeful enough to come anyway. That's the best pre-date attitude. I found it very attractive.

Esther: Adam, you said you knew almost immediately if you fancied someone. Is that how you felt about Iris?

Adam: Yes. I thought that she was hot [laughs] in that cool dress.

Esther: And then?

Adam: When she started talking, I thought she was hot and sweet. Then a bit after that it became hot, sweet, smart and funny. I relaxed then because I thought there was no hope of her fancying me back, so I could be myself. [laughs]

Esther: You're joking but I sense you're not entirely.

[silence]

Esther: How did you enjoy the date, Iris? What made you want to see Adam again if you couldn't be bothered with dating?

Iris: He was funny and he was sweet and yes, I instantly fancied him too. I liked that he'd made an effort with what to wear and his choice of outfit. He had good taste – a nice denim shirt that matched his grey eyes, and he'd picked a bar that was perfect for a first date. Close to a tube station, and not so quiet as to be dead but not so busy that we didn't get a seat. He let it slip that he'd researched how long it would take for both of us to get there, which came across as thoughtful, and that gave me those flutters without any red flags. I liked him as a person and wanted to see him again. When you've been on enough internet dates you want to leave the second you arrive, you value that.

Esther: So it was a good date?

Iris: Well, we did get married.

Adam: [laughs]

Esther: When was the last time you went out somewhere like that, together?

Adam: We went to the pub last month.

Iris: I don't count that. It was an emergency summit about whether to end our marriage or come to counselling, so not exactly a date. Before that . . . I don't know.

Adam: Maybe our anniversary last year.

Iris: I don't think we did. It wasn't that long after Mum got sick. Even if I'd felt like it, Mum was our usual babysitter and I wouldn't have asked her.

Esther: So it's been a long time?

Both: Yes.

Esther: You've both told me how much you enjoyed meeting each other, and how surprising that was after romantic disappointments. I wanted you to remind yourselves what you liked about each other to begin with. With that in mind, I'm going to set you some homework. I'd like you to schedule a regular date night. I know it's not easy when you have children, but aim for once a month. Carve out some time together, out of the house, to reconnect. Do you think that's doable?

Both: OK.

Chapter Fifteen

5 February, 9 p.m.

'Hi Fran, we're back,' I call as we enter the house. Adam and I take off our coats and head into the living room, where the TV screen is paused on a particularly gruesome moment from *Breaking Bad*. 'Thanks so much for watching the kids,' I say, seeing Fran's eyes track Adam around the room as he puts his laptop case on the coffee table and plucks his phone charger from the mantelpiece, concentrating much harder on plugging it in than anyone needs to, because doing so means he doesn't have to look at Fran. This is the first time they've been in the same room since a boozy pre-Christmas lunch with Fran, Liam and their kids. The atmosphere is much less jovial. 'Sorry, we're later back than we were supposed to be.'

'Don't be daft,' Fran booms, her Warrington accent coming through the forced cheer of having to be outwardly pleasant to Adam, while fixing him with the kind of stare that's kept Joe Pesci in awards for several decades. 'Whenever you need me. I know these appointments are going to be regular. And anyway, it gives me an excuse to leave Liam and the kids at home and enjoy a nice leisurely drive back. Alone. God, I love silence. I never appreciated how much until I had three kids.' She starts collecting her stuff together, shoving her phone in her bag and winding a scarf around her neck. 'Jack and Sav are in bed, although I doubt Jack's asleep as he's been out three times to ask for water, then a wee, then more water. I expect he'll need another wee any minute now.' She hugs me and throws another look in Adam's direction before letting me walk her to the front door. 'That was one long therapy session,' she says to me quietly. 'I thought you'd be back at about half six. Is everything OK?'

'We've been prescribed a date night,' I tell her, trying not to cringe at how lame it sounds. 'So we went for a drink afterwards. Now Dad's gone home I wasn't sure when we'd be able to fit it in, but as you were already here . . .' I smile apologetically. The last thing I want is for Fran to think I'm taking the piss.

'It's fine! As long as you're all right. Did you have a good time?'

Adam comes out of the living room and goes into the kitchen, before coming back out again and saying, 'I'm making a tea – do you want one, Iris?' A moment passes and he adds, 'Thanks for coming, Fran.' He sounds like Jack when he's being strong-armed into thanking someone for his birthday presents.

She tilts her chin at him in response, acknowledging it but without saying 'you're welcome'.

'I'm OK for tea, thanks,' I say, and he potters back into the kitchen. I'm glad he's having one, though. That means I have enough time to go upstairs by myself.

I drop my voice. 'The drink was OK,' I say to Fran. 'I can't talk now, but I'll see you at the weekend.'

Fran nods back. 'Understood,' she says, in the same quiet tone. 'And I cannot bloody wait for the weekend, by the way. Thanks for the invite.' She raises her voice again. 'Right, I'm going to sit outside your house in the car for ten uninterrupted minutes, scrolling through Instagram, before I even consider turning on the ignition. It'll be like going to a spa.'

I laugh as I wave her off, before popping my head around the living room door where Adam has now set himself up on the sofa with his cuppa.

'I'm tired, I'm going to go up.'

'Really? Already?' He gestures to the TV screen where the Netflix homepage is auto-playing some documentary about murderers. 'I thought we could watch that show we were talking about in the pub.'

'Maybe tomorrow night. It's a bit late to start it now. I'm knackered. But you stay up and watch something if you like.' Adam looks disappointed but I don't give him time to respond and instead practically sprint upstairs, grabbing my pyjamas and locking myself in the bathroom to get changed. With Dad here, Adam and I had no choice but to stay in the same room, but even though he's gone now and I could kick Adam into the spare room, I feel awkward about changing the set-up. Besides, the way I've managed to arrange it, we might as well be platonic flatmates. My nightly routine now involves either beating him to bed by heading up inordinately early, or staying up later than I want to so that I can make sure he's in bed and asleep by the time I get there. Basically, I go to great lengths to ensure that come night-time we're rarely conscious simultaneously – but without him knowing that's what I'm doing.

I brush my teeth and shake out the new astronomically priced 'sleepwear' I bought from some trendy Instagram fashion brand last week. Whatever I wear for bed at the moment feels wrong. If I'm in my old flannel pyjamas it looks like I'm making no effort at all, and if I wear something impractical but a bit sexy it looks like I'm trying to entice him back with some bargain-bin Ann Summers, so my compromise is a pair of pyjamas styled to look like that casual 'hey, I'll put your shirt on' moment in films when a woman has stayed over at a man's house for the first time. It's the no-make-up-make-up of clothes and priced accordingly.

As I come out I almost barge into Adam, and I jump in surprise.

'I thought I'd head to bed too,' he says in explanation, clocking the look of horror on my face.

'Right, sure. Well, I'll see you in there then.' Like I told Fran, our drink in the pub was fine. We ordered some food and talked about the logistics of doing a date night regularly by drafting in my dad or Fran, and then moved on to all the shows we haven't been watching together recently. We studiously didn't talk about 'us'. It was almost like the old days, except with the draining undercurrent of having to try.

I get into my side of the bed, and not for the first time thank past me for insisting on a king-sized bed when we bought a new one five years ago. Heavily pregnant with Sav, and knowing how much time Jack spent co-sleeping with us by accident rather than design, my priority was having room for as many family members as possible. Neither of them tend to come in at night any more, but the acres of space mean I can literally keep Adam at arm's length.

I hear the toilet flush and the bathroom taps start running, so I nervily pick up one of the six books I have stacked on my bedside table, before realising it's one of my self-help specials. I grab another, the Sally Rooney that I'm the last person in existence to have read, before jettisoning that too and turning off my bedside lamp. It's better if I'm asleep when he comes in, or at least appear to be. That way we don't have to talk, or touch, or talk about why we're not touching.

I lie down, my back to Adam's side and my neck strained from resting my head not quite on my pillow but a little above it, my reflexes on high alert. A couple of minutes later he pads in, and there's a thud as he bangs something, I'm guessing his foot, on the side of the door in the dark.

'Shit.'

'Are you all right?' I turn over, pretending he's woken me up, despite him seeing me wide awake and attempting to creep out of the bathroom mere minutes ago.

'Yes, just cracked my toe,' he says, in a tight voice that's trying to mask the pain he's in. He switches his phone to torch mode to make his way to the bed, shining it right into my eyes. He's wearing his usual pyjama bottoms and an old band T-shirt, which was on regular wardrobe rotation when we first met and has been relegated to nightwear over the years. The duvet wafts as he gets in, letting in a chilly draught. I tense again but he stays where he is, on his side, nowhere near close enough for the shared warmth of our bodies to heat the no-man's-land patch of mattress between us.

'Do you mind if I put my light on and read for a bit?' He sounds so formal it's as if we're in a play.

'No, it's fine.' My voice is all muffled from where I have the duvet bunched around me, as though to protect me from – what?

The bedside lamp on Adam's side snaps on, and I hear him flipping open the Booker winner he's been ploughing through for weeks now. He usually only manages a couple of pages before he falls asleep. Meanwhile, I'm starting to overheat and feel weirdly deflated, almost foolish. What is this set piece I've acted out? Did I think that because we managed a civilised drink together, he'd try to initiate sex? My reaction shows how far I am from being ready for that to happen. But then, what if he never tries to initiate sex again?

Chapter Sixteen

9 February

Fran sits down on the double bed in our luxury cottage and fixes her gaze on me. 'Are you sure you're OK?' she says.

I'm smoothing my outfit down in front of the mirror and analysing my eyes for any stray traces of make-up that have seeped into the crevices.

'Yes, just nervous. After what happened at the last one, I need this visit to go well.'

We're on the Isle of Wight so I can do another Trust site visit, this time with Emmett and Viola Banks, an elderly (and rich, of course) couple who have been donating money for decades. They're lovely and I always enjoy meeting up with them, not least because they're keen to see places all around the country, so I get to travel a bit to see them. But after the Lucas Caulfield debacle, I feel off my game so am anxious that it runs perfectly.

Thankfully there's no rush this time, though. I'm being put up for the night, and Adam is home with the kids, so I drafted in Fran for some moral support. She's at the stage where she would – as she's told me several times – sell her own mother to sleep in after 6 a.m. I'm just looking forward to sleeping somewhere I can stay up until the same time as my roommate.

She appraises me. 'You look good. Like a wise art student.'

'Thanks.' I'm wearing some high-waisted black trousers and a grey polo neck, and have paired them with some velvet Chelsea boots. My red lipstick is in place, my favourite fifties glasses on.

'Do you want me to get you into the manor house so you can look around while I'm working?'

'Nope.' Fran wanders into the bathroom and then comes back out holding a miniature body lotion with the lid off. She gives it a sniff and picks up the remote control for the wall-mounted flat-screen TV. 'Sitting in this tidy, clean room for two hours with a coffee and some biscuits I don't have to share is enough of a holiday for me. I might even have a nap. Oh my God, a NAP. No shushing or patting required.' She looks at her watch. 'You should go. I've got a lot to do in my remaining twenty-four hours of holiday. Come back here after and we'll go for lunch.' She gives me a little salute. 'Good luck, you're going to be great.'

I throw on my coat, a more substantial wool number than last time – at least that's one lesson I've learned – and scurry out of the door, stopping briefly to admire the view of the sea from the cobbled path of our cottage. There's a strong wind coming off the water, but even when the sea is as blustery and roiling as it is today, it's stunning. Another pocket of the UK with a history to absorb. Not to mention another previously unvisited property to tick off my list. That makes me think briefly of Lucas and the runner I did, and my stomach twists with angst.

Not now, I tell myself, willing myself to be 'on'. I force myself to throw my shoulders back, even though it means I'm soon getting slapped in the face by the cold. At least it wakes me up during the brisk walk to the manor house, so by the time I meet Emmett and Viola Banks in the lobby of Atherford House I'm invigorated, if a bit bedraggled. This time I have Charlie, the chief curator of the house, with me and everyone is fully aware of the Bankses' generous contributions over the years, so I can openly defer to her superior knowledge of the house and grounds and let her give us all a tour. But I've also planned a big surprise, because the reason the Bankses wanted to come here today is that they honeymooned on the Isle of Wight sixty years ago. A touch of sleuthing taught me their diamond wedding anniversary is next week, so we've arranged a special 'diamond lunch' for them in a room that's usually shut up to the public.

★

'Hello, Iris,' says Viola, hugging me warmly before I do the same with Emmett. They're both in their eighties, and Emmett is dressed smartly in a three-piece suit, holding a stick that matches the dark brown of his brogues. Viola is in a long purple floral dress, her hair in a gunmetal-grey flapper bob, and wearing a shade of red lipstick that immediately makes me ask her where it's from.

'I was going to ask you the same thing,' she says, laughing. 'Mine's the famous Revlon Fire and Ice.' And then she adds, 'I used to wear it in the seventies and then decided I was too old for it. Then a couple of weeks ago I decided to resurrect it.'

'Good decision,' I tell her. 'It looks fantastic. Mine is NARS Manhunt.' I cringe at a name I've never given much thought to, until I had to say it in front of two octogenarians.

Emmett chuckles. 'Shouldn't think you'd need to hunt for long in that lippy,' he says, and Viola swats his arm.

'Behave, Emmett,' she says with a laugh. 'I'll have a look next time I'm in John Lewis.' She links her arm through mine as we begin the tour.

Charlie starts us off in the lobby, and I let her knowledge wash over me. She's such a brilliant guide; everything she tells us is imbued with warmth and humour, even her story about the painstaking restoration of the ballroom after a fire ripped through the building in 1867. I love being immersed in places that are so different from my life now. Stories told through old buildings, especially grand houses like this with an upstairs-downstairs legacy, places I'd never have got within a whisker of living in if I'd been around in the olden days. Adam would probably disagree – he's always teased me about my private school education, and Mum and Dad's big detached house – but he wouldn't dare say something about it in front of Dad, who's always proudly declared himself to be self-made as he ran his own building firm for many years. 'I come from trade,' I always joke when Adam tells me I'm posh.

We make our way into a large room that looks out onto the lawn before giving way to a rugged view of the sea. It's absolutely stunning and will be even more so come the summer. Charlie and I stop the Bankses there for a moment and let them admire the view, then hit them with the other surprise we've discussed.

'I know how excited you were to come back to the Isle of Wight after all these years,' I start tentatively. 'So we were wondering if you might like to have a small party here in the summer to celebrate your diamond wedding anniversary. All at the Trust's expense, of course,' I add quickly. 'You don't have to decide now, but we'd love to host you and your family as a thank you for your support all these years. Atherford House isn't usually available for hire, but we're happy to make an exception in your case.'

'What a lovely gesture,' Viola says. She nudges Emmett. 'What do you think?'

He's smiling and looks a little damp-eyed. 'Could we pick the date?'

'Of course,' I say.

'One of our sons lives in Australia but is coming over later this year. We could do it when the whole family is in one place.'

'That sounds wonderful,' I say.

Viola turns to Emmett. 'Maybe we could . . .' She breaks off and grabs my hand. 'Would we be able to do a vow renewal? It's something we've talked about before, but this would make it such a lovely occasion.'

'Absolutely,' I say. 'Let me know what date you're thinking and what numbers, and we can sort everything else.'

'We didn't have a very big wedding the first time around,' Emmett explains, 'so we've always wanted to have a proper do. It almost makes more sense to do it now when we've made it this far together.' It's Emmett's turn to nudge Viola. 'You must admit, there've been times when we probably didn't think we'd make it this long.'

'Till death us do part and all that.'

'Even if my death was at your hands,' he jokes. Suddenly my eyes pool with tears, and I have to keep repeating the word 'lovely' to them so they think I've been swept up in the emotion of a long and enduring marriage, rather than lamenting that my own marriage might not even make it to sixteen years, never mind sixty.

'Will you wear white, Viola?' I ask.

'God, no,' she says. 'Never was my colour. We got married in the early sixties but it was before everything started "swinging", so my dress was very plain and proper. At least this time round I can wear something jazzy.' We all laugh and Charlie moves them to another window, revealing a neatly manicured patch of lawn with wildflower beds dug in on either side.

'I've always thought that would be a lovely place to have an arch for an outdoor ceremony,' she tells them.

Viola looks thrilled at the prospect. 'Are people still into cupcake towers instead of wedding cakes?' she asks. 'Or is it something else now?'

'I'm not sure,' I reply. 'The trend was for cake pops when I got married.' I finger my still-bare left hand and my smile starts to droop.

'My grandson had a cake made out of cheese, if you can imagine,' Viola says, raising an eyebrow. 'Well, I didn't know what to think.'

An hour later, we deposit them in the house's orangery, where a bottle of champagne greets them and there's a five-course tasting menu to work through. I'm completely beamed out but give one last push to make sure they're happy and settled for their lunch, before reiterating that they should get in touch as soon as they decide on a date.

They both hug me again heartily, and Viola dabs at her eyes as Emmett draws her seat out for her. 'Call me if you need anything else this afternoon,' I say, making a mental note to order a NARS lipstick and have it sent to Viola. Then Charlie and I leave them, hurrying back to her office for coffee and a debrief. On the way, I fire off an email to Vanessa.

The Bankses don't just want a party here, they want a vow renewal! Consider them nurtured!

★

'Fran, are you awake?' I call as I get back to the cottage. The curtains are closed and the lights are off. I flip on a side lamp.

'Just about,' she murmurs from somewhere inside the super-king bed. 'I made it through about four pages of my book before I decided that my brain would be far better improved by sleeping. Also, there's a child murder in it and I couldn't go on. I threw it across the room.'

She points to the corner, where her book is cover-down on the floor.

'Lunch?' I say, and she pulls herself out of the bed, her jeans and jumper still on.

'How were the generous benefactors?' she asks, pulling on her biker boots.

'It went well, thank God,' I say, meaning it. 'They're going to renew their vows here later this year and were thrilled with the surprise lunch. They're such a great couple – I'm glad to do something nice for them. Plus, touch wood, there's no way they'll drop their contributions after that.'

'Good,' Fran replies. 'You nailed it. Not that I ever doubted you, but I know you needed a work boost.' She picks up her bag, pausing to swipe open her phone.

'Oh, look at them, they're so cute,' she says, showing me some photos Liam has sent her of the kids in the soft play near their house. 'I miss you,' she says to the screen.

'But I also don't want to see *any* of you in person until tomorrow afternoon.'

My own phone stays resolutely quiet. Despite the effort we're supposed to be making on the date front, Adam and I aren't in a casual photo-swapping zone right now. We're more about practical logistics: drop-offs, pick-ups, whose turn it is to do certain chores, and slotting in our therapy appointments around all of that. I consider sending him a friendly message, then think about what I'd even say if I did.

'One thing I *have* had time to do is look into where we should go for lunch,' says Fran, opening the door for me and pointing in the direction of the front gates. 'There's a wanky gastropub not far from here that does all manner of small plates and artisan courses – all things my children would turn their noses up at. Yours might not though, being so very bourgeois.' I've told Fran about my dad's criticisms, which she thinks are hilarious.

'As though your children subsist on Fray Bentos pies and Findus Crispy Pancakes,' I reply.

'God, do you remember them? I used to bloody love a Findus Crispy Pancake in the eighties.'

'They probably do an artisan version of them in the posh pub. Repackage all those eighties classics for the millennial small-plate crowd.'

'Vegan. And with added wellness.'

'Exactly.'

When we arrive, the pub doesn't do a Fray Bentos, but its stripped wood, sharing tables and soft lighting offer the perfect place to hole up on a cold February afternoon, while the seared scallops with chorizo foam and the extensive cocktail list more than make up for it. There's a huge room at the back with an open fire, a library of books and magazines, and a floor-to-ceiling window that looks out onto the blustery bay, where we can see a few committed sailors tending to their boats. We assume two side-by-side armchairs, Fran grabs a pile of magazines, and we settle down with a couple of Old Fashioneds, before passing the next few hours in a comfortable daze of food, warm fire and only the odd bit of conversation, usually to do with Jennifer Aniston or *Love Island*, depending on which tier of celebrity magazine each of us is reading at the time.

It's only when we're onto our second drink that Fran says casually, 'So. You were going to tell me about your post-therapy date. How's it all going?'

I've been doing a good job of not thinking about Adam until now, concentrating instead on the glow of the fire and the whisky. I sigh. 'I keep thinking about things we said in therapy and wanting to tell you all about it, but then again I feel . . .' I try and think of the word.

'Disloyal.'

'Exactly. Like I'm disrespecting the process if I thrash it all out with my best mate afterwards.'

Fran nods. 'Fair enough.'

'But if I'm honest, at the moment therapy feels like a waste of time.'

Fran's face is neutral. 'In what way?'

'In that I don't know how I'm supposed to therapise my marriage back to life when I hate him most of the time. Is that normal?'

'Of *course* you hate him. I hate him. I can't think of anything more normal than hating him right now.'

'I don't know. I mean, I've agreed to give my marriage a year, but right now it's like all I'm doing is mentally gathering evidence as to why it's not going to work out.'

I can see Fran trying to control her neutral face, but there's a twitch.

'What?'

'You don't *have* to stay for a year, you know. That's just an arbitrary amount of time you've come up with.'

I sigh again. 'I know, but I owe it to us to try. Or, I owe it to the kids, if nothing else.' I look into my drink. 'A year feels like the right amount of time.'

'For what?'

I take a shaky sip. 'Long enough to give it a proper go. Not so long as to flog something that's dead if it's over.' My voice is more glib than I feel.

'And he's trying to make it up to you? Grovelling, begging, proving he's changed and that you are bloody amazing for even entertaining the idea of giving him another chance? That sort of thing?'

I think about it. 'He keeps making a big show of leaving his phone and laptop open, making it clear there's no contact with' – my voice snags on her name – 'her. But who knows if he has been? I mean, how can I be sure?'

'Are you not tempted to get in touch with her?'

I think about how many times I check her Instagram page in the average week and how many times I've Googled whether it's possible for someone to see how many times another person has checked their Instagram page. Then I think of all the scathing messages I've mentally composed to her. Entire commutes taken up by devastating and well-worded DM take-downs. 'All the time,' I admit. 'My search history is an embarrassment.'

'Let's see,' she says.

I'm tipsy enough for this not to seem like a terrible idea, and I pull up Jules's Instagram.

'She's in Oman at the minute,' I say. 'There was a photo of her sandboarding on desert dunes there this morning. See, she doesn't just fly to these places; she makes the most of her time there when she arrives.'

'Oh Christ, she's one of them,' Fran says, the second I pass her my phone. 'Oh, here's me all casual in a bikini doing yoga next to an infinity pool.' She rolls her eyes. 'What's this one?'

I look. 'A mountain climb for charity.'

'Course it is.' Fran's derisive tone would be more appropriate if I'd said, 'It's her skinning animals for their fur.'

'She's not only beautiful, smart and well travelled, but she's also a good person.'

'No, she's not!' she shouts back instantly. 'She's a home-wrecking bitch. And she can't even claim she didn't know Adam had a wife because you told me about that message.'

Go back to your wife. It hits me again like a punch.

'True. You're right. Fuck her. She is a complete bitch.'

'What's her Facebook like?'

'Locked,' I say instantly. Of course I've checked. Fran looks her up on my phone anyway.

'You should get in touch with her. Make sure Adam has cut off contact.'

I nearly spit out my drink. 'How would that play? "Adam, I know we agreed to try and move on and you assured me you'd broken it off, but I don't believe you so I've asked Jules myself."'

'Yes, exactly like that. You're well within your rights. I would.'

I think of Fran and Liam and how much he adores her. 'You wouldn't need to.'

The smile she gives me is almost apologetic. Is this how my friends are going to be around me from now on? All 'sorry my marriage isn't shit'?

'If you need some sort of proof that they're no longer in touch, don't let Adam make you feel like you're mad or weird for wanting to hear it from her.'

'He hasn't.' We haven't even discussed it. 'I don't know if I want to talk to h—'

'I've friend-requested her,' Fran says, and as I dive to get my phone off her, it's as though the walls are closing in on me.

'What the fuck, Fran? Why did you do that?'

'Power move,' she says, as though that explains everything.

'She'll know I've been looking her up like some loser wronged wife. How is that a power move?' My armpits prickle with stress sweat. What will she think when she sees the friend request? What will Adam think if he finds out?

'Because she'll see you've looked her up and know you know all about her.' She looks smug but I have no idea where she's getting this from. 'Then she has to decide whether to accept your request and face a humongous bollocking or leave you in request purgatory, always knowing you could come for her at any time.'

'That is *not* how I would interpret what I – *you* – have done.' I'm so pissed off with Fran right now. 'Can you rescind friend requests?' I fret. I keep glancing at my phone, panicking about what's going to happen when Jules sees the notification.

There's a buzz and I jump, throwing my phone onto the table in front of me. 'I can't look, what is it?'

'Oh!' Fran sounds relieved herself. Power move, my arse. She's a bit drunk and trigger happy. 'It's a WhatsApp from Nat to the group.' She passes my phone back and reaches for her own.

I read the preview.

Been trying to get hold of you two for a while but I guess I'll have to do it over WhatsApp . . .

'Er, we've been right here,' Fran grumbles. 'She's the one who cancelled the last drinks, which isn't really on considering what you're going through.'

I open the message, which turns out to be an ultrasound image.

I'm four months, so due in July!! 😊

'I guess that explains Dry January,' says Fran. 'And being all about solidarity with husbands even when they're useless.'

Fran is typing . . .

She fills the reply window up with hearts, baby emojis and celebration streamers, while I summon up the part of me that can be happy for someone else without turning it into a misery fest about me. It's got to be in there somewhere.

Such AMAZING news, Nat. Massive congrats! We need to celebrate soon – Seedlip for you, obvs.

'God, I feel terrible,' I say to Fran, while I match her emoji for emoji. 'She'll have wanted to announce it to us back in January, and then I sucked all the joy out of her baby news with my marriage woes.'

'Hey,' Fran says sharply. 'Don't be daft. How were you to know?'

I contemplate the picture. 'Her year will end very differently to mine. The happiness of a new baby compared to the potential death of a marriage.'

'If you think the newborn months are happy, you're in a worse place psychologically than I thought,' says Fran, standing up and wobbling. 'Besides, your marriage isn't dead. Not unless you want it to be. Hold that thought while I go to the loo. I'll order a bottle of wine, some soda water and a sack of ice on the way back. It's drinking but diluted. Win-win. God, how are we in our forties,' she mutters, disappearing around the corner in search of a toilet, which is when my phone buzzes once more. I pick it up expecting Nat again, but steeling myself for it to be Jules. It's neither.

It's a Facebook friend request from Lucas Caulfield.

Chapter Seventeen

'Why have you got that weird look on your face?' Fran plonks a bottle of Chardonnay in an ice bucket down on the table and I turn the screen to show her.

'The charismatic millionaire!' she shrieks. 'Are you sure it's not a bot?' She grabs the phone to take a closer look and swiftly presses 'accept'.

'Fran!' I shout. 'Seriously. Stop fucking with my phone.'

'What? He requested you. It would be rude not to accept.'

'It's unprofessional,' I say weakly. I'd have at least left it an hour before I accepted.

'Pfft.' She waves an arm at me. 'Only if you have unprofessional motives towards him.' She rests one eye on me in a penetrating yet tipsy way. 'And on the plus side, this means he definitely isn't pissed off about the Chatterstone visit.' She fixes me with a squinty look and puts on a teasing voice. 'Level the playing field.'

'Oh God. Shut up about that.'

'Fine.' She pours us each a very full glass of wine, with a token ice cube in each. 'Then let's have a totally professional deep dive into his social media. You know, so you can tailor your relationship building – *work* relationship building – to him and his interests. Oooh, which include' – Fran's flipping through his photos so quickly I'm terrified she's going to hit the 'like' button and expose that I've been looking at his holiday photos from 2014 – 'bike riding, craft beers, and going to massive conferences with other venture capitalists in San Francisco, by the looks of things.' We hunch over my phone.

'No one who you'd pick out as a girlfriend in any of the photos,' Fran says.

'That doesn't mean anything. Adam's got hardly anything on his Facebook page. He's had the same profile picture since he went to watch the 2012 Olympics and took a picture with the flame.'

'You're right. Some people keep their pages deliberately hard to read.'

My hackles go up. 'What do you mean? That Adam has purposely made it unclear that he's married with kids on there?' Fran shrugs. Has he? I think of my feed. Photo spam of my family: first days at school, World Book Day, the Christmas tree going up, all the clichés. And then I think of Adam's: just the bare bones. I thought he couldn't be arsed with social media full stop, but maybe he was doing it on purpose. The mini revelations never end. I have to keep revisiting my opinion on everything, even his Facebook page. Is he lazy or calculating?

My phone buzzes again. This time with a message. From Lucas. Fran screams. Thank God we're tucked away in this little alcove, away from the other punters.

Hi Iris, I know you were behind the NT gift and wanted to thank you personally. I hope everything turned out OK with your dad.

It's so innocuous.

Not unlike that first message from Adam to Jules.

I place my phone gently on the table. Then pick it up again. Then press it face down.

'You have to answer him,' Fran says, watching me push my phone further away from us as though that will solve anything.

'I will. But not now.'

'If Adam can "connect"' – the quote marks Fran's making are wildly exaggerated, her Warrington accent getting stronger by the second – 'with old flames, why can't you make some new friends?'

'He's not a friend, he's a work contact. A very important work contact.'

'Who has Facebook friend-requested you, which implies he wants to be friendly outside work. You know *I* think you're a total catch, but I also recognise that what you need right now is external validation. And what could be better than the external validation of a mysterious millionaire?'

I give a bitter laugh. 'As though it's that simple. And as though that's the answer to my marriage problems.'

'I know I keep joking' – is she joking? – 'about beating Adam at his own game, but in all seriousness, no one could blame you for thinking about moving on, or having a look to see what's out there,' she says carefully. She's fiddling with the angle of the ice bucket, pretending she's barely interested in the conversation. I know this because it's exactly the kind of thing I do when Sav's in the bath, has half told me about something that's happened at school, and I want more information. If I show I'm too interested she clams up, so I concentrate on something – anything – else while I 'casually' question her.

'I'm not thinking of moving on.'

'Maybe you should,' she says. Still not looking at me. Still uber nonchalant. 'I mean, not necessarily with this Lucas, but in general.'

The air has been sucked out of the room. 'What? Why? How long have you thought this?'

Fran finally looks at me. I can tell by the expression on her face that even as she's speaking, she's not sure it's a good idea. 'Since you told me. And since Adam didn't get on his hands and knees and beg for you. You're being so hard on yourself, and I hate watching you blame yourself for what that bastard did and trying to fold yourself into therapy sessions that so far just seem to be making you feel bad. I want you to be sure that promising him another year of your life is what you want when you could get back out there and move on.'

'I don't know what I want. Besides, I can't think of anything worse than "out there". Right now, Keanu Reeves could Facebook friend-request me and I still wouldn't be interested.'

'I think we *all* know that's not true,' Fran says, in an attempt to lighten the mood. 'But I get it. You want to fix it. You want to see if you can protect the kids from a nuclear-level break-up. But *I* want to make sure you know that if you can't come back from his affair you're not to blame, you're human, and the best thing for the kids is for you to get out as painlessly as possible. It wouldn't mean you've failed. I don't want you to waste the next twelve months of your life with him when you could be happier on your own.'

Ten minutes ago, we were laughing and teasing each other. Now both our voices are clipped and curt. I know she's trying to be supportive, but I feel judged. How does she know how I should deal with this? Liam adores her, always has. She's never had anything to worry about. But then neither did I, until I did.

'So you're saying I *should* get divorced and that there's no point in trying to salvage our marriage?'

'Only you can decide that. And whatever you choose I'm on your side.'

It doesn't sound like that from here. I angrily tip some more wine into my glass. 'I don't want to get a divorce.'

'Are you sure about that?' She stops and fiddles with the stem of her glass, as though there's something else she wants to say.

'What is it?' I snap.

'It's just, you've been angry with Adam for a long time.'

'Having an affair will do that to a person.'

'No, before that. Last year. Remember how angry you were with him.'

I open my mouth to retort, but I stop, instead letting the words sink in. 'My mum was dying. I was angry with everyone,' I say finally. It's true, I was. Before she got ill, I saw Mum all the time. She was always there. A constant. In the background mostly, but front and centre when I needed her. Until the rampant cancer got her, and she went from force of nature to a hospice in four months. I'd seethe with resentment when I saw mother-daughter couples out for lunch together and was quick to lose my temper with everyone at home. I can remember getting mad with Sav over something stupid the day Mum had to go into the hospice. She'd dropped cereal on the sofa, and I properly shouted at her, ranting about how she needed to take responsibility for her actions. She looked at me like I was a crazy person before bursting into hot, hysterical tears. I felt guilty for days afterwards.

'Not the kind of angry you get when the world is unfair. The kind of angry you get when someone deserves it. You were livid with Adam, and you'd tell me about it every time we met up. He wasn't helping enough, he wasn't doing enough. You needed more support.'

'It was hard.' That's an understatement, but it's a can of worms I don't want to open here, now.

'That's what I mean. Your mum was dying, Iris. It was shit. And he *wasn't* doing enough. He was barely there while you were running yourself ragged travelling between home and your parents'.'

I think back to last summer. Adam and I hardly saw each other. I rushed from home to work to holiday club pick-up to Surrey. Mum refused to get a cleaner right up until the end, so I'd go over on Sunday morning to do their house. Then I'd go back to my own house, which was invariably in a state, and have a go at Adam for letting it turn into such a tip.

'I shouted at him all the time. It must have been horrible.'

'Are you kidding me?' Fran's entire face is going red, the effects of either booze or animation, or both. 'It was hardly a normal situation. It was grief and it had to come out somehow. Anyone who loves you would understand that and give you a bit of a free pass. The way I see it, he was used to you being the strong one – case in point, all the time you've spent helping him clean up Gabe's messes – but when you needed him to do the same, he let you down. He ran off to someone less "complicated". It's unforgivable.'

'So you hated Adam even before the affair.' I'm drunk now, and muddled.

'I didn't hate him,' she says more gently. 'But I wanted him to look after you more than he did. At the time I put it down to him being a shit bloke, but in light of what he was doing, I want to kill him.'

'You think I don't want to kill him?' I laugh bitterly.

'So you can see why I want to make sure that if you stay together, there's something in it for you. Something binding you together, more than the fear of being without him. You're strong enough to start over if you want to.'

'Am I?'

'You've already got through your mum dying, practically on your own. You're strong enough to do this, I promise.'

Fran's words are like a punch to the gut. I lean my head back in the chair and close my eyes, grief for my mum and my former secure life washing over me.

Then I pick up my phone and tap out a reply to Lucas.

Glad you liked it. I figured I owed you a decent coffee! 😜

Chapter Eighteen

24 February

'Why don't you like Daddy any more?'

Sav's nervy little face looks up at me from below the worktop, and my hand freezes right at the point I'm about to stick a lemon into the arse-end of a chicken.

'What do you mean? Of course I like Daddy.' The faux-jollity in my tone makes it even more obvious I'm lying. Sav has never been anybody's fool.

Her mouth wobbles. 'No, you don't. Whenever you speak to him you use your cross voice and we never do anything together. Sinéad's mum and dad don't live together any more because they don't love each other. Is that what's going to happen to you and Daddy?'

Sav's face collapses so completely that I realise she's been holding this in for some time. I have no idea how to handle it, because on the one hand, she's right – completely, utterly and devastatingly right – but on the other, there's no way I can burden her with the hideous truth of the situation.

I think back over the last few weeks. I can't relax when it's the four of us spending 'family time' at home, so I end up finding some washing to hang up or an errand to run to save me from the pressure of it. It's far easier when we're going about our business; Adam taking Jack to his gymnastics class on a Saturday while I take Sav to tae kwon do, and only passing each other in between. Some of it's down to the inevitable division of labour when you have two kids with no shared interests, but the rest, like our sleeping set-up, I've been happy to mastermind. No wonder Sav's picked up on it. But now I'm stuck with the blame as well as the burden of coming up with an explanation, because Adam isn't here. He's outside, having made a big show of doing the 'first mow of the year' during the sort of weekend that makes you hopeful the shitty weather is over, and spring is on its way. The sort that almost guarantees it will start snowing within forty-eight hours. Jack is out there booting a football into our feeble daffodils as Adam alternately ignores him and tells him off.

I pull Sav into a hug while inwardly berating myself for not Googling how to talk to the kids about this. When Mum died, I spent ages trawling the internet for the right way to explain death, so maybe this needs the same approach: blunt honesty. Except the part about the affair and the messy explanation that we may or may not be together in a year, obviously.

'Mummy and Daddy have been falling out a lot recently,' I say slowly into the side of her head. She smells of gummy worms, probably because she managed to get one smushed into her hair yesterday and it won't comb out. 'Like you and Jack do, but that doesn't mean you don't love him any more, does it?'

'I don't like him when he's mean though,' she says in a low voice.

'No, but mostly he's not trying to be mean, he just doesn't think. Sometimes grown-ups are like that too.'

It occurs to me that I've done this all wrong. Not only have I likened our marriage to being siblings, but Jack is outside, uninvolved in this conversation, so now I'm going to have to explain it again to him. And I also need to tell Adam that she's onto us. We've only had one conversation about what to tell the kids, and we decided not to tell them anything, so if we're talking to them about it at all it should be with a united front. Plus: *do* I still love Adam? This conversation could come back to haunt me in December if I decide to leave. But I'm committed now, and all I want to do is reassure my little girl that her world isn't going to change. Not yet, anyway.

'Nobody is going to live anywhere else. Everything is exactly the same. Daddy takes you to school, Mummy picks you up, and we all live here together.' I remember that I still haven't found the time to reply to that email from her teacher about a catch-up. I add it to my mental to-do list.

'If you keep falling out, I think you and Daddy need to do better listening and be kind to each other,' she says, pulling away from the hug and parroting one of our choice phrases back at me. Her earnest face threatens to unravel me completely.

'I think you're right,' I reply, tears pricking at my eyes. I scramble through the archives of my brain to think of something else to comfort her. 'We are a family, always, remember that. But if you're ever worried about anything, come and speak to Mummy about it, OK?'

Predictably, now I've hit my stride and dredged up something that might make her feel secure, Sav's lost interest and wandered over to the other side of the kitchen.

'What's this?' Sav asks, pulling off the top of a cardboard box and looking inside.

'It's some . . . of Mummy's stuff,' I say, whisking it away and plonking it in the hallway. Given the conversation we've just had, I can't tell her the truth. *This, Sav, is Mummy's visualisation box. Her marriage therapist mentioned them in our last session, and I looked it up online. It's full of things she is using to represent the 'her' she wants to become and the marriage she wants to have. Yes, I'm hoping a tat-filled box is going to save my marriage to Daddy.*

No.

'Morning, Iris.' Dad makes me jump as he comes into the kitchen, whistling, and plonks a frozen Sara Lee cake on the counter. Another Mum special; he must have picked it up on his way here. I'm pleased because he's been popping over semi-regularly for Sunday lunch and has let himself in with his key, so he's obviously more comfortable about coming and going, but I didn't hear the door.

Dad looks thin, but then so do I. I've lost weight without even trying since New Year, although I haven't so much slimmed down as deflated.

'I'm prepping the lunch. Adam and Jack are in the garden if you want to head out there.'

'Play with me, Gan-Gan,' Sav shouts.

'Right-o,' Dad replies, pleased to be needed.

'I want to do a treasure hunt with Grandad.' This is shorthand for wanting some chocolate, seeing as the 'hunt' consists of finding chocolate buttons wrapped in foil that have been hidden around the living room.

I don't have it in me to say no. After the conversation we've just had, I want to make her happy.

'Fine.' I pull the foil out of a drawer and start tearing bits off. 'Dad, you start wrapping and Sav, you go upstairs while he hides them. He can shout you when he's done it.'

A couple of minutes later, Dad takes the 'treasure' into the living room to hide. I notice he's got his slippers on. Hopefully he brought them with him to change into, otherwise the kids will have another field day.

'Ready for you, Savvy,' he shouts from the other room, and she comes thundering and shrieking down the stairs. I calculate I've bought myself enough time to finish the lunch.

I shift to autopilot, sticking on the radio and concentrating on peeling to a soundtrack of blues chosen by Cerys Matthews. I used to go to gigs a lot when I was younger but can't remember the last time I did. My most current musical references are at least a decade old. I hum along to Etta James, occasionally looking up through the patio doors to see Adam and Jack examining something outside, while I keep checking the dinner. It could almost be a normal Sunday morning, one where Mum will wander in to pour us a cheeky glass of white wine as soon as it hits noon, or the weather will start making me think about where we could book an overpriced family trip for the summer holidays. Almost.

'MUMMY!' Sav's ear-splitting shout snaps me out of it. 'I'M BORED.'

'What?'

What sounds like 'HOOIUIOUILS' comes back at me.

'Come in here if you want to talk to me.'

'WHAT?'

'Come in here! Oh, for God's sake.' I pull the chicken out of the oven to rest and go into the living room, where she's on the floor surrounded by foil detritus and sofa cushions, with *Minions* on the TV. There's no sign of Dad.

'What is it?'

'It's BORING on my own.'

'Where's Grandad?'

She does that exaggerated shrug small children do when you question them about anything specific.

'He built me this den' – that explains why the cushions are all over the floor – 'and then he left.'

'He's probably gone to the toilet.' I step into the hallway and shout up the stairs. 'Dad!'

Nothing.

'Hang on, I'll find him.' I rush up, checking quickly in the kids' bedrooms before I get to the end of the hall and see the bathroom door is open. 'Dad?' He's not there. I run down again.

'Where is he?' Sav asks, as I go back into the living room.

'You weren't playing hide and seek, were you?'

'No.' She beams. 'But can we?'

'After lunch,' I say, distracted and making for the kitchen. He must have slipped past me into the garden.

'Adam,' I shout. 'Is Dad out here with you?'

He and Jack look up from a patch of soil where they're planting lily bulbs. 'Your dad? I didn't even know he was here. Has he gone to the shop or something?'

I get a weird fluttery sensation in my stomach from Sav being left on her own without me knowing. It's not like I wasn't in the house, but it's off. It's strange that he wouldn't pop in to tell me if he had to leave.

'Not sure.' I run to the front door, step out and scan the street. When I step back inside, Adam, Jack and Sav are all in a row looking at me, worried.

'It's all right, I'll ring him.' His phone is off, obviously. It's then that I realise the box has disappeared from the hallway. 'Did you put that box upstairs?'

Adam frowns. 'What box?'

'Mummy's treasure box,' Sav explains.

'It's not—' I stop, embarrassed and not wanting to explain. Why have both Dad and the box gone missing?

'He must have popped out,' I say, more to reassure myself than anyone else. 'Lunch is ready now anyway, so I'm sure he'll be back by the time we sit down.'

Adam ushers the kids into the kitchen, shooting me another anxious look. 'Let's get your hands washed for lunch,' he says, as Jack protests he doesn't need to, despite his being caked with mud.

I call Dad's phone on and off while wrestling the potatoes out of the roasting tray and dumping half a bag of frozen peas into a pan.

By the time we're all sitting around the table, Dad still hasn't reappeared. How long do we leave it before we do something? What do we even do? He can only have been gone for an hour max, so I can't call the police, but it's so odd. As I bring over the gravy, Adam makes a big show of putting his phone face up on the table, which I know is for my benefit but annoys me all the same.

'*No* phones at the table,' Jack says, instantly fiddling with it, because he's never met a phone he doesn't want to play with.

'You're right. Put it away,' I snap, and Jack places it on the seat next to him, grinning cheekily at Adam as though he's got one over on him.

'Where's Gan-Gan?' Sav keeps asking as we eat, peas dribbling off her plate and onto the table. Jack flicks one onto the floor.

'Stop it!' I shout. 'He's gone out,' I say to her, not sounding very confident.

'I've finished,' Jack announces, all of two minutes after we start eating. 'I want an ice cream.'

'Nice try,' Adam replies, flipping up a bit of chicken on his plate, under which Jack has hidden most of his veg.

Jack pouts and goes to work stuffing as much of the veg into his mouth at once.

'Chew it, Jack. You'll choke.'

As lunch degenerates into a telling off, I hear the front door open and catapult myself into the hallway, where Dad is taking off his coat.

'Where have you been?' I shout, almost hysterical. Dad freezes halfway through hanging up his coat and looks at me like I'm a crazy person. The crazy-person voice obviously doesn't do anything to dispel that.

'I took that box for you,' he says carefully. 'Thought I'd get it out of the way.'

'Get what out of the way? Took it where?'

'To the charity shop.' Dad passes me on the way to the kitchen and sits down next to Sav, where his plate of food has gone cold while we waited for him. 'Ah, lunch is ready. I didn't realise it would be so soon.'

None of this conversation makes any sense. 'Dad, no one knew where you'd gone. Or why.'

He chuckles as though *I'm* being dense and ruffles Sav's hair. 'I told her where I was going.'

I can see Adam watching him, eyes a bit narrowed, measuring up whether or not he should chip in.

'You didn't,' I insist. 'But even if you did, she's four. You didn't tell me or Adam you were going out.'

'Ah well, it's done now.'

'Where did you even take it?'

'I told you, the charity shop.' This conversation is making me feel like I'm spiralling into madness, as though there's a vital component of it that I've missed but everyone else knows.

'Which charity shop?' I think about the box and what was in it. Nothing valuable but things with sentimental importance. A limited-edition Fleetwood Mac T-shirt Adam bought me that you can't get any more, ticket stubs from a spontaneous weekend to Venice that we booked before I had Jack, a scarf Mum gave me which I always seem to be wearing when I do something that makes me happy.

I need to get it back.

I'm trying so hard not to shout at him. He genuinely thinks he's done me a favour.

I frown at Adam, who flicks his eyes at Dad and then back at me with the same unreadable expression on his face.

'YES!' I hear Jack shout. Taking full advantage of the kerfuffle, he's now playing some game or other on Adam's unlocked phone.

'What are you doing?' Adam snatches it off him, swiping through the screen. 'Jack, you've downloaded fifteen quid's worth of games here. What were you thinking?' He glares at me. 'This is exactly why people have passcodes on these things.'

'Sure, it's my fault,' I retort, picking up Dad's plate to put it in the microwave. 'You *can* put child locks on the content, you know.'

'That's the voice I meant, Mummy,' Sav says, 'your cross one.' She turns to the rest of the table and says, 'Mummy and Daddy haven't been very good friends recently, but it's OK, Mummy says they're not getting divorced like Sinéad's mummy and daddy.'

Chapter Nineteen

Transcript of session with Adam and Iris Young by Esther Moran, 26 Feb

Esther: How are you feeling tod—

Iris: [interrupting] Stressed and scared. The kids know there's something wrong, and I completely messed up talking to them about it properly.

Adam: Iris told them we were having problems, which wasn't something we'd agreed to do.

Iris: I was put on the spot. What was I supposed to do? I couldn't lie to her. That's not me.

Adam: What's that supposed to mean?

[silence]

Iris: Also, I'm under a lot of pressure at work at the moment. I'm worried about being made redundant.

Esther: It sounds like there are a lot of elements whizzing around at the moment. Let's take one thing at a time.

Iris: OK.

Esther: One word I picked up on a lot then was 'I'. Do you feel like you have to take on a lot of this stress yourself, Iris?

Iris: Adam wasn't there when our daughter Sav asked me if we were getting divorced, and then there was this whole situation with my dad going on too which confused everything even more. We talked to Sav – and Jack – again together that evening and they seemed to understand.

Esther: OK. And what about the stress of your job being under threat? Has Adam helped you with that?

Iris: Well, it's my job that's at risk, and I've been given targets to meet so it's only me that can do anything about it. We haven't discussed it that much, to be honest. I mean, he knows about it, obviously, but what can he do?

Adam: She's not going to lose her job. They're getting antsy about donation levels at her charity, but it will pick up again. They won't lay Iris off. She's too good to lose.

Esther: It's positive that you have confidence in Iris, but that's not exactly what I was asking. Iris, do you feel like you have Adam's support with the whole situation? That he understands you, or that he'll take care of you emotionally if you do lose your job?

Adam: Ye—

Iris: Not really, if I'm honest. I'm anxious about what might be ahead. Not that there's ever a good time to be unemployed, but I have feelings of dread when I think about what the strain of it might mean for me and Adam. After all, last time things got tough for me, when Mum got ill, Adam had an affair.

Adam: Whoa, hang on, that's not fair.

Iris: It's true.

Esther: Why do you think that's unfair, Adam?

Adam: Because that hasn't got anything to do with [pause] with [pause] what happened.

Esther: But your affair did coincide with Iris's mum's illness?

Adam: Yes. But—

Esther: From what you've told me, Iris, your mum's death has been an enormous event in your life. You're still grieving for her.

Iris: Yes. I'd say the whole thing – her illness, her dying so quickly – was the worst period of my life so far. I think about her all the time. I miss her all the time. [pause] Sorry, it's hard for me to talk about her without getting upset.

Esther: Don't worry. Take a second.

[silence]

Esther: Without thinking about it too much, how supported did you feel by Adam during your mum's illness?

Iris: [quickly] I didn't. I felt abandoned.

Esther: Can you explain that a bit more?

Iris: He just wasn't there – emotionally, but also physically, now I look back. I was snappy and irritable at home, I know I was, but I couldn't help myself. I felt guilty for driving him away, but he withdrew and left me to get on with it. Maybe I deserved it, but there was no one to cut me any slack. It was very lonely. I was so stressed with travelling to Surrey and trying to hold it together for the kids. But it was only later, when I saw the dates of his first contact with Jules, that it made sense.

Esther: What made sense?

Iris: That I wasn't being a good wife, so he went elsewhere. And that I shouldn't count on him for emotional support; that's obviously not our dynamic. [quickly] My friends were great, though. I got a lot of support from my friend Fran in particular.

Esther: Let's rewind for a moment. You've just said that your dynamic isn't to expect your husband to empathise or support you when you're going through a difficult time. Adam, how do you feel when you hear Iris say that?

Adam: [pause] I'm shocked, if I'm honest.

Esther: But do you disagree with what she is saying?

Adam: She was really angry during her mum's illness, so I took a step back. I thought it was better if I kept out of her way because she'd take her anger out on me.

Esther: You didn't think that you could have done something else when your wife was more angry and emotional than usual? You mentioned in a previous session that one of the things you liked about Iris was that she was 'together'. Did it frighten you that for once she wasn't?

Adam: I thought she'd say if she needed help.

Esther: It can be difficult for someone to ask for help, particularly when they're going through a tough time, and particularly when their role as the caretaker has been ingrained. That's a lot to put on someone. What I'm hearing from Iris is that she's scared that any expression of negative emotion pushes you away. Iris, if a friend told you what you've just said to me, what would you say back to her?

Iris: [pause] I'd tell her the husband sounds useless and how dare he make her feel like that. You should be able to rely on your partner when it's hard, not only when things are good.

Esther: So why are you prepared to accept that for yourself?

Iris: I didn't realise I had. Like I said, it's only in retrospect, and because of something my friend said to me about it, that I see how little he was there for me.

Esther: And how do you feel about it now?

Iris: When I think about it, I'm so angry I can barely breathe. Not least because [pause].

Esther: Go on.

Iris: Because of all the times he's leant on me with his family stuff. Letting him use money from our joint account to pay debts his brother has run up. Juggling everything to make sure he didn't have to worry about the home front when he dropped everything to go up to Sheffield. And talking things through with him. What to do, how to deal with Gabe or his mum. Well, trying to. He's never been very good at letting me in.

Adam: But that's what I mean.

Esther: What's what you mean?

Adam: I'm not as good at talking things through as Iris. I didn't know what to say or how to help.

Iris: So you ran away and found someone else.

Adam: No. That's not fair. I didn't know what to do to help with your mum. There was nothing I could have done to make it better. Why didn't you say anything at the time?

Iris: Why didn't *you* say anything to help? You left me, Adam. I have never felt so alone in my entire life, and you left me. It was bad enough when I thought it was because you're bad at emotional stuff, but then I found out you had literally left me for someone else. I hate you for that.

Esther: Adam, you're looking at me. Why?

Adam: Because I thought this was about being on the same team. I didn't think she'd be allowed to say she hated me.

Esther: It's about everyone feeling heard. I'm not here to shame you but it *is* about accepting responsibility for your share. That's about being on the same team too. Iris is telling you, now, how your actions have made her feel. That you weren't on her team during her mum's illness. And that she feels emotionally unsupported by you in the marriage, which is making her anxious about the future. What do you want to say – and do – in response?

Chapter Twenty

6 April

Adam's phone is vibrating on the kitchen counter. Of course I look.

Gabe Young WhatsApp Audio . . .

Christ, what does he want?

'Hello?'

A silence. 'Ad?'

'It's Iris. Adam's upstairs.'

'Can you put him on? I need to talk to him.' He doesn't ask me how I am, or the kids, but what's new?

Good to speak to you too, Gabe. I'm surprised he can't see the roll of my eyes as I run upstairs shouting, 'Adam! Gabe's on the phone.'

He's in Jack's room where he and the kids are playing Monopoly. Jack pockets some of the bank float as Adam turns to intercept his phone and Sav loudly protests. Jack gives her a shove in response.

'Hey, Jack, stop.' I go to pull them apart and Adam

leaves the room in the ensuing fracas. He comes back minutes later with a face like thunder.

'Oh God, what's he done?' I ask. 'Don't tell me you need to go to Sheffield.'

'Did you send my mum a Mother's Day card?' Adam's voice is terse. The question throws me.

'What? No.' I completely avoided going anywhere near the card shops this year, because for the first time ever I wouldn't be buying one for Mum, and seeing all the displays made me hate everyone with a mum to buy one for. There was no agonising about an overpriced afternoon tea at a hotel in Central London or cajoling the children into making a card for Grandma; I just blocked it out by muting all mention of it on social media and unsubscribing from about forty thousand brand emails all pushing their Mother's Day deals. I was so successful I forgot about it completely, until I was presented with a card and a squashed bunch of flowers on Sunday from Jack and Sav.

'Because you usually do.' Adam's tone is accusatory. Right, that's what this is about. I do usually send his mum a Mother's Day card along with one for my own, but this year I haven't so Gabe has pulled him up on it.

'It wasn't that high on my list of priorities this year.' My response is clipped but I'm not apologising. I mean, why was I even in charge of that job to start off with?

The children are both watching this back and forth, and I'm aware of my 'cross tone', the one that upsets Sav. Even Jack has stopped counting his ill-gotten money in favour of staring at us.

'Daddy needs to talk to Mummy about something.' Adam pulls me out of Jack's bedroom and into the hall where he hisses, 'I get it, Iris, you're pissed off with me, but that doesn't mean Mum should be punished. Gabe was on his high horse saying she was upset at not getting something from the kids, like he's in any position to have a go at me.'

I now realise what he's getting at versus the actual reason I haven't been all over the Mother's Day admin this year. 'Adam, I didn't deliberately not send your mum a card because of' – I'm not saying 'affair' within earshot of the children – 'all this. Jesus Christ, not everything is about you. Do you think I'm that petty?' I briefly feel bad for Anne, expecting something from Adam and Jack and Sav, and nothing arriving. Mother's Day was almost a week ago. She's obviously waited to see if the cards would come in a later post before mentioning it to Gabe.

'But you always send the cards.' It's as he says 'cards', plural, that it dawns on him. His eyes widen and he goes very still. 'Shit, Iris, I'm so sorry. I didn't even think.'

'No.' My voice is cold. 'You didn't.'

Chapter Twenty-One

11 April

'Then she shouted, "Stop being such a dick!" to Walter.'

I wince, but there's a bit of me that's trying not to laugh, recognising the phrase both Adam and I are guilty of bandying about on occasion. I feign a surprised expression and try to concentrate on what Mrs Hayward – Sav's very young, very keen and very trendy Reception teacher – is saying to us.

'I see.'

The infants' part of Orchard Primary School is plastered in brightly coloured artwork, letters to influential people on issues they're worried about – climate change features heavily, although the children seem to think Iron Man is the person to sort it out – and photos of the children. Sav's classroom – 'Pear' – is empty except for Adam and me, sitting side by side on unstable, infant-sized chairs and listening to Mrs Hayward, who has finally managed to pin us down and guilted me into sneaking out of work early, catalogue the myriad ways her behaviour has gone downhill this term. I'm holding a notepad and pen in my lap, which I diligently brought along. I look down at it. The only thing written there so far is the word 'dick'. Mrs Hayward hasn't finished yet.

'Not listening, disrupting other children. She's smart but her stubbornness is proving to be problematic. When she was challenged on the swearing, she shouted, "You'll never take me alive," and sequestered herself in the outside climbing frame.'

Adam starts to shake with laughter next to me and I nudge him, even though my own face is crumpling into badly suppressed mirth. We are terrible parents.

'I'm so sorry,' I try to say, my voice going all squeaky as I hold in a laugh. 'I promise we're not being disrespectful.' We clearly are.

'It's the way you're describing it,' Adam adds, snorting and trying to pull himself together.

It's true. Mrs Hayward's deadpan delivery is somehow making it funnier. But I know it's not funny. You're not supposed to draw such distinctions between your children – and I wouldn't to *them*, obviously – but of our two, Sav's always been the obedient and relatively quiet one. Not like Jack. We're already resigned to the next nine years of school reports telling us that he talks too much. But Sav's a rule follower. She gets anxious if she thinks we're going to be late for anything, or even if we don't stand up quickly enough on the bus when approaching our stop.

'We spoke last year when she started school as she hadn't settled, but I don't think you understand how much of a change I've noticed in her since Christmas,' says Mrs Hayward. Her face is soft, but her glare is hard. The teacher thinks we're useless, I can tell. A brilliant start to Sav's school career.

'Before that she was withdrawn and shy, which can be the case when children are a little overwhelmed with starting "big" school, but now she's gone the opposite way and is acting out. Has anything changed circumstantially at home?'

Our mirth dies in the air.

'There are a few things going on at home, yes,' Adam says carefully. 'Her grandmother died last September, and her illness was unexpected, so we're all still coming to terms with it,' he adds. His cheeks look a bit pink. He's obviously having trouble keeping the main issue in our home life a secret from the teacher. Shame he didn't have the same physical reaction when he was lying to me. It could have saved a lot of time.

'And Iris is under threat of redundancy at work. There's a bit more . . . tension than usual.'

That's only the half of it, I want to say.

Mrs Hayward's expression slackens as she nods sympathetically.

'And also, in all honesty—' he starts.

'We're feeling the pressure of it too,' I interrupt, sensing Adam is about to come clean and deciding that's enough. I *do not* want every primary school teacher in this place discussing my marriage. I'd rather they thought we're foul-mouthed parents with semi-feral children.

'That's understandable,' says Mrs Hayward. Her voice is a couple of degrees warmer now. 'It might be an idea to discuss all of this with Savannah. Children can pick up on stress and internalise it. They have a tendency to think things are their fault.' Sav seemed reassured after our conversation with her and Jack about it all, but now Mrs Hayward is telling me that some 'upheaval' is making her misbehave. What else can it be other than bad vibes radiating from the people who are meant to make her feel safe?

'You're right, we need to take some time to make sure the kids feel secure,' I say. 'I'm so glad you're discussing it with us. Is there anything else you think we should be doing – educationally – at home to support her?'

'Teaching her what is and isn't appropriate vocabulary for a four-year-old would be a top priority,' she says. She's smiling but she means business.

'Understood,' we say in unison. I go to pull my jacket from the back of the chair.

'I need a drink,' Adam mutters as his tugs on his own.

*

It's barely seven o'clock when we leave the school, but we rush home to relieve Fran and get the kids in bed. The second it's all quiet, Adam hands me a glass of red wine and brings the rest of the bottle into the living room.

'I think she's acting out because everything's gone mental,' I say, moving up so he can sit down on the sofa next to me. Guilt slices through me. I've been too busy thinking about how it's all affecting me to notice how it's affecting Sav or Jack.

Adam nods, looking over to the TV screen in the corner, where the news is playing in the background at a low volume. I flick it off. 'I've fucked everything up, haven't I,' he says eventually.

Every cell in my body is screaming at me to agree with him. To confirm that what he's done has made me insecure and him edgy, which Sav has picked up on, turning her into a confused little girl who is being naughty at school because she doesn't know what all these weird churny feelings are or where to put them. But right now, I don't want to have another fight. More than anything, I want us to be kind to each other. For him to be kind to me.

'It's not just you, Ad. It's everything. How are Jack and Sav supposed to be OK when we're not? They can sense it. I miss Mum. And as for us . . .' I trail off, not knowing where 'us' is right now. Esther asked about our future. For me, it's like a big black hole that sucks the breath out of me if I think about it too much. I can only think day to day.

We sit in silence for a minute.

'Gabe started getting in trouble at school when he wasn't much older than Jack,' he says gloomily.

'Sav isn't Gabe,' I say sharply. 'And you're not your dad.'

'I was always a bit jealous of him, to be honest.'

'Your dad?' Adam and Gabe's dad is the epitome of a deadbeat. The only thing to be jealous of is how few shits he gives about anything. It must be liberating to care about nothing but yourself.

'Gabe.'

'Oh,' I say. 'He got expelled when he was eleven for throwing a blackboard duster at his maths teacher's head and ended up at the roughest school in Sheffield, which was more of a training camp for petty criminals. It's not like he got into the BRIT School.'

Adam gives me a grim smile. 'Not that bit. More because he did whatever he wanted.'

'Did he though? The way you tell it, it's always seemed involuntary to me. He wasn't making choices; not when he was a kid, anyway. Acting out was the only way he could think of to get your dad's attention. So in a way, you *were* both doing the same thing.'

'I was a complete swot.'

I shrug. 'If you got the best grades, won every prize at school, maybe you'd get his attention. Same feelings, different behaviour. Makes total sense.'

'Plus, Gabe never seemed to feel as though he should be Mum's rock like I did. I love her, but . . .'

'It's exhausting. And you were a kid. You shouldn't have had to do that.'

I resolve here and now to make sure Jack and Sav never feel responsible for my happiness. Taking that on for Anne has been one of the defining experiences of Adam's life; diligently watching to see how his dad and Gabe's behaviour was affecting her and overcompensating for both.

'It's equally possible Sav's just overheard me swearing in the car and that's where she got the language from,' I say, trying to lighten the mood.

Adam allows himself to laugh. 'Your road rage is bad.'

'Bad,' I agree. 'Maybe we can spin swear-gate as a feminist thing. We're giving her the skills to take up space and express her emotions. Women will not be silenced, that sort of thing. Isn't that what you teach at your equality workshops?' I'm being facetious but it feels good to tease him and be playful, even more so when his forehead unfurrows and he smiles.

'Yep. Now listen up, kids. Boys and girls are equal, which is why it's fine to call both boys *and* girls dicks.'

'Exactly.' I sip my drink. 'We'll talk to her again,' I say more seriously. 'Together. Find out if she's worrying about anything in particular or responding to our stressed-out frequency.'

'Something is definitely not right if Jack's being the good one,' he agrees.

We sit in silence for a minute, before I get up and potter around putting the lamps on, which bathe the room in a more flattering glow than the overhead light.

'Speaking of workshops, did Veritas sign on for another year?' I ask, remembering Adam was worrying about funding for his charity the other day. The non-profit Adam works for relies on corporate donors to keep it going. His targets don't keep going up like mine, but it's something he has to think about at the beginning of every tax year.

'Yes, but we managed to get almost double their donation from that hedge fund, Pecunia.'

'How did you manage that?'

'Did you see the story about the court case?'

I shake my head.

'They've been done for a massive sexual harassment case. There were hardly any women working there to start off with and the culture was hideous. Three senior male staff members have been convicted. It was a huge scandal. After I read the story, I got a meeting with the MD and managed to convince him that an annual donation would be a good way to rehabilitate the company, seeing as the press were using their name as shorthand for toxic bro culture.'

'Well done,' I say. I clink his glass, impressed, but also a bit sad that he's pulled off a huge work coup without me knowing anything about it. The therapy seems to be enabling some 'big' conversations, but I'm missing the day-to-day intimacy. Being the first port of call for some work news or something funny he saw on the internet.

'I didn't tell you about it as I'm aware of my own hypocrisy, by the way,' he adds softly. He pulls at some dry skin on the back of his hands. He gets eczema. So does Jack. For both it gets worse when they're stressed. Patches of Adam's skin look red and livid.

'You're not a hypocrite,' I tell him. 'An affair isn't the same as the systematic groping of colleagues.' I chance a dark joke. 'Unless you've got something else to tell me.'

'No! Of course not.'

A silence stretches out. It inflates, filling the room, sucking in all of the joy and magnifying the space between us. Adam clears his throat.

'I was thinking we should book a holiday,' Adam says suddenly. 'For the summer. I could do it.'

Now it's my turn to laugh. 'We should' usually means Adam suggesting something and me adding it to my to-do list. I check my snark. Nice evening. No cynicism.

'OK. Good idea.'

I leave it there, to see where he goes next with this. I'm not going to shoot the idea down, but I'm also not going to do the legwork if he wants us to go on a family holiday. Particularly because the pressure of that – me, Adam, the kids, all in a tiny hotel room for a week – makes me nervous.

'I've got a few ideas, but is there anywhere you really don't want to go?'

'*Not* on a city break,' we both say at the same time. After Jack was born, we were in denial about what constituted a holiday with a baby and for some reason decided to go to Berlin. It rained for three days. Our hotel room was hip but totally inappropriate for two knackered parents and a baby that would only sleep if it was pitch black and completely silent, meaning we couldn't even watch a film on our laptop after we finally got him to sleep because he'd immediately start wailing. We took it in turns to go downstairs for a drink in the hotel bar and swiftly revised our expectations about family trips.

'Self-catering apartment, pool, kids' club, warm but not too hot, nice food for us but not too "challenging" for Sav . . .' I tick the specifications off on my fingers, trying not to hate myself for sounding like a complete cliché. Jules pops into my head. She'll be off somewhere she can Instagram herself standing under a waterfall like the Timotei ad. She might even be flying *herself* there. Jules will not be picking olives out of a pasta dish because her four-year-old has decided she doesn't like them today.

'Not cheaply priced because it's located next to the most popular Irish bar in the Algarve,' Adam chips in. Another mistake we made, not long after Sav came along. 'Maybe all-inclusive, which I know we swore we'd never do, but . . .'

We pull a 'kill me now' face at each other and then laugh. I like it. I like him looking at me with warmth, with an expression of anything other than annoyance or concern.

'Europe, though,' he says, taking out his phone and pulling up Google. 'Somewhere that isn't the seventh circle of school holiday hell.'

I nod. There's a flutter, sparked by the idea of planning something for four months in the future. Not excitement exactly, but perhaps a little bit of hope.

Chapter Twenty-Two

13 April

'Hi, hi, so sorry I'm late.' Nat rushes in and up to our table at All Bar One. Well, as much as an almost-six-months-pregnant woman can rush anywhere. 'The tubes were all messed up and I had to wait for three to go past before I could squeeze on one. The Baby on Board badge got *no* traction because I couldn't get anywhere near the seats to be offered one. Hell, I hate being pregnant. I hate the tube, and I hate everyone *on* the tube. Plus, I can't even have a drink now I'm here.'

Fran and I let her burn herself out before Fran places a glass in front of her. 'However, you *can* drink this non-alcoholic gin and tonic we've got you. It's made with one of those hipster teetotal gins. Almost as good as the real thing. And it should be, considering how much it cost.'

Nat takes an experimental sip and sinks into the chair we've saved for her. 'Ooh that's nice. I don't think I'd know the difference if you hadn't told me.' She turns to me and does the wrinkled-up face of pity I knew was coming but have been dreading. 'How are you, Iris? I can't believe

I've barely seen you since it all happened, but I'm so glad you've worked it out with Adam now.'

Next to me, Fran splutters.

'Thank you, although I wouldn't say we've worked it out,' I correct her. 'More that we're working on it.'

'That's what I mean. I know you guys can get through it.' She scrunches up her nose. 'Because it's so weird – I mean, what would make Adam do something like that?'

My own (alcoholic) gin and tonic sticks in my throat. All the weeks of thinking and agonising about whether or not I'm doing the right thing. Weeks when I haven't seen Nat and have felt guilty about not celebrating her baby news properly. Meanwhile, she's been theorising about how I could have driven Adam to infidelity.

'What would *make* him?' I spit out before I can stop myself.

Nat's face flushes. 'No,' she stutters quickly. 'That's not what I meant. It wasn't a dig at you, honestly. But . . .' The 'but' of doom. 'They do say that usually cheating isn't the problem in itself but a symptom of something else, don't they, which is why I think it's good that you're working through it with a therapist.'

I hold her gaze, forcing her to be the one to look away.

'It's a symptom of him being a massive dick,' says Fran, giving Nat a look that could shatter glass. 'And of him neglecting Iris and being arrogant enough to think he can do whatever he likes. Not sure which part of that you think is her fault, Nat, but sure, nice to see you.'

'That's not what I meant!' Nat looks agonised, but I can see she's not going to let it go. 'I always say the wrong thing. That's why I've been giving you some space. I didn't want to slag Adam off if you're making a go of it, because if you want to be with him, then there's got to be something redeeming about him, right? That's all I meant, I promise. I'm on your side.'

She smiles at me in what she must think is a reassuring and supportive way but instead makes me feel like a pitiful being.

'What if he's the villain but they're also working on it?' Fran isn't going to let this go either. I remember the conversation we had on the Isle of Wight. She thinks I should leave him. Nat clearly believes that by staying I'm acknowledging I'm at least partly at fault. I have no idea what the truth is. 'And Iris is seeing how things go while looking into her options,' Fran continues.

'What options?' Nat turns to me, concern radiating from her eyes. 'That she still might leave?'

'Yes. And thinking about moving on. Dating. Meeting someone else.'

What's she on about? I sent one totally above-board message to Lucas that has resulted in two or three further work-related emails. 'Can you both stop talking about me in the third person? I'm sitting right here.'

'You're dating,' Nat says, in a voice saturated in judgement, all concern gone. 'Then why are you bothering with therapy?'

'I'm not dating.' A surge of defiance pulses through me. I watch the bubbles fizzing in my glass and force a nonchalant shrug. 'But so what if I were?' It comes out chilly as the ice in my drink.

'Well, exactly,' Fran practically shouts.

'I thought you were in therapy to sort it out – you know, the kids and everything.'

'Please, Nat, do *not* bring up my kids. Do you think I don't think about the kids constantly?' All day, every day, wondering whether it's better or worse for them if I spend a year in a marriage that might be dead. 'I can't stay with Adam only for the kids. I have to see if there's still an us in there too.' I throw a glare at Fran. 'However, I'm *not* dating. I'm doing everything the therapist tells us to. I've committed to a year.'

There's a noxious silence filled, no doubt, with their own thoughts. Of what they would do differently from me; of what they would do better.

'So how does therapy work?' Nat's voice is curious rather than critical but I'm too exhausted to get into the ins and outs of marital therapy, the constant vigilance over Adam's phone use, or how I look for hidden meanings in whatever he says or does.

'She's given us some exercises to do,' I say before clamming up. It feels treacherous to talk about it, plus they're hanging on my every word about how we're having to be taught what should come naturally in relationships.

'What, like homework?'

'Yes. So, things like a regular date night. Or concentrating on actively prioritising each other,' I mumble.

'I don't think it's you that needs to work on that!' Fran bursts out loudly, before apologising. 'Sorry, sorry. Go on.'

'My part is to tell him what I need, so I don't get resentful if my needs aren't being met, because he doesn't know anything about it. I find it hard to ask for help and he sees me as self-sufficient, so we're trying to meet in the middle.'

'Shouldn't he know to check in with you?'

'In an ideal world, yes. But it's only recently I've realised that's not how we've related to each other in the past. Which is fine when things are cruising along nicely but apparently doesn't work when my life is being shat on from a great height.'

'So you're helping him work on that?' says Nat thoughtfully. 'That sounds good. But what if you tell him when you need him, and he still doesn't prioritise you?'

I shrug, attempting to be more blasé about it than I am. 'Then I guess I know the limits of our relationship.'

'It's kind of bollocks,' Fran says loudly. 'Why is it *your* job to help work on him? I can't believe he had an affair while your mum was dying and you're now saying it's because you didn't ask him for help.'

'That's not what I'm saying!' It was so clear when we talked it through with Esther. 'It's not as black and white as that. And neither of you are saying anything I don't already ask myself on a daily basis. We're seeing if we can evolve from unhealthy patterns.'

'I think it's great,' says Nat. Finally, someone being supportive. 'You *should* put the other person first in your relationship.'

'That only works if you're both doing it,' Fran says, looking at her pointedly. 'I don't think Iris is the only person who's ended up in that trap.'

'Anyone want another drink?' I jump up, desperate to escape the atmosphere. 'And then can we talk about something else? How's work, Nat?'

'Busy and stressful. Mass redundancies on the horizon in the City.' All that does is remind me of my own precarious work situation. 'Also, I'm going to have to go after this one,' Nat says. 'Mark always has a nightmare getting Georgia to bed when I'm out.'

'Maybe if he did it a little more often . . .' Fran mutters, before saying to me, 'I'll have one.'

I grab my bag and head to the bar, automatically checking my phone while rooting for my purse.

A text from Anne, Adam's mum, sent ten minutes ago.

Can you get him to call me? It's urgent.

I sigh. Rub my face. She only ever comes to me when she can't get hold of Adam.

I'm out, but Adam's at home with the kids so try his mobile.

. . .

I have. He's not picking up.

I let out an irritated breath. Adam's not answering because this is probably something to do with Gabe and he can't be bothered. But instead of actually saying that to his mum, he's ignoring her.

Easy is not a word I would associate with my relationship with Anne. She calls me The Duchess. She thinks I don't know, but I do. I'm sure she blames me for Adam not being as available as she'd like (which is constantly) for every Gabe-related crisis: she's decided I 'won't let him' visit enough because he's busy down here with us. And he's happy to let her think that because it saves him an awkward conversation. I get it – he doesn't want to be on call every time Gabe gets fired or into a fight – but that means I have to accept being painted as the bossy wife to make his life easier. It's not my fault Adam feels bad about telling his mum he needs space. Besides, as far as I'm concerned, Adam *had* been dutifully going up there to visit them. It's just that instead he was with Jules. I wonder what Anne would think about that if she knew.

Fear pricks at my insides and doubt seeds itself. Perhaps he's not answering because he's on the phone with someone else. Would he call *her* when the kids are in the house?

I call his mobile and he picks up on the second ring. The relief that he's there and available is cancelled out by my annoyance that he's screening his mother.

'Where are you?' I say reflexively.

'At home.' He sounds annoyed. 'Where else would I be?'

'Can you call your mum, please? She's texting me.'

He grunts in frustration. 'Gabe's drunk and belligerent, saying he's going to find my dad and sort him out. She wants me to talk to him but there's no point when he's like this.'

I knew it. All she and Adam talk about is Gabe. She never rings to see how we are. Her name appearing on my phone always means something ridiculous with Gabe is going on. Usually, I'd tell him to put her off, let Gabe sleep off whatever drunken mood he's in and check in on Anne tomorrow, but tonight there's a stab of sympathy for her. She doesn't have anyone else to lean on. She never did. She kept getting back together with Adam's dad but even when she did, she was basically a single parent doing her best, and worrying if she was doing the right thing for her children. I think I finally get why she didn't just kick him out and cut her losses.

I glance back at the table, where Fran and Nat are locked in conversation. The look on Fran's face suggests she's giving Nat a good talking to about what she said to me earlier. Nat looks like she's arguing the toss right back. They're so sure about what I should do. What's best for me, what's best for my kids, what the magic formula is.

'Call your mum,' I say to Adam. 'I know you can't do anything about Gabe, but she needs to know someone's listening.'

Chapter Twenty-Three

Transcript of session with Adam and Iris Young by Esther Moran, 16 April

Esther: In the last session we talked about support – or the lack of – for you, Iris, while your mum was ill. I'd like to pick that up today and talk about it from the other perspective. Has Iris always been supportive to you, Adam?

Adam: Yes. I'd say so. She's always encouraged me to be there for my family, but also told me not to let them take advantage. She always makes situations seem clearer. As you mentioned before, I've always liked how together she was.

Esther: And what do you mean by 'together'?

Adam: That security in herself I talked about. An innate confidence.

Esther: Do you think you have innate confidence, Iris?

Iris: I'm not sure. I've always been relatively happy with who I am, I suppose.

Adam: I have a theory that it came from her parents. She never had a moment's worry that they didn't love her and wouldn't look after her. I think people from happy homes don't realise how much for granted they take that, because they don't know the alternative. I always thought if I had kids, I wanted them to be so sure I loved them that they'd be almost careless with it. They'd never have to check. I hope that's what's happened. That's why I'm so ashamed about the [pause] the affair.

Esther: And you didn't feel secure about that love in your family as a child?

Adam: No. I'm saying it all wrong. My family do love me. Mum and my brother Gabe do, anyway – my dad's not around. My family is more complicated than Iris's. Gabe is [pause] Gabe.

Iris: That's his younger brother. Adam is basically a father figure to him.

Esther: In what way?

Iris: In every way. Bailing him out of trouble – once literally bailing him out – encouraging him to find jobs or stick at jobs, helping his mum to keep him on track, or find him when he goes on a bender. Money—

Adam: [interrupting] He's not a bad person.

Iris: No, he's not. But he's not easy to be around. Their mum spends a lot of time and energy trying to look after him, even now he's in his thirties. Between Gabe's [pause] antics, and their dad turning up and disappearing, there wasn't a lot of time left for Adam when he was growing up.

Esther: Is that true?

Adam: Mmmm.

Esther: You don't seem sure.

Adam: It's hard to hear it like that. But yeah, my brother is complicated. He's been getting into trouble since he was a kid. Sometimes I can get through to him, other times [pause].

Esther: You don't seem to have much patience for Gabe, Iris.

Iris: I used to. But after ten years of him disrupting our lives, letting Adam down and monopolising their mum's attention [pause] Don't get me wrong, I like him – when he's not doing any of those things – but since we had the kids I can't deal with the constant drama. It's draining, and when something happens Adam is out of sorts for days afterwards. Gabe's thirty-seven. There's not a lot we can do for him now if he won't try to help himself.

Adam: It's not that simple. They're my family, not just a problem. Gabe being in trouble is like Jack being in trouble. I want to fix it for him.

Iris: But Jack's seven. Plus, there's messing up and there's throwing your life away. And everyone's got their own stuff, you know. He's not the only one who gets to have problems.

Adam: He makes bad choices. People who make bad choices sometimes keep on making bad choices.

Iris: But then how can anything, anyone change?

[silence]

Esther: Yours and Iris's backgrounds are very different.

Adam: Yes.

Esther: Do you find that it sometimes makes you see situations from different stances?

Iris: No—

Adam: [interrupting] Yes.

Esther: Why don't you explain why you think that?

Adam: Gabe is self-destructive and it's frustrating. I know that more than anyone. He can go weeks or months when I think he's finally pulled himself together and then he flips again, goes out drinking or gets in a fight or quits his job. Then my mum is upset. He still lives with her most of the time – occasionally he moves out into his own place but he boomerangs back and forth. At least when he's living at home, she can keep an eye on him, but it means she's too involved in every crisis, however big or small. Iris thinks he needs to move out, but then again Iris sometimes thinks situations are clear-cut when they're not. That he should be 'better', or Mum should be harder on him to get him to change.

Esther: Do you think that, Iris?

Iris: No, I disagree with that. I actually feel as though Adam wants me to be the baddie when it comes to them.

Esther: What do you mean?

Iris: He wants to be able to say, 'Iris said we can't do that,' so that it's not his fault if he sets a boundary. But he also gets to be rid of some of the responsibility he feels for them.

Esther: What do you think, Adam?

Adam: Sometimes, yes, I use Iris's name to set a boundary when I think I'll offend my mum if I tell her I don't want to do something. It was claustrophobic growing up with all that going on.

Esther: So now you're in London and they're in Sheffield.

Adam: [quietly] Yes. But it spills over. They can be a lot to deal with. Plus, my dad is there. I wanted to get away.

Esther: Would you say there is guilt associated with that? Sometimes relief is counterbalanced with the feeling that you've been disloyal.

Adam: I don't know. [pause] At the time I just wanted to leave. Had to. I'm not sure what this has got to do with me and Iris.

Esther: When did you leave Sheffield?

Adam: At eighteen. For university. I got the grades and a student loan, so here I am. It's true, I wanted to leave my family far behind for a while.

Iris: That's not the whole story though, is it?

Esther: What do you mean?

Iris: They were supposed to be coming to uni here together. His whole London life was supposed to start with her. Then at the last minute she changed her mind and went to Durham instead.

Esther: Who?

Iris: Jules.

Chapter Twenty-Four

4 May

The picture of me on the poster was supposed to be my headshot from the Trust's website, the one where I look approachable yet professional, but instead someone – Sophie? – has swapped in a 'candid' (read: side-eye and double-chin) shot from last year's summer mixer, where I look about as professional as someone trying to flog my amateur crafting store on Etsy. As if I'm not nervous enough about giving a talk at a 'Fierce Women's Retreat' in Kent to 'high net worth businesswomen' about why the National Trust is here to meet all of their philanthropic needs. It was my idea to try and rustle up interest in this demographic, so I hope I haven't oversold them as potential donors. Vanessa keeps telling us that any time out of the office needs to 'translate to targets', and this is an all-weekend event. I won't be getting the time back in lieu unless I make some money.

I peer through the glass of the double doors into the conservatory to see how many high net worth women are here. There's a smattering – seven to be exact – all in their forties and fifties, I'd say, and wearing expensive-looking athleisure wear. The rest of the weekend consists of yoga classes and workshops with names like 'Blasting Burnout', which are targeted at affluent but time-poor women who want all their wellness requirements met in one handy five-star, heritage-heavy location.

It's only 10 a.m. but it's the hottest day of the year so far and I'm sweating. My floaty calf-length dress keeps sticking to my thighs, but I don't have time to change now, so I walk in, trying to appear as upright and commanding as possible while making for the stage area at the far end of the room.

'Morning everyone,' I say brightly, trying to channel some of that inner confidence Adam told Esther I have. I think of the sort of people who can work a room; ideally I need to be a cross between Brené Brown and Amy Poehler. 'I'm Iris from the National Trust. I hope you're already feeling the benefit from the activities. I saw the runners go out early this morning, so it looks like some of you are going to be smashing your PBs as well as the patriarchy this weekend.'

There's a pleasing ripple of polite laughter, but the sun is shining through the conservatory roof directly into my eyes. One lady gets up and leaves, meaning there are only six left. Bollocks. I need these women to listen and spend money. I decide to change tack.

'Shall I rearrange the chairs so it's a bit less formal?' I encourage everyone to stand up and then pull the chairs into a loose semi-circle so that we all have our backs to the sun. 'And I'll order some teas and coffees so that it's all a bit less talk-y. I don't want to bore you to tears with PowerPoint presentations if you're just looking for an overview and a chat.' The assembled women awkwardly rearrange themselves in the way people do when they don't know each other very well but are being forced closer together, while I make a coffee order. When I come back, they seem to have relaxed and I launch into my spiel. Most of them listen politely; a couple keep checking their phones – either the peril of being an always-on high-flyer, or they're bored – and only one, a woman around my age with dark hair, seems to be listening properly. As we reach the 'any questions?' stage, I smile encouragingly and there's a silence.

'I'm so sorry,' a middle-aged woman with a severe bob says as she stands up, 'I thought this was a trust workshop – as in, learning to trust. But thank you.'

My rictus smile fades, and I force out a small laugh. 'I can see how the confusion might have happened. Not this one, I'm afraid, but if there is a trust workshop happening this weekend, let me know as I could do with that myself.'

I hand out my card to the remaining women. 'I'm staying overnight to experience the retreat for myself, so I'll be around. Please do come and grab me at any time if you'd like to know more.' They file out, nodding and smiling but not meeting my eye, the universal sign of 'I'm not going to give you any money' if my own experience with street chuggers is anything to go by. Stress sweat prickles in my armpits. Beneath my clammy thigh, where I've stashed my phone on my chair, I feel it buzz. Vanessa.

Let me know how you get on.

The rest of the line is filled up with money bag emojis.

*

The sound of the gong bath is supposed to be calming, but instead the reverberations are making me more tense. I'm cocooned in a soft blanket with my head on a lavender pillow, sound waves vibrating around me and the other twenty women in the room. The teacher is encouraging us to relax and let the chimes heal us, but it's *a lot* louder than I was expecting, and the noise is causing my mind to focus on all the things I should be doing rather than lying here. Each fresh 'dong' reminds me of another task.

Dong!

New school shoes for Sav, after realising yesterday that she has blisters from her current ones being too tight.

Dong!

Go and see Dad. I've been so caught up with everything that I haven't seen him for weeks.

Dong!

Reschedule our next drinks meet-up, because Nat's morning sickness has come back with a vengeance in her third trimester and she's been signed off work.

Dong!

Why do none of these women want to donate money? I *have* to go into work with some positive news for Vanessa. Sophie already accused me of coming here on a jolly; I can't go back without any leads.

Eight thousand years later, the session is over. The teacher – a middle-aged lady in a combination of designer leggings and handcrafted batik – is handing out peppermint teas. Everyone else looks bleary-eyed and tranquil, so of course the teacher pounces on me for feedback. 'How did you find that?' she asks.

'Lovely,' I say. 'So relaxing.' I have pins and needles in my arm from the effort of trying to stay still for an hour.

She gives me a penetrating look. 'Your aura is telling me otherwise. There's a transformational breathing class at five that might help.'

'Sounds great,' I say feebly. 'I'll look it up.' I have no intention of looking it up. My lacklustre aura and I were planning on having a glass of wine at five and shaking down whoever's in the bar for donations.

'Iris?' There's a tap on my arm and I turn around to see one of the women from earlier. The dark-haired one who seemed to be listening to me.

'Oh hello, nice to see you again.'

'I'm Liv,' she says. 'I came to your talk. I was wondering if I could chat to you a bit more about the National Trust?'

'Yes, of course!' I'm so relieved I forget to use the hushed tone everyone seems to have automatically adopted since coming here. I throw the teacher what I hope is a 'we'll carry this on another time' look, and we move to the side of the room to fetch our shoes.

I slip on my red Birkenstocks. Liv has the same ones but in white. In fact, practically everyone here has them in one colour or another. This whole place is a metaphor for middle-class women in self-care crisis.

'I wasn't sure what to expect with this gong class, but I enjoyed it. I thought I was going to fall asleep at one point. How did you find it?'

I say nothing and she laughs. 'I'm sensing the gongs didn't do it for you. Don't worry, I went to a yoga session once where the teacher pulled out an accordion during savasana and started singing. My heart rate was through the roof. And meditation, forget it. The more they tell you to let your mind go, the more I fixate on my most embarrassing moments or the pithy comebacks I could have said to my ex.'

‘So you’re not going to be signing up to the inner harmony class tomorrow?’

‘I think two yoga classes in a day, one gong bath and an upcoming silent nature walk basically makes me Gwyneth Paltrow, so I can skip tomorrow’s inner harmony in favour of a lie-in. What’s in here next?’

I consult my schedule. ‘It’s called “Yoga for Feelings”.’

Liv pulls a face. ‘Oh God. Do you have some time now? We could go for a walk and explore the grounds, and you could tell me a bit more about your legacy package.’

‘Definitely.’

We duck out of the sleek studio, walk past the indoor swimming pool and spa treatment rooms, up through the lobby and out of the heavy front door. The gravel crunches under our feet as we head across the driveway towards the central lawn where a path breaks off, leading to the rest of the grounds. The retreat is being held in a Georgian country house, set in ten acres of countryside, which is having a soft relaunch after undergoing a multi-million-pound renovation. The retreat is part of reinvigorating more widely what the National Trust ‘brand’ means, which is why I thought it would provide a new audience for us to infiltrate.

‘God, it’s boiling, isn’t it?’ Liv pulls a pair of sunglasses out of her bag and puts them on as we pass the organic vegetable garden.

‘It is,’ I agree, doing the same. It’s twenty-six degrees and humid, with light bouncing off the ornamental pond and the smell of herbs in the air from the kitchen gardens. Topiary hedges line the walkway, culminating in an archway where a thousand incredibly tasteful and hope-filled marriages will begin once wedding season starts.

‘When you say you’re interested in our legacy package, is that for yourself?’ I try to keep the disappointment out of my voice. Legacies are sums of money willed to us. As Liv is late thirties, forty at most, signing her up is unlikely to reap any dividends for the next few decades, but at least it's something to report back to Vanessa. Plus, rich people always know other rich people, so maybe she'll spread the word – with my name attached to it.

She laughs. 'Not yet. I've barely got enough money to leave to my daughter, never mind to the National Trust. My break-up wiped me out financially.'

My heart sinks further, and Liv clocks my confused face.

'Sorry, I should explain. My dad passed away a few months ago and left some money to be donated to charity. He stipulated that I should decide who to give it to. I've been agonising over whether it should be a children's or animal charity, and then you turned up here and something clicked. He was a card-carrying Trust member so I thought it worked perfectly. Particularly as you were talking about all the extra value people could get. I thought maybe a bench or a tree in his name would be a way to have somewhere to come and remember him? He loved visiting the places nearest to where he lived, and exploring. I can almost see him here, roaming around the gardens and looking up any species of plant he didn't recognise in his trusty book.'

'I'm so sorry about your dad.' My throat tightens. 'My mum died last year so I know how hard it is.' I can't see Liv's eyes behind the sunglasses, but the look on her face is that fixed jovial expression people adopt when they're letting your words wash over them to avoid an outpouring of emotion.

'And of course we can look into a memorial for him at one of the properties. They obviously all have rules about what can and can't be planted or constructed on their grounds, as it depends on the era of the architecture or the species of plant, but I'm sure we can make something work. Do you mind me asking how much the donation is?'

'Five thousand pounds,' she replies. 'He worked so hard his whole life, I want to do something special for him.' Her voice is steady, but I can sense she's trying hard to make it that way. I can almost feel her sadness when she talks about her father.

We usually have a five-figure minimum donation to take on someone as a client in our department. This isn't going to make a dent in my target or help in my competition with Sophie, but I keep quiet and instead nod. I like her. I'll make something work. 'Why don't you have a think about which property meant the most to your dad, and we can stay in touch. Let me know what you decide, and I'll make enquiries about a tribute. Then perhaps we can meet up there to have a look around.'

We've arrived at a fountain in the middle of an enclosed garden. Shrubs line the perimeter, along with little hedges buzzing with bees. We head for a bench flanked with lavender and sit down, holding our faces up towards the sun's warmth.

'That works. He was a Londoner like me, so once he retired, he was a regular at the places within about an hour of there.'

'Which part of London are you from?'

'East originally, but I'm in Finsbury Park now. I'm a GP there.'

'Ah! Near me. I'm in Harringay.'

'I'd rather move back east, to be honest, because I don't have brilliant memories of the area I'm in now. But my daughter is enrolled in school and my ex isn't far from us, so I don't want to disrupt her life any more than I already have.' She grimaces. 'I have to make it work.'

'Is your break-up recent?' I try to keep my tone nonchalant, but I'm curious about how post-break-up parenting works.

'Not really, but it took a long time to work through it. We broke up when Cilla was nine months old, so let's see, about four years now. I think I knew we weren't right for each other before I got pregnant, but I was thirty-four, he was thirty-eight, and we'd been together three years. Deep down I knew I was settling, but my biological clock ticking drowned out the voice telling me it probably wasn't right. Then once we had Cilla, the niggles turned into things I couldn't ignore any more because we were both knackered and had even less patience with each other. He felt the same. Of course,' she adds, rolling her eyes, 'it took him about twenty minutes to meet someone else, who was only thirty, and now he has another daughter. Single dad who can commit is obviously a much better prospect than single mum who's getting on a bit and might want to steal your sperm to quickly pop out another one.' She swipes a hand through her hair, wafts her face in an attempt to create a breeze. 'Sorry, I think either the heat or the sharing atmosphere of the retreat has got to me. You didn't need to know all that.'

'No, no, don't be silly.' There's something about Liv that makes her easy to talk to. Maybe because she's a doctor and used to absorbing people's innermost concerns. Or maybe it's because she doesn't know me and Adam at all so isn't judging us as a couple. 'It's reassuring for me to listen to someone who's been through a break-up and come out the other side. I'm not in a great place in my own relationship and I'm wondering how I'd make it work if we divorced. We have two children together and a massive mortgage.' Worry spikes under my skin. I have no idea where I'd be able to afford to live if I was on my own. Not in a four-bedroom house in North London, that's for sure.

'It's hard, for sure. Working out access and money. I was on maternity leave when we broke up and absolutely shitting myself about how I was going to go back to work, manage financially and get my life back together.' She gives me a sympathetic smile. 'But my relationship with Cilla's dad is much better now. In the sense that we can speak to each other without needing mediation, and I can hold entire conversations with him without gritting my teeth. It mostly works, except that I miss Cilla madly when I'm on my own in the house.'

I nod, thinking of my kids. I miss them already and I've only been here for five hours. I imagine them not being there when I get home. 'Your ex is pretty involved then.'

'He is – now,' she says. 'As I said, he's got another daughter and I think, weirdly, doing it second time around has made him feel bad about everything he missed out on with Cilla, when we were breaking up and could barely speak to each other. There was a phase when he left me in the lurch and wouldn't commit to a proper routine. When he did have Cilla for the weekend, he needed hand-holding over everything. But he got better. Eventually. Plus, Cilla's five now, so she can tell him what she wants rather than me having to text him instructions on how to get her down for a nap or use the potty. Although he texted me the other week to ask how I get her to go to bed at the weekends. I was like, "Figure it out yourself. I'm her mum, not yours."'

I know I'm prying but I can't help myself. She hasn't just come through it; she seems happy.

'Do you ever regret it – splitting up?'

'God, no. But am I jealous of him finding someone else? Fuck, yes.' She pulls a vape out of her bag. 'Sorry, do you mind?' She gives a long pull on it. It's vanilla-scented. 'I mean, even if I do meet someone new, my life will have to fit around all the other arrangements. Cilla comes first, of course, but she has her routine with me and another one with her dad and step-mum and sister, and my job is full-on too – partly because that's the nature of it, and partly because I'm a single-income household and I need the money. Then who knows what baggage the other person would have themselves, whether that's a messy divorce, kids of their own, or a job as all-consuming as mine.'

I nod in what I hope is a supportive way, but it's making me anxious just thinking about it. Time for myself is rare enough now, and I have Adam to pick up the slack if I want to go out for drinks or for a run

Liv gives another pull on her vape and laughs. 'Oh, and I've got to meet this mythical person first. Sometimes it doesn't seem worth trying.'

'Are you on all the dating apps?' I ask.

'Yep,' she says, sounding resigned. 'On and off, anyway. Every few months I get a renewed enthusiasm and reactivate my Tinder account. Whereupon I field a load of messages from man-babies who ask me if I'm a "real" doctor or if I "just" have a PhD. And then that drives me to a women-only retreat.' She blows out another plume of scent. 'So here I am, surrounded by scary professionals. Believe it or not, one of the school mums – she's head of press for a record label so she's always jetting around the world at the last minute – couldn't make it and offered me her place at a discount. I think she felt sorry for me because I'm always so harassed and broke. Anyway, I was supposed to be picking your brains about the National

Trust and now you know my life story. What's going on with your husband?'

My insides churn up as I summarise the last few months. It all comes out: Adam's cheating; how lonely I was during Mum's illness, even though we were together. As I struggle to hold back tears, I even pour out the story of that stupid visualisation box going missing. She listens to me until I reach the end, a sympathetic expression on her face.

'It feels like an omen, you know?'

'I don't know what a visualisation box is,' she says, fiddling with her vape in one hand, 'but if you think losing the box is the same as losing your marriage, it's not. The box won't fix it. I went through a mad phase when I thought vocalising affirmations about love into the mirror would fix mine. It didn't. If your marriage is fixable, you'll fix it without any potions or secret contracts you make with the universe.'

We watch a bee hovering over the lavender, bobbing down onto a bud before moving on to the next one. 'I think I might need that transformational breath class after all,' I say, laughing through the tears I'm struggling to contain.

Liv laughs with me. 'Worth a try. I've been where you are and honestly, I know how crushing it is. The weight of wondering whether or not you're doing the right thing and how it will affect your children. You're probably drowning in well-meaning advice right now' – she rolls her eyes as she says 'well-meaning' and I can't help but smile – 'so I won't add any more platitudes to the pile. But for what it's worth, you'll get through it, either way. And it sounds like we're almost neighbours in London too, so keep in touch, especially as our daughters aren't far apart in age.' She nudges a thigh against me in a gesture of solidarity.

'If nothing else, it's always good to recruit someone new to trade babysitting with.'

I wipe my eyes. 'Deal. And thank you. Who needs yoga for feelings, eh?'

'Oh, there's still plenty of time for that too.'

We get up and head back down the aisle away from the archway, then follow a trail that leads further away from the house, through a thicket of trees, and opens out onto a cycle path that stretches around a huge lake. Little fishing jetties lie at intervals between trees and wildflowers and there are ducks, swans and moorhens gliding around on the water with their ducklings in tow. It's so still that we both pause and gaze out onto the view. I think again about the box, and the opinions I seem to attract unsolicited from my friends, then bat away the sense of foreboding. Liv is right. Adam and I need to save our marriage ourselves. Or let it sink.

Chapter Twenty-Five

6 May

'Five grand? Actually, scratch that – *maybe* five grand? Is that it?' Vanessa stops there. There's no need for her to continue. I get it, I am officially being bollocked. And it's happening in our weekly catch-up meeting so it's also happening publicly. I daren't look at Sophie, but glancing around at the others – my supposed allies – is even worse. Even Taylor won't catch my eye, which makes me paranoid. After all, what additional information is she privy to? 'Can I see you in my office after this?' Icy eyes from Vanessa.

'Of course,' I say, as brightly as I can manage when my cheeks are burning.

Vanessa works through the rest of her update list, studiously ignoring me. When she calls on Sophie, she smugly reports that she's got two new donors 'in the bag', who are good for fifty grand apiece, and the rest of us are forced to give her a round of applause. Finally, the whole painful thing is over, and I follow Vanessa meekly as she strides back to her office. Inside she flips the blinds, and I register the shock in Taylor's eyes at her desk outside. A closed-blind meeting is bad. Very bad.

There's no preamble from Vanessa. I'm not even sitting down when she starts talking. 'What happened?'

'Well,' I say carefully, lowering myself into the chair in front of her desk. 'The talk wasn't as well attended as I had hoped. But' – I interrupt myself before she can point out why that's not an acceptable response – 'I spent the rest of the weekend chatting to the women more informally and made some excellent contacts.' I did. At the evening drinks, steeled by a few cocktails, I mingled. Liv and I chatted all night and were quickly joined by a group who were as keen to balance all the wellness with wine as we were. After two bottles the trust workshop woman, Penny, confided about the ex-husband whose secret gambling debts caused her to seek out such a workshop, and after that no one stopped sharing. I don't think this is the sort of connecting Vanessa wants to hear about, though. 'I have numbers and email addresses so I can follow up with them all over the next week or two.'

Vanessa's expression softens a shade. 'Well, that's good news at least. Although I'd have thought you'd have something more concrete for me by now. You still have another two hundred thousand pounds to go.' I try not to flinch as she reminds me. Three hundred thousand pounds of donations have already been credited to me for this year, but they've come via my historic relationships. My target is half a million and I'm only going to get there if I bring in some new money. Sophie is trouncing me on the new donor front. 'This is a big year for us, so we all need to be working at full throttle,' she says, as though I don't already know.

'Believe me, I'm chasing every lead and constantly looking into ways to engage new or existing supporters.

I think the retreat was worth a shot and good things will come of it.'

She gives me a penetrating look. 'Is that where you've been going on Tuesdays? Meeting leads?'

My heart drops. Shit. It's been noted. I can't tell her I'm leaving early to see my marriage therapist, proving that I'm clearly not as focused on work as she would like me to be.

'That's for physio.' I waft a hand along my side, which could indicate any area between my knee and upper spine as the problem. 'I've been trying to change the time but it's the NHS, what can you do?' I say, mentally apologising to the NHS.

'And there was some school thing you had to leave early for too, wasn't there?'

That'll be the meeting with Mrs Hayward. 'Yes, but that was a one-off,' I say quickly. 'In terms of donors, I've had a run of bad luck,' I continue, forcing cheer into my voice. 'You know how it is. Some weeks even getting a small amount is like pulling teeth, and others, people can't stop throwing money at you.' I thrust a note of confidence into what I'm saying and think of Liv's money, a gesture from her beloved dad. 'Which is why I know the confirmed five-thousand-pound donation isn't as high as we'd like, but I think it deserves the same nurturing as fifty thousand pounds. After all, some of our highest contributions have been legacies from family members from different generations. It's up to us – me – to convince new donors that they're part of the Trust community, so perhaps we'll increase that donation in the future.'

'And you think this . . .' Vanessa looks at her notes. 'Olivia Logan could be one of those people?'

As far as I know, she has zero money, but I nod vigorously. 'Absolutely. She's a doctor and knows all sorts of people, from areas like . . .' I grasp for something, anything. How did she get her place at the retreat? 'The music industry. A totally different crowd than we usually target, but you know what it's like now. Taylor Swift's into baking and Demi Lovato knits.' I'm pretty sure I read that somewhere. 'Why shouldn't the National Trust be the next old-fashioned hobby to become cool?' I start throwing ideas out. 'We could have Noel Gallagher in the adverts. Or Adele—'

Taylor knocks on the door before popping her head around apologetically. 'Sorry to interrupt, but your ten o'clock is here.'

Vanessa nods. 'If you say so, Iris, then I trust your instincts. One last thing. Where are you with Lucas Caulfield? You said after Chatterstone it was going well, but he still hasn't confirmed for any donor dinners or shown interest in future visits.'

'He . . .' Again, the truth won't wash. 'He's sent me a few Facebook messages' is not what she wants to hear. 'He's been in touch a couple of times but I'm still trying to reel him in.'

'Well, do it. Whatever he wants. God knows we all enjoy going home on time when we can, but out-of-hours liaison is the nature of the job, physio or no physio.'

I'm mortified. It's the only chastising I've had since I was an assistant in my first fundraising job, and I forgot to order lunch for a conference of fifty people.

'Understood,' I tell her and get up. An apology is on the tip of my tongue, but I know Vanessa and she's the kind of boss who wants you to bring her a solution when you deliver bad news, not expect her to sort it out. That's the kind of team member I've always been. It would only make me look weak to concede that I'm fucking up.

I take a couple of deep breaths before I walk back to my desk, an attempt to cool the blotchiness I know has crept up my embarrassed face, and to calm the nerves that have left me shaking. Taylor mouths, 'OK?' as I pass her desk. I give her a feeble approximation of a smile in response.

'Your phone rang while you were in there,' Sophie says as I try to slip unnoticed onto my chair, but she's been watching for me coming out. She has literally no charm. How has she managed to convince any new contacts to part with their cash? I pick up my phone but there's nothing on the landing screen. No missed calls or voicemail alerts.

'Are you sure it was mine?'

'Oh sorry, yeah. I answered it and took a message. The ring went on and on, so it was disturbing everyone.' The volume is set to three bars above silent, but whatever.

I look at her and try not to sound impatient. 'Who was it then?'

'Someone called Esther.'

My heart skips. 'OK. I'll give her a call back,' I say briskly. 'Thanks.' I swipe at my phone and make it look like I'm going to do it now, even though there's no way I'm calling my therapist with Sophie listening in.

'No need. She said she had to push your session back by fifteen minutes next Tuesday and if she didn't hear from you then she'd assume that's fine.'

'Great. She's my physiotherapist,' I say, as breezily as I can manage. I might as well stick to the same lie for everyone.

'Really? Because she said Adam could call her back if need be.' The note of triumph in her voice gets louder by degrees as she speaks. 'I didn't know they did couples physio.' Loyalty is preventing the others in our office from openly listening in, but as I can no longer hear the background hum of mouse clicks and keystrokes, they clearly are.

'Great. Thanks, Sophie. Excellent message-taking. What a wonderful PA you would make.'

I'm still holding my phone impotently in my hand when it buzzes with a message, making me jump.

Facebook Messenger. Lucas.

The NT mailshot tells me that Bray House is hosting a pop-up bar and I'd be keen to visit. Next Tuesday night?

Several emotions compete for my attention. Hope that there's another chance to impress Lucas Caulfield into parting with some cash, and to wipe that smug look off Sophie's face. Confusion at why he's using Facebook to contact me about this and bypassing Vanessa. And anxiety because I can't say no to Lucas, even though it's on Tuesday. Which means I'm going to have to ring Esther back and cancel that therapy appointment after all.

Chapter Twenty-Six

13 May

'What could be more important than our session?' says Adam. The way he's stirring the pasta sauce – very, very carefully – would tell me how annoyed he is, even if he wasn't using the same impatient voice he usually reserves for the fifth time he's asked Sav to put on her shoes.

'I didn't say it was more important,' I reply, immediately defensive. 'Just that I have to go. It's a work thing and you know how much pressure I'm under right now to deliver.'

Stir. Pause. Stir. 'I don't understand why you can't do it on literally any other night.'

I'm trying not to snap. 'Because it doesn't work like that with these high rollers and you know it. The guy is loaded, he works all the time, and we have to fit a hospitality visit around his schedule. Come on, Adam,' I plead. 'This year is important for us, of course it is, but I still need to have a job at the end of it.' Particularly if I'm a single mum. 'There's no way I'll be happy if I'm broke and unemployed.'

I can see him relent, which was the entire point of me guilt-tripping him, but now I feel bad, although I can't say the idea of going to a cool new bar isn't more appealing than wading through my emotions in therapy.

'I'm sorry,' I say. 'Cancelling sessions isn't something I'm going to make a habit of, but this is a one-off. You should still go.' Can you go to couples therapy on your own? 'It could be good for you.'

He looks sceptical. 'There's no need for that. Maybe Esther can fit us in later in the week. I can see.'

'I think we should leave it,' I say quickly. 'Sorry, I don't mean to be negative but I can't do another time if it's during the working day. It's already been noticed that I'm having to leave early on Tuesdays. Can we please skip this week and let me focus on work?'

He stops stirring. 'Because you never do that.'

'Well, my boss thinks my head isn't in work – I wonder why – and you think I'm not focused on us, so it looks like I'm failing on all fronts, doesn't it?' For something to do, I stalk over to the fridge and pull out a lettuce to start shredding for the salad. I could throw everything I have at my marriage, but then I'd almost certainly get made redundant – and there's still no guarantee we'd make it – or I could be an exemplary employee and get the blame for not making enough effort in my relationship. So much for women trying to have it all. *Some* of it would be nice.

'Sounds like the crusty old businessman needs to make some friends, rather than getting a complete stranger to meet him for a drink.' Adam's crap joke shows me he doesn't want to fight about it either, and my relief outweighs the small point that the 'crusty old businessman' is in fact my entire office's fantasy boyfriend. I contemplate telling him, because of full disclosure, but also because I want him to experience the sharp thwack of jealousy I carry around with me near constantly. Although Adam would probably think I was doing it purely to *try* and make him jealous, and that's worse.

I settle for a truth, just not all of them. 'He's actually not much older than us.' If Adam asks me anything else, I'll tell him, and then reassure him that it's all above board. That of course it's not a date.

But he doesn't ask.

*

The austere Tudor manor house in Barking has been temporarily transformed by glowing candles, red drapes and tarnished silver goblets, into which curated cocktails are being poured. A waitress walks past us to the next table with a drink encased beneath a smoky glass cloche, before elaborately lifting it and wafting the fumes around the glass as the three people sitting there all coo.

'We must get one of those,' says Lucas, glancing up at it from the drink menu, which is printed on an aged paper scroll. The overall effect is part *Game of Thrones*, part Parisian speakeasy, which should be hideous but, sprinkled with a knowing layer of irony, it's made a pop-up in a National Trust stately home one of the hottest bars in London right now.

I scan the list of ingredients. 'I'm not going to last very long if I start drinking whisky from the off,' I say with a laugh. 'I'll start with something I know I can handle.' I watch the mixologist pouring liquid from a cocktail shaker into a copper mug. 'A gimlet, I think.'

A waiter approaches and I order, suddenly shy now we don't have the common ground of dissecting the drink menu to fall back on.

'I've spoken to the estate manager here and she said they can arrange for a private picnic in the grounds over the summer, if that's something you'd be interested in,' I begin. I've done dozens of visits with donors over the years, but the combination of how much is riding on me impressing Lucas and being in a dimly lit bar with him is bringing my nerves to the surface. It all seems too intimate, and so to compensate I've started talking to him in an ultra-formal way. My speech belies the fact we've exchanged emojis in our now semi-regular messages. 'I know you wanted to go back and see the rose garden at Chatterstone, and this place has its own walled gardens which have been rewilded by the Trust, as well as an amazing Japanese garden commissioned by one of the former owners. This property is a complete mish-mash of its previous owners' tastes, and it's quite wonderful.'

'There's a virtual tour you can take on the website, I came across it the other day,' he replies. 'I was in a meeting with one of our clients – an artificial intelligence company – and they used it as an opportunity to show off their latest headset. It was as though I was really here, exploring the grounds. It was fantastic.'

'Artificial intelligence?' I ask. 'Can it do that?'

He nods, enthusiasm firing in his eyes as he starts to tell me about one of the companies he's invested in. 'It's a travel platform and they mainly use AI to make recommendations and book trips for customers. They find deals by cross-referencing room prices and flights, and then create personalised itineraries – it's scarily accurate at predicting taste – but the tech guys are also developing a virtual travel arm, which is going into beta testing.'

'What, sightseeing without leaving the house? Is there a market for that?' It sounds a bit depressing to me, not least because I'd probably be out of a job. 'Wouldn't that mean people just sitting in their houses plugged into the Matrix?'

Lucas shrugs. 'Not everyone has the time, the money or the physical capability to travel wherever they like. It would be a godsend for someone like my mum, who's a wheelchair user. Accessibility has got better in recent years, but there are places she's never going to be able to go in her lifetime because there are steps, or the entrances are too narrow, or simply because they're not going to add an accessible toilet onto some ancient ruins. I've been looking for a company that can bring the world to her and other people with conditions that limit their ability to travel.'

'I hadn't thought of it that way.' Loves his mum: another tick registers.

'It might not be a substitute for the real thing, but this way she can have a taste of it, and the technology is only going to improve. It could even help with things like over-tourism and sustainability. Think about the environmental impact if people cut down how much they flew.'

At the mention of flying, the unwelcome image of Jules comes into my head. Maybe this AI tourism will put her out of a job, I think. Although I much prefer thinking about her being on a different continent, rather than anywhere near my family.

Lucas's eyes widen as his drink appears before him and the elaborate cloche-lifting ritual is played out, for our benefit this time. The smoke dissipates and the waitress returns with my more humble drink, so we clink our glasses together.

'How is it?' I ask, raising an eyebrow.

Lucas takes an experimental draw, pursing his lips as the liquid hits the inside of his mouth. I have to force myself not to stare at them. They're full and pink and—

'Smoky,' he replies, and I pull myself out of the moment. 'It's definitely more of a sipping liquor. By the way, I hope your dad is completely recovered now.'

'He is, thank you.' It's a subtle reminder of my unprofessional behaviour at our last meeting. 'Luckily it wasn't a bad scald, but I think the shock panicked both him and the children, and once you've shown fear there's no calming kids down, is there? I'm so grateful that you let me take your car to get back. I hope it didn't put you out, and I'm sorry I had to leave so suddenly.'

'Honestly, I'm glad I could be of help.' He pats my hand as he says it, and the pressure points of his fingers make my nerve endings fizz. Adam and I are so careful around one another at the moment that no one ever touches me any more. Well, the kids do, but that's in a rough-and-tumble kind of a way. The brief brush of Lucas's hand feels . . . well, considering my hand is still tingling, it feels suggestive.

He takes his hand away and has another sip of his drink. 'I think I'm getting used to it now. This drink, I mean, not women running out on me. Hopefully I won't make a habit of that.' He smiles, and there's a weird thump in my stomach. He's flirting with me. He is. And I'm flattered. 'You didn't need to send me the coffee in thanks.'

'It was the least I could do. And I don't make a habit of running out on men either.' Yep. I'm flirting back. Is this how it was with Adam and Jules?

He's still looking at me intensely. I don't dislike it, but I know a flush is working its way up my body. It's the gimlet, I tell myself.

'Was it easy for you to get away this evening? I imagine it must be difficult with children to consider,' Lucas asks.

The mention of the children snaps me out of it. 'Yes,' I lie. 'Totally fine.'

'Who have you left them with?'

'The kids?' He nods. 'Adam,' I say, a bit confused, and then I remember I told him I was separated at Chatterstone.

I look at my left hand. My wedding ring is still off. It's the moment I should clarify things and add 'my husband'.

But I don't. Instead I say, 'Their dad.' Not a lie, more a deflection. Lucas doesn't press me any further and I don't offer him any more information. Does he think this is a work meeting or that we're two acquaintances, potentially friends, meeting up for a drink? His work schedule doesn't seem to allow much time for socialising, so maybe he doesn't have that many mates, particularly ones who like hanging out in National Trust properties like he does. Or perhaps he thinks there could be more to this.

Either way, I need to tread carefully if I'm to nurture this relationship into one that can be quantified by Vanessa towards my financial target. I need to sit here, have some drinks with this charming man, and find out all the things I should have at Chatterstone so I can hit him up for some money. If I enjoy it, that's a bonus, right?

I swallow the rest of my gimlet and pick up the menu again. 'Let's order another drink,' I say conspiratorially. 'And you can tell me more about your journey from Liverpool to Silicon Valley.'

Chapter Twenty-Seven

Transcript of session with Adam and Iris Young by Esther Moran, 21 May

Iris: I want to talk about sex.
Adam: [splutters]
Esther: OK.
Iris: Maybe not just sex [pause] intimacy. I'm nowhere near wanting to do it with Adam, but I also miss being touched. The few times he has, it's seemed like an accident, and I can't work out if it's a new thing, since the affair, or if we stopped touching each other a long time ago, and that's [pause] that's one of the reasons why.
Esther: Adam?
Adam: [carefully] I don't think it's a new thing. But because of everything that's happened, I'm aware that Iris needs to be comfortable with the pace of our [pause] physical relationship. I'm cautious when I'm around her, in case she thinks I'm forcing her to do something she's not ready for.
Iris: It makes me think you don't want to touch me. That you don't care. That you're comparing me to Jules and I'm losing.

Adam: It's not that. I don't want there to be a sense of obligation.

Esther: Adam, you look as though you have something else to add.

Adam: [clears throat] I suppose I'm also worried that if I reach for your hand or a hug, you will reject me. Iris, do you think I haven't noticed that you treat bedtime like a military manoeuvre to get into bed without having to go anywhere near me?

Iris: I don't! [groans] OK, I do. I feel awkward, all right? I don't know how to be around you. Why didn't you say anything?

Adam: I thought I owed it to you to go along with it.

Esther: Tell me more about that.

Adam: If me having sex with another woman was the crime, then in my head, perhaps the punishment is that I have sex withheld from me.

Iris: That's why *you* think I wouldn't want to touch you. Not why you wouldn't want to touch me. It's different.

Esther: Can you try and hear what Iris is trying to tell you, Adam? Please continue, Iris.

Iris: I feel as though the physical part of our marriage is lacking and that you're OK with that.

Adam: I'm not. But I also don't know what to say. For the reasons I mentioned, I'm not going to make you feel like you have to have sex with me.

Esther: Iris, what was your physical relationship like prior to Adam's affair?

Iris: I thought it was OK. I mean, we'd been together ten years, so we weren't at it all the time, probably once a month if we were lucky. Less while Mum was ill and in the aftermath. Well, less for me anyway. Adam was obviously [pause].

Esther: Did you consider yourself sexually compatible with Adam?

Iris: I thought so. Maybe not adventurous. [pause] I was so angry and sad when Mum was ill that I didn't want to do it then. Maybe that's why you went elsewhere. Maybe it's as simple as that cliché.

Adam: No. I'm not having that.

Esther: Why not? Can you explain a bit more?

Adam: I think our – uh – physical intimacy was lacking during that time, but it wasn't a case of me thinking, 'Iris isn't up for it, so I'll find someone who is.' I'm not that cold.

Iris: You kind of are. Because that's what you did.

Adam: Not because of that.

Iris: Sure.

Adam: I'm just answering the question.

Iris: [muttering] Fucking good for you.

Esther: Can we take a moment right now.

[pause]

Esther: Iris, I understand this is upsetting for you, but Adam, can you clarify what you meant?

Adam: [takes a breath] I didn't sleep with someone else because I thought mine and Iris's relationship was physically lacking. I think maybe it's more because – and I don't think I knew this at the time, it's only since thinking about it through these sessions – because I didn't feel emotionally close to her during that period. [quickly] Which I do take responsibility for. I wasn't there for Iris emotionally, so she backed off, and then I felt even more distant from her. From everyone.

Esther: This might be painful for you, Iris, but Adam, can you tell us how you reconnected with Jules?

Adam: I first ran into her at the tube station on the way back from a work conference when I was rushing to pick up the kids, because Iris had to go to her mum's. I hadn't spoken to her for years before that and she was so happy to see me. We only spoke for a moment because I was late to pick-up, but she gave me her number to catch up.

Iris: I don't get how you go from catching up like two old friends to sleeping together, just like that.

Adam: We sent a few messages and then she invited me out for a drink, and I went. It was another weekend when you'd taken the kids to your parents'. I'd like to say I would have told you if you'd been around, but I wouldn't have, which is how I knew I was doing something wrong. I think she represented what she always has been to me. Escape. And then we drank too much and then [pause] well.

Iris: And then [pause] well? That's it? Wait, was it in *our house*?

Adam: No! We went back to hers.

Iris: [bitterly] Well, that's OK then. It sounds like you had it all planned perfectly. That's the bit I don't think I'll ever be able to get over. It's so calculated. I feel sick every time I think about it. And she knew you were married. She *knew.* You both disgust me.

Adam: [quietly] I know. I didn't say it was right, but that's what happened. I felt neglected. I was upset about you spending all your time with your parents. And I was being reckless. Being more like Gabe, I guess. Not thinking of the consequences.

Esther: I think it's important to acknowledge that you have owned this moment, Adam. But Iris, it's unlikely that you're going to find satisfaction in any of the 'answers' Adam gives you about what he did. It sounds like he wasn't thinking about you at all, just about himself. Would you say that's the case, Adam?

Adam: Yes.

Iris: [tearful] How could you look me in the eye when you came back from her? That's what I don't understand.

Adam: I couldn't. But it wasn't an issue, because the way I saw it, you weren't looking at me either.

Chapter Twenty-Eight

5 June

Sav is eyeing us as though she's in a hostage situation, flicking her gaze from one to the other as if she's trying to get the measure of what is happening, and who is more likely to be sympathetic to her cause. Answer: neither of us. Not least because it is she who has hijacked us, from our mandatory date night. Jack is at Fran's on a playdate with her eldest, and instead of being at the cinema watching a film without a U rating before heading to an affordable mid-range chain for dinner, Adam and I are at the local ice-cream parlour trying to bribe Sav into telling us why she's still not getting on with school. Two scoops of chocolate chip have so far not loosened her lips, but according to Mrs Hayward, while her behaviour towards other pupils has improved, she now seems unhappy again. Twice this week she's claimed to be ill, only to swiftly recover once she's been picked up from school and deposited on the sofa at home. Of course the school rang me rather than Adam, and having to leave work to collect Sav went down brilliantly in the office. I cannot risk this becoming a regular thing.

'Is there anything that's worrying you in particular?' Adam tries again. He's wearing a pale grey shirt I bought him for his birthday two years ago. One he keeps separate from his smart-casual work wardrobe to wear on smart-casual special occasions. It brings out his eyes. He goes to give Sav a hug, and her sticky little mouth makes the perfect brown imprint of an O on it.

'I just don't like school,' she says bad-temperedly. 'I don't want to go any more.'

'Why not?'

'Because I don't.' She looks away, refusing to engage with us. 'I want to stay at home with Mummy and Daddy.'

'But that's not an option, chick,' I say with a sigh, my heart tugging to look after her at home, even as I know that within three days we'd both be going nuts. 'Mummy and Daddy both have to go to work.'

'I could stay at home with Gan-Gan then.'

Adam snorts with laughter and I raise an amused eyebrow at him. Dad probably thinks he could 'hang about with the children all day', as he has referred to stay-at-home parenting, but even with his now-established childcare regime of telly, sausage rolls and park, he'd swiftly revise that viewpoint if he had to do it for more than one day every few weeks. I decide not to try and explain home-schooling to her because I have far too much respect for actual teachers to pretend I could do it.

'You have to go to school, Sav, it's the law.'

She looks stricken. 'Would a policeman take me to jail?'

One of those moments when you don't know the right answer. Say yes and it might shut down the current issue but make her scared of the police; say no and we're still locked in this circular conversation where there's no reasoning with her.

'No one would go to jail,' I start. Adam looks like he's going to interrupt with the facts about truancy laws, but I stop him with another eyebrow. 'However, you wouldn't learn how to read or write, and one day that would make you very sad. Plus, we wouldn't be able to do anything fun if we stayed at home because we wouldn't be earning any money to pay for it.'

'And what about all of your friends?' Adam chips in. 'You wouldn't see them any more because they'd all be at school and you wouldn't. They wouldn't remember who you were and invite you to their birthday parties.'

'I don't like any of them anyway.' Her face is fixed. Little mouth in a straight stubborn line. She looks so much like my mum when she was about to tell me off for something that I almost gasp.

'How about . . .' I take a second before I decide to break one of our most basic (only) parenting rules: not to bribe them to do everyday things that are non-negotiable. But this is an emergency. 'If you go to school without complaining for the rest of this year, we'll get you a treat at the end of it.' I pull an apologetic face over her head to Adam. He reciprocates with a shrug of what I take to be agreement.

Hostage eyes from Sav. 'What kind of treat?'

'To be determined,' Adam says, closing ranks with me. 'Let's see how we get on.'

'Can I come for ice cream with Mummy and Daddy again?'

Another heart squeeze, this time undercut by a stab of guilt. She looks happy just to be here with us.

'Yes.' I look into Sav's empty bowl. 'But we can do that anyway, not just as a reward for going to school.' Adam looks at his watch. We've missed the start of the film now and, while I could still drop her at Fran's so we can go out to eat, to be honest, I want my babies with me. Both of them. Maybe it's letting Esther down to jettison our couple time, but family as a unit comes first, it just does.

I'm grateful when Adam seems to read my mind and says, 'Shall we go and pick up Jack? It's a nice evening and we could walk there instead of getting the bus.'

He opens the overly ornate wooden parlour door for us, and Sav stations herself between us, ready to hold both of our hands as we walk down the street. I hear Adam's phone ring in his pocket. He pulls it out, sighs, and shoves it back in again.

Adrenaline immediately surges through my body. We're six months into our year and I still react this way whenever I don't know who's calling him. 'Who's that?'

'Mum,' he says in a surly teenage tone. He sounds cross – not as though it's my fault exactly, but as though I'm bothering him by asking.

'Aren't you going to answer it?' My voice is sharp and suspicious in response.

'I've already spoken to her today.'

'About what? She must need something if she's calling again,' I say. 'And you don't need to say it to me like that. How am I supposed to know that you've spoken to your mum if you haven't told me?' Our sentences bat back and forth like little darts. Rat-a-tat. Rat-a-tat. I'm holding on to Sav's hand so we can cross the road, and I feel her tense up. Mummy and Daddy are cross. Again.

'It'll be about Gabe. He's on one again.'

'What now?' Why is he making me ask every little thing rather than telling me? A thought strikes me: is it even his mum? The second I acknowledge the suspicion, I realise it has always been there.

'The usual—' He stops.

'What usual, Adam? It could be anything. What's he done?'

He doesn't answer and forces us to walk in silence halfway along the street to Fran's house, when his phone starts up again. He pulls it out and presses 'cancel', but too quickly for me to confirm the name on the screen.

I content myself with snapping, 'Answer it. At least then she'll stop ringing.'

'She won't though, will she. There's always another crisis.' He's right, but that's not the point. 'I'm trying to take a step back. Set boundaries. All that stuff we talked about.'

'Does *she* know that? It's one thing setting boundaries, but you have to tell the other person, Ad, otherwise it's just ghosting your mum.'

I can't help thinking it's Jules, or Jules-related. I could demand to see his phone, but what if he's changed Jules's name to 'Mum' to cover his tracks better?

Why would he do that?

Why wouldn't he?

'It's not as easy as that, you know it isn't.'

'I know.' Another tug. The therapy seems to have convinced Adam that he needs more space from his mum at the point where I'm starting to see her in a new light.

But I'm still not convinced it's her, or that this is about Gabe.

His phone rings for a third time. 'Give it to me,' I order. I don't want to remind him of the phone transparency rule in front of Sav, but I will if I have to. He sees the look on my face and hands his phone over. I press the 'accept' button.

'Hi Anne, it's Iris. Is everything OK?'

Then she does something she has never, ever done before. She starts to cry.

Chapter Twenty-Nine

6 June

A frantic dash through St Pancras station after the school drop-off. Two Pret filter coffees leaking from their keep-cup lids. Sweating at both the price of two bought-on-the-day 'supersaver' (snort) return tickets to Sheffield and the sprint from the tube station, up from the bowels of the Victoria Line, along the ludicrously long pedestrian tunnels to get to the National Rail station, and up another escalator where we stand gasping for breath as we stand beneath the great iron roof in the shadow of Tracey Emin's neon pink 'I want my time with you' sign, waiting for the delayed 09.47.

Once we're on the train, Adam and I passive-aggressively offer each other the window seat, which offers a premium view of the retail parks of North London and blurring station signs – West Hampstead, Borehamwood – as we zip north.

'Has she said she's found him yet?' I ask for the fifth time this morning.

'His phone was off all night apparently, and he still hasn't been back.' Adam looks tired, exactly like he's had a night of broken sleep waiting for an update about his brother, who came home ranting about a job interview that was 'rigged' against him and then promptly went out to 'clear his head' (Gabe-code for going to get drunk), before disappearing completely. Bloody Gabe. Just when you think he can't make any more trouble, he absents himself, thus making yet more trouble. All I could get out of Anne before I passed her over to Adam was 'he's ruining his life' and that she was worried what he might do. He's been known to go out looking for a fight, but then Anne suggested he was so down he might hurt himself, and that spooked all of us. Angry Anne is one thing, but crying Anne made me think we needed to go up and see her.

I should say something reassuring. 'He'll turn up. He always does. He might even say sorry for freaking your mum out.' Unlikely, echoed by the look of despair Adam shoots me. Gabe once borrowed a van from his mate to go and pick up something he'd bought on eBay, and when he dented it, he tried to blame his friend for not warning him about the 'heavy steering'. Taking responsibility is not high on his list of personality traits.

Adam pulls out his laptop. 'Sorry. To take a day off at short notice so soon after half-term, I need to get some planning stuff done on the train.' I look at my phone, waiting powerlessly for Vanessa to get back to me about my own last-minute annual leave request, which comes hot on the heels of those two early exits for Sav's mystery illness. My WhatsApp message has been blue-ticked but not responded to, and she sent a terse 'fine' to my email reporting on my cocktail evening with Lucas. Well, the bits I told her about. How he was keen to set up more meetings but not interested in group dinners, and how he likes eighteenth-century properties in particular and anything with impressive gardens. I haven't told her about how our hands brushed together several times at Bray House, or the few messages we've batted back and forth since. His latest was a picture of this month's featured coffee from the subscription we bought him, arranged in a wanky flatlay with a book next to it and the caption 'This is how the Grammers do it, right?' I sent a response telling him to be 'more extra'. *I want to see peonies, a bowl of homemade granola and chia seeds, or at the very least some coffee spon-con.*

It's nothing dodgy, but objectively speaking, it looks more like flirty chit-chat than the professional courtship of a millionaire. The professional boundary has got . . . fuzzy. I know that because I wouldn't want Adam to read the messages. I consider sending him one now, but something worky, in the vain hope I can give Vanessa some good news from the train and relieve the gnawing unease that my absence at work is being used as a black mark against me.

Yesterday, I sent out a load of new emails to CEOs and rich former Trust members who've let their membership lapse, but it's too soon to follow up. Anxiety laps at me as I think what else I can do, who else I can target.

Next to me, Adam pulls up a Word document where he's been writing role play scenarios; moral dilemmas teen boys might find themselves in where they have to work against a conditioned or expected response.

For something to do, I tap out a message to Nat. I haven't heard from her for ages. Not since the awkward night in the pub in April, despite a couple of simpering messages from me. I try again now.

How's that baby cooking? Drinks soon?

As I type it, I think, *When? When do I have time for drinks?*

Her reply is quick and closed.

Sure.

No suggested date or location, no chat at all. The thought nags at me: *So the onus is on me, is it, to keep this friendship going? Haven't I got enough going on?*

'Would a fifteen-year-old say "smash that"?' Adam asks, looking up. He's got his glasses on. He looks cute in them.

'I have no idea. But I don't think you should try to write it in the same way teens speak, especially if the corporate volunteers are going to be reading them out to their groups. No one needs Rupert from Mergers and Acquisitions saying "lit".'

He nods, then focuses on his screen and carries on tapping away. His profile is so familiar; forehead wrinkled in concentration and jaw speckled with two days' worth of stubble.

It doesn't take Esther to work out how Adam ended up working for a company dedicated to helping angry young men make sense of the world. Ninety per cent of the boys in the under-privileged and under-served schools his charity works with are growing up without a strong male role model in their lives; Gabe would probably have benefitted from the kind of sessions Adam now teaches. Although I imagine most of the top fee-paying boys' schools would also benefit from a course in how to avoid growing up to be a sexist prick, which is what one of Adam's sessions covers. (It may not officially be called that, but that's the gist.)

I scroll through my emails, checking again to see if Vanessa has responded there, or if there's anything else work-related I can jump in on to look like I'm on it, even if I'm technically on leave. There's an invitation from Emmett and Viola.

From: emmettandviola@us.com
Date: 6 June
To: Iris Young
Subject: Vow renewal
Dear Iris
I do hope you are well. Thank you so much for your time back in February (and for sending the lipstick – I'm a convert! V), it was a joy and a pleasure to see you again. And thank you for sorting out the date for our vow renewal, and all your help with suppliers and decor. I know you said you would be on site, but we'd like to invite you and your family as our guests rather than as a staff member – the invitation is attached.
Warm wishes
Emmett and Viola

There's an attachment with the full invitation for 7 September, where their names are drawn out in a tasteful floral design and 'Iris and family' are invited to the sit-down dinner.

I think about Emmett and Viola, the ups and downs they must have had during a sixty-year marriage, and make a note to ask Adam later about us all going. Maybe it would symbolise something about our future. That we have one.

A calendar invite pops up. Another one-to-one with Vanessa, scheduled for tomorrow with 'donor catch-up' in the subject line. It's swiftly followed by an email from Sophie, cc-ing in practically everyone in the company, asking me if I've updated the shared document about donor activity because it doesn't look like it on the one saved on the server. I have, but the most recent version is on my laptop, where I was working on it last night. And I forgot to bring my laptop with me, because I got distracted scheduling the three birthday parties Jack has coming up over the next few weeks into the family calendar just as we were about to leave the house. The noise of frustration I let out is enough to make Adam look up.

'Everything OK?' he asks.

'Yep, fine. Work stuff.' A moment passes and I change my mind. Something has to give. I'm supposed to ask when I need help. 'I've messed up something at work and it's because I'm juggling too many other things.' Adam looks at me over his glasses and half closes his laptop to show he's listening.

'OK. What do you need me to do?'

I take a breath. 'I need to be able to take a step back from the mental load of school admin for a while – the WhatsApp group for birthday parties, the present buying, the dress-up days – all that.'

He nods as if to say, 'Is that all?' so I elaborate. 'Not as in, I tell you when those things are happening and then you deal with them; as in, you need to be on top of them completely.'

Adam smiles gently. 'I know that's what you mean, and yes, of course. Invite me to all the groups and then mute them, delete them if you want.' As if – but there's a tiny weight lifted, even if it doesn't solve my immediate shared doc problem.

Working on it on the train today so will share the most up-to-date version later.

Send.

Yes, working on my day of annual leave. A small victory but I still need a bigger one.

I decide to message Lucas after all.

Let me know when you next want to see an NT property. I'm still working my way around them too, after all.

I add a smiley face, delete it, add it again and then press send, shoving my phone into my bag, turning to look out of the window and watching the landscape blur past.

*

It's as though last night's phone call never happened when we arrive. 'You didn't have to come,' Anne snaps, when she opens the neat green door to her red-brick terrace in Manor Estate. 'All that way from London. Must have cost you a fortune, seeing as visiting me isn't something you've planned for.' There's no safe way to respond to that so I don't say anything. 'You'll both want a tea,' she adds. We follow her static permed hair as it bobs down the hallway to the kitchen and through the eighties time warp that is Adam's childhood home. Woodchip wallpaper, hard-wearing swirly patterned carpet, and kitchen lino that's a slip hazard due to how meticulously cleaned and polished it is, but unmistakably old by virtue of B&Q discontinuing this particular line back in 1992. Anne's in her best 'house' outfit: a white cotton shirt with military-grade creases ironed into it and cropped 'slacks', paired with minimal, tasteful make-up. Anne does not approve of slobbing out, even though she has been retired from her job as a home-help for five years and no longer needs to look professional on a day-to-day basis. The few times she's stayed at our house in London, she's been appalled if we're not dressed by 10.30 a.m. at the weekend.

'Any word from him?' Adam asks, once we're sitting at the breakfast bar and she's stewing a teabag in the pot.

She shakes her head almost imperceptibly, before lobbing another question back. 'Who's with the children?'

'They're at school,' I say. 'My dad is going to pick them up later.'

Anne's face softens at the mention of him. 'How's he getting on, you know, without your mum?'

Over the years, she and Mum always kept in touch, especially when Jack was first born and my mum was visiting all the time. She was better at keeping Anne furnished with news and photos than Adam was.

'He's OK,' I say. 'He misses her. We all do.'

'Shocking shame,' she says, pulling the bag out and sweeping it into the bin, before pouring us all a cup of very strong tea.

'So what happened with Gabe?' I ask. Any warmth evaporates. Even my mention of his name is taken as a dig.

She directs her response to Adam. 'It's the job interview he went to last week. He got called back for a second interview, which is supposed to be this afternoon, but said they've stacked it so that he's got no chance. He'd already had a drink when he told me about it and then, well, you know how he gets. By the time he left here, he was still angry but more maudlin, and saying "What's the point in anything?" I haven't seen him since seven last night.'

Gabe isn't definitely an alcoholic, but he's also not *not* an alcoholic. He's one of those. Drink often seems to be involved somewhere along the line, but whether it's the cause of all his drama or just a component is difficult to work out. And obviously, we're not allowed to address it.

Adam nods as though that all makes sense, but I'm clearly missing something.

'A second interview is . . . positive, isn't it?' I ask.

'The interview is with someone Gabe has had trouble with in the past.'

'Right. What sort of trouble?' It could be anything, anyone.

'They were at school together. The first high school.' She looks at Adam and says, 'Dave Slater,' who I guess is someone he's had a fight with.

'School was a long time ago now, though.'

'I know that,' she snaps. 'But some people hold every little thing against you. Never mind that he's talented and they'd be lucky to have him.'

He is talented. He's always been into art and graphics, according to Adam, but his employment history is all over the place. Maybe if he didn't burn bridges with every single person who crossed his path, or self-sabotage at every opportunity he gets, he wouldn't find it so hard to stay in continual employment. Or if he started again, in an area where he hasn't fought a good proportion of the population while he was still at school.

'Has he ever thought of moving out of Sheffield?' I say, realising the second I do that it is categorically the Wrong. Thing. To. Say.

'Why would he do that?' The temperature in the room drops several degrees, just as the front door opens and then slams. Everyone jumps.

'Mum!' Gabe bowls in as she shouts, 'Where have you been?' at him. Five years younger than Adam, with the same grey eyes rimmed with long lashes and dark wavy hair – Gabe's is a bit thicker around the temples than Adam's and without the trace of silver – but he doesn't look it. His sallow skin and the crinkles at his eyes speak to both a hangover and a smoking habit he should have kicked at least a decade ago, not to mention the chipped front tooth from one of his pub scuffles. They say having children ages you, but Adam radiates health in comparison to his unencumbered sibling.

'What are you doing here?' he says when he spots us. Gabe's face is sullen, teenage, the chip firmly on his shoulder. We both turn around uncomfortably on our stools. I give him a half-smile but keep quiet to let Adam do the talking.

'We popped up to see Mum,' he says. Gabe looks unconvinced that we'd traipse up here on a Thursday without the children, just for a cup of tea. I'm wondering what we're doing here myself, but Adam carries on as though it's totally normal. 'And to see how you are. She says you've got a second interview at Proctors.' I see we're ignoring that he's been out all night, worrying his mum to death.

'Didn't realise you were an employment agent now.'

The air crackles. Adam doesn't rise to it, but I can see his face tense. His mum doesn't tell Gabe off for being rude, which in turn makes me prickle with annoyance. Somewhere deep inside, I know she makes digs at Adam and me because, unlike Gabe, we'll take it, but knowing that doesn't stop it from pissing me off.

Adam starts patiently. 'It just seems' – *ridiculous*, I want to chime in, but that would get Gabe's back up. It's like dealing with Jack – 'unnecessary to skip it because Dave Slater is on the interview panel.'

'He wouldn't just be on the panel, though. He'd be my boss.'

'OK,' Adam agrees. 'But if you get the job – which you have a strong chance of doing if you're through to the next round – that means he has no interest in rehashing any sort of beef with you from the past.'

'Or he does, and he's only calling me in for interview to humiliate me.'

I make an involuntary snorting noise, and three sets of eyes swivel to me. Anne's alarmed expression screams 'don't fuck this up', while Gabe looks openly hostile. It's insane how much of a baby he's being about this. I have to say something.

'I don't know anyone who has time to conduct a hoax job interview, purely to get back at someone they fell out with in school—'

'Gabe got suspended for cracking Dave's head against a football goalpost,' Adam interrupts.

'OK, well, even so. If he wanted to rub your face in how much better his life is than yours, he'd friend-request you on Facebook and show off about his house or wife or salary or something. That's why it's there. To prove to your enemies that your life is far better than theirs, all without having to leave your house or get HR involved.'

'It's humiliating,' Gabe repeats. 'Having to beg him for a job.'

'You're not begging for anything!' I shout. 'You're qualified. They need a graphic designer – is that the job?' Anne confirms it with a nod. 'And you are one. It's a transaction. If you don't get it, it's not personal. Well, it might be; he might just not like you on the day.' I think of Sophie. 'We've all worked with someone whose personality we're allergic to.'

'Not helpful,' Adam mouths.

'But I promise you there's nothing humiliating about it. Certainly nothing worth flouncing off all night over, to ruin any chance you might have of getting the job.'

'I didn't flounce anywhere.' Gabe twists his mouth into a sneer, and I resist the urge to chuck my piping hot tea in his face.

'You didn't tell Mum where you were going or when you were coming back,' Adam says. 'She was worried. We all were.'

'Why? I'm not nine years old,' spits Gabe. 'I can go out for a drink whenever I like.'

There's a pause, where I assume we're going to brush over the bit where Anne was worried enough to think he was going to do something, but Adam clears his throat and says, 'Mum said you sounded different, and then she couldn't get hold of you. She thought something . . . bigger might be going on. But I can see you're *fine.*' The emphasis on 'fine' shows he's being sarcastic. 'It's not OK, Gabe, to do that to Mum, or us.'

'I needed to blow off some steam,' he says, in a voice that's meant to make us all think we're total squares who are overreacting. 'You'd get that if you knew anything about humiliation.'

'I know quite a bit about it, actually,' I reply, rage biting at the back of my throat. In my peripheral vision, I see Adam's eyes widen. *How about your sainted older brother cheating on me with the girl that got away*, I want to scream, even though I know giving Gabe this information is a bad idea. 'You don't have the monopoly on it. I've been rejected from plenty of jobs, I didn't get into my first two choices of university, I've been humiliated by men, dumped by one of my good female friends, and once I was rejected on the door of a cool new bar by a woman who said my outfit was too frumpy and I couldn't come in.'

Gabe almost smiles. 'I wouldn't have stood for that.'

'And therein lies the difference between us,' I say. 'I went to another bar. You'd burn the first bar down. Or let the people who care about you think you might be dead.'

The room collectively holds its breath. I never speak to him like this. I rarely speak to him at all these days, but however Adam and Anne have been 'handling' him clearly hasn't worked. Plus, there's a small part of me blaming him for Adam's infidelity. Without Gabe's constant misbehaviours, he wouldn't have had a watertight excuse to disappear 'up north' for weekends at a time. It's almost reassuring that Gabe has been as troublesome as ever; at least some of Adam's M1 dashes have been genuine.

Gabe holds my look for a second. I might be mistaken but I'm sure there's a glint of respect there. It disappears as quickly as it arrived, and he turns back to Adam.

'Nice to see you up here anyway,' he says, in a tone that implies the opposite. 'It must be at least seven months. Drafted the wife in to have a go at me this time, have you?'

I do the maths. Before his fake New Year with Gabe in Sheffield, Adam came up here to see them in November. He said he did anyway. I know Gabe is doing this on purpose, to needle Adam, but at least it confirms for me that the November trip was real.

'No one's here to have a go at you, Gabe,' Adam says quietly. 'Like I said, Mum was worried, and we wanted to come here and see her, and yes, speak to you. This job sounds like a good opportunity and there's still time to make it to the interview. But I can't force you to do something you don't want to do.'

Gabe examines his hands. The knuckles on his right hand look swollen.

'Does that hurt?' I say.

'Nope,' he says, emphasising the 'p' and crossing the left hand over it so it's covered up.

'Let me look at it,' Anne implores, standing up and reaching for it.

He bats her away. 'Fuck's sake, Mum, get off, it's nothing.'

'Don't talk to Mum like that,' Adam thunders at the same point I snap.

'What is it you want, Gabe? Do you want a perfect job handed to you, one where you're the boss – even though you've spent years destroying every chance you've been given? Stop whining about how everyone is out to get you because – guess what – you're not the victim in this situation. If anything, Dave Slater is probably worried you'll kick his head in if he doesn't give you the job.' I pause. 'That was a joke.'

When I look over at her, Anne's face is murderous, and Adam looks like he's about to have a stroke.

'Could you give me a minute with Gabe on his own?' Adam says, trying to regain control of the situation. Anne practically drags me into the front room.

'I wish you hadn't done that,' she hisses, the second I'm ensconced in her ornamental crystal collection. She has one of those display cabinets they have in H. Samuel, and it's full of the stuff people got as wedding presents in the seventies and eighties – a decanter no one ever uses, a hideous clock with light bouncing off its glass prisms, three whisky tumblers. The fourth, Adam once told me, was thrown at his dad by Gabe in the nineties, the day he left for good. For once I'm in agreement with Gabe's poor impulse control. Best thing for both their dad and the glass.

'Why?' I say truculently, chucking myself onto the squashy leather sofa.

She eyes me warily. 'The interview is in two hours but now he'll dig his heels in about going even more.'

'Will he? Based on what? Gabe digs his heels in based on anything at a given moment – how much he wants attention, whether Sheffield Wednesday have lost at home, whether Brad and Angelina are on speaking terms.'

'Who?'

'Doesn't matter. He'll do what he wants, so why shouldn't I – or *you* – say what we think?'

'You don't understand,' she says, sinking down onto the sofa next to me, her face showing a chink of that vulnerability from the phone call. She starts rearranging her already immaculate pile of newspapers and magazines on the side table.

'I wish everyone would stop saying that to me,' I snap back before I can stop myself. Anne catches the tone and latches on to it.

'Adam could do with some support when it comes to Gabe, you know.'

Right. Because I'm the inadequate wife. Adam hasn't told his mum about Jules or that we're giving ourselves a year to decide if we can stay married, and there's no way I'm going to – I'm not mad – but being told *I'm* not supportive enough makes me livid.

'One thing I do know, *Anne*, is that secrets can be toxic. Perhaps you're doing Gabe no favours by protecting him from the reality, which is that he's caused most of this himself. He's been hurt by his dad, I get it, even though no one thinks I do, but aren't you a bit insulted that everyone constantly blames his issues on his upbringing? You've worked so hard to provide for them and done your best, yet it's still not his fault when he messes up.'

Her mouth is a straight line. 'He's not as strong as Adam. You'll understand when your own children are older.'

'Yes. Adam. *Such* a role model.' It just comes out. I pick up the *Sheffield Star* and start flicking through it. The words swirl around on the page in front of me, but

I concentrate on reading about the council's controversial tree-felling programme and Jarvis Cocker heading up this year's film festival.

'Is everything all right?' Anne says slowly. There's an expression on her face I've only seen once before. It was a few days after Sav was born, while I was relaying the saga of her arrival and describing the anaesthetic wearing off halfway through the midwife stitching me up. I think it's sympathy – or disgust. Hard to tell. 'You know, all marriages have their ups and downs – God knows I know that – but you and Adam are all right, aren't you?' She sounds tentative, worried. 'You're solid – together?'

I think about all the time Anne wasted with Adam's dad over the years and wonder if the happy parts were happy enough to make it worth it. I want to ask her, *Did you think every chance you gave him would be the last one?*

'Some marriages are better off over,' I say carefully. 'Yours was.'

Anne and I lock eyes. For once she doesn't have a retort ready to fire at me. I feel instantly guilty for what I have suggested to her. Another branch of her family splintered off. A life where she sees even less of her London-based grandchildren than she does already.

'And some are worth a second chance,' she says in the end. Quietly. 'Whatever it is, and I don't expect you to confide in me, it makes me feel better knowing that Adam . . . that your life with Adam, down there, with the kids and your high-flying jobs . . .' She shakes her head and looks away. 'I'm proud of what he's done, that's all.' Then she gives me – not a smile exactly, but a look of support. 'Besides, Gabe can't have the monopoly on second chances. Granted, he's had about forty of them, but surely there's one left for Adam.'

That was almost a joke. I'm stunned. Are we bonding?

Adam bustles into the room, interrupting the moment. 'He's going to the interview,' he says. 'He's made it sound as though he's doing me a favour, but whatever. He's going to get showered and changed, and then we can drop him in a cab before going to the station.' He looks at me. 'That OK?'

I glance at Anne again, sitting there. Another crisis averted. Another visit from Adam orbiting it. The push/pull of two sons, one who demands all of her energy, the other who she never gets to just *be* with. I always had my mum close by for both the dramas and the everyday. I never needed anyone else.

'If I get the train back down now, I'll probably make it in time to pick up the kids with Dad. You come back here after we've dropped Gabe off and spend some time with your mum.' I go over and hug him. He tenses, surprised. I'm a bit surprised myself.

'Are you sure?' The look on Adam's face tells me he doesn't know if this is a test or a trap. Is he supposed to stay or to extricate himself and come home with me?

'Yes, honestly. Spend some time here and get a later train. It'll be nice. I'll see you when you get home.' I squeeze his hand, hoping he takes it as an olive branch and not a threat.

Chapter Thirty

20 July

'There's a sixth birthday party that weekend, so we could go to the vow renewal but we'd have to be back for the Sunday lunchtime,' Adam says, as he rummages under the seat for any more stray Matchbox cars that have dropped there over the course of the flight.

'Whose sixth birthday? How do you know that?'

'Ella's. The invite was in the Reception class's Facebook group. Although, I guess it's a Year One Facebook group now. I've said Sav's going anyway.'

I look at him. 'Oh.' It's not that I wanted him to fail at being in charge of school admin, more that I wanted him to know what it's like to be on a knife-edge all the time, juggling, and occasionally dropping, some of the balls. 'Thank you,' I say instead, before being immediately annoyed with myself. No one ever said thank you to me for getting on with it.

But wouldn't it have been nice if they had?

'Anyway.' I look at the swarm of people attempting to get off our easyJet flight to Palma despite the fact that the doors aren't open, and the seatbelt signs haven't gone off yet. Sav is one of them. She's made a break for it under someone's arms as they reach to get their bag from the overhead cabin.

'THE SEATBELT SIGN IS STILL ILLUMINATED,' roars a member of the cabin crew, and Adam darts from his seat, grabs her, and straps her screaming back into her chair. The other people do that half-standing half-sitting action that's supposed to show they're doing what they're told when they're not.

'Where are you trying to go without Mummy and Daddy? We're not allowed to get off yet,' he says in his most patient voice.

'Everyone else is,' Sav shouts back.

'I know,' Adam reasons, 'but we have to wait for them to park the plane safely.' Two more people get up and Adam gives in. How are you supposed to explain rules when the so-called grown-ups are flagrantly ignoring them?

'Are these people all naughty for standing up?' Sav asks. A bespectacled woman holding at least two more bags than are allowed as hand luggage throws her a dirty look. I exchange a glance with Adam and try not to laugh.

'Yes,' I say sadly. 'I'm afraid they are. They'll probably call the plane police about that lady when she gets off. That's the risk you take. Anyway,' I say again.

Sav furrows her brow. Jack so far hasn't looked up from the iPad. Which is fine by me on a two-hour flight that would be hell without it. But it probably won't be fine by me tomorrow when the rest of us want to go to the beach, and he wants to sit in a darkened room and watch YouTube.

'Anyway what?' Adam asks.

I've completely lost my train of thought. 'No idea,' I say. 'It's gone.' The seatbelt sign finally goes off. The entire plane stands up simultaneously while we restrain Sav and wait for it to clear.

*

'Oh, I've remembered,' I say thirty minutes later, as we clear passport control. 'Which car rental company desk do we need to look for?'

Adam looks at me blankly. 'I don't know,' he says.

'Well, where's the confirmation voucher? It'll say on there even if you booked it through some random broker site.'

'I didn't book it,' he says slowly, 'you did.'

'No,' I say briskly, narrowing my eyes a shade. '*You* did.' A moment passes in which I bark 'NO!' at Jack, who is surreptitiously trying to edge towards the arcade inside the airport. 'Unless you didn't?'

'I thought you were doing it.'

'Despite the fact that you said you were going to sort out this holiday, I booked the flights, the travel insurance, the car park at Luton and the excursions at the resort. I specifically said, "Can you sort out the car hire for Mallorca?"' I look at the car rental desks dotted around the circumference of the arrivals area. The pick-up queues are all massive. We were up at 4 a.m. in order to make our 6 a.m. flight. We ended up running sweating to security because there was a crash on the M1 and we were going to miss boarding, before our plane was delayed for two hours on the tarmac without even the Pret breakfast we'd promised the children because we didn't have time to buy it. I am hungry, I am tired, and I am SICK of having to project manage everything. Keeping an eye on the fucking school Facebook group does *not* make up for this.

'Right,' I say, dropping Sav's monkey rucksack onto the floor and fighting to keep my voice level. 'Then you'd better book us one now. I am going to the toilet – *alone* – and then I am going over there to get a coffee and a pastry and to sit down. If anyone wants to come, they can, but I will be sitting at a separate table for no less than fifteen minutes reading my book. I need a moment.' I'm using an Esther technique: setting a boundary and being clear about it. I am asking Adam for what I need to get through this situation, which is making me feel anxious about the rest of the holiday.

Adam is nodding desperately as he scrambles for his phone to get onto the airport wifi. Jack whines, 'But I want a pastry too,' and I walk away, surprisingly calm. Adam may have come through on the school admin, but this was his responsibility too. I am not going to sort this out and then act like a martyr for doing it. Instead I'm opting out and going to enjoy a solo wee without Sav trying to open the door while I'm mid-wipe. Frankly, that's already a holiday.

When I come out, the others have moved over to the airport café. Jack and Sav are stuffing chocolate twists into their mouths while Adam takes quick, nervous sips of a coffee and looks harried as he taps at his phone.

'MUMMY!' Sav shouts as I approach.

I hold up one finger. 'I'm going over there. Fifteen minutes.' Something in my voice tells her not to push it. I head for the table furthest away, around the corner, with a view of the departures entrance and the families returning after their weeks away, looking alternately tanned and sunburned, all loaded down with suitcases and inflatable crap and impatiently ushering their children into the airport. I scan the back of my book, this summer's highbrow must-read, according to the *Guardian*. I'm probably not going to read it, as I also have two thrillers more suited to being read four pages at a time while I've got one eye out for my children drowning in the apartment building's swimming pool.

I do some deep restorative breaths. It turned out the yoga teacher at the retreat was right (of course) about the benefits of transformational breathing. It's come in handy on more than one occasion when I've wanted to, say, punch Sophie at work, or clear my head of how much I resent my husband.

I blow all the air out of my lungs through pursed lips – five seconds, really experiencing the breath – and go back over to my family. The airport is air-conditioned, but Adam's brow looks damp.

'There's not much available but I think I've found one.' He points to the queue for 'Despesas Cars', which is almost out of the door. 'You lot wait here, and you can come and join me when I get to the front.' I nod, trying to smile through the tension headache nudging at the corners of my brain. Sav hands me her rucksack, which is my cue to start dealing the cards for what I anticipate will be many games of matching pairs while I wait for Adam to pick up the car.

An hour and a half later, we have secured what seems to be the last hire car in the whole of the Balearic Islands. It is, however, without a child's car seat, which means Sav can't travel in it. I can see Adam trying to hold it together as he signs for the car, the insurance, the extra insurance that wasn't included in the already ludicrously priced insurance but no one ever explains why, and for Jack's booster.

'There is another rental office in the town where your apartment is located,' the rental man tells us with a helpful smile. 'I have called them, and they are holding a child's car seat for you. You can pick it up when you get there.'

'But it's a forty-five-minute drive away,' says Adam. He looks down at where Sav is standing – bored, restless, and desperate to get to the outdoor swimming pool we've been dangling as a carroty bribe to get her through the final six weeks of school. Her hatred of school subsided as the term went on, but our reward system became less and less sustainable, not least because when Jack found out, he was livid that Sav was getting a prize for simply going to school without a fuss. 'I guess one of us could drive to the other office, pick up the seat and then come back for the others,' Adam says. He looks uncertain, because it's a lose-lose situation. Either navigate yourself to another car rental office and back, with a round trip of an hour and a half, all the while knowing your spouse is waiting with two thoroughly fed up children for you to return, or remain in the airport with two thoroughly fed up children asking every five minutes when your spouse will be back.

I make a snap decision. Despite my boundary setting, I will in fact project manage the situation. I just won't be a martyr about it. I summon up another of Esther's teachings and repeat it inside my head.

We are on the same side, we are on the same side, we are on the same side.

'Get the keys and wait here,' I say, as I run over to where a group of holiday reps from various rival companies are waiting for the next flight to land. I explain our situation to the person who seems most likely to be sympathetic to our plight, and ask for a lift to our apartment building in their transfer coach.

'We're not supposed to,' I'm told by a Geordie in full fake-eyelash, facial-contouring glory, who looks barely old enough to have done her A-levels. The name badge on her red polo shirt reads 'Catrina'. I open my mouth to offer her money, but before I can, she drops her voice and whispers, 'They think the company is going to go bust soon though, so if there's room on the bus, then sure. Could you vote for me in our Rep of the Year competition? It'll look good on my CV when I'm applying for other jobs.'

I almost hug her. 'Yes, of course. And I'll get everyone on the bus to do it too.'

'Hang around here until the flight lands and I know how many we've got in terms of numbers. It's not supposed to be a full coach, but I have to wait until we've fully boarded to offer you a seat.'

'Thank you, thank you.' I rush back to tell Adam I've found a solution, and he looks as relieved as I am. 'We'll get on the coach and you take Jack in the car.'

'I'm sorry, I know this is my fault.'

'It's fine,' I say, meaning it. 'Let's get to the resort.'

What I decide not to tell him, once we're on the coach and I've looked over twenty-five people's shoulders as they voted for Catrina on their phones, is that our mode of transport is relaxing compared to how I imagine he's faring in the rental car, even if we will have to stop off at every hotel in the region before we get to our apartment. I neither have to drive nor navigate, and the coach driver doesn't make any noises of exasperation because of me doing either of those two things unsatisfactorily. The suitcases are with Adam (I checked) so we don't even have to deal with the luggage, just sit here and be taken to our destination. This must be what it's like to be Taylor Swift. If Taylor Swift travelled on her tour bus with twenty-five people on an over-fifties 'solo silvers' package holiday and a small child who threatens a meltdown every time she's hot, hungry or bored (approximately every five and a half minutes).

The motion of the bus and the tension of the trip releasing lull me into a doze. Sav manoeuvres my rucksack into a position where she has easy access to the snacks and leaves me to it, and the next thing I know, two hours have passed, and Catrina is shaking me awake and telling me we've arrived at Casa Marina.

There's a moment as we're about to get off the bus when it crosses my mind that we're on one of those trips where everything that can go wrong does, and that when I emerge down the coach steps it will be to a building site with a crack den next door. But my first view is of a two-storey white building with small balconies dotted along its perimeter, which is arranged around three swimming pools that have intricate slides and fountains twisting through them. The sky is bright blue and cloudless. My phone tells me it's twenty-six degrees, and the combination of the sun and breeze on my face tells me it's the perfect temperature for a holiday with children that will involve as much running around with them as a day in a London park.

'I've checked us in and we've been looking out for you. Jack's been dying for you to get here so we can go down to the pool.' Adam appears next to the coach and leads us to our apartment on the second floor, which has a view of the pools in one direction and the marina in the other. It's simple but chic, with one double bedroom, a twin for the children, and a kitchen/living room hybrid with glass double doors at the end, and a tiny balcony that looks perfect for relaxing with a book and a glass of wine once the kids go to bed. Meanwhile, Jack is sitting in his swimming shorts on the sofa, looking like he's got a right grump on.

'You've been ages,' he says in a sulky voice.

'We had to get the bus and it took a while,' I reply. 'We're here now though, so we can get changed and go down.' I turn to Adam, who looks no less stressed than before. 'How was your trip?'

'Yeah, all right,' he says, and I give him a meaningful look. 'We got lost twice, I almost went the wrong way around a roundabout, and Jack screamed every time I crunched the gears – which was *a lot*. We haven't been here much longer than you. Sorry you had to wait around for the coach.'

I bite my lip and try not to laugh. 'We're here now.' The only thing tugging at my nerves is that he thinks I'm going to hold a grudge about the car rental fuck-up. The wife-as-nag narrative. I brush it to one side. 'Right, choices time. Would you rather take the kids down to the pool or find the nearest supermarket and get some supplies, which can also include a bonus solo coffee or' – I check my watch; it's 4 p.m. – 'Aperol Spritz for your troubles?'

We smile at each other. One of the good smiles. The 'we're on the same team and we made it' smiles. 'Are you sure? After you had to hang around for the coach and everything? Thanks again for sorting it out, by the way. My solution would have taken ages and been a nightmare.'

'We all made it and the coach was completely fine. Honestly.' It was, but I'm still pleased Adam has acknowledged that I sorted it out. A year ago he wouldn't necessarily have noticed, never mind thanked me. I want to believe it's more than us being on our best behaviour. It feels like he's seeing me. 'Sav has decided that the solo silvers have the right idea and she only wants to go on holidays by herself from now on.'

'CAN WE GO TO THE SWIMMING POOL?' Jack screams.

'PLEASE!' Adam and I scream back at him simultaneously.

'Please,' he mutters, startled.

'Yes, yes, we're going. Let me find my cossie. Daddy's going to get us some food, so we'll see him in a bit. Sav! Where's your swimming costume?'

The suitcase has been ransacked by Jack and Adam, putting paid to my carefully organised packing system that gave everyone their own section. 'Right, there's Sav's,' I say, pulling her dinosaur all-in-one out from a corner, 'now where are mine?' I've brought two. A sporty cover-me-up-and-suck-me-in one that I wear whenever I have to go near a kids' party in a swimming pool, and a new royal blue fifties-style bathing costume, with a halterneck and ruching all the way down the front. It was an impulse buy one lunchtime and flattering when I tried it on, but I'm a bit self-conscious about it now. We're in a family-friendly resort, not an Insta-holiday. I find them both and consider them in my hands.

'That one looks cool, is it new?' Adam asks.

I nod.

'Very Jane Russell.'

'Who's Jane Russell?' Jack asks, rolling his eyes.

'She's someone who's almost as pretty as Mummy.'

Jack makes a sick face.

But it's a gesture.

'Right.' Adam slaps his leg, the way men seem to start doing when they turn forty. 'I'll get going to the shop and see you back at the pool in about an hour. I saw a sign for a Spar on the other side of the complex – it's just down there.' He pulls his phone out of his pocket and puts it on the kitchen counter. 'I don't think I'll need this. You'll know where I am if you need me in the meantime.'

Going anywhere without a phone seems unthinkable. Jack looks appalled. But I recognise it. It's another gesture. I pick up the royal blue costume and go to get changed.

Chapter Thirty-One

26 July

'I'm cold.' Sav shivers, and I wrap her in a towel as the catamaran accelerates through the Med. Two hours into our 'dolphin watching' experience and we're yet to see one dolphin. Jack has cycled through excitement at being on a boat, excitement at being on a boat that's going really fast, to boredom as all we've seen is a 'few rubbish caves'. That'll be the fascinating pre-historic rock formations, but fine. Admittedly, even I'm a bit nippy as we whizz along to follow a tip-off about some bottlenecks further out to sea.

'I'm hungry,' she adds.

'Sav, we've been through this. You didn't eat your breakfast – again – and now you're after snacks. No, you'll have to wait until lunch.'

'I'm hungry too and I ate all my breakfast,' wails Jack. He did eat his breakfast. And Sav's. Jack is a bottomless pit of hunger. But I can't give him a snack and not her. I fold and pull out two squashed bananas from my bag. They both pull a face.

'If you're not hungry enough to eat a banana then you're not hungry,' Adam tells them, as he shoots me a look of solidarity. It's the last day of the holiday and we're in the zone where no matter what activity we do, the children whinge about it being too hot or too cold or too far or too boring. The bananas are either too squashed or not forthcoming. I knew the kids would never let us have a completely picture-perfect holiday because they're, well, kids, but I was also worried about a full week with Adam, without the distraction of work to escape to. Just us, a two-bedroom apartment, two children to entertain and twenty-four hours a day together – but overall it's worked. We haven't only got through it, we've enjoyed it. And almost relaxed, at times. As relaxing as a holiday can be, with a healthy fear of the peril two children can get into at the seaside. I've barely thought about work; I've even pushed Vanessa's 'circling back' emails about where I am with my donor activity and 'particularly Lucas Caulfield' out of my head. I've been ordered to ensure he agrees to a summer meet-up, but I'll deal with that when I get home. It's easier to pretend the target stress and the not-quite-appropriate messages from Lucas don't exist when I'm in a different country.

We bounce along the waves a bit longer before stopping at a spot so far out that the coastline is tiny, far in the distance. I can just about make out the beach we drove to yesterday, spending all day broiling on the sand while Sav dug for shells and Jack hurled himself in and out of the sea. Adam spent approximately a thousand hours patiently playing beach tennis with one child who got pissed off if he lost, and one who could hardly hit the ball but still got pissed off every time she missed. One of those days when I was nostalgic about our family time even as it was happening, knowing they won't want to play games on the beach with us forever. We finished the day pink-faced, sweaty, gritty and exhausted, but despite the endless requests for ice cream and nuclear-orange Fanta, we had fun. As we carried our mounds of towels, sun cream, beach balls and bags back to the car, Adam hooked his hand into mine as though it was the most normal thing in the world. I didn't even realise he'd done it until he let go to unlock the car door.

Two more catamarans from other tour companies pull into view. There's obviously been some sort of alert if they're all congregating in the same place. We bob here for a few minutes, the passengers all scanning different parts of the sea in the hope of spotting something.

'I'm bored,' Jack whines. 'Can I have the iPad?'

I sigh. 'Why would we have brought the iPad on the boat with us—'

'There!' Adam shouts. About twenty metres ahead there's the ghost of a spray. Was it a dolphin or a lapping wave?

'Where?' says someone else in the boat, just as a pod of four dolphins leap out to the left of us, only a few feet away.

A dozen phones are fixed on them, and the only thing that can be heard above the collective coos of this magical moment is Sav asking for another snack.

*

'So then did you have to do a wee on Mummy's leg?'

Adam is regaling the kids with the time I got stung by a jellyfish in Thailand. Obviously, they have no interest in the fact that I was in immense pain.

'No,' Adam laughs. 'We were near a café, so we got some vinegar.'

'You're supposed to wee on it!' Jack hoots.

'You don't *have* to wee on it – that's just that one episode of *Friends*.'

'I didn't wee on Mummy,' Adam reiterates.

'No one weed on anyone.'

Sav yawns, almost falling asleep into her unfinished ice cream. A sign of exhaustion if ever there was one. She'd never normally leave any pudding. Our last meal of the holiday, and we're all knackered and delirious from a week of constant activity and late nights. Bedtime has gone completely out of the window and the kids have been falling into bed when we do. Not exactly conducive to any alone time but conducive to letting go of the daily grind, which is what we needed; a break from the rigidity and routine.

Adam asks for the bill, while I make a futile attempt to clear up some of the breadcrumbs and dinner debris littered in a splash zone around our table. It's our third time here and we've claimed El Menaje as our favourite restaurant in Mallorca, through the combination of its cute decor, no stag dos, and the family that run it not minding when our children – along with all the others in the place – hurtle around their patio while waiting for the food to come. It's also located on the top of a cliff with a view over the sea.

'Come on then,' Adam says, having paid. He picks up Sav for the walk back down the hill.

Jack runs ahead, poking into hedges and peering into cracks in the walls before shouting, 'Lizard!' every time he spots one.

'What do you reckon – shall we get these into bed and stay up for a drink on the balcony?' Adam asks, shifting Sav's weight from one side of his body to the other. 'Won't be able to do this much longer,' he adds, looking down at Sav's head as we amble along. 'But you probably won't want me to carry you when you're a big girl anyway.'

'I will,' she says sleepily.

'OK then. I'll carry you up to collect your university diploma when you graduate, if you want me to.' Sometimes comments like this – about the future, about my children growing up, about things that might happen fifteen years away – make tears spring to my eyes. This is one of those times. I can't work out if it's nostalgia for a childhood that isn't even over yet, or because I don't know if Adam and I will be sitting side by side at that graduation ceremony. I quickly lift my sunglasses and swipe at my eyes. Sav is absent-mindedly tugging on Adam's hair, the way she used to for comfort when she was settling down to sleep as a baby. Adam's forehead is all red, the result of a week sweating off his own suntan lotion while running after two kids to make sure they're covered. I've got two-tone arms from when we ran out of factor thirty by the pool and I grabbed the kids' nothing-will-shift-it factor fifty to finish my shoulders. The creases around Adam's eyes have also got tan lines. Paler in the crinkles where he's been squinting into the sun. But aside from the patchy tan, he looks good. I fancy him, I think, something I haven't thought about in ages because I've been so busy wondering if I like him or if I can forgive him, but that I realise now is important. He's in a thin white shirt and tailored shorts, and his hair has got a bit longer which suits him, especially lightened a little by the sun. He catches me checking him out and I quickly turn away, my face burning red even beneath the bloom of sunburn on my cheeks.

When we get back to the apartment, the tiled floors are covered in a week's worth of sand from the beach but they're still blissfully cool. We all kick off our shoes the second we walk in the door, and Adam carries Sav straight into the kids' bedroom. 'Jack,' he whispers, 'you need to come now too and be quiet.'

I know Jack must be knackered when he puts up no argument about being older so should be allowed to stay up later. Instead, he follows his dad zombie-like into the room.

I grab two glasses and a bottle of white wine from the fridge and head out to the balcony, moving semi-dried swimming trunks and costumes from the backs of the plastic chairs. The resort has been busy all week, but they've designed it well enough so the tiny balconies give enough privacy to not feel like you're sitting outside with all your neighbours.

I pour myself a glass and sit back into the chair, enjoying its cold bite as I take a sip, and looking out across the horizon. There are still a few stalwarts sitting by the pool, eking out the last few rays before the sun sets. Brits, probably. According to Fran, it's pissing down back home and everyone is going mental cooped up in her house. Actually, her exact words were, 'I'm three episodes of *Bing* away from faking my own death.'

Adam wordlessly appears at the patio door. He's doing the exaggerated tiptoeing walk of someone who's aware he could get called back by a lone 'Daaaaddy' at any second.

'That was quick,' I say, as he softly pulls the sliding door shut as far as possible, while still allowing us to hear any rogue cries from inside.

'They're completely exhausted. Even Jack had no fight in him tonight.'

'A full week of spending eight hours a day swimming and going to bed no earlier than 9 p.m., that's *all* it takes to tire our son out. Who knew?'

We both laugh as Adam's phone buzzes. Instinctively I tense up.

He checks his messages, a surprised look on his face.

'It's Gabe,' he says. 'He got that job.'

'God, your mum must be thrilled,' I reply. 'And I mean, obviously well done to Gabe too.'

'Christ knows what the other candidates must have been like,' he adds with a wry look, tapping out a reply.

'I wasn't going to be the one to say that,' I say, and we laugh again. I pour Adam a drink.

'Congrats to Gabe, and cheers.' We clink our glasses together and lapse into silence, watching the sun set and the sun-lounger stalwarts collect up their towels. An easy moment. I've been so fixated on the parts of our relationship we've been told need to change that it's made me question the familiar parts. Not everything needs to change, and hanging out with Adam on a slightly-better-than-budget-holiday balcony drinking wine while our children sleep is one of those things.

'It's been good, hasn't it?' His voice interrupts my thoughts, but there's an uncertainty in it that makes it more of a question than a statement, as though he can't commit until he knows what I'm thinking.

'It has,' I agree. 'Hasn't it?' Now he wants confirmation from me, I'm suddenly unsure.

'I promise you, there is nowhere I would rather be than here with you and the children. It was stupid, *so* stupid—'

I cut him off. 'I don't want to talk about it – her – now. Let's keep this week about us.' I mean it. This week has been a safe space. Just us, as a family, recalibrating our time together with as little of the outside world as possible. Also, that was the one good thing about having to book a cheap and cheerful airline. At least coming with easyJet, I knew for sure that my husband's former mistress wouldn't be flying the bloody plane, because she works for a prestige carrier.

The balcony is so small that our knees are almost touching as we sit side by side. There's probably less than two centimetres in it, and I have an overwhelming urge to bridge the gap. Adam's arm is resting on his chair, the wine glass in his other hand. I think of our session with Esther where we talked about sex. We're still cautious around each other physically, and it's aeons since we've touched properly, deliberately. Slowly, tentatively, I rest my knee against his, apprehensive that he'll take it as a request for more space and move his away. But he doesn't. There's a slight build-up of pressure as he pushes back gently on the side of my knee with his. We sit like that for a minute. I'm too nervous to move at all and he's stopped drinking from his glass. He's too still to be comfortable. We both are. Still looking in the direction of the pool, he moves his hand from his own armrest to mine, gently resting his fingers on top of mine. My heart is pounding as though I'm on my first ever date, and the palm of my hand on the plastic armrest is clammy. I can feel the heat radiating from him into the tops of my fingers.

'Iris.' We finally look at each other. There's a shift in energy, but his eyes are a question. I understand. It has to come from me.

Gently, I take the wine glass from his hand and put both of them on the rickety balcony table, resisting every urge to be sensible and carry them, plus the half-full bottle, back inside to stop them getting warm and/or full of flies. I pull him up by the hand and lead him back through the balcony doors, one ear out for the children interrupting the moment with an ill-timed cry for attention, half hoping one of them will, because I'm scared. There are so many thoughts jostling for attention inside my head, number one being that the last time Adam had sex it was with no-strings Jules and her Instagram body. Close behind is the memory of the last time Adam and I had sex, which I think was in November but can't be sure. It wasn't that memorable. Not to say it was bad. Rather, two people who know how to get each other off efficiently, but with the pressure of several other deadlines to juggle along with the semi-regular sex-life box to tick. That attitude isn't going to cut it tonight. This needs our full attention, time to be taken, desires to be nurtured . . . but it's also faintly absurd to pretend we're characters in the soft-focus, power ballad soundtracked sex scene of an eighties movie.

As we get into our bedroom – which is in complete chaos having half packed for our flight tomorrow morning, with piles of dirty laundry lining the floor – Adam presses the door closed and then pulls me in for a hug that whips my breath from me. It's somehow more intimate than the sex we used to have even before the kids, when we could take as long and be as loud as we liked.

'I've missed you,' he murmurs, his head buried in my hair. I concentrate on his warm, soft breath. His touch, which over the years has made me feel at different times weak-kneed or safe.

'I've missed you too,' I reply. I have, but I don't want this to turn into a tender heart-to-heart. That's not what we need right now. This moment has to blow our minds. Really quietly, so we don't wake up the children. I start undoing his shirt, my fingers clumsily missing the buttons. In the end, Adam tugs his shirt over his head and then slides down the straps of my sundress, kissing me across the shoulder as he works the zip at the back. It sticks. It always sticks, but it's not usually this urgent for me to get it off. He patiently pulls it up and then tries again, more slowly. Meanwhile I'm undoing his shorts, and gently scratching my nails along the small of his back the way I know he's always liked.

'You're so beautiful, Iris,' he tells me, dragging his hand through my hair before stroking the fabric of my dress down so I'm standing in front of him only in my pants. He looks at me. *Really* looks at me. And starts tracing his hands along the contours of my body, starting at the top of my shoulders and working his way down, skimming my boobs and my hips and the top of my thighs. I go to take his shorts off, but he stops me.

'No. Let me concentrate on you first.'

It's cheesy, but I'm so turned on I'm embarrassed. With my own husband. But my mind is straying to Jules, to what they might have done together, to the bad place that makes me want to halt this now and run away. I can't let the doubt in. Not if I want to rescue a part of our relationship that was important to me, to us, before all of this happened. I'm too young for companionship or a sexless relationship. I want to be *desired.* And I want to have sex with my husband. I silence my inner doubting voice by sheer force of will and try to channel Sharon Stone, or Samantha Jones, or anyone who can deliver a femme fatale line without laughing, the words rushing around my head and building up to a pep talk.

You know what he likes. You can tell him what you like. Use it to your benefit. Be assertive, Iris.

Stepping out of the puddle of my dress, I push him back onto the bed and sweep another pile of washing out of the way.

'Stop talking,' I say.

Maybe we should have the soundtrack of an eighties power ballad after all.

Chapter Thirty-Two

9 August

The new tapas restaurant on the high street is all distressed tables, tasteful succulents and fairy lights that hang from the exposed crockery shelves. It smells deliciously of garlic, paprika and lightly frying sardines – ideal for an attempt to recreate the Spanish buzz from our holiday – but right now we're too wound up to enjoy any of it, instead staring intently at the menu and trying to decompress from the act of trying to leave the house.

Dad was supposed to be babysitting, but when I called to get his ETA on the way back from school holiday club he said I'd never asked him – another dropped ball on my part – so then he was late and harassed when he finally arrived. Then, the kids had a sixth sense we were trying to ditch them so proceeded to behave as badly as possible to try and thwart us. The stressed-out energy meant we almost didn't come, and now we feel guilty that we're here.

'Wine,' I say as a statement, catching Adam's eye.

'Yes,' he replies, flagging the waiter and knowing without asking me that this is a bottle rather than a mindful glass situation. It arrives quickly, and we both give a fixed impatient smile as the waiter goes through the rigmarole of showing us the label and letting one of us taste it. I'm practically rocking with anticipation by the time he's finished and we both take a grateful swallow. Wine as a parental relaxant is a cliché, but it's a cliché for a reason.

'You look great,' Adam tells me.

I blush a bit. I'm in the green shift dress from our first date, which I fit into again; a bittersweet victory because after two kids and ten years, it's the stress weight loss of this year that has got me into it.

I don't tell him any of this. 'Thank you.'

'How are you?' Adam asks, giving me a tired smile.

'You sound like Esther,' I reply. 'Between the general burning-bin state of the world, the work stuff and the school holiday juggle . . .' I always feel Mum's absence more keenly when I can't rely on her for childcare. The kids are seeing this summer through with a combination of holiday club, favours called in with other parents, and a mish-mash of annual leave Adam and I are taking separately. 'Plus, I haven't heard anything from Nat since she had the baby.' Marnie was born while we were on holiday, but since the round-robin birth announcement she's been totally silent; to me at least. It's not so long ago that I can't remember those newborn days – having acres of time each day yet without any time to do anything, a phone charger at the opposite side of the room when you're trapped on the sofa under a feeding baby with one per cent battery – but it's off somehow. She hasn't even responded to my asking to come and visit them both at some point when they're settled, and we never did sort out that pre-birth meet-up. I sigh. 'Then that scene at home. I'd say I'm definitely tense . . . How about you?'

'About the same.' He eyes his phone warily, which is resting on the table next to mine, primed to be swiped up if Dad decides he can't cope with wrestling the kids to bed. 'I'm struggling to keep track of where the kids are supposed to be on a given day, and I'm already worried about Sav going back to school even though it's not for another month. Plus, I haven't heard from Mum about Gabe all week, which is making me more stressed rather than less.' Gabe started at Proctors this week, and it's as though we've both been waiting for the fallout ever since. Holding our breath until he does something to mess it up. 'I've also had to turn BBC news alerts off, because every time one comes up it's something else that makes me anxious.'

Adam briefly looks down at the menu and then back up again. His voice is hesitant. 'Where do you think I – we – are on the burning-bin scale right now?'

'Right this second, I think *we* are the least burning-bin thing in our lives,' I say, meaning it. 'Eight months into our year, and I feel like we might be getting somewhere, Adam. It made me want to celebrate our anniversary this year.'

Adam grins. 'Well, one of them anyway.'

I couldn't get a sitter for our actual wedding anniversary – 1 August, the same as our first date – but tonight is the anniversary of our other 'first', which happened a week later, when I went back to Adam's neat bedroom in a Shoreditch flat-share, where he lived with Calum and their other friend 'Webbo' at the time. There were enough furniture flourishes to indicate that they gave a shit about their surroundings; the only red flag was a giant glass bong on the coffee table, which Adam assured me belonged to Calum, who probably still has it. The sex was . . . well, it was OK. The first time, anyway, when we were both overly horny and overly nervous so performed rather than participated. It was probably the second, or maybe the third time – which took place over that same night – when we clicked, relaxed, enjoyed it. *Well, for the next ten years.* I inwardly berate myself for being negative. At the moment, things are good. We've even had sex twice more since Mallorca, which in Fran's words is 'twice more than she had with Liam in the six months before he got his vasectomy'. She's taking no chances when it comes to future family planning, seeing as last time she accidentally signed up for a BOGOF.

'I'm glad we came here,' I say, looking around. 'I've wanted to try it for ages.' We used to be the type of people who did things. We looked at *Time Out*, made a note of its cool new restaurant suggestions and then actually went to some of them. These days I pick one up from a vendor outside the tube station and flick through it on the way to work, with rising anxiety about the never-ending amount of *stuff* in the world I'll never have time to experience. The closest I've got to doing something zeitgeisty in recent times was the pop-up bar with Lucas. The not-date. 'Let's order too much food for us to feasibly eat.'

'Yes.' He busies himself examining the menu again, and I do the same. The waiter comes over to light the candle in a wax-covered Rioja bottle that punctuates the space between us on the rickety round table.

'OK,' Adam says decisively. 'Patatas bravas are a given. And then meatballs, gambas, something chorizo-y, plus some token veg.'

'Yep, and let's have calamari, croquettes and pimientos de Padrón. And then let's see.'

Satisfied, we close our menus. The tension lifts now we've chosen our food. My shoulders relax a bit and I take another sip of my wine, less like I'm hoping for it to anaesthetise me.

My phone vibrates and we both look down, tensing as we prepare for the word 'Dad' to light up my screen. But it doesn't. All the breath leaves my body as I see a Messenger notification from Julianne Shepherd.

Jules.

Chapter Thirty-Three

Iris,

I've agonised about sending this message, because when I saw your request on Facebook I didn't know what you wanted from me: an apology or the truth. But I realise now that you deserve both. Adam told me you knew about the five months we were together last year and that he came clean to you, but I wonder if you know he was going to leave you? I'd want to know if I were you. After all, if your marriage was so great, he wouldn't have cheated to start off with, would he? Who knows how many lies he's told you before or since. I'm sorry it happened behind your back, but I'm also sorry if you've been led to believe it was nothing. Adam was the best thing in my life when I was 17 and I genuinely thought he could be again, but I can at least thank him for making sure I never make the mistake of looking back again. He lied to both of us. Maybe this message will help you decide if you want to leave him in the past too.

Jules

Adam's face is stricken with panic. I see it as I throw my full glass of wine at him.

'YOU PIECE OF SHIT!' I screech, as the waiter appears next to the table, his jolliness evaporating when he clocks the liquid dripping down Adam's face and white shirt. Adam sits there, letting it.

'I'll give you another minute,' says the waiter tactfully. He withdraws, no doubt to consult with his colleagues about whether they let us play out whatever this is here or ask us to leave.

I can't think for the roaring sound in my head. *What what what what what what.*

'What the fuck, Adam?'

'I swear I have no idea why she's messaging you.' Each word is a stutter, as though he can't get the syllables out quick enough. He wipes at the wine running into his eyes, squinting at me as it's obviously stinging. Good. 'I haven't spoken to her for months, not since I told her I couldn't contact her again. What does she say?'

I shove my phone under his face. 'Read it.' He looks at it as though it's a loaded gun. It is. And the target is our marriage. 'Or shall I read it to you? "Iris,"' I begin, before he snatches it, his hand quivering. I'm shaking with fear and rage. I want to see what his face does as he reads, so I look at him, on high alert for an involuntary twitch or clenching of the jaw that would indicate he's having to suppress how he really feels. But all I get is a widening of the eyes followed by pursed lips. He puts it back in front of me wordlessly.

'Anything to say?'

Adam exhales deeply. 'I think we've already established that I'm the baddie, but at least this proves I ended it with her. I haven't been in touch with her. But it looks like you have.'

'That's your main takeaway, is it?' There's another rush of nausea. How did he break it to her? What did he say when he broke it off? Was there longing and regret, or just a cold goodbye? 'Yes, I –' OK Fran, but we don't have time for that now – 'friend-requested her on Facebook. I wanted to ask if she'd been in touch with you. Whether you responded or not.'

Guilt passes over Adam's face – briefly, but it's definitely there. 'She's sent me a couple of emails before now. But not for ages and I've never replied.'

'You could have blocked her. I told you to block her.'

We both look at his phone. I'm itching to snatch it and then scroll through every single email folder he has, before contacting the server and asking them to recover everything he's deleted from the past year. I want evidence, I want facts, while at the same time I want more than anything to take his word for it. But I can't, so here we are.

'You're not even going to address it?' I ask. 'It says here, "he was going to leave you".'

His expression immediately becomes one of desperation. 'I told you I'd thought about it.'

'When?'

'After our first therapy session. When we had that fight in Sainsbury's.'

'You said you'd thought about it, not that you'd told *her* you were going to.'

'But I didn't. Leave you. Did I?'

'Why not?' I point to another sentence on the screen, where Jules has depth-charged to the crux of it all; hit upon the murmur that is forever in my ear, even when Adam is assuring me there's no place he'd rather be than with me and the kids.

If your marriage was so great, he wouldn't have cheated to start off with, would he?

'What if she's right?'

He looks at me straight in the eye, more intensely than he's done all year. 'Maybe she was,' he says, and fear slides down my spine.

The roar in my head becomes a blast. He's finally said it. 'Well, that's it then, isn't it?' I say, slumping into my chair, my voice becoming a whisper. 'It's done,' I repeat.

'What I mean is—'

From the corner of my eye, I see the poor waiter tentatively start to approach again, pad in hand, obviously taking the quiet for some sort of truce rather than a defeat. 'Are you ready to order?' His face is kind and concerned, and it's about all I can do not to burst into tears.

'No, I'm leaving,' I decide. I stand up and grab my phone, my bag. The restaurant, formerly so cosy and kitsch, is smothering me. 'I'm so sorry,' I say to the waiter, extreme politeness a habit, but the words are dry and dusty in my mouth. 'My husband will pay for the wine. I have to go.' In that moment, it's very important the waiter doesn't think I'm crazy. In case I need witnesses, for the custody hearing my imagination has already jumped forward to.

I've tried, I think. I've tried so hard, but how many times am I supposed to be humiliated? Tears are coming as I think about it, and I shoulder-barge another couple as I turn to leave. 'Sorry, sorry.' Then Adam is getting up too, pulling his wallet out, but I'm ahead of him, weaving through the parties of people arriving here to enjoy a carefree Friday night meal out.

'Shit, I don't have any cash,' I hear him say behind me. 'Take what you need from there. Contactless. My card's in there. Add a good tip.' His voice gets fainter as I speed up.

In the street, the sun is still out. It's nearly eight o'clock and the bright light and street noise seem like an affront to the moment; the restaurant I'll never be able to walk past again without thinking, *That's the place my marriage ended*. There are people outside the pub next door enjoying a summertime pint, their lives blissfully un-torpedoed. I shuffle past in the direction of our house, without wanting to go back there. I can't face Dad, *the kids*, right now. What will I tell them? *How* will I tell them?

Then Adam grabs my arm. 'Iris, stop. You didn't give me a chance to finish talking.'

'What else is there to say?' My voice is as cold as I can make it and I won't meet his eye, won't let him take any more of me. I keep moving, twisting to get his hand off me as I do.

'Everything. There's everything.' The pub-goers are spread across the pavement. I step through them, laughs and wisps of chat puncturing the air between us. 'Please listen, *please*. What I was trying to say was that maybe at *that* moment, our marriage wasn't as happy as it had been. Or as it could be again.' Adam's voice is soft and imploring. The peripheral noise is drowning him out. 'Can we go somewhere quieter and sort this out?' I don't say or do anything, but he takes that as assent, guiding me through the foot traffic until we turn onto a side street only minutes from our house. I slow down, but something is preventing me from stopping completely. Pride, adrenaline, both.

'I did think about leaving,' he says. 'The freedom to start again with someone I hadn't had the same old arguments with a thousand times before, and had built up in my head as this perfect woman.'

'Stop it, just stop it. It makes me feel sick. I don't want to hear about it any more.' It was bad enough hearing about how they ended up having sex in that session with Esther, without dragging it up all over again.

'No, listen, please. Then you sent that message saying you were going to see a solicitor and it hit home. Big time. I was frightened. I realised what I had to lose and what "freedom" would mean. I wanted my kids. I wanted my imperfect marriage. The marriage that was now saying it might not want me. So I cut her off. And you and I decided to try, to go to the counselling, and every month that has become more and more obviously the best decision I've made for a long time.'

He looks at me as though that explains it, but I still can't believe what I'm hearing. 'My split-second decision to see a divorce lawyer all those months ago was your wake-up call? What if I hadn't?'

He doesn't say anything.

'You'd have been willing to chuck away a decade of marriage for a five-month fling? You were going to leave me.'

'But I didn't. It quickly became about much more than me being worried I'd end up as a weekend dad who doesn't know what's happening in his kids' lives. I got to know more about *you*, and I wanted to make you happy again. As well as live up to being the kind of person who could make you happy. Isn't that what matters?'

Fucked if I know. Does he really want to start a debate about intentions versus deeds? I finally stop moving and look at him. 'I don't know what we do now. You can't tell me I'm not allowed to be upset about this.'

'I'm not telling you that. I wouldn't. But it's in the past. It's what happens here and now that matters.'

'It's not in the past for me. I only just found out,' I retort. 'It's not nothing.'

'Then what is it?'

I look away, down the street, as though the answer might emerge from one of the shutter-clad bay windows lining the road.

An elderly man rounds the corner and then starts to cross the road ahead of us, before seeming to change his mind and climbing back onto the pavement. His odd movements get my attention, even before the jolt of recognition.

'Dad!' I shout, starting to walk again, away from Adam and towards him. 'Where are the kids? Were you coming to get us?' He turns towards me, and as I get close I see his eyes are cloudy with confusion. 'Dad, what are you doing out here?'

'Iris?' His hands reach for me, his fingers worrying at my arm as he makes contact. 'Is that you? I don't know how to get home, Iris. I don't know where I am.'

Chapter Thirty-Four

13 August

The smell hits me, along with a building sense of dread, the second Dad opens the door to his and Mum's house. As I steel myself to go in, I calculate how long it's been since I was last here.

I've been dropping him off from ours pretty regularly over the past few months. But inside? It was probably last year, maybe before Christmas. Before Mum got ill, we came here every fortnight for Sunday lunch, but without her as the glue to hold us together, I've neglected to visit, preferring to get Dad over to ours where I'm not surrounded by memories of Mum all the time. The thought smacks me in the face along with the smell: fifty miles away from us, Dad's been quietly getting on with living without his wife of fifty years, not wanting to make a fuss. Not wanting to bother us. And he hasn't been able to cope.

Adam is beside me, holding the comically big suitcase we got as part of a set years ago but have never used, because it's an excess baggage charge waiting to happen. He fetched it from the loft especially and insisted on taking the day off work with me so that, once we'd taken the kids to holiday club, we could come here together and sort Dad out with a few bits while we work out what's going on. We never finished the conversation about Jules, about our divorce. The pause button was pressed the second we found Dad wandering around confused in the street. The smell is worse in the dim hallway that never did get enough light. I'm almost afraid to turn the light on. Adam catches my eye.

'Terry, why don't I come upstairs with you and help you get some stuff packed?' he says tactfully. 'Iris can see what's what in the kitchen.' He guides Dad up the stairs, leaving me to locate the source of the smell. It doesn't seem to be one thing; it's everywhere. Fusty and fungal a million miles from the overpowering floral plug-ins Mum was keen on. I see one of them, long empty, on the floor. I press on, past the door to the living room and through to the kitchen.

I want to weep when I see Mum's beloved sanctuary. Plates everywhere, some with beans or porridge concreted on, and mugs speckled with mould. The bin is overflowing and there's another full binbag tied up next to it. The bottom is split, and liquid trickles out onto the tiles. There's dust ingrained into the grease on the hob and dried-on spills covering the worktops. It's filthy. It's heartbreaking. Dad's not lazy. He's always taken pride in his house, refusing to pay people to fix things he knew he could deal with himself. So this is not right. It's a snapshot of a man who can't cope, or can't see what needs to be done any more.

I barely know where to start.

I wrinkle my nose again. With the bin. I feel marginally better once I've taken it out and opened the windows, even though bin juice has dripped onto my jeans. Maybe if I wash up, the smell will subside a bit. I check the cupboard under the sink but there's no washing-up liquid, then remember that Mum always used to bulk buy from Costco.

The under-stairs cupboard is the jackpot, where I find washing-up liquid, dishwasher tablets, fresh scourers, and even some of her plug-ins from a shop she must have done before everything. With the taps running scalding hot water, I start separating the dishes into ones that need pre-washing and ones that can go straight into the dishwasher, although when I open the door, I realise there's already a full unwashed load in there. I stick it on and move through the house, collecting mugs and plates while picking up discarded leaflets and bits of dropped food from the floor.

The living room isn't as dirty as the kitchen, more neglected. Dust flies off the heavy Laura Ashley curtains as I open them, and yellowing free newspapers are piled up next to the telly. Bills and letters lie unopened on the heavy sideboard, some with angry red FINAL DEMAND stamps on them. I sweep them all into a carrier bag to deal with back at home, and for a moment I close my eyes tightly against what's in front of me. I'm hoping the view will have changed when I open them, but it hasn't. This is in no way the quick clothes pick-up we thought it was going to be. I hear Dad and Adam moving around upstairs and perch on the corner of the settee. I don't think I can face going up there. God only knows what state the bathroom will be in.

Mum would be horrified, and even though I had no idea what state their house was in I'm ashamed that I've let it get this bad. The Mum part of me is also too embarrassed to get a professional cleaner in to sort it out. She wouldn't want that. We'll have to do the deep clean ourselves.

The thought of Jules's message slides into my head unbidden.

We.

Or *I*?

'Iris?' Adam calls from the stairs. I come out to meet him, and I can see from the look of alarm on his face that he's as shocked by the house's deterioration as I am. 'We've packed your dad's clothes,' he says, before dropping to a quiet, urgent voice. 'Are you OK? I think we need to come back and do a tidy up.' He comes to the bottom bannister and reaches over, giving my arm a quick squeeze. A tiny shot of warmth and pressure before he pulls his hand away again. How strange to have such an intimate moment in the midst of something so shitty. The memory of it lingers on my skin after he's pulled away.

My brain reacts reflexively. *He stayed. He's here.*

Is that enough?

I breathe out a big shaky sigh. 'It's pretty bad down here,' I say. 'I should make a start on it while you get Dad back to ours. I'll come back on the train later.'

'I can stay and help if you need me.'

Do I need him? I don't have time for philosophical questions so I shift into practical mode.

'I think it might upset Dad to see the extent of it. Also, I think I should go and see the new next-door neighbours, tell them what's going on.' The old neighbours, Suzanne and Paul, downsized a year ago having lived here for forty-odd years. They were good friends of my parents and would have kept an eye on Dad if they'd still been around.

'I think that's everything for now.' Dad comes down the stairs, clutching his leather washbag from Debenhams. Everything in this house could have come out of a time capsule from my youth, and the longing is stabbing at my insides. I scrutinise him as he descends. He's a little shakier on his legs, definitely grasping the bannister more tightly than he used to, but overall he seems physically fine.

'We can always come back if you've forgotten something,' Adam says.

Dad nods. 'Your mother should be down in a sec.'

Adam and I lock eyes and freeze. 'What?'

My tone of voice seems to reset something and the look on Dad's face is fresh raw grief. His voice quavers. 'Sorry . . . I forgot for a second.'

'It's all right, Terry, I do that too. I expect Mary to walk in any second whenever I'm here,' Adam says, saving the moment. A surge of appreciation rushes through me. 'It's hard not to with the way she used to rule the roost here, isn't it?' he adds. Dad nods, his eyes swimming with tears or confusion or maybe a combination of the two. 'Iris says she wants to do a spruce up before she leaves, so I thought we could go for a pub lunch on the way home and meet her there – what do you think?'

Dad turns to face the living room door, but doesn't go in. There's a tiny twitch next to his left eye and he takes a deep breath, setting his jaw before that look vanishes from his face. Whatever he was thinking, it's gone.

Chapter Thirty-Five

20 August

'I told you this would be a great place for a picnic.'

Lucas is lounging on the checked blanket that has been laid out by the staff, an empty plate that was previously loaded with smoked salmon, cream cheese, tiny cucumber sandwiches and mini artisan quiches beside him. The crockery is china, with real glasses on hand for the champagne that was at the bottom of the hamper. We're back in Barking on a glorious summer's day, and after preparing the picnic in a plum spot in the garden, the staff silently withdrew in the way I imagine all 'help' is taught to on large estates. It's like being in *Downton Abbey*, aside from the wireless speaker that's been set up in case we want some music.

'You're right. It is. Thank you so much for the invite.' Vanessa ordered me to come up with an appealing summer invitation for him, but that wasn't my only incentive. Since Jules's message, work has been a welcome distraction. And not just work. Lucas's light-hearted emails have been one too.

The day is thick with heat. Parasols have been erected, and my only task this afternoon is to stay here and hobnob, before joining Lucas on a private walk-through of Victorian art that will be open to the public as of this weekend. Not a bad gig for a Tuesday afternoon, and one that gives me another excuse to put off mine and Adam's therapy appointment until next week. Last week was cancelled due to Dad, but I still cannot face a session disseminating the bomb-shell from Jules. I need some time before I'm expected to 'show empathy for his feelings'.

There's the tiniest wisp of breeze, enough to fragrance the air with the smell of the wildflowers in the house's 'secret garden', but instead of serving as a further relaxant to the idyllic surroundings and easy company, the citrus scent is translated by my synapses into the artificial lemon of the antibacterial spray I used a whole container of at Dad's last week. Six hours to do a superficial clean of the kitchen, bathroom and living room, with a bigger clear-up and clear-out to come. The second I think of Dad, I think of the doctor's appointment we're waiting for. And as soon as I think of that, I think of Adam again. Our holiday seems so long ago; it reminds me that any happiness is fleeting, temporary.

'Are you OK?' Lucas asks, propping himself up on his elbows. He's so relaxed he's literally horizontal. He angles his face towards the sun, linen shirtsleeves rolled up and tanned forearms sticking out. Next to him I'm sitting bolt upright.

'I'm fine,' I say, picking some grapes out of a Waldorf salad and popping one into my mouth, hoping it doesn't stick in my throat on the way down.

'This was a good idea, Iris, thank you,' he says again, squinting to take in the view.

'You're welcome. We like to look after our VIPs at the Trust, as you know.' I offer a small laugh.

Lucas gives me an inscrutable look. 'So, you're under the Trust's orders to be here, are you?' His tone is light, but there's that undercurrent again. The one I pretend isn't there when it suits me.

'Technically, yes,' I say carefully, 'but it's not as though I'm going to picnics every week.'

He smiles. 'That's good to know. I was hoping I was more than another wallet to keep happy.'

A warm flush spreads across my body.

He clears his throat and looks away, a Hugh Grant-type gesture without being so bumbling. 'What I mean to say is, I've enjoyed meeting you, Iris. I hope this isn't too awkward, but you've told me you're separated from your husband, so I was wondering where that put you in terms of dating. I'd like to see you again, and not just at locations you've arranged for us to visit through your job.'

So many contrasting emotions are battering into each other, but I'm not saying anything, so the moment stretches out into an uncomfortable silence. Right now is when I should be saying thanks but no thanks because – surprise! – I'm not separated, not yet anyway, even though I've let him think that's the case. But I'm not. And the longer the silence goes on, the more I realise it's not purely because I don't want my rejection of him to impact on any potential financial contribution he might make to the Trust this year.

Lucas's expression is morphing between embarrassment and concern as to why I look like I've received some very bad news, rather than the offer of a posh cocktail in the Shard (which is where I assume millionaires take you on dates). 'Sorry, sorry,' he mutters, 'I've overstepped the mark. Put you on the spot. I shouldn't have . . . I don't meet many people – women – that I connect with. I just thought that you . . . I was getting a vibe.'

He's trying so hard to be nice that I feel even worse.

'No, no, honestly. The thing is, I'm very flattered . . . it's just . . . I'm not separated, at the moment.'

Lucas's eyes bulge out of his head and he sits up sharply. 'But you said before – back at Chatterstone.'

I take a deep breath as I'm speared with shame. 'I did, yes.' Not to mention all the deflections and misdirections I gave so I could enjoy some ego-boosting attention, without technically doing anything wrong. Technically. 'It's all such a mess,' I say. 'My husband and I have been having . . . issues this year, which we're trying to work through, but I don't know if we can. I didn't mean to mislead you in any way.' Another half-truth – OK, an out-and-out lie, but a necessary one. 'I haven't even told any of my colleagues what's going on at home.' That bit is true, even if Sophie's shit Miss Marpling means she knows something is up. 'We *were* separated, for a while' – sorry, Adam – 'so if I've given you the impression it's just me and the kids, it's because there's a part of me trying it on for size.'

It occurs to me that Lucas could get nasty. Rejected men sometimes lash out. There's every chance he could put in a complaint about me at work as a reaction against his bruised ego, and there's no way I can start talking to him about percentage increases in his donation now.

He gives an embarrassed laugh and looks everywhere but at me. 'Typical,' he says. 'I've been doing a lot of app dating over the last year or two, but it's pretty soul-destroying at times. My sister told me I should be proactive when it comes to meeting women in real life. She met her now-husband in the queue for a taxi during a tube strike.' He catches my raised eyebrow. 'I know, it's like a

Richard Curtis movie, sickening. Anyway, she thinks it's all about grabbing opportunities, and when I met you, I thought that might be one of those things.'

I can't help it. It gives me a little buzz that he's definitely interested in me. Options. I have options.

'Under other circumstances, it would be, but at the moment . . .' I leave the sentence hanging; it ends on an inflection. A question rather than a statement. A moment passes.

'So you're back together?' he asks. His persistence is attractive, but then, you don't get to be a rich venture capitalist without developing an instinct for knowing when to persevere and when to walk away. Lucas can obviously sense that with me it may not be cut and dried.

'Sort of. We're in therapy, and we're giving ourselves until the end of this year to see where the chips fall,' I say, trying to ignore how intently he's still looking at me. I take a small sip of champagne to steady myself, but the bubbles leave my head fizzing. 'There were some issues – well, one main one – and we're trying to see if it's ruined or just corroded, by peeling off the layers and seeing what's underneath.' I give a self-deprecating laugh. 'That's the kind of thing you learn to say in marriage therapy.'

Lucas nods, his eyes still on mine.

'I don't know what the issues you're referring to are, but he's a bloody idiot if it's what I think it is.'

'He is,' I reply. My ramrod posture has weakened along with my resolve, my spine curling as I've moved closer to him on the rug; as if while I've widened the emotional distance between us, my body has rebelled and craved being closer to him physically. 'He says it was a mistake,' I blurt out. 'My husband.' Lucas looks at me steadily.

'Everyone makes mistakes,' he replies, his voice cracking a bit. The heat, his voice, the idea of revenge – it's all so seductive.

My blood is pumping. And Lucas's face is now only inches from mine. Less, as he leans a little closer. The line. It's there. Right in front of me.

He was going to leave me, I think again. And: *How come Adam is the only one who gets to make mistakes?*

It's millimetres now. I can imagine Fran telling me to even the score.

At the last moment, I jerk back as though we're two repelling magnets, seeing his look turn from desire to confusion. I feel a spike of disgust. At him, at myself, at the whole situation. This mistake won't cancel out Adam's, just throw another onto the pile. I open my mouth to apologise again, but instead stand up, grab my bag and run.

Chapter Thirty-Six

Transcript of session with Adam and Iris Young by Esther Moran, 27 August

Iris: I'm not exactly sure why we're still coming here. It all seems a bit futile now I know he was going to leave.

Adam: But I didn't. I don't know how many more times I can say it. And also—

Iris: [interrupting] What?

Adam: [exhales] It's something you say, isn't it?

Iris: What do you mean?

Adam: It's something you say when you're [pause] having an affair.

Iris: You were lying to me *and* to her? [mutters] Just when I think it can't get any better.

Adam: I massively fucked up. It's the one thing we can all agree on. But it's like now you know I thought about leaving you're fixated on it. You won't listen to anything else I've been saying. Something I considered – but didn't act upon – *months* ago is somehow more important than how I feel now.

Iris: It's not that easy for me. You might have considered it months ago, but I'm still processing it. When my brain isn't jammed with everything else.

Esther: What else?

Iris: My dad, I'm worried about him. Work stuff . . .

Esther: Is your job still under threat?

Iris: Yes. I'm trying so hard to bring money in, and it's not working, and so much of my job is about relationships and chemistry. It can lead to misunderstandings.

Esther: In what way?

Iris: [pause] It means being constantly 'on', needing people to like me. It can be draining. It can also feel very personal.

Esther: It sounds as though there's a lot.

Iris: But that's it. There's *always* a lot. There's never a time when I can think, 'Right, this week all I need to do is concentrate on my marriage and get things back on track.' This year was supposed to be about us, but how am I supposed to prioritise us when my dad is living in squalor, or when I need to throw myself at my job to avoid losing it? I'm not saying this isn't important, of course it is, but those other things don't go away and they're not *not* important. [starts to cry]

Adam: I'm trying to support you with all of the other stuff, Iris, but after telling me you need me to be there for you, you're now pushing me away. You're the one who's cancelled therapy appointments, not me, and I asked if we could arrange another date night so we could talk alone, but you said no.

Iris: We can't leave Dad with the kids right now, and Fran is overloaded.

Adam: So we ask someone else. Calum has said he'll babysit.

Iris: [snorts]

Adam: Or we pay a babysitter. I know you're worried about redundancy but we can afford it.

Iris: Something always seems to happen when we go out. It's like we're jinxed.

Adam: This is what I mean. You're making excuses, pushing me away.

Iris: I'm not.

Adam: You are!

Esther: Adam, you said you didn't feel as though Iris was listening when you explained how your feelings have changed about leaving your marriage. Why don't you try it again now?

Adam: [deep breath] I can't take back anything I've done, or even anything I've thought, but I hope you can see that I'm taking responsibility for it. And I *have* done a lot of thinking about marriage. I've started to think that it isn't a constant state of happiness.

Iris: So you accept the misery of marriage? That's not a reason to stay together.

Adam: That's not what I said. [sighs] It's not a constant state of happiness and nor does it need to be. It's more like having a baby. You spend a lot of time thinking, 'Why did I sign up for this? I'm knackered, it's relentless, it's too much responsibility.' But when they eventually smile at you or, I don't know, you arrive to pick them up from nursery and they run into your arms, it's a happiness you'd never have known without them. Maybe marriage – a good marriage – is like that. You're not always happier in the moment but your life is better overall. Fulfilled. Even if sometimes you forget that with babies when they're like, teething, and you want to throw them out of a window.

Iris: You were going to throw our marriage out of the window, though.

Adam: Yes, I thought about it. But you would never have known that if she hadn't messaged you, because I never acted on it. You must have thoughts sometimes that you wouldn't want me to find out about. Things you wish you had done or said, or things you wish you hadn't. If Fran emailed me and told me what you've said about me over the years, would it all be positive?

Iris: [defensively] That's not the same. Confiding in my best friend isn't the same as promising to run off with your lover.

Adam: I know, and I'm sorry. But over the past months I've done everything you've asked me to, Iris, and I'm telling you now, I don't want her. I am all in when it comes to saving our marriage, but right now you're the one holding back. It's not enough for you to forgive me, you have to want to be with me too.

Chapter Thirty-Seven

7 September

The gardens at Atherford House look stunning. A gentle sea breeze cuts through the late summer heat hanging in the air, and everywhere I look there are flowers: curled around the iron backs of chairs, festooning the arch a master carpenter created as a bespoke piece for the event, and gathered in wild displays that flank the outdoor aisle. Sav was given a basket of petals when we came in and is giggling as she throws them in the air for Jack to run through. I think the idea is that she waits until the ceremony starts, but the other children here all seem to be doing the same thing and no one is stopping them, so I let her crack on.

There are a fair number of people milling about before Emmett and Viola's vow renewal begins who look like they could be relatives. I've had a few people glance at us with curiosity as we stand towards the back, waiting for others to take their seats so we don't inadvertently end up sitting in the spots reserved for the family. I know they have four children – the eldest is in his late fifties, I think, then two daughters, and the youngest son is about our age.

They also have several grandchildren, including the one who had the controversial cheese wedding cake and has since divorced, I've learned. I try to work out who they are, while occasionally hissing at the kids to get up off the floor. Jack is in black chinos, a white shirt and a jacket, with a tie he has promised Adam he will put on before the ceremony starts. Sav had a meltdown because she wanted to wear her cheap princess fancy dress costume, but I told her she had to wear something that wouldn't make her collapse in the freakishly warm twenty-seven-degree heat. She disagreed, strongly, and is now sweating in said princess dress, because if we hadn't set off when we did we'd have missed the whole thing. We've only come down for the day, not wanting to leave Dad alone overnight, so they're already hot and knackered. They're both back at school in a couple of days, which at this stage of the summer holidays frankly cannot come soon enough, even if my nerves about whether or not Sav will embrace Year One are through the roof.

'I bet that's their son,' I say to Adam, pointing at a man in his forties who is the very picture of Emmett if you knocked forty years off. He's with a little girl wearing a frilly white dress, and an incredibly glamorous-looking woman in a structured blue dress that makes her look both sexy and efficient at the same time.

'The one who lives in Australia?' Adam replies. He's in a grown-up version of Jack's outfit, by which I mean uncrumpled and with his tie on.

'Yes.' I smooth down the front of my dress. It's a mint green, sweetheart-necked fifties prom dress I spotted on eBay a few weeks ago, and I thought Viola would get a kick out of it, but as it's made of taffeta it's about as aerating as Sav's polyester number in today's heat.

I glance over at the children and see Jack try to hurdle the flower-lined aisle. He catches his foot on a neat row of violets, treading them all over the place. Adam leaps into action, scrambling to rearrange them and pulling the kids away. Jack seems to have inspired every other under-ten in the place though, and within seconds children are everywhere as parents jump up to pat down what must be hundreds of pounds' worth of floral artistry.

I check my phone. Again. I sent Lucas an apology by email for ditching him for the second time at a property, but there's been only silence. A hurt ego, or a businessman too hectic to respond now there's no chance of taking our professional relationship any further?

'Surely work can't be asking you to live tweet the ceremony for them?' Adam says, nodding down at my phone while strolling back over with Jack and Sav. Jack doesn't look happy to be leaving the carnage behind.

'What?' Sweat prickles under my arms and on my top lip. I tell myself it's the weather.

'You've been glued to your phone all day. It must be Vanessa, right?'

There's a flutter of movement as some staff members come over and jolly people into their seats. It must be about to start.

'We'd better find somewhere to sit.' I corral him, plus Jack and Sav, to some seats at the back, just as Ella Fitzgerald's 'Let's Fall In Love' starts drifting out of the discreetly concealed speakers. The guests all look around to see Emmett and Viola walking arm-in-arm towards the gardens from the main building; Viola in a cobalt blue, long-sleeved top with a matching floor-length silk skirt and a slick of red lipstick, and Emmett in a light blue suit with his top shirt button undone. As they arrive at the aisle, they start waltzing, waving and nodding at people as they pass. Viola catches my eye and gives me a broad smile, acknowledging Adam and the children with a nod. I smile back, tears immediately pooling in my eyes; happy tears for a couple clearly besotted with each other after sixty years. I think of Dad at our house and wonder if he's OK. He's under strict instructions to use only the microwave and not the hob, and Fran's going to swing by later but I'm still worried. After finally getting him in at the GP's, her referral to the Memory Clinic at the hospital was swift, too swift for it to be nothing.

As the service begins, my tears morph into full-blown sobs; less about Emmett and Viola now, and more for the long retirement my own loved-up parents didn't get to experience together. They just didn't make it that far.

'Mum, stop crying, it's so embarrassing,' Jack says loudly while rolling his eyes. I press my lips together, and Adam produces a tissue and passes it to me. I dab at my eyes, and he slips his hand into mine, giving it a squeeze as we sit down for the vows.

Chapter Thirty-Eight

19 September

It's the way the air smells in here that reminds me most of the hospital appointments with Mum. It's the same place but a different department, so the posters on the hard-wearing beige-painted walls are advertising different charities and helplines, but the way the air settles – too warm and completely still, medicinal while also seeming not quite clean – is exactly the same. The floor is blue marbled lino, the chairs are fixed to the floor in a neat row of four, and there are sanitiser dispensers at regular intervals along the corridors with instructions about good hand hygiene.

Dad is jiggling his leg in nervous anticipation. The appointments are running forty-five minutes behind schedule and we were already here early. I wish Adam was here. He offered to come but I told him not to. I was convinced that this was something I ought to handle myself, but that seems stubborn now. He wanted to support me, and I told him not to.

'She was always getting cross with me, your mother, for losing things,' Dad is saying to me. 'My memory's like a sieve.'

'It is.' I don't want to deflate the Mum-memory moment with a dose of realism. Leaving your packed lunch at home when you're in a rush isn't the same as living in squalor because you can't remember to look after yourself. Absent-mindedly calling your daughter by your wife's name isn't the same as forgetting your daughter has two children of her own, as Dad did earlier this week when I explained I couldn't run him down to the shops because Jack and Sav were both in bed and Adam was at the gym.

'But I'm not forgetting everything. Iris, I wanted to talk to you about me and your mum, and about you and Adam—'

'Terence Phillips.'

Dad grabs my hand as we're called in to see the consultant and I help him up, clinging on to him even once he's steady on his feet.

Dr Shantir is kind but brisk. She's about my age and overworked in the way any NHS employee is, while being mindful that we're anxious and frightened. Her office consists of a rectangular wooden desk and ergonomically designed chair, and the same selection of posters that are in the corridor. A laminate badge dangles around her neck and she's in a smart shirt and trousers rather than a white coat. As she examines Dad's file in front of her, I try to gauge from her expression how bad the news will be.

'I'm going to have you complete a memory test, Terence.'

'I've already done one of those,' Dad fires back gruffly.

'I know, at the GP's. This is another one, if you wouldn't mind doing it again. It's more in-depth so will take a little longer.'

I nod encouragingly at them both, trying to cajole Dad into doing it, and into getting on the right side of the doctor. As though pushing Dad into being the model patient will have any impact on the result.

'Once we've done that, I can decide if you need any further tests. Sometimes it's worthwhile to get an MRI scan before diagnosis. On that note, my first question is: would you like to know your diagnosis?'

We must both look a bit surprised. 'That's why we're here,' I say.

She gives us a quick smile. 'Some people prefer not to know. Of course, in terms of being able to plan and managing your symptoms as much as is possible, knowing your diagnosis is helpful.'

I turn to look at Dad. 'It's up to you, Dad.'

He looks very old sitting in the chair, and sagging, as though the weight of the decision is bearing down on him.

'Yes,' he says quietly. 'I think it's for the best we find out. My wife passed away last year and that was all very quick. Too quick.' He swipes roughly at his eyes as the fleeting image of my mum in the hospice, her breathing laboured, trying to communicate something to us when she could no longer speak, flashes through my mind. 'But because we knew roughly how long we had left with her, we got the chance to talk through her wishes before she was too far gone to tell us. I'd like Iris to have the same opportunity with me, so she knows—' He stops, and my heart does too. How the doctor holds it together on a daily basis I have no idea. Dad clears his throat and starts again. 'Before I'm no longer capable of telling her what I want, I'd like to be able to work it all out.'

'Of course.' Dr Shantir pulls some materials from a folder beside her. 'We'll start with the memory test.'

They begin with an activity involving a clock where Dad has to place the hands at quarter past ten. My stomach twists into the knot of apprehension I get when I see Sav struggling with a task; torn between wanting to rush over and sort it out for her and knowing intellectually that I have to let her try, and even fail, by herself. Dad starts confidently, placing the hour hand at ten, but then quickly starts to look distressed when his fingers hover over the minute hand.

'If you'd prefer to have it as a digital unit, it's ten fifteen,' Dr Shantir says gently.

Dad nods, his face a picture of gravity, and he goes to place it again, faltering as he does.

Dad frowns. 'I'm not sure.' He looks up at me, the minute hand at the three. 'Is this right?' he asks in a small voice. It's all I can do to give him a tiny nod, and he places it down, relief apparent in his entire body language. He thinks he's passed and that's even worse.

Dr Shantir gives me a small, ambiguous smile. 'It's important to let your father complete the tasks on his own.'

'Yes. Of course. Sorry. Is it better if I leave the room?'

'It depends if your father is more comfortable with you here. Terence, should Iris step out?'

I look at Dad and he gives me a slight nod.

'OK,' I say, opening the door and making for the waiting area. I force myself to tune out the thought of Dad struggling through the exercises, and concentrate on my inbox with blurring eyes. I scan through a couple of meetings that have been put in for next week, and automatically check for anything from or about Lucas. Still nothing.

There's an email from Liv, thanking me for my help organising her dad's tree and asking if I fancy going for a coffee sometime.

It would be great to have another mum mate in North London. Thanks so much for your help with Parr

House and Dad's memorial tree. I felt like we clicked at the retreat and I don't think it was just the crystals (and wine) aligning our chakras. Is that weird to say? Not sure of the etiquette of making new friends in my 40s! I hope you're feeling OK about your marriage but if you ever need to talk – divorcee here ✋.

I smile, starting to tap out a reply when a discreet cough interrupts. It's Dr Shantir. She's finished the test.

*

The drive home is mostly silent. Dad's damp-eyed and clutching the leaflets we've been given, while I negotiate the school-run traffic and will myself to think about the task at hand, rather than the bottomless pit of uncertainty that has come with a concrete diagnosis of mild dementia.

I was on autopilot, unconsciously holding on to Dad's hand as the doctor explained what it meant and how the illness would likely progress. Listening without taking it in and without writing any of it down as I'd planned. All I could think about was how it meant I was going to lose Dad too, but twice. First as his memory of us, me, everything, dimmed. Then once the illness had cruelly robbed us of who he was, he'd die. *I want Adam*, I think again.

'If you have any questions at any time, please do get in touch,' Dr Shantir told us, before we left the relative safety of her office to grapple with what we'd been told in the real world.

'We've a lot to sort out,' Dad says in the end. We're stuck in traffic outside the Tesco on Stroud Green Road in Finsbury Park. A busker is playing the blues outside, which with the windows down is adding an even more ominous air to the conversation. It's warm and muggy, humidity hanging in the air. My entire body is clammy and too hot.

'My will is in order, but I need to look into one of those living wills and transfer power of attorney over to you,' Dad is saying. 'I'll need you to make a list of all the things I need to remember to do because I can't be trusted now.' The traffic moves on and I set off again.

'Slow down, Dad. You can be trusted. It's mild, that's what she said.' I know Dad is processing what we've been told in his own pragmatic can't-possibly-leave-a-mess-behind-for-Iris-to-deal-with way, but I don't want to think about this, any of this.

'Mild *now*. Dementia only gets worse. We don't know how quickly it will progress.' I indicate to turn right, desperate to get home, put the kettle on, then ring Adam at work to tell him. There's nothing he can say to make this any better, but I need him to know. I wish again that I'd let him come to start off with. He could have looked out for me while I looked after Dad. I stop to let a bin lorry turn up the street, and we wait, unable to get any further while the men drag wheelie bins over to the truck and empty them.

'One thing I do know is that I can't live with not knowing where I am or who anyone is. Before they can say I'm incapable of making a decision, I want to look into . . . where is it people go? Switzerland?'

The lorry passes, the sour backdraught of rotting food wafting through the windows as I pull out and carry on down the road.

'Please don't talk about that, Dad,' I plead. 'Not now. We're nowhere near that stage, and you could have years before you're that' – I don't even know what the polite phrasing is – 'far gone. I don't even know how we would decide if that was something we should do or how I would explain it to the children.' I'm getting het up, and my voice is rising higher and higher in panic. It's early days, but Sav seems to be settling into Year One better than Reception. How will this latest bomb-shell affect her behaviour? 'In fact, until I've spoken to Adam and we've researched what to say, don't mention the dementia to Sav or Jack, please.'

I turn into our street, clicking my tongue in annoyance as I see that next door has nipped into 'my' space on the road outside our house, and I'll have to park on the other side.

'Who's that?' Dad asks, as I reverse park into the tiny, snug space opposite. It takes me two goes before I clear it.

'The person I don't want you to mention it to? Jack. He's your grandson.' Is this how it's going to be? Shifting from lucidity to confusion from one moment to the next?

'I know that, Iris,' he says impatiently. And then he points across me and out of the driver's side window, where I look across the road to our house. 'I mean, who's *that*?'

Gabe is sitting on our front doorstep. And he's covered in blood.

Chapter Thirty-Nine

'It's OK, Dad. It's Gabe, Adam's brother,' I say, with an assurance I don't feel.

Gabe looks up as we approach and I get a better look at the source of the blood, a cut along his eyebrow that's leaking at an alarming rate, and a swollen cheek with bruises blooming along the bone. He's in smart trousers and a shirt that was originally white but is now stained red and grubby from God knows what. There's a hole ripped in the knee of his trousers. Dad's met Gabe a few times but not for years. Unsurprising that he didn't recognise him when he looks like this.

'What's happened, son?' Dad asks as we reach him. As I hear the word 'son', I wince. I know it's a generic term but it's the sort of thing that could needle Gabe, and as he angles his face in Dad's direction, I smell the alcohol on his breath.

'Hurt my head,' is all Gabe says, before slumping against the door.

'I think we should call an ambulance,' I say. What if he has a brain injury?

'No!' Gabe shouts, his body stiffening. 'Don't do that. It's just a cut. I'll be all right in a minute. Then I'll go.' He's slurring. Is that booze or concussion?

'Let's get you inside,' Dad says. His voice is soothing. He's completely rational. 'We can clean it up and take a proper look.' Dad reaches out to take Gabe's arm, but I hesitate. Adam was right. Gabe might have got the job but of course that wasn't a permanent fix. Here we are, a few months later, in the midst of another drama. Only this time he's brought it to our front door.

'There's a train at . . .' Gabe pulls his phone from his pocket. The screen is smashed and unreadable beneath the criss-cross of glass. He squints at it. 'Well, they go every hour anyway.'

'Don't be daft, son.' I wince again, but Dad is oblivious and Gabe is looking at him with benevolence rather than aggression. 'You're here now. Besides, if we send you off in this state, you'll scare all the kids coming out of school.'

Thank God ours have tea-time club today. I've no idea how I would explain this. Especially as I have no idea what the explanation is.

'Dad, I'm not sure we should . . .' Gabe is drunk and has clearly been in a fight. I don't want him inside, but Dad shushes me and then proffers his arm again. This time, Gabe takes it. I grab his other side, realising that Dad isn't strong enough himself to bear the weight of a fourteen-stone man, and together we lead him into the house, before depositing him at the kitchen table.

'Why don't I put the kettle on?' Dad moves off, leaving me with Gabe. I let him sit there for a while, hopefully sobering up, and try to get a better look at the cut. Jack cracked his head on the slide in the park once and I thought he was going to die from how much blood came out of it, but it turned out to be a tiny wound. Perhaps this is another one that looks more dramatic than it is.

'I'll be one sec,' I tell him, rushing to the bathroom to see what we have by way of a first aid kit. There's some cotton wool and plasters, and a bottle of TCP that's been there since Adam had tonsillitis a couple of years ago. It'll do under the circumstances. I tap out a quick text to Adam.

Come home. Please.

Then I grab one of his T-shirts and some jogging bottoms for Gabe to change into.

Gabe is still sitting in the same position as when I left. If anything, he looks like he's trying to contain his entire body into as small a space as possible. He looks so uncomfortable. As I busy myself filling up a bowl with warm water, Dad sets a mug down in front of him.

'Tea,' he says. 'Strong and sugary. That'll help.'

'Thank you,' Gabe replies in a quiet, obedient voice.

I pull up a chair in front of him. 'We need to clean the cut and see how bad it is.'

'It's all right, I'll do it in a minute,' he says. He leans over to pick up his tea and blood drips from his head onto the table. Gabe freezes. 'Sorry, sorry.' He goes to wipe it off with his hand but only succeeds in smearing it around. 'Fuck. Sorry.' His hands are shaking.

'Gabe, stop,' I say as gently as I can. 'Drink your tea. Can you tell us what happened? We didn't even know you were going to be in London. You should have said.'

The look Gabe gives silences me. Less an accusation and more a 'yeah right'. He takes a sip of his tea and his eyes widen. I wonder how many sugars Dad put in it.

'I wouldn't mind a tea, if you're having one, Dad. No sugar for me though.'

'Right, yes. I'll see if I can rustle up some biscuits too.' He bustles off again. I know for a fact that the only biscuits in the house are behind a stacked wall of tinned tomatoes in the pantry, because I was the one who hid them there from Jack. I dip some cotton wool in the bowl of water and dab it around the wound, tackling the blood on his face before I start trying to clean his injury.

'You know I got the job at Proctors?' he slurs.

I nod.

He tells me in fragments. 'We had a training session at head office down here today. It was me and a few others from the other offices around the country.' He stops and looks around the room until I prompt him.

'Then what?'

'We finished at lunch and went for drinks after.' He shrugs as though that explains everything.

'And you got in a fight with one of them?' I say slowly.

Gabe stiffens. 'No,' he says coldly, batting my hand away from where I'm pressing the cotton wool. It hovers there. My face is very close to his face and I briefly see the hurt in his eyes before it hardens. 'You always expect the worst, don't you?'

Will the truth or a lie antagonise him more? 'You've kind of conditioned us that way.'

He gives a wry smile and then winces as the action pulls at his eyebrows. 'Touché,' he says softly. 'I didn't get in a fight,' he continues emphatically. 'The others all went to catch their trains, and I hung around thinking I could buy Adam a beer when he finished work. I dunno, do something nice . . . surprise him that I could afford to buy him a London-priced beer. Didn't have the guts to text him, though, did I? So I stayed in the pub drinking and building up the courage.'

'Oh, Gabe,' I say, but he keeps talking over me.

'Next thing I know, it's four o'clock and I'm battered, so I thought I'd start walking up here, get something to eat and sober up. Then I could catch Adam when he got home. But someone had one of those briefcases on wheels and I tripped over it and then smacked my head on a wall. Fucking bloke had the audacity to shout at *me* even though he's too pathetic to carry his own bag.' His Sheffield burr gets more pronounced as he criticises Londoners. 'Then, even though I was the one bleeding, everyone in the street looked at me like I was a crazy drunk trying to mug him, so I legged it and waited here. I didn't know what else to do.'

He looks so forlorn. I nod and carry on cleaning up his face. I don't know what to say. I'm embarrassed that I assumed he'd started a fight, but this is still a classic Gabe story. He's the only person this sort of thing happens to. Most people stop sniffing out any potential drama within a five-mile radius when they're twenty-five.

'I can't remember the last time I had all afternoon to sit in the pub,' I say instead. Gratifyingly, he laughs.

'Kids are a bit of a bummer like that. They really cramp your all-day-drinking plans. That's why I don't have any. As far as I know. Ow!' He flinches as I start working on the cut.

'Hold that on there for a minute,' I say, passing him a length of bandage that I think is from Sav's doctor's kit. Probably best not to dwell on whether or not it can be classified as sterile. 'Let's see if we can stop the bleeding.' I have no real idea what I'm doing, but I'm sure this is what you're supposed to do; I read about it in an article once. True, that was about the American public being trained to administer first aid if they ever got caught up in an active shooter situation, but I'm pretty sure the same wound-stemming principles apply. If necessary, I think I know how to create a makeshift tourniquet anyway. I busy myself with that for a while and drink the tea Dad deposited before disappearing. 'I don't know where Dad's got to,' I say worriedly. I hope he hasn't gone out.

'Does he come here a lot?' Gabe says. The hand holding the bandage is covering his left eye.

'Sort of.' I busy myself with rinsing the bowl out and refilling it with fresh water, the diagnosis hurtling to the forefront of my mind. 'He's staying here for a bit. I've been at the hospital with him.' I realise my message to Adam sounded panicked but didn't explain anything. He'll think it's about Dad. 'He's got dementia. We just found out. Early-ish stages, but we've got a lot to sort out.' My voice is much more matter of fact than I feel.

Gabe nods and swaps over the hand he's using to press the bandage. 'I'm so sorry,' he says quietly, sounding more sober than when he first arrived. 'That's got to be rough. He's a good man, your dad.'

'He is. It's hard. It's only going to get harder.'

Gabe clears his throat. 'Truth is . . .' He pulls the bandage off his head. It's soaked through. 'Is there any more of this?' I root through the kitchen cupboards for anything resembling a bandage. I come up with kitchen roll and a tea towel. I take the tea towel over.

'Use this.'

He looks uncertain. 'It'll be ruined.'

'It's a tea towel, Gabe, not the Turin Shroud.' I hold it up to his head. 'What were you saying?'

He gives a light shake of his head and then seems to reconsider. 'I was going to say that I've always admired your family. Well, more than that. Been jealous. Mum too. That's why she can be . . . well, you know how she can be.'

I give him a small smile. 'The Duchess couldn't possibly comment.'

He laughs. 'She'd be upset if she knew you knew she called you that. The last time I saw my dad was in a pub on Ecclesall Road. About a year ago,' he says softly. 'He was with a load of blokes. I'm guessing they were his mates, but I wouldn't know because he's never introduced me to any of them. He blanked me. And not because he's got a condition that makes him forget who I am.'

'Shit. What did you do?'

Gabe looks away with his good eye. 'Downed a pint in there, and then left and got wasted somewhere else.' He shrugs. 'Can't remember anything after that.'

I try to think of something to say that doesn't sound patronising. 'Your dad's a shit, Gabe. It's OK to be mad at him. I would be. Adam is.'

'Adam?' He sounds genuinely surprised. 'Adam couldn't give a toss.'

'You're joking, aren't you? Adam has so much anger towards your dad. He's spent his entire life trying to prove a point against him. I knew that even before we started—' I stop, not wanting to say 'therapy'. He hasn't told his mum or Gabe about it. You're never sure with stuff like that if they will be supportive or consider it a bit sad, like online dating at the time when Adam and I were doing it. It took a bit longer for its acceptability to spread to the north.

Fuck it. I've had enough of secrets, and if by the end of this year Adam and I can't work things out, it's better for them to know we tried. Otherwise I'm sure I'll get the blame.

'Even before we started marriage therapy.'

He's sipping his tea again and he looks up sharply, a frown on his face. 'Why are you and Adam in therapy?'

I don't respond immediately, not knowing how to articulate it.

'Everyone has their problems, Gabe,' I say in the end. 'You, me, Adam.'

He looks like he's going to say something else before half nodding. 'That's true enough. But—' He stops himself. 'Is it all right if I have a coffee instead of this?' he says quietly, looking around for Dad. He must not want to offend him.

'Of course. We only have instant, is that all right?'

'Perfect. I feel a lot better now, thank you.'

I put the kettle back on. It's on the counter at the other end of the kitchen, which puts some space between us and makes it easier to switch the conversation back to Patrick. 'Adam is not OK with your dad and how he was. How he still is. I thought you knew that.'

Gabe shakes his head. 'He never talks about him.'

'Because he can't. He buries it all. Plus, he thinks it's disloyal to your mum to care.' I pour boiling water onto the granules. 'But believe me, he hates him. That's one reason for the therapy anyway. Why do you think he moved so far away?'

I tip in some milk and bring the mug over. It says 'Best Mum Ever' on it.

'We thought he'd come back. Eventually.'

'Your dad? He did.' *Again and again and again*, I think. Until he didn't.

Gabe slurps at his coffee. It's too hot. 'No. Adam. Mum and I always thought he'd move home after a bit of time in London. Especially when his ex didn't end up coming to uni here, which is what we thought it was all about. Thought he'd enjoy the Big Smoke for a few years and then come back to settle down. But then he met you.'

There's an awkward pause. I don't know what to say to that.

'Your mum would probably like it if he came back, wouldn't she?' I say eventually.

A noise escapes from Gabe, a cross between a strangled snort and a harrumph. 'Course she would. He's Goldenballs.'

I channel Esther. 'I guess it can seem that way to you.'

'Do you reckon? It's bad enough being the black sheep of the family, the eternal disappointment, and having Adam swooping in to fix things, without your mum wishing he was the one living nearby while you disappeared to London, possibly forever. But because he lives so far away, he's like some sort of mythical figure. "Have you seen Adam's lovely house?" "Look at Jack and Sav's school photos." "You know Iris has been promoted at work?"' His impression of Anne is surprisingly accurate. I laugh and he smiles.

'I highly doubt your mum would say that about me.' The mention of work makes my stomach lurch. Not so much to be proud of, if in a few weeks I'm in the dole queue.

Now it's his turn to look sceptical. 'If anything, you're on a bigger pedestal than Adam is. With your swish job and your parents being so tight with you. She thinks Adam "married up".' He shoots me a look over his mug. 'We're the poor relations.'

'I'm losing relations all the time at the moment,' I say, gloom descending. 'First Mum, now Dad. I always liked being an only child. Never having to share, getting all the attention. I wasn't lonely like people always warn you you'll be. Never bothered me. Until now. Having someone else to help make the hard decisions and look out for you doesn't stop when you leave school. You – and Adam – are lucky you'll have each other if anything happens to your mum. The stuff with Dad is all on me.'

He looks away but I swear his eyes are damp. He pulls the tea towel off his head. 'How's it looking?'

'Pretty terrible, but it's stopped bleeding at least. We're going to have to wash it again though.'

The whole right side of his face has puffed up, and there are streaks of blood stretching from his forehead to his chin where it's smeared off the tea towel. It looks shiny, swollen and sore. As I pick up the bowl again, I look down at my hands. They're covered in blood too, and so are the sleeves of my Breton top. I squint at my reflection in the window above the sink and can see that flecks of blood have worked their way onto my face too. So much blood from one cut. Still, the tension seems to have dissolved. This is the most relaxed I've been around Gabe for years. 'You know, Gabe, you don't have to only get in touch when you need Adam. Your mum too. It would be nice to hear from you when there's nothing going on. Just for a chat. You could come and see us.'

'Maybe,' he says uncertainly. 'Adam always sounds stressed when I ring him.'

I wonder why, I think but don't say.

I hear shouting.

'Iris! Iris! What's happened? Is it your dad? Why aren't you answering your phone? Why is there blood all over the doorstep?' Adam flies into the kitchen wild-eyed and looking crazed with worry. 'Are you all right?' he shouts at me, then stops dead at the sight of Gabe. 'What have you done?' he says in a hard voice. 'What the fuck have you done now?'

Chapter Forty

'What did he do to you?' Adam grabs my hand, looks into my face. 'Where does it hurt?'

He wheels around, yanks Gabe by the shoulders and slams him against the kitchen wall, pinning him there. Drops of blood fly off his face as he smacks his head, speckling the white metro tiles behind him. The room is starting to look like a crime scene, but I'm too stunned to move. Adam pulls his right arm back, hand fisted, as Gabe's look of shock morphs into something else; a hardening, a down-twist in his mouth that says: burn it down.

'Did they teach you how to manage your anger like this in therapy?' he sneers.

The unexpected retaliation causes Adam to falter, and the room falls so quiet I hear my own intake of breath. It only takes him a second to recover.

'What did you say?' Adam says, in the tone of a man who's accused you of looking at him funny in a pub on a Friday night. His arm is still poised, ready to punch, but his angry eyes flit to me, burning with betrayal. 'Why would you tell him what I did? Why would you do that?'

'I didn't,' I stutter out. Gabe is still flat against the wall. 'I told him about therapy, nothing else. Please get off him. Get *off*.' I finally seem to get through to him, as he lets go and takes a step away.

'What else is there?' says Gabe, sounding full of bravado now he doesn't have a fist in his face. 'What did you do to Iris?'

'Nothing. It's nothing. We're working some stuff out, like I said,' I say. 'That's why we're going to therapy.'

Adam takes another step back, his hands rubbing his face as though he's awoken from what he was about to do. He won't have liked losing control like that. It's a Patrick trait, one he abhors.

'No. He said that he did something to you,' Gabe wheedles. He can't leave anything. This is why people are always hitting him. 'What was it? You said he had repressed rage towards Dad.' I wince as he tosses out another mangled fraction of our conversation, one that makes it sound as though we've been having a long personal tête-à-tête here about Adam. 'He better not have laid a finger on you.'

'Of course not,' I say crossly. 'He wouldn't do that.'

'So, what then?' Why won't he shut up?

I can't look at Adam. I'm not going to grass him up, but I'm not going to cover for him either. He has to be the one to either lie or confess.

'Adam. What was it?' says Gabe again.

'Just leave it, Gabe, OK.'

Adam mutters something I can't hear. Neither can Gabe. 'What?'

'I had a fling with someone else, OK?' The back of Adam's neck and the side of his face are all red. Flushed with embarrassment, or shame, or both. I wonder if he's relieved about getting it out in the open. Many times over the past few weeks I've wanted to tell Adam about my almost-kiss with Lucas, wondering if putting it on him would lessen the guilt.

'You cheated on Iris?' Gabe's eyes flick to me questioningly. He looks genuinely shocked and upset. 'When? With who?'

'Last year,' I say, as Adam says, 'Jules.'

Gabe looks at him blankly before the name registers. 'Jules Shepherd? From school? Are you serious?'

We both nod, me as I'm looking at the floor.

'Who dumped you twenty years ago and made it clear she wanted no more to do with you once she went to uni?' Gabe's eyes widen and he shakes his head as though he can't believe it. 'You fucking idiot. Why would you do that? You're always coming up to Sheffield to tell me what I'm doing wrong with my life, when the whole time you're throwing your own down the toilet. The fucking nerve of you.' Now he's squaring up to Adam. He's five years younger and two inches taller, plus he's got much more experience when it comes to scrapping. He pushes him, jabs two fingers into his shoulder, hard. 'You wanted to fight, you prick, so let's go. See how hard you are when you haven't taken me by surprise.' Adam pushes him back, slamming him into the wall again, and before I know what's happening there's some argy-bargy going on where they're both in each other's faces, years of poorly suppressed anger and resentment oozing from them.

'GABE. ADAM. STOP!' I scream, wheeling away from the sink and tugging at their tops, the classic woman doing the ineffectual 'leave it' routine.

'ADAM!' I shout again. It's like he can't even hear me. Next I try, 'DAD!' Where is he?

Dad meanders in, looking like he's in no hurry until he sees what's happening in the kitchen, then drops the newspaper he's holding and puts himself between their bodies. Physically he's no match for either of them, but replacing Gabe's face in Adam's eyeline with his seventy-something one has the desired effect. Even in this wound-up state, Adam isn't going to go through a pensioner to get to his brother.

'Adam – over there, son.' Dad waves a hand in my direction as Gabe rubs the back of his head.

Breathing heavily, he says, 'How could you? You have the perfect family, man. The *perfect* family. And you're supposed to be the golden boy. Maybe we're not so different after all. Or maybe you're more like Dad.'

Adam flinches. He's storming up and down the kitchen, a coil of jittery energy, his face pale where Gabe's words have hit the mark. I intercept him and guide him to a seat at the table.

'Can we all take a moment,' I say, trying an Esther technique. My voice is shaking and there's adrenaline pulsing through me.

'I made a mistake,' he mutters. 'It was a mistake. I'm not like him. And then *you* turn up—'

'I haven't done anything,' Gabe says quietly, the fight suddenly deflated from him. Dad helps him into a seat at the other end of the table, and the two brothers glare at each other. 'I can't believe you think I'd be capable of doing something to Iris. To any woman.' He looks into his lap, and his expression breaks my heart. So much anger, so much hurt, constantly spilling out of him. 'Especially when you've done what you have to her. She's too good for you, Adam, she always was.' Gabe looks up at me. 'And you putting up with it. What are you even still doing with him?'

Chapter Forty-One

Excerpt from transcript of session with Adam and Iris Young by Esther Moran, 8 October

Esther: And how is your relationship with your brother now?

Adam: [silence]

Iris: I think it's fair to say it's strained. Gabe walked out. I spoke to their mum on the phone and he made it back to Sheffield OK, but he didn't tell her what had happened. I think he was trying to protect her from the truth.

Adam: How good of him.

Iris: You know what I mean.

Adam: What, so she can think she has one OK child rather than two fuck-ups?

Iris: Just that it would upset her to know—

Adam: [interrupting] What? That at the end of this year we'll be getting a divorce? We'll all be upset about that.

[silence]

Chapter Forty-Two

16 October

'Iris, can I have a word?' Vanessa is next to my desk, having appeared wordlessly as I'm scrolling through Rightmove, seeing what's 'out there' in terms of three-bedroom houses in the same area I live in now, but magically affordable on one salary. I quickly minimise the window and flip to my Excel spreadsheet of donor activity, where she can see highlighted in green all the leads I've been chasing.

'Now,' she adds.

As I stand up, my phone buzzes with a message from Nat and my eyes automatically flit down. It's the first one I've had in weeks. All I can see from where it lies on my desk is the preview.

Can we meet up . . .

I don't swipe for the rest. Vanessa's tone is grave enough for me to know that fiddling with my phone is a hard no, so I follow her to her office. She closes the door behind us. Blinds down again.

'I put in a courtesy call to Lucas Caulfield yesterday evening.'

I nod, the dull thud of being busted registering as relief rather than the panic I was expecting. I've been waiting for this moment since August, when I reported back to Vanessa that the visit was fine but I hadn't been able to get hold of him since. Aside from my apology I've been too cowardly to even try, but that's not what Vanessa has been led to believe.

'He told me he hasn't heard anything from the Trust since' – she glances at her notepad – 'late August.' She fixes her eyes back on me. 'And asked who he should get in touch with if he wants to arrange visits in the future. As you can imagine, I was more than a little surprised as I was under the impression you were in regular contact with him, and it was only a matter of time before he increased his annual donation. Iris, what's going on? Why have you ghosted one of our most important donors?'

My heart starts hammering. The relief has given way to something else, a survival instinct that knows my body needs adrenaline, even if my head is too overloaded to register it. 'Can I be honest?'

She nods. 'Please do.'

Deep breath time. 'The visit in August was . . .' I filter the options. I mean, I said honest, but obviously I mean honest-adjacent; I'm not a complete fool. 'Awkward. You're right – at one point, Lucas and I were in regular touch, friendly even, but it seems he got the wrong impression when it came to personal-professional boundaries, and it came to a head at Bray House in August.'

Vanessa pales and concern passes across her face. 'Are you telling me he did something inappropriate? Because let me assure you, there is protocol in place to deal with that and we will support you all the way. There are two historic claims being investigated right now, and as you can imagine, the Trust wants nothing to do with money from parties who have committed offences, whether past or present.'

'No, nothing inappropriate,' I squeak. Shit. 'Nothing like that. More a misunderstanding I'm embarrassed about – I imagine he is too – and wasn't sure how to broach in the office.' Oh God, do I have to relay who did what? The meaningful looks and brushes of skin?

Her expression relaxes and approaches something akin to sympathetic. 'So why didn't you say anything? Instead of leaving it to fester.'

Why? Because this year has been one long series of fuck-ups, that's why.

'Because there's been so much pressure this year regarding our targets,' I say. 'I didn't know how to handle it because I worried a rejection would make him pull his donations altogether, and then I'd be in big trouble.' Vanessa likes solutions, I remind myself. 'So I apologised in case I gave him the wrong idea and tried to distance myself. I've been panicking that he was going to make a complaint about me in retaliation – not that he's like that necessarily, and not that he would have a case for it' – I'm garbling – 'but I'm relieved he still wants to work with us. He deserves to be treated as the VIP he is, but I'm not the right person to do it.' As I remember the sensation of his face near mine, I cling to the fact that I didn't act on it. Wasn't that Adam's defence for not leaving me? It seems you can apply the same reasoning to work and marriage if you manipulate it enough. Morally dicey situations might arise, but it's what you do about them that matters.

That seems like a good theory.

I rack my brain for a way to make this less of a car crash. There's only one thing I can think of. 'It might be better if Sophie takes over on this.' The words stick in my throat, but I choke them out. 'It needs a rescue mission but not from me.'

Vanessa sits back in her chair, contemplating me. 'You do realise that if Lucas decides to up his donation, it will then count towards her target and not yours.'

I don't trust myself to speak; instead I press my lips together and nod. Am I prepared to sacrifice my job to Sophie? But what if getting Lucas far away from me helps save my marriage? I try not to resent that it feels like it has to be one or the other.

'This . . . misunderstanding does seem like the latest in a long line of blips for you, Iris.' The pause tells me she's not entirely convinced by my explanation, but she holds up a hand as I protest. 'I'd be more inclined to overlook this situation with Lucas Caulfield as an unrequited crush on his part' – I flinch again – 'if there hadn't been plenty of other incidents this year. The last-minute days of leave, going home early, being distracted in meetings. None of these things are significant when taken on their own, but they are when the biggest one is your failure so far to secure much in the way of new donations.'

She leans forward in her chair. 'Is there anything else going on?' This is where I should tell her about Adam and me, or my dad, or that everything has seemed more pointless since Mum died, but I can't. Work is the only place where the other stuff is somewhere else, and I can't trade it for some pity, not least because at the end of the year Vanessa will still be judging us on numbers, not intentions.

'No,' I say. 'Like I said before, I've had a bad run.'

She holds my look and then pulls out a printout. 'You remain a hundred grand short of your target, while Sophie is only ten thousand pounds away from hers.' My stomach lurches. 'Even without Lucas Caulfield being passed on as a contact, I remain confident that she'll surpass it by the end of the year. You, not so much.'

I nod weakly. Sophie has been on fire. Focused, pulling late nights at events and early mornings at her desk, and generally looking like a woman who is dedicated to her job and the Trust. I can't claim my lack of dedication is due to being a parent, because the kids existed last year and I wasn't off my game like this.

'She is great at her job,' I agree. 'But I know I can pull this back, Vanessa. I have irons in the fire.' This is patently untrue.

'If you say so, Iris,' she says with a dubious look. 'There are three months to convert your contacts into cash. I suggest you do so as a matter of urgency.'

Chapter Forty-Three

26 October

I spend the next few days and late nights perfecting a pitch to send out to all the rich, professional and/or well-connected women I've ever met – as well as plenty I haven't – outlining my idea for a nomadic women's members' club held at different Trust properties. My 'vision' (as I call it) combines the wellness of the Fierce Women's Retreat with business networking opportunities and a 'Trust Talk' series of speakers. Considering it's an idea born of desperation, I think it's pretty good, but when my inbox is barren of responses a week later, I have to conclude the recipients disagree.

I take to avoiding Vanessa whenever I see her, rushing past her in corridors or if we end up on the same loo schedule, and checking my emails even more often than when I was waiting for a response from Lucas.

As I arrive at the café to meet Nat and Fran at the weekend, I check again. Tumbleweeds.

'I'm so tired,' Nat bursts out the second I take a seat, tears leaking down her face. Fran is already there, coming back from the counter with two lattes, and we exchange a 'do something' look as she passes them to me, before rushing back for the other coffee and some slices of cake. She sits down and, through a mouthful of half-chewed cake, Nat sobs, 'I don't want to do it any more.'

I start to say, 'Which bit?' but she interrupts.

'Any of it. I don't want to pretend it's all fine and I'm coping when it's shit. And I hate Mark, like really hate him. I hate his stupid face, and how he gets to go to work in the morning, and how he complains about being tired as though he and I are the same in terms of exhaustion. He hasn't got up at night once. He doesn't even get Georgia ready for school in the morning, because he has to leave for work and I'm "at home anyway" – as though bickering with an eight-year-old about getting dressed after being woken up every hour through the night by the baby is a simple task for me right now.'

'Of course it's not,' I murmur, but she ploughs on.

'He doesn't understand that having the freedom to run out and grab a sandwich at lunchtime is nine thousand per cent more freedom than I have right now.' She waves her fork around. 'I don't even eat lunch most days because I'm trapped underneath Marnie while she naps. And the worst part is, I enabled this because the first time around I did everything. I sucked it up. But now we have two children and I don't want to. I'm stuck in some 1950s gender role marriage, and I am knackered and I *hate* it.' She stabs at her cake with her fork as though it has personally offended her. Dark circles ring her eyes, and she has the kamikaze look of someone who has started to let out her feelings and now can't stop. Three-month-old Marnie is asleep in the carrier on her front, with crumbs all over her head.

'He made it seem like he was some sort of saint for taking Georgia today so I could come here. Oh, how generous of you, I only need to look after *one* of our two children today. God forbid you have both of them, like I do every single day. I don't want to do it any more. I just want to run away from my life.' She chokes out another sob then looks down at the baby, her lip wobbling and beyond caring that we're sitting in a busy café in Crouch End. Although it's such a popular hangout with NCT groups that another emotional outburst from a new mother is nothing to them. 'I'm a terrible person,' she carries on, changing tack. 'A terrible mother. The number of people who would love to be in my position. Two gorgeous daughters. I shouldn't be so ungrateful. How did you do it with two, Iris? And you, Fran, with twins? Why am I so shit? Why can't I do it?' She looks at each of us in turn, her eyes flicking frantically, searching for an answer.

It's been three months since she had the baby, but Nat is now back, physically anyway. And now I see her, I realise that whether or not she was dodging my texts, her disapproval hasn't been the only reason. She's a woman who has been avoiding the outside world while pretending everything was fine.

Fran is the first to react, sweeping the cake debris from the baby as she leans over to give Nat a hug. 'I did it pretty much the way you are now. By going through the motions, thinking I was messing everything up, and then having a complete breakdown. Then I drafted in Liam's mum, my sister, you two, and Liam himself, who, if you remember, hustled me off to the doctor at six months, and I was diagnosed with postnatal depression. So first of all, you are not a bad person or a bad mother. You need some help and you need some sleep, because I guarantee you will feel four thousand per cent less mental if you can rack up more than two hours in a row. Once we've got you that, we can work out if you're totally knackered or if there's more to it.'

'But Marnie is waking up all the time at the moment,' Nat counters. 'And I'm breast-feeding.'

'Well,' I say, treading carefully. The tricky line of trying to offer her choices without judging the one she makes. 'Will she take a bottle? And if she will, you could express, or Mark could give her some formula.'

'I don't know.'

'About formula? Well, that's up to you, of course.'

'Don't feel guilty about it,' Fran interrupts. 'The twins were combi-fed. It was the only way I had a hope in hell of sleeping.'

'I meant more, what if Mark won't do it.' Her face is pensive, and I freeze with my latte halfway to my lips, not knowing what to say.

'Well, he'll have to, won't he?' Fran says. 'What kind of person would he be if he'd rather let you go out of your mind than get up and do a few night feeds?'

'Maybe.' Nat looks utterly defeated. 'But what if . . .' She starts again and then turns to me. It comes out almost as a whisper. 'Iris, I owe you an apology. Being all judgy about you and Adam, and behaving as though your break-up was catching' – is *that* what she thought? – 'and now I hate Mark, and all I can think is what could be more normal than wanting to ditch your shit husband?'

I smother a smile.

'It's OK, Nat,' I say, trying to soothe her. 'Speaking as someone who's been told she's bad at asking for help, you need to ask him – and us – for help when you need it. And,' I add, 'just because you think he's a shit husband now, doesn't mean you will always think he's a shit husband.' I see Fran raise an eyebrow in my direction and I deliberately ignore her. 'You won't necessarily feel these feelings forever,' I tell her, before quickly adding, 'but that doesn't mean they aren't valid or true right now.'

Nat nods, not looking like she's taking it in, but definitely looking like she's using everything and anything as further evidence of how terrible she is. She's clearly out of her mind with tiredness, but it doesn't mean I don't appreciate the acknowledgement that she hasn't exactly been supportive about Adam. And there's also, I admit, relief that I'm not the only one whose marriage isn't rock solid. Vindication that maybe things for everyone are messier than they'd like to admit.

Chapter Forty-Four

30 October

By the fifth visit, you'd think I'd have got used to coming to Mum and Dad's house, but it still feels weird – wrong – being here without them. For the last couple of days, I had Adam to help me, but he's saving the rest of his leave for the Christmas holidays so I'm facing the last of the clearing out alone. I took a week's annual leave; not only for this, but also to escape the impending-doom atmosphere of the office. Even if coming here is for the saddest of reasons, the lure of immersing myself in the past, where everything was safe and cosy, is more appealing than another week of smug Sophie bragging about the money her donors can't stop throwing at her.

As I walk through the downstairs rooms, they look familiar but somehow different, like when you see a person you recognise in the street but can't quite reach for their name. It smells of fresh paint and new carpets, which make a whispering whoomphing noise as I pad around to check the decorator's handiwork from yesterday. Once I'd tidied up and cleared out everything down here, blank-slate, estate agent-friendly neutrals replaced Mum's favoured Laura Ashley florals, before I moved on to the rooms upstairs. In a couple more days I'll have finished the upstairs, and the decorator and his team can spruce everything up before the agent comes to take photos. To rent it out or sell is yet to be decided, as is where Dad will go. I have brochures for sheltered housing and specialist homes all over our kitchen table, have spent every evening poring over them – sometimes with Dad, sometimes without – and still not come to any decision. One thing we do know is that he can't come back and live here alone. He's gone downhill, even in the weeks since his diagnosis; the gaps in his memory and our worry about his welfare have increased in direct proportion.

I get to the dining room, which faces the back garden, and stop to gaze out of the window.

Adam and I managed to get Dad over to help us with some of the initial sorting out, but whether from his condition or being overwhelmed by having to sift through the sheer volume of *stuff* that comes part and parcel with the house you've lived in for fifty years, he got frightened and upset very quickly. It was too much. Adam ended up putting on a DVD of the FA Cup Final in 1997, when Chelsea won, on the advice of the dementia charity we've spoken to. They told us we're better off trying to evoke positive feelings than exact memories because emotional memory clings on longer than the detail of everyday occurrences and since then we've been searching for Dad's happy place. It turns out it's his beloved Chelsea FC. Reliving a match whose outcome made him so joyful at the time – he always used to talk about dancing Mum around the kitchen when Roberto Di Matteo scored only forty-two seconds in – makes him feel safe, so we've both got the whole thing downloaded on our phones, the same way we used to load them up with emergency episodes of *PAW Patrol* for Sav.

I watch the afternoon light fade in the garden, Dad's shed disappearing from view as it gets dark. We've taken the tools to store in our own shed; not because Adam or I have any idea what to do with most of them, more because they represent Dad so perfectly. He used to turn up at our house to fix something we would almost certainly have paid 'a man' too much money to deal with. I didn't know what else to do with the tools. At least they will be nearby, even if he never uses them again. Thinking about them makes me hope our house can be the refuge for Jack and Sav that this one has been to me: always a place to run to, where there's a full fridge, no rent to worry about, and a parent who can fix almost anything.

I head upstairs, where my parents' bedroom looks as it did when I left it yesterday. The furniture has already been separated and delivered into storage or to the charity shop, and the floor is covered in the piles of stuff I pulled out from the wardrobes, cabinets and drawers.

I can't deal with Mum's things yet; instead I start with the stuff from Dad's side of the room, which seems to be an explosion of the type of things you see middle-aged men studying very seriously at car boot sales: Haynes manuals for every vehicle he's owned dating back to the seventies, packets of screws, a bag full of miscellaneous wires. Safely impersonal in theory, but even sifting through wires feels like a violation. Every object is a decision to be made on Dad's behalf. I consider shoving the lot into boxes to put in storage and deal with at a later date, but Dad told me to do what needed to be done, and Mum would want me to do it properly. I sort through it all for anything meaningful, find nothing, and dump everything into the area for the recycling centre before turning to the next pile.

What does he need right now, what will he never need again, and what for my own sake will I regret throwing away? These are the questions I meditate on as I work methodically through each area, filling binbags. As an only child, I've always known this task would fall to me one day, but I wasn't prepared for doing it while one of my parents was still alive.

Clothes next: from the safe grey suits he used to wear for work, dry-cleaned and wrapped in the polythene bags that have covered them since he retired, to every pair of thin-kneed cords that had been downgraded to odd-job trousers over the years. Such mundane items, but I'm crushed by the memories of each of them.

'Stick to the plan,' Dad tells me occasionally. 'The plan' was made after his diagnosis, when Dad specified that all his loose ends should be tied up to make life as simple for me as possible. Easy for him to say; he's not the one here worried about betraying him by chucking out the wrong things.

After two hours, Dad's stuff is bagged up and I prepare to tackle Mum's. Ever organised and determined, Mum's already done some of the work for me. She took it upon herself to systematise all the household documents so Dad would know where everything was when she was no longer able to run the house; birth certificates, marriage certificates and all other crucial paperwork are neatly stored in one box file, with another one dedicated to utilities, bills and household accounts. Although finding a typed A4 page of internet account passwords makes me grateful that no one has yet robbed the house. A third file stores everything left over from when she executed the wills for both her own and Dad's parents when they died. There are photos stuck carefully into albums and labelled in the handwriting that makes me ache when I see it. I force myself not to get distracted by looking through the pages and concentrate.

I turn to her clothes, which still smell faintly of her, and bag up the immaculate trousers and blouses she favoured for the charity shop. They're so her that I long to keep them, but she'd berate me for hoarding them when someone else could benefit. The same goes for her shoes. I remove her special occasion dresses from more polythene bags and sift through the memories attached to them. The pastel mother-of-the-bride frock from my wedding, the black velvet dress from Dad's retirement party, the boxy skirt suit she wore to Jack's christening. A maxi-length black-and-gold brocade gown stops me in my tracks. I've only ever seen this dress on Mum in a picture, glammed up for someone's wedding in the seventies. She always says it was old-fashioned even at the time because it was more fifties in style than the bell-sleeved boho designs of the seventies, but I've always loved the way she looked in the fitted bodice and sweetheart neckline. I didn't realise she'd kept it. I'm taller than Mum and bustier, but I can't let this go. I put it to one side for myself.

Among some dried-out bits of make-up from her dressing table there's a half-empty bottle of her favourite 'for best' Estée Lauder perfume. I keep it. Then there are the child-hood pictures I drew that she's been storing all this time, along with every birthday card, Valentine's and Mother's Day card Dad and the kids and I ever gave her, meaningless to anyone but us, charting the decades of her life. I flick through them, watching the years of Mum's life in reverse, from 'World's Best Grandma' to 'Happy 40th!'

'I love you Mummy' is written in my childish scrawl. I was probably about ten at the time; forty seemed so old even though she was two years younger than I am now. You read about young mums dying of cancer, who write birthday cards for their children stretching right up to their eighteenth birthday. My next milestone is fifty, and I'm secretly hoping there's a card from Mum secreted among this lot to be opened when I reach a half-century, telling me what I should do and how to live my life.

Another card catches my eye. It's a cartoon, saucy in a Benny Hill, eighties-seaside sort of a way. A sexy woman kneeling in front of her broken-down car saying, 'Can anyone take a look at my rear end?' as several men salivate over her shapely bum. It's so at odds with all the others and not Dad's sense of humour at all. I look inside.

Mary,
Never not checking out your rear end . . .
M xx

I frown, sifting through my mental file of family and friends. I can't think of anyone, not even someone who would write this as a joke. Who's M? And why would Mum keep this tacky card?

Chapter Forty-Five

14 November

'Don't be ridiculous, I'm not selling the house.' Dad looks baffled. I try my hardest not to cry through a combination of frustration and sadness as he splashes milk into his tea, his hands shaking slightly. 'Besides, how could someone make an offer on it when it's not even on the market?'

My heart plummets as my mind cycles back over my latest round of Google research. I make my voice quiet and steady as I reply. 'It is on the market, Dad. It's been up for sale for a week now.'

'We'll see what your mother has to say about that.' He picks up his mug and walks off into the living room, leaving me standing alone in the kitchen. I dunk my own teabag a few times, the familiar gesture giving me a few moments to collect myself, before fishing it out and dropping it into the bin. What sort of day is it? One where he's in there somewhere or one where he's going to stay out of reach?

Picking up my tea, I follow him into the living room where he's sitting on the settee in front of the news.

Remove outside distractions.

'Dad,' I say, flicking off the telly. 'Can I talk to you?' At any given time, I have tabs on my phone open from the NHS, Dementia UK and the Alzheimer's Society, as well as about four other charities and blogs that deal with how to relay the same information to someone over and over again, when they'll be hearing that information as though it's for the first time. They lay it out in simple steps, clinically, so you can absorb how to do it. It's very helpful, but the one thing they don't talk about is how you will feel while you do it. How frightened and impotent and upset. How passing on certain information will crush them and how that in turn will affect you.

'Mmmm?'

'I need to talk to you about the house.'

Speak slowly and clearly. Don't rush.

'Your house has been on the market for a week. We – together – decided you were going to sell it. Today someone has made an offer just above the asking price that the estate agent thinks we should accept. It's up to you, it's your house, so if you want to hold out for more that's fine, but the house is for sale. That's not the part under question.'

Dad is looking at me with suspicion. I've been getting this look more and more. As though I'm trying to trick him. It's hard not to take it personally.

Deep breath, Iris.

'And Mum . . .' I hate this. It's not happened that often yet, but still more frequently than I'd like. And it will only become more frequent. If I could talk about her without getting upset myself, it might be easier, but even thinking about Mum can set me off on a crying jag. The sort where I can't get any words out for sobbing. One of the other tips is to make eye contact, but right now I can't. Instead I clear my throat and focus on a spot in the corner of the room. A literal spot where Sav had a go at the wall with some purple crayon. 'Mum died over a year ago. Last September. She had cancer and we all really miss her.' My voice has gone all high and thin, and the last bit comes out as a squeak. I force my gaze back to Dad in time to pinpoint the moment it sinks in, because disbelief, shock and pain all register on his face and it collapses. It's as though it's just happened and I'm the one who has broken the news to him.

We're both crying now. Another shitty part of this shitty thing. Dad's emotions are so close to the surface, on a hair trigger. As a British man of a certain age, his stiff upper lip has always run through him like a seam. Not that I'm advocating men burying their emotions, but that's always been my dad. Stoic. Now his emotions swing this way and that: frustration that manifests as extreme anger, and deep wrenching tears when he's upset. He's so vulnerable, it's heartbreaking. And often it feels like I'm the one doing this to him. Would blissful ignorance be better, or more confusing? There's no way to know what's cruel and what's kind. I find myself reassessing it constantly, sometimes on a minute-by-minute basis.

'Your mum died?' He's stock still, his tea clasped between his hands, tears running down his cheeks.

I sniff. Wipe my eyes on my sleeve. 'Yes. Last year.'

'Of cancer?'

'Yes.'

'Why didn't I know? Who was with her? Was I not there for the treatment?'

'She didn't have much. It happened so quickly and there was little the doctors could do. But you were there when she died. We both were.' *It was horrific,* I think but don't add. Something I'd rather forget. The films lie. People don't 'go to sleep'; they struggle for breath and they rasp, and it drags on until you will them to go while at the same time willing them to make a full recovery and to never leave you. 'I think the problems you have with your memory make you forget sometimes.'

He physically slumps, and I put both of our teas on a side table and hold his hand. 'Because you're not well either. You have dementia, and we agreed that we should sell your house and you'd stay here with us while we work out what to do next. Do you understand that?'

Dad nods slowly, the shock of the loss still written all over his face. It's so unfair that he experiences this pain afresh, every time Mum's death is relayed to him. No wonder he's devastated. His partner is gone. In his head, he only saw her minutes ago. I carry the knowledge with me all the time and still can't outrun the grief. What must it be like for him?

He looks at his lap, looks up again. 'Did I tell you what she said to me when I first met her?'

He has, many times. Their love story has always been wheeled out as some sort of legend. They were both still teenagers, at a local London disco where one of The Kinks apparently once asked Mum's mate out, and where Dad had a reputation as some sort of ladies' man (I suspect he wasn't entirely above pretending he was a lesser-known member of The Kinks himself). Mum already knew of him when he came over to chat her up and wasn't sure she wanted to date someone with that rep, so she instigated her own seventies version of pick-up artistry on him until he was wrapped around her little finger. They got married twelve months after they met. 'I'm not sure,' I say, trying to draw out what I know is a positive memory for him. 'Remind me.'

'She said, "If you're going to take me out, you're going to have to get better taste in shirts than that."'

I laugh and Dad joins in, genuinely delighted to relive the sass Mum was full of when she was nineteen.

'She's been buying my shirts now for fifty years,' he says, wiping fresh tears from his eyes.

'I know.'

'I don't know what I'm going to do without her,' he says. His lip is trembling.

'I don't know what I'm going to do either. We'll manage though. I know I can't replace the happiness you had with her, but I promise we'll look after you.'

There was always a part of their relationship I couldn't compete with. I may have been the doted on only child – wanting for nothing but the pony, as Adam has been known to remind me – but there was also their unit of two, which preceded and didn't always include me. As a child I was sometimes jealous when they went out together without me, or one of them would start singing a lyric before the other joined in and laughed. A balloon of self-pity would swell and fill me up, because I was party to the perfect relationship, but merely as an observer. Only as an adult can I appreciate that they needed their own protected area, a part of their relationship that was theirs, for the sake of their marriage. I think of the bags of their belongings being stored in our loft, the old cards among them.

Who's M? I wonder again. I've wanted to ask Dad about that card since I found it, but I couldn't; either scared that he wouldn't recall it or scared that he would.

In front of me now, he wrinkles his forehead and closes his eyes. I can see him ordering himself to think, to remember. 'Yes, she died. September twenty-seventh.' He gasps a bit as it all comes back to him, the memories of her sad decline I'm constantly trying to hold at bay.

All I can do is squeeze his hand again. As someone who feels as though I've spent most of this year on the verge of a panic attack, it's never closer to bursting out than in these moments. Dad feels like he has lost his partner all over again, and right now it's tapping into my own fear about losing mine. He watched the person he loved get sicker and then disappear. He had his support system and all those shared times taken away, and now can't always remember them. Throughout this year, I couldn't imagine Adam being gone from my life, even when I haven't liked him much. I itch to text him to come and help me, to carry some of this weight, more confident than I've been for a long time that if I did text him right now, he'd drop whatever he was doing for me.

'I know what it's like to be scared, Dad. I'm scared about what's going to happen to you as your illness gets worse, and I'm also scared I'm never going to be able to fix my marriage.' I blurt it all out and then immediately regret it. I can't burden Dad with this. I'm supposed to be supporting him. He barely spoke to me back in January when I told him what Adam had done. Who knows if he can remember it now, never mind process it?

'What I mean is, there's a lot going on.' I start babbling to try and cover it up. 'But don't worry about any of that. We – I – can handle it.'

'You're here, aren't you?' he says suddenly, his eyes looking clear again.

'What do you mean? In the house? With you? Yes.'

'You're here. You stayed. You and Adam are still together.'

'Well, yes. But it's not as simple as that.'

'It's the first thing,' he says, and then lapses into silence.

'OK,' I say slowly.

'I've been thinking a lot, and whether to tell you, ever since you told me about your . . . situation earlier in the year. It's not just – uh – my problems with my memory that have stopped me saying anything until now. I needed to work out what was for the best. And to be honest, it might now all come out anyway, without me having any control over it if I leave it much longer.'

I have no idea what he's rambling on about. 'What is it?'

'I tried to tell you at the hospital, before we went for the test, but well, then my diagnosis came and I didn't get into it. I want you to know I understand your fears about your marriage. I know how hurt and confused you must be.'

'Thank you, Dad,' I say automatically. It may have taken almost eleven months for him to acknowledge what I told him, but at least he got there in the end.

He blinks again, screws up his mouth. 'No, I truly understand how you feel.' He gives me a look loaded with meaning. I just don't know what the meaning is. 'A long time ago – you'll have only been about six or seven at the time – me and your mum almost split up after she had a wobble about me, about us. And, well, there was another chap involved.' He chokes on the last couple of words, and I automatically hold out a hand to comfort him, even as my own heart is racing.

'What *chap*?'

'At the leisure club she used to go to, for aerobics and squash and whatnot. He worked there.'

'The Manor Club?'

'I can't remember what it was called.'

'The one I used to go to for swimming lessons?'

'That's the one.'

I don't know why this seems relevant, but it does. It wasn't a big place; a private gym and health club attached to a local hotel. We went often enough to say hello to the staff if we saw them out and about, but which one fits the description of this 'chap'? They were all just grown-ups to me.

'How come I never knew anything about it?'

'Why would you?' Dad's voice is gruff. 'It was a fling, she always claimed, and the fellow . . .' He squints as he plucks the name from his memory. 'Max – that was it – packed in working there and moved away shortly afterwards. My threatening to kill him if I ever saw him in the area again may have had something to do with it.' He flashes me a ghost of a smile.

Max.

M.

I can only look at Dad and wonder if he felt as lonely and humiliated as I did about Adam. If he wondered whether he would ever feel normal again or if the spectre of it would always be there. 'I'm so sorry. It must have been hideous.' And then: 'How did you get over it?'

He's looking past me, out of the window and into the back garden where there are a few birds pecking at the nuts and seeds in the feeder. It's freezing outside, so they must be rock hard. My first thought is that he's lost the thread of the conversation and his attention is now elsewhere. 'I think there're a couple of blue tits out there,' he mutters, more to himself than me, before turning his head back in my direction. His eyes are red-rimmed.

'I'm not going to lie to you, it took a long time. Months and years. It being over didn't stop me thinking and worrying about it. The whys, the hows – God, I was obsessed with the details. There were more than a few nights when I punished her by working late and not coming home, to make her wonder where I might be. I don't recommend that as a course of action, by the way, it only made things worse.'

I'm still stunned that we're even talking about this. Mum? Loved-up Mum cheated on Dad? I always thought my parents were the epitome of first love turned happily ever after. Instead, she wasn't sure he was The One, if she ever believed in that concept to begin with.

'Was she ever going to leave us?' It comes out all wobbly. I'm not sure I want to know the answer to this.

'She said not. She seemed almost relieved when I found out.'

Morbid curiosity gets the better of me. 'And how did you find out?'

'He told me. From what your mum said later, she ended it and he said he'd tell me if she broke up with him.'

Another silence while I absorb this information. 'Why did she do it to start off with?'

Dad pulls a face. 'I'm probably not the one who can answer that question. She told me she felt neglected and bored, but once she started up with him, she felt guilty and wretched and didn't want to carry on. I promised her I'd never tell you. We didn't want you to think badly of her for it, but I think she'd forgive me for telling you now.'

'Forgive you? How could you forgive *her* for doing it?'

Dad makes a noise. Not a laugh, but almost. 'I didn't, not straight away. But it was thirty-five years ago. That's a lot of time to get back on track. If you want to.'

'That's the part I'm struggling with,' I admit. 'What *do* I want to do? There are days when I think I've moved on and then it hits me. What he did, that he's capable of doing it. Some days I still hate him so much I don't want to forget about it.'

'You won't forget about it. Well, I might now.' He gives a low chuckle. 'But one day it might not seem like the be-all and end-all any more. If what you have together is still there.'

'But how?'

Dad shrugs. 'Only you can decide that. You've been together for, what is it now, ten years?'

'Together for eleven now. Married for nine.'

Dad nods, as though weighing it up in his mind. 'You still have plenty of time to start again if that's what you want. I considered leaving your mother. I thought about it for a long time.' He gives a wry laugh. 'You know me, I like to think things over before I make a decision.'

'So why didn't you?' I need to know the alchemy. The thing that flips a horrible relationship back into a desirable one.

'It wasn't one thing, and it wasn't one decision. I had to decide every day for a long time to keep going. We made a decision to prioritise each other, to try and repair the hurt on both sides. If I was looking out for her and she was looking out for me, then everything was working.' He takes a big breath, glances towards the blue tits again. 'All I can tell you is that when I look back on fifty years with your mum, her infidelity wasn't one of the defining events of our marriage. *An* event, yes, but for me, our life together overall was worth it. I loved her.' He chokes up again. 'And I think that she loved me.'

'She did, Dad. I know she did.' I pull him into a hug. My cynical, bashed-up heart can't believe it's that simple. That love will win out.

'And she loved you too. What I will say is this. You're not stuck. If you need money to start again, I will look after you. It's what your mother – and me – would want.' I nod into his shoulder, incapable of doing anything else. 'Once I sell this house, my money will be freed up. You can get set up with the children. If that's what you decide to do.' I start to protest but Dad shakes his head. 'Now,' he says, pulling away. 'Show me the pictures.' That conversation is over, but it's hard to get used to the non-sequiturs. I let the thread about Adam and me drift away, rub a hand over my tear-stained face and follow the new direction.

'Which ones?' I take a couple of deep breaths, trying to calm down. I've created a folder on my phone where I store information and photos that might help him remember things or evoke positive feelings. Pictures of his and Mum's wedding day, notes I've taken when he's been reminiscing about holidays or TV shows he likes. My idea was to have a stockpile of information that he can scroll through when he's reaching for something in his mind – a name, a memory – but can't connect the dots. Sometimes he gets lost in the folder, scrolling through moments from his life as though he's watching a film, but other times it does help prompt him to remember, for example, that he wanted to say something about Rod and the time they watched the BDO World Darts Championship at Lakeside in 2010.

'The house.' His tone is tinged with impatience, as though I should know. I swallow down the urge to bite back.

I pull up the page from the estate agent's website that shows the wide-angled shots of the house's pristine interior. It's had a steady parade of well-off couples and young families coming to view it and several offers, but nothing anywhere near the asking price until today. Dad swipes through the photos, pausing on each one, before slowly going back through them for a second time.

He stares at the image of the exterior of his house. The bushes have been cut back, the fence fixed and the lawn neatly mown. The drive is empty of the Citroën he sold within hours of getting his diagnosis, preferring to offload it before he was told he had to. He sets his jaw. 'Sell the house.'

'I want to make it clear that we don't have to,' I reply. 'We can hold out for a higher offer if you like, or we can look into renting it out. It's your house. It's up to you. And I don't want you to think you have to do it for me, Dad—'

'No,' he interrupts, his voice firm. He looks steady, like the Dad I know. 'We should stick to the plan, Iris.' He takes one last glance before handing my phone back. 'It doesn't look like our house any more anyway.'

I nod. 'I'll call the estate agent then.'

It should be a relief to know it's sorted. But as I'm learning, dementia doesn't work like that. I screenshot each picture he's been looking at, so that when the house is taken off the market and the web page disappears, I have a record of them. To show Dad the next time we have this conversation.

Chapter Forty-Six

Excerpt from transcript of session with Adam and Iris Young by Esther Moran, 17 December

Esther: I know you were going to see how your relationship went over the course of the year and, as we're coming to the end of it, I wanted to check in with you both.

Adam: It's been challenging. Not least because in recent weeks a lot of family stuff has overtaken prioritising our relationship. I think what it has shown, though, is that we have pulled together.

Esther: Would you say that's true, Iris?

Iris: Yes, in many ways. We've reconnected with Adam's family recently and we've sorted a few things out. Gabe apologised.

Adam: [mutters] If you can call it that.

Iris: Well, it was a text saying he was sorry for storming off and telling Adam to protect what he had.

Adam: It was basically a threat.

Iris: It was better than nothing. And I've started texting pictures of the kids to his mum, to include her more in our day-to-day lives. My dad's dementia diagnosis has brought it home to me that we need to make an effort. The parents we have left aren't going to be around forever. And it's also made me realise that we need to try if we're going to be happy. That takes effort.

Esther: And you think Adam has been making that effort too?

Iris: Yes. We've been on the same team when it comes to all of the family stuff.

Adam: I'm glad. You know I love your dad, and I'm happy for him to stay with us until we work out where the best place for him is. I'll come with you to visit the different housing options. I've told you, Iris, I'm all in.

Iris: Are you? [pause] Because you might not want to stay when you hear what I suggest.

Adam: What's that?

Iris: [long pause] I don't want Dad to have to live in sheltered housing. I think he needs to move in with us. Permanently.

Chapter Forty-Seven

23 December

I've been waiting my turn all morning, but Taylor coming over to my desk and telling me Vanessa is ready for me still makes me jump when it happens. Eleven twenty-five. With any luck I can take my 'feedback' and disappear for an early lunch straight afterwards. That's if Vanessa wants me to come back at all. There's a reason companies wait until it's almost the end of the year to make redundancies. The Christmas holiday spans two weeks, so by the time everyone else comes back in the New Year, you're gone. People put you out of their minds and start afresh with a new team. Less New Year, New You and more New Year, No You. Sophie took today off as annual leave so had her meeting last thing Friday. She came out looking delighted and asking if anyone fancied some Christmas fizz at the bar around the corner. So no bad news for her.

I take a deep breath and stand up, smoothing down my power outfit – a fitted plum-coloured dress paired with my trusty Manhunt lipstick. I'm channelling the poise of Joan from *Mad Men*, who always looked perfectly put together even when she was being screwed over by her bosses. It seemed appropriate.

'How do you think this year has gone, Iris?' Vanessa asks when I'm seated in front of her. Great: the old self-review routine, allowing me to dig my own grave. The desk in front of Vanessa has no printouts on it, so I can't gauge anything about what might be on the agenda. There's no one from HR here at least, which would be the worst sign of all.

I make myself pause before I respond. 'Mixed bag,' I reply, deliberately vague. Vanessa will have no qualms about filling me in on the specifics of my failures. 'Plenty to learn from in terms of what works when it comes to attracting new donors, but also a strong reminder of how much money my regular donors bring in on an annual basis and how much I enjoy working with them. I've worked hard to ensure their continued support.'

'I think you're right. Your relationships with donors is one of your biggest strengths. Only today I had an email from Emmett and Viola Banks singing your praises.'

'Their vow renewal in September was lovely,' I say, thinking back to the ceremony. 'I still feel a bit tearful about it, if I'm honest.'

'They were thrilled to bits. Which is why they have decided to donate an additional fifty thousand pounds to the Trust this year, along with giving us written notice of a legacy pledge to the tune of a quarter of a million.'

I cough awkwardly. 'Fifty thousand? That's brilliant.' It is, but not good enough to hit my target. I'm still another fifty grand shy of half a million.

'Didn't you say they're in their eighties? So that's three hundred grand altogether if one of them . . .' She doesn't finish the sentence.

I wince. 'I'm sincerely hoping we don't have reason to cash that in any time soon.'

'Yes, yes.' Vanessa flaps a hand as though she's agreeing with me, but in her trademark all-black outfit she looks more like the Grim Reaper waving his scythe. 'And I entirely agree with you about how pitching for new business has been hit and miss.'

I nod. 'I think it's important to have tried different things, even if they don't always work. As you said, following every lead—' Vanessa cuts me off.

'The Nomadic Members' Club was a stroke of genius! I can't believe you didn't come to me with it in the first instance – I'm going to need you to email me the presentation so I can get up to speed. However, the women you already have interested are a fantastic start.'

It takes a second to sink in. I listed Vanessa as Director on the information pack, but I was the one who emailed it out. Not one of the recipients has contacted me. 'Which women are interested?'

Vanessa turns to her computer screen and scrolls down her inbox. 'There were two. They said they met you at the Fierce Women's Retreat back in May – another great call, Iris. Penelope Charles and Mandeep Kaur. Do their names ring a bell?' Through my shock, I nod my head and stifle a laugh. Penny of the severe bob and trust issues has come to my rescue. She and Mandy were two of the women I bonded with while slagging off men over wine.

'They said they wanted to take the idea to the entire female contingent of their company, which is why it's taken until close of business at the end of the year to come to a decision.'

'And?' I hear myself ask faintly.

'They want a breakdown of how the members' club will work, plus an assurance that we're working to get high net worth women from all the blue-chip companies on board – I don't think that will be a problem now we have their bank in the bag. But roughly' – she pulls a weighing-it-up expression – 'I think we're looking at half a million if we – you and I, that is – can make it happen. To start, I'm thinking we go with a tiered membership fee system; the more someone pays, the more access is unlocked.'

I nod with my eyes, feeling a bit like I'm having an out-of-body experience. 'Like Scientology,' I whisper.

'What's that?' she says. 'We'll iron out the details in due course, but with this on the horizon you've absolutely smashed this year's challenge. I must admit, when you told me back in the autumn that you had irons in the fire, I thought you were bluffing, particularly after that business with Lucas Caulfield, but I'm utterly delighted to be proved wrong.'

I've never seen Vanessa smile like this before. She doesn't just look happy; she looks *impressed* and that's even better.

'That's great.' I still don't really believe what's happening but I allow myself to smile back and continue cautiously. 'Can I ask what this means in terms of redundancy? I'm guessing I'll still be here if we're going to be working on this project together.' There's no way Sophie would have looked that pleased with herself yesterday if she'd been canned, but then again, I hadn't won this money for the company yesterday.

'That's the fantastic part,' Vanessa says. 'The entire team has stepped up to the plate so brilliantly this year that we're back on track, and we won't have to look at cost-cutting. You and Sophie have been particularly valuable in terms of new business, so I'm thrilled that both of you will be here to nurture these new relationships.'

I let out a breath I didn't know I was holding. 'Wow. Right.' That's one bit of good news to end the year on, although continuing to work with Sophie, not so much.

Vanessa reaches under her desk and picks up a bottle of champagne. 'So take this, have a great Christmas, and come back in January ready to get seriously stuck in to phase two of operation Club Nomad. We'll be going in to present to every company in the City and beyond, so I'm going to need you on your A-game with the ideas and time to devote to it.'

Her eyes sparkle as she talks about how challenging and rewarding it will be, and how we're going to be bigger than Soho Farmhouse because we can offer history as well as luxury. 'Americans will love it. We should offer an overseas package.' She registers the shell-shocked look on my face. 'Sorry, I'm thinking out loud here. We'll get into the meat of it next year. Clear the first two weeks for strategy as this is going to monopolise Q1 and Q2.' She gives me a little conspiratorial look. 'There are going to be some late nights, so buckle up.'

'I'm so excited about this, Vanessa, I can't even tell you. I've always wanted to build something like this from the ground up, that links our fantastic properties with amazing women, and I *am* dedicated to making it happen.' Another surge of adrenaline pulses through me, half excitement and half fear at what I'm about to say next. I was so prepared for being made redundant that I'd started considering what the benefits of being at home more for a while could be, and I need to see this thought through. 'But—'

'Don't "but" me, Iris,' she warns. 'Oh God, don't tell me you're pregnant.' She claps her hand over her mouth. 'Sorry, I know I'm not supposed to say that.'

'No, I'm not. But you're right, there is a but.'

Her smile fades.

'This year *has* been very challenging, and it hasn't only been the stress over work targets. I have some things going on in my home life that are going to make it difficult for me to be here for every late night. Not just because of my children – although that too – but I need to be at home more.' I let it hang there for a moment while I weigh up how much to spill. Not me and Adam. I still can't bring that into work. 'My dad, he's not well. He has dementia and is going to need a lot of care over the coming months and years. He's living with us now and I need – want – to be there for him. So while you will have my hundred per cent dedication during working hours and I can take part in a certain number of out-of-hours meetings, I have other commitments that are non-negotiable.'

Vanessa looks contemplative. 'I'm sorry to hear about your dad,' she says. 'That must be difficult.' She stops. I can almost hear her mentally counting how long her sympathy pause has to last. 'What are you suggesting?'

Always solutions with her.

Think, Iris.

'Taylor,' I blurt. 'I think she's more than ready for a step up, and I'll need a lot of support if I'm going to balance everything.' The more I talk, the more convinced I am that this is the right suggestion. Vanessa's interest is piqued and Taylor deserves a promotion. 'She can gain a lot of experience very quickly and I can act as a mentor to her. I know I can rely on her to work hard and know the project inside out, so when I occasionally can't be here she can be the point of contact.'

Vanessa is nodding, her mouth pulled together as she thinks it over.

'If we're good for as much money as we think, surely we can give Taylor a new title and a salary bump and then hire a new PA for you. It will be well worth the investment.'

'And this will ensure you're available for all of the essential work?' she asks.

This is the most I've ever asked for help in my entire career, and I'm worried I've gone too far. My heart is pounding but I commit to it. 'Yes.'

'Understood. Leave it with me so I can look at the numbers.' She stands up, effectively dismissing me. 'See you in January.'

'Thank you.' I stand up, dizzy from how this meeting has turned out. 'See you in January.'

I wink at Taylor on my way out, depositing the champagne on the desk in front of her. 'Merry Christmas,' I tell her.

Chapter Forty-Eight

25 December

I inhale two segments of chocolate orange and sit back on the sofa, closing my eyes now there's a lull in all the present-opening and shrieking. The rat-a-tat sound of automatic gunfire pierces through my skull.

'Can you please turn it down a bit, Jack?' I ask, deliberately not looking at the game he's playing on his new PlayStation that by rights should be called *Inhumanity*, judging by the fact that the goal seems to be killing as many people as possible. Gabe bought it for him despite the sixteen-plus rating we only clocked once he unwrapped it. Naturally Jack loves it.

He knocks the volume down an almost imperceptible amount. Across the room, there's the shooshing of Lego being raked through the carpet as Adam helps Sav build her new pet parlour, the sound punctuated by Anne yelping as she steps on an upturned Lego poodle while collecting the wrapping paper debris in a binbag.

'Don't worry about that now, Anne, come and sit down,' I tell her.

She shakes her head and carries on stuffing the paper in. Having been up since 4.30 a.m., when the kids jumped on Adam and me on the sofa bed in the living room to declare Santa had been (funny how Jack keeps his Father Christmas atheism to himself when it comes to reaping the benefits of his existence) and we dragged ourselves out of bed, I don't even feign making like I'm going to get up to help her. We let them open one (big) present each, and then spent three hours holding them off from opening the rest until the others got up. Or, in Gabe's case, was physically dragged out of bed by Adam because we were losing our minds and couldn't wait any longer. I can't tell if Anne's happy tidying or just can't relax amidst the chaos, but as I insisted that she didn't help with the Christmas lunch, it seems she's making up for her lack of productivity in that area by doing a deep clean of the house.

I was nervous about inviting Anne and Gabe down to spend Christmas with us. If last year was upsetting because of the Mum-shaped hole, this year it's because of the maelstrom of uncertainty. Will Dad even know us by next year? It was that, in part, that convinced Adam to let me do it. A guilt-trip over how our family is shrinking and that we need to cling on to the bits we have left. He agreed, with the caveat that Gabe is out if he even alludes to our marital problems in front of Anne, so here we are, on a knife-edge, with everyone Making An Effort in capital letters. With Anne sleeping in our bedroom, Gabe on Jack's floor, and us ushering everyone out of the living room each evening so that we can make up the sofa bed in here.

'Shall I open some Prosecco?' Adam calls across the room. It's midday, just. His mum looks mildly disapproving, but less than I'd expect, and Gabe practically leaps up off the floor – of course he's playing the murdery game with Jack – to fetch some glasses.

'I'll do it,' he shouts, disappearing. 'Jack, pause the game.'

'Sure, why not?' I reply. I feel as though I've got up for an early flight; buzzy, eye-burny and disconnected. A drink will either help or send me right over the edge.

I hear a cork pop in the kitchen before Gabe reappears with a tray of booze, plus wine glasses filled with orange juice for the kids. He starts serving them out around the room. 'I wanted a Coke,' Jack says immediately, before the whole room choruses 'no' at him. Dad pauses before plucking his glass off the tray.

'A small one won't hurt, I don't think,' he says, looking to me for reassurance, and I nod and smile, not knowing if he should drink alcohol with his condition and trying not to berate myself because it's something I *should* know, while resenting the fact that it's something I have to take into account at all. So far, today seems like a good day in terms of his lucidity but I'm still on high alert for things changing, the front door banging and Dad wandering out onto the street. Jack and Sav both know to tell me if it happens when I'm in the other room and they're with Grandad. Adam and I have agreed to let Dad stay indefinitely, without tackling the permanency of it with him yet. How quickly I have assumed the role of carer. I'm not sure I'm up to the job.

'Do you like your presents, Mummy?' Sav asks me, and I look down at my feet where I'm wearing some hideous unicorn slippers she picked out for me and insisted Adam buy.

Then I glance at my wrist, where Adam's present to me dangles. A chunky gold vintage bracelet with tiny jade pieces set into it. He obviously went to a lot of effort; it definitely surpasses the pair of running trainers he bought for me last year in terms of romantic idealism, but ungratefully I wish he hadn't bought it for me the year he had an affair. It feels like a bangle of guilt.

'I love them,' I say to Sav instead. 'We've all been very lucky this year.'

'We have,' Adam chimes in. 'I love my presents too.' He pulls up the brim of the 'Best Dad Ever' cap Jack decided was perfect for him. It's leaving a black mark on his forehead where the material is reacting with his skin, but he looks cute in it. I wish I had been as sure as Jack about what to buy. I spent ages trying to pick something cool and 'him', something that expressed that I cared about him without being too gushing, seeming insincere, making it about me or being burdened with having to represent 'us' as a concept. That present doesn't exist, so in the end I got him a pair of boots I knew he wanted but hasn't bought himself as he thought they were too pricey. Then when he opened them, I couldn't help but tell him I'd managed to find them cheap online. My other gift was telling him I'd contacted Calum and his uni mates to organise a weekend away, something they used to do all the time but fell by the wayside when we all started having children, moving out of London, or, in Calum's case, spending 'more time in the studio'. The message was supposed to be that I trust him to go and do things without me, but who knows if it translated. It's too much to always be on the lookout to see everything from every angle, and analyse why each of us is behaving in a particular way.

I take a sip of Prosecco and the bubbles catch at the back of my throat, making me cough. 'I'll check on the lunch,' I say, adding, '*please* sit down, Anne,' as I pass her, now at the mantelpiece and standing up the Christmas cards that fall over every time there's a draught from someone opening or closing the living room door. I feel bad the second I do. She's doing her best and probably feels as awkward as I do, which is exactly why she can't just have a bloody seat.

In the kitchen I stand at the worktop, picking at the foil of a mince pie with my fingernail and staring into space. The windows have misted up on the inside from the heat coming from the cooker. I've become the type of mother who hides in the kitchen during any sort of occasion. I take a cursory glance at the food in the oven to justify coming in here. There's nothing to do; it's all in, and it'll all be fine as long as I don't mess up the timings. I deliberately bought everything pre-prepared so I wouldn't have to worry about it, but now I wish I had some pastry to pound or pigs to wrap in blankets, just for something to occupy me.

'Can I do anything?' Adam wanders in, his glass already empty, and rummages in the fridge for the bottle. 'I've managed to get Mum to play Guess Who with Sav. I told her the house will be a bomb-site for the next week regardless of whether or not she keeps hoovering, so she might as well give up. I give it about ten minutes before she says she's going to run a duster over a few shelves.'

'I'd be insulted that she finds our house so filthy, but I'm grateful she can be arsed to clean when I can't,' I say. I take the mince pie out of the foil and nibble at the pastry. It's Tesco Finest. After extensive taste-testing of every supermarket brand, we decided that these ones were the best.

Adam pulls off his cap and wipes uselessly at the black dye on his forehead. His hair is all sweaty and flat, so I go over to the sink, run a bit of kitchen roll under the tap, and then come back to rub the mark off. He holds on to my hand as I move it away, and we look at each other for a moment.

'Thanks.' He smiles at me. 'Do you really like your bracelet?'

'Yes, I do. It's very me.'

'I wanted to get you something special.' He smiles sheepishly. 'Fran helped me choose.'

That he had to enlist my best friend to double-check my taste feels more normal somehow. 'Thank you. And Fran too.'

'She also told me she'd beat me to death with it if I hurt you again.'

I pull my mouth into a smile. 'She would too.'

'I know. She won't have to, though.' Adam looks around the kitchen, seeming to realise I'm not doing anything in here. He frowns. 'Are you OK?'

I nod, ignoring the tension headache forming behind my eyes. 'It's a lot,' I admit. 'It's nice all being together for Christmas, but the reality is hard. I feel like I need to be constantly "on".'

'Same. Gabe and I are being overly polite to each other, which is making Mum even more tense than if we were bickering. I've got half an eye out for him getting drunk and starting some trouble. I can't work out if it's better or worse that he's spending most of his time with Jack.'

'Jack thinks he's the coolest person ever.'

Adam raises his eyebrows in mock alarm. 'That's because basically they're the same age emotionally. I'd be worried about Gabe being a bad influence, but maybe Jack stands equal chance of being an influence on him.'

'Good or bad?'

'Not sure.' I try to smile but it doesn't land. He cocks his head to one side. 'Are you sure you're OK?'

I look down at the counter so he can't see the strain on my face. 'Yes.' If I say it enough, it will have to be true. 'It's just . . . Christmas, you know. Hard without Mum. Hard to know what Dad's condition will be like next year. Or' – I decide to say it – 'what next year will bring for us. It's making me a bit melancholy.' I pick up my glass. 'Probably need a few more of these.'

He tops up my Prosecco, even though I've barely touched it.

'I got you another present,' Adam says. 'Nothing big,' he adds quickly. 'Bit stupid.'

I laugh. 'You're really selling it to me. What is it?'

'I was going to burn it onto a CD, until I realised we don't have a CD drive on our laptop any more, so it's on my phone.' He holds it out to show me. 'It's a playlist.'

I scan the names. 'I literally have no idea who these people are.'

Adam smiles. 'That's the point. You're always saying you never have time to listen to anything new except songs the kids ask for, so I got the sixth-form students at my last school to recommend some new artists.' He raises an eyebrow. 'I listened to *a lot* of terrible music on their recommendation – I'm not sure how into grime you're going to be – but I whittled it down and some of it's pretty good. Loads of different genres, weird little bands and rappers I had to look up. To start off with, I think they thought I was trying to be cool and ingratiate myself with them, but then when I said I was making a playlist for you, they all started telling me the songs of theirs that their mums like.' He laughs and I swat him with a tea towel. 'Anyway, see what you think. We used to go to loads of gigs, didn't we? Maybe if there's anyone you like among this lot we can see if they're playing sometime.'

Tears spring to my eyes and he looks at me in alarm, as if to say, *What have I done now?* 'No, no, I'm not upset about anything to do with us,' I say quickly. 'It's this . . . it's so sweet.' It is. I'm touched. More by this than by the swanky bracelet, because it's something he's spent time on, trying to foster a connection. 'I can listen to it while I sort the rest of this lunch out.'

'Sure.' He sets his phone on the worktop. 'It's not locked,' he adds, and then clears his throat. 'About us though—' he starts, but I cut him off.

'Please, Adam. Not today. Let's get through Christmas. We've got a week to go, so let's save it for then.'

He doesn't look satisfied.

'We're not in *EastEnders*. I don't want the Christmas Day episode to be the big showdown,' I add, trying to make a joke of it. 'For the kids. Let's keep things going for them.'

He sighs, and then nods. 'OK. Next week.' His voice is light but the expression on his face betrays him.

'Go and see if you can get your mum a bit pissed,' I say. 'Then she might even let us leave the washing up, rather than jumping up the second we've finished lunch.'

He nods again, his mouth set in a straight line. 'Shout if you need me to do anything.' He disappears through the door, calling behind him, 'I'll be back to do the gravy in a bit.' Gravy is his 'thing' and he spends ages perfecting it, even though everyone would be happy with Bisto. A couple of seconds later, I hear Christmas songs pipe up in the living room. I push the kitchen door closed to drown out the strains of 'Last Christmas' and press play on the playlist Adam has made for me. The first track is some singer-songwriter with all the vowels deliberately removed from his name.

I squash down the guilt about batting Adam away. I just can't today. It's too much. Why do I feel like this? Is it because of the usual mental-load bullshit around Christmas – the food, the decorations, the presents; not just for the family but for friends' children, the kids' teachers, and the random people who come into our lives and would be offended if we didn't shove a box of Quality Street in their direction? Or is it the juggling of festive parties, on top of the niggle about whether to trust Adam at his office Christmas party, while also acknowledging that we'll never move on if I don't trust him to do anything? Do I not want to be here or does *no one* want to do all of this crap? Why is it that every time I come to a decision I start second guessing myself again?

I don't know I don't know I don't know.

I look down; I've massaged the remnants of the mince pie into a sticky mass in the palm of my hand. I rub them together to wipe it all off, letting the crumbs drop onto the worktop in front of me. One more week to decide the future.

Not just mine but the future of everyone in this house.

Chapter Forty-Nine

31 December

'Will someone get the door?' Liv shouts. She can barely be heard over the competing noises of music, drunken conversation, and ten children under the age of ten who should definitely be in bed by now but aren't and are reaching critical mass on the temper-tantrum front. That no one is policing the fizzy drinks being used as mixers – due to the fact that everyone has been demolishing the spirits those mixers go with – is not helping matters. The last time I saw Jack, he was underneath Liv's dining room table having a biscuit-eating competition with her daughter Cilla. Despite him having two years on her, Cilla was very much holding her own.

'I'll do it,' I shout back, pushing myself up from where I'm perched on the armrest of an armchair talking to one of Liv's doctor mates. I shove past reams of people loitering in the hallway where it's quieter, and wonder if I should have left the kids at home with Anne, who was already staying in with Dad, but as Liv said everyone else's would be running feral I brought them along. She's become a good friend over these last few months, and I jumped at an invite to a party that would get Adam and me out of the house for this last night of our year-long challenge.

The bell bleats again and I rush to get it before whoever it is leaves, opening the door to find a pizza delivery man standing there. He shoves a mountain of boxes at me, already walking away as I ask who ordered them and what we owe.

'Pre-paid. Happy New Year.'

I carefully turn around, a tower of pizzas in front of my face, blocking my view.

'Here, let me help you.' Liv's face appears as she lifts half the pile from me. 'These are for when everyone's pissed and starving at midnight. The first time I've ever thought ahead about that in my life, which proves I *must* now be a grown-up.' She waves to a couple of people, the pizzas wobbling on her other hand. 'I'll come and say hello properly in a minute,' she calls. 'God, I forgot that when it's your party all you do is circulate and have the same conversation for five hours about how people got here and how they plan to get home again. You look great, by the way. I love this skirt.' I smile, pleased that the high-waisted, three-quarter-length skirt I had made from the brocade gown I found at Mum's has had an impact. It's a bit of her with me. 'And thank you for bringing a single man with you,' she stage-whispers at me as we make our way to the kitchen. I look over at where Gabe is standing, deep in conversation with Adam and one of Liv's neighbours, who is on some decks mixing one chart hit from our teenage years into another. They've all spent a very long time this evening staring at and discussing vinyl.

'Adam's brother? That's not why I brought him! I mean, sure, if you're interested, but I'm not sure I could write him a good review so please don't ask me what he's like. I won't be able to lie.'

'Oh, thank God you said that,' she says, as we make it to the kitchen and clear enough space among the party detritus to put the pizza boxes down. 'I thought you were trying to set me up, and don't take this the wrong way but he looks a lot like Adam, and it would be weird.'

I laugh. 'None taken.' I tipsily think of any other eligible single men I know. Calum? Single, yes. Eligible? That depends on how Liv feels about being the breadwinner and spending her evenings listening to him trying out new 'arrangements' of Coldplay songs. What about Lucas? I press pause on that. Definitely not the time to revisit getting in touch with him, even for someone else. Besides, Sophie's apparently getting on 'so well with him' maybe she'll snag him for herself.

I make my way back to the living room and lean against the wall for a moment, taking an inventory of the assembled children. I think we're missing at least two, until I see that they've joined Cilla and Jack under the table and are playing an aggressive game of Hungry Hippos.

'Can we talk?' Adam asks, appearing beside me. He looks nervous, and I instantly feel the same. It's five minutes to midnight. One year. Almost over.

'Yes, let's go upstairs where it's quieter. Hopefully it's not the sort of house party where there are people having sex so there'll be a free bedroom.' We make our way through Liv's terraced house, neither speaking nor looking at each other. Only a few streets from ours, it's almost identical in layout, but right at the top, in her loft conversion, she has some French doors that open onto a tiny roof terrace and look out to central London – if you stand on your tiptoes and squint far enough over the neighbouring rooftops, that is. I lead Adam up there, where we won't be disturbed, and we squeeze outside, me taking nervous sips of my drink and Adam picking at the label on his bottle of East London micro-brewed ale.

'I know I should probably wait until tomorrow, but I can't stand it any longer, party or no party,' he says. 'What's your answer?'

I watch a group of young women in the street below legging it in high heels and short skirts towards the pub at the end of the road. 'COME ON,' one of them shouts as she edges in front of them. 'We're going to miss it.' She yanks open the pub door, and the intermingled sounds of chatter and music waft up to us. As the door shuts the countdown to midnight starts, before a few beats later it begins downstairs, slightly out of sync. Even two floors up I can feel the vibration of people's voices buzzing through my feet.

Ten . . . nine . . .

'How do *you* think this year has gone?' I ask.

'It's been hard,' he admits, ripping a long strand from the label before rolling it between his fingers. He realises there's nowhere to put it so stuffs it into his jeans pocket. 'I didn't expect you to forgive and forget straight away so I knew it would be, but if I'm honest I can't pretend there haven't been moments when I haven't wanted to walk away, especially when you seemed so sad and angry. Sometimes I thought we'd be better off putting ourselves out of our misery. Do you know what I mean?'

'A fresh start.' I nod, before echoing Dad's words. 'We're both young enough.'

Eight . . . seven . . .

With the size of the terrace it isn't really possible to get much closer to each other, but Adam angles his body towards me and reaches for my hand. 'But you said to give us a year, and you were right. Everything about this year – my stupidity, all the bloody counselling – it's all driven home to me how much I love you and that I'm prepared to wade through the hard stuff, whether that's with us, or with our parents – to hang on to it. And it's not been all bad, has it?' He looks at me. Properly looks at me. 'When I think about the future, Iris, I always see you there.'

Six . . . five . . .

I squeeze his hand and look back at him, thinking about how the nine years we've been married is such a small percentage of Mum and Dad's half-century. Still time to start again. Twice over.

Four . . . three . . .

'You're right, we agreed to give it a year. So what I think is . . .' I take a deep breath. 'That we should give it another one.'

Two . . .

Adam's hand loosens, his fingers gently resting on mine, but no longer intertwined.

One . . .

'I'm still on probation,' he says, his voice dejected. 'Please, Iris, I don't know what else I can do to prove how much you mean to me.'

'*HAPPY NEW YEAR!*'

The chorus echoes from all directions. I see the flash and crackle of the official fireworks at the Thames, along with a load of rockets and bangers being let off by amateurs in their back gardens which will no doubt have local pet owners and new parents cursing them.

I grasp for him, holding his hand tighter as I pull him towards me to explain. 'No, you're not on probation. Or if you prefer to think of it that way, we both are.'

He searches my face, rightly looking confused.

'We've worked harder on our marriage this year than any other time – both of us – and I agree, it has been hard work. Our relationship changed. It's still changing. And that's because *we've* changed.' I can tell Adam thinks this is a drawn-out dumping so I get to the point. 'I thought that after what happened I had to fall back in love with the man I met all those years ago, and remind myself who you were, but I didn't. Instead I had to fall in love with who you are now.'

His face has softened but there's still doubt in his eyes. 'And did you?'

I smile, thinking of how supportive he's being with Dad, and the commitment we've made to being on the same team. Prioritising each other. And then I think of the sex. OK, maybe not so regular as it once was, but we're trying. 'Yes. Even though I was hurt, even when my brain was full up with worry about how we'd make it work. I loved who you were when we met, and I love you now – differently, but just as much. We're evolving. And I want to evolve together. What I'm trying to say is, let's keep working on us, next year and *every* year. What do you think?'

He responds by kissing me, hard, before whispering, 'Happy New Year, Iris.' And then, 'OK, let's give it another year, for an entire lifetime.'

Acknowledgements

Considering the way 2020 has panned out, the title of this book could apply to anyone, not just the fictional Iris and Adam. For me, it has certainly thrown into sharp relief the people I am beyond grateful for in my life.

For my mum, who died while I was writing this book. Despite suffering a life-changing brain haemorrhage in 2001, she remained infinitely supportive, my bookworm idol and a hilarious quipper to the last, as well as teaching me the fine art of dressing down useless politicians during TV phone-ins at an early age. I couldn't have asked for a better mum.

For my dad (I know you will already be emotional by this point!), who was my mum's full-time carer for eighteen years and who I have spent hours in hospitals with over the years. I love and admire you more than you will ever know, Denge (if not your lack of a decent kitchen bin system).

For Ian, who is the best of the best and who is always on my side. I know we sometimes wish we had met a bit earlier in life, but you were worth the wait. I hope I keep making you laugh forever (and that I can one day keep you in the manner you hope to be accustomed via my successful writing career).

For Ikey, who may have provided some of the inspiration for Jack and Sav's mischievous moments. As you might say, 'I love you berry berry much'.

For the dream team: Sarah Hornsley, Sam Eades and Phoebe Morgan, who made this book happen and made it a thousand times better with their editorial notes (and in Sam's case made me laugh out loud with some of them). During its lifespan, they have been promoted, changed jobs, had babies, moved house, coped with a pandemic and generally demonstrated the exact sort of non-stop juggle I wanted to write about. I hate to break it you, but you're the reason women are so stressed about having it all, because you don't just make it look possible, you do it with aplomb.

Thank you to my copy-editing team Claire Gatzen and Clarissa Sutherland for saving me from myself and to my cover designer, Rachael Lancaster. And a special mention to Rachael Bull for telling me enough about her job for me to make up the rest for dramatic purposes.

And for all my family and friends who have championed me and my writing, who inspire and support me every day.

CREDITS

Trapeze would like to thank everyone at Orion who worked on the publication of *I Give It A Year*

Agent
Sarah Hornsley

Editor
Sam Eades

Copy-editor
Claire Gatzen

Audio
Paul Stark
Amber Bates

Contracts
Anne Goddard
Paul Bulos
Jake Alderson

Proofreader
Morag Lyall

Editorial Management
Clarissa Sutherland
Charlie Panayiotou
Jane Hughes
Alice Davis
Claire Boyle

Design
Rachael Lancaster
Joanna Ridley
Nick May
Clare Sivell
Helen Ewing

Finance
Jennifer Muchan
Jasdip Nandra
Rabale Mustafa
Levancia Clarendon
Tom Costello
Ibukun Ademefun

Marketing
Tanjiah Islam

Production
Claire Keep
Fiona McIntosh

Publicity
Alex Layt

Sales
Jennifer Wilson
Victoria Laws
Esther Waters
Lucy Brem
Frances Doyle
Ben Goddard
Georgina Cutler
Jack Hallam
Ellie Kyrke-Smith
Inês Figuiera
Barbara Ronan
Andrew Hally
Dominic Smith
Deborah Deyong
Lauren Buck
Maggy Park
Linda McGregor
Sinead White
Jemimah James
Rachael Jones
Jack Dennison
Nigel Andrews
Ian Williamson
Julia Benson
Declan Kyle
Robert Mackenzie
Imogen Clarke
Megan Smith
Charlotte Clay
Rebecca Cobbold

Operations
Jo Jacobs
Sharon Willis
Lisa Pryde

Rights
Susan Howe
Richard King
Krystyna Kujawinska
Jessica Purdue

Help us make the next generation of readers

We – both author and publisher – hope you enjoyed this book.
We believe that you can become a reader at any time in your life,
but we'd love your help to give the next generation a head start.

Did you know that 9% of children don't have a book of their
own in their home, rising to 13% in disadvantaged families*?
We'd like to try to change that by asking you to consider the role
you could play in helping to build readers of the future.

We'd love you to think of sharing, borrowing, reading, buying or talking
about a book with a child in your life and spreading the love of reading.
We want to make sure the next generation continue to have access
to books, wherever they come from.

And if you would like to consider donating to charities that help
fund literacy projects, find out more at www.literacytrust.org.uk
and www.booktrust.org.uk.

Thank you.

*As reported by the National Literacy Trust